Books by Bill S. Ballinger

Portrait in Smoke
The Tooth & the Nail
The Longest Second
Wife of the Red-Haired Man
The Fourth of Forever
Forty-Nine Days of Death
and
twenty other novels of
adventure and suspense

The Corsican

BILL S. BALLINGER

Copyright © 1974 by Bill S. Ballinger

All rights reserved. No part of this book may be reproduced
in any form without the written permission of the publisher.

Reprinted by arrangement with Dodd, Mead and Company

ISBN: 0-931773-61-X

Manufactured in the United States of America

. . . to Lucy with love for keeping the home-fires burning during my long absences while working on this book

Glossary

bande	gang, mob
bandit	gangster
belote	a common card game
blé	dough (money)
bousiller	to rub out (kill)
cabane	jail . . . can
camelote	junk, shoddy goods
carte nationale d'identité	identification card, or papers, carried by all French citizens
casseur	mug, strong-arm, muscleman
cavaler	to beat it, scram
cette merde	this crap
commérage	gossip
commissaire	chief inspector of detectives
con	"nuts," crazy
copain	buddy
dur	tough one
filou	a sharp operator
flic	cop
flingue	gun . . . heater, gat
foutre	sexual intercourse (gutter)
fric	money
frigo	jail . . . cooler
gourbi	hole up, hide out
gorille	gorilla
informateur	informer
inspecteur	detective

liquider	to knock off
mec	guy, fellow
merde	crap, shit
milieu	French underworld
mouchard	squealer
nana	a gal, chick, tomato
Le Patriarche	head of a family (honorary title)
pianque	hide-out
pote	pal
poule	broad (slur); whore
poulet	cop. Poulaille - cops
relégué	small-time criminal; repeater of petty crimes
sulfateuse	automatic revolver
tapineuse	prostitute
taule	jail . . . tank
videur	bouncer

The situations in this novel are based upon true facts, although the characters are fictional.

Part
One

Chapter 1

From a vantage point concealed beneath the *maquis* covering the rising foothills, a pair of eyes studied the activity on the beach below. Khaki-clad figures labored on a stretch of sand lapped by the Tyrrhenian Sea. They struggled with massive rolls of heavy steel mesh—unrolling the perforated strips of metal, interlocking them end to end, then concealing the landing sheets with a thin covering of sand. At intervals, long metal spikes were being driven through the mats to reach the hard ground beneath and hold the landing sheets firmly in position. The distant ring of sledge on spike reached the ears of the young Corsican who was watching from the hills above Ghisonacia.

After some minutes of intense observation, Cesar Satisanni rose to his feet and started a circuitous descent to the small fishing village located inland from the beach. Although in his early twenties, he moved with the practiced ease of a mountaineer down the difficult slope. He slipped through the dense coverings of heatherlike *maquis* and rockrose shrubs and made his way through stands of cedar and pine entangled with mastic and buckhorn, dropping from one stony outcrop to another with little more effort than descending a staircase.

Over young Satisanni's shoulder swung a vintage single-shot rifle, slung in a worn leather strap. Carefully hoarded bullets jingled in a pocket of his loose full trousers which bagged below his knees and were wrapped tightly around his ankles and partly up the calves of his legs by thongs. A large sheathed knife snuggled against his belly beneath a broad leather belt.

The June sun blazed overhead in the blue-white sky by the time Cesar arrived behind the village of Ghisonacia. He concealed his ancient rifle beneath flat stones and scraps of brush, for the Germans had decreed a death penalty to Corsicans carrying arms. Although the scores of uniformed men laying the landing sheets on the beach did not look like Germans or Italians, young Satisanni was cautious. American and British uniforms were not yet familiar sights. In their three-thousand-year history the Corsicans had learned to be suspicious of all strangers.

Cesar started for the village, which lay quiet in the noonday hour. Along the serrated coasts of Corsica—tucked in small bays, beside lagoons, at the ends of fingered inlets, or in the lee of rocky peninsulas—were scores of costal villages similar to Ghisonacia. Each village comprised clusters of fieldstone houses, many of them plastered and painted in weathered hues of yellow, blue, or pink and topped by roofs of orange tile; each also had a tiny white church with an ascending square tower. All sucked their very lives from *Mare Nostrum*. In the summer of 1943 Ghisonacia had a population, possibly, of one hundred and fifty persons.

Cesar Satisanni had not visited Ghisonacia before. For other reasons he had ventured so far east on the island and stumbled on the activity beside the Tyrrhenian Sea. His own home was inland from the west coast, in the mountains behind Piana which faced toward the Mediterranean. Near it were the great Calanches, whose gigantic rocky spires sometimes seemed to impale the sun.

Young Satisanni walked down the narrow, unpaved street between houses shuttered against the heat. He stopped a small boy who was lugging a tin of water from the public well. "Which is the house of Signore Marc Calevecchio?" The boy stared warily in a combination of reticence and curiosity. "Are you so dumb that you can't speak?" Cesar asked. The boy pointed a grimy finger at a peeling, mustard-colored house further down the street and continued staring at the stranger.

After repeated knocking, the heavy door was opened by an old man. He stared dimly, through eighty-year-old eyes, at the young

4

man standing on his doorstep. Indistinctly he made out the lean, dark face and the dark eyes and hair of his visitor. But these were common characteristics among the inhabitants of the small island, where inbreeding had developed a "type" of dark olive skin, brown eyes, black hair, and intense hawklike features.

Cesar nodded politely. "Signor Marc Calevecchio?"

The old man said, "It may or may not be . . . depending on who stands at the door and asks." The conversation was conducted in Corsican, a dialect of somewhat archaic Italian mixed with heavy southern French intonations.

"I'm Cesar Satisanni. My mother is Angela Andrea Fennechi." He displayed no irritation, or embarrassment, with the old man.

A thin, shaking hand went to an ear and rubbed it briskly until it flushed a dark red, while the old mind rummaged through the attic of involved genealogies. Families were of first importance, although if carried back far enough, it seemed almost everyone on the island was related in one way or another.

"Fennechi . . . Archino . . . Vallica . . ." Cesar prodded quietly.

The old man pounced. "Vallica, Tasera, Calevecchio!" Marc stood away from the door, holding it open. "Come in, come in!" he welcomed. His wrinkled face, pitted like bark from a cork oak, broke into a toothless smile. Marc Calevecchio had identified Cesar as a far-removed nephew—possibly a great-grandnephew on the young man's maternal side of the family. The exact degree of relationship was unimportant. That it existed *was* important.

Marc gestured Cesar to seat himself at a heavy wooden table in the old-fashioned room of rude furniture, then shuffled to a cupboard. Taking out a partly filled bottle of white Corsican wine and two heavy glasses, he shouted in a thin voice, "We have a guest, a relative from . . .?" The old man paused and peered at Cesar for an answer.

"Col Pieto."

"Of course. Col Pieto!" Marc sat down beside Cesar and poured wine into the glasses. Another ancient, a woman, hobbled into the room with a chipped plate on which were slices of ewe's cheese, small quartered tomatoes, wrinkled black olives, and several thick chunks of coarse gray bread. Silently she placed the plate on the table in front of the two men and hobbled out again—a slow-moving figure completely clothed in black from her neck to the hem of her skirt, which barely cleared the top of her black shoes. From the air of complete indifference with which Marc treated her, Cesar guessed that she was the old man's housekeeper.

Cesar ate the food hungrily while his uncle tore bread into small pieces, dipped them in wine, and gummed them in his toothless mouth. The young man politely answered questions regarding the health, well-being, and state of social and economic success of various members of his own family, whom the old man began to recall with increasing clearness: Yes . . . his father, Victore, was in excellent health. No . . . his mother had no other sons—only himself, Cesar. Yes . . . he had six sisters; that was indeed unfortunate. Yes . . . his mother's brother, Angelo Fennechi, still attempted to smuggle tobacco from North Africa. No . . . the crops—if such they could be called—were not good this year.

Young Satisanni replied patiently to the old man's flood of queries. Behind the eyes, so dark as to seem one with the irises, was a fathomless depth. Occasionally he turned them on Marc, glancing up from the table or over the brim of his glass. The eyes looked, absorbed the image of what they saw, but gave no reaction. In time it would be Cesar's turn to ask questions. He had not called on Marc Calevecchio through a sense of family duty, but because the distant uncle was the only person he knew in Ghisonacia.

The old man looked sleepily at the empty bottle before them. It was time for his midday nap. Cesar grasped his opportunity. "Out there . . . on the beach. What are they doing?"

"It's the war," Marc replied.

"Yes, it's always the war. But what are they doing?"

"Who knows," Marc said, his voice fretful. "And so long as they leave me alone, I don't ask. . . ."

"They aren't Germans."

"No."

"Or Italians."

The heavy door opened, flooding the shuttered room with sunlight as a young man stepped in. Seeing Cesar seated at the table, he paused, then closed the door behind him. Without taking his eyes off Cesar, he addressed the old man, "Nonno . . . grandfather . . . who is he?"

6

"A cousin. Cesar Satisanni from Col Pieto," Marc said vaguely, leaving the exact relationship of third or fourth cousin to be examined later.

The newcomer nodded to Cesar. "I'm Joseph Tasera."

Marc's thin voice stretched with irritation. "You're late. I've waited for you all morning."

"I didn't forget. I've done my best." Joseph smiled at the old man. He placed a package of Lucky Strike cigarettes on the table, together with several tins of meat and a bar of soap—taking the items one by one from his pockets. Marc clawed open the cigarettes, placed one between his thin, dry lips, and looked around for a light. Joseph lit it for him with a GI lighter.

Marc inhaled deeply, holding the smoke in his lungs for a long moment. Exhaling, he said, "The smoke has no bite. This is tobacco to be fed to babies. It does nothing to a man's blood, but it is better than smoking nothing." Grumbling, he stood up slowly from the table and started feebly toward an interior door. "I'm going to rest now," he said. "Will you be staying?" he asked Cesar.

"I don't know."

"If you leave and I don't see you go, carry my respects to your family."

"I will, *Zio* . . . uncle."

The old man left the room. The two young men regarded each other warily. Joseph was neither as tall nor as physically sound. He appeared to be several years older than Cesar, and the features of his face were finer and more sensitive. Although the two distant cousins had much the same coloring, Joseph's eyes reflected a warmth and alertness in contrast to the impenetrable stare of Cesar. The thin, mobile face of young Tasera displayed intelligence; the immobile features of Cesar concealed the shrewdness that lay behind them.

Joseph took the wooden chair recently vacated by Marc. He placed a crumpled pack of cigarettes and his lighter on the table. Both men lit up in silence. Cesar examined the pack. "American?"

"Yes." Joseph jerked his head in the direction of the beach. "They're building an airstrip."

"I saw them from up in the hills. They didn't look like Italians or Germans. I thought they might be British . . . or Free French."

"No. They're Americans . . . that's what they are."

"How many?"

"Two hundred. Possibly two fifty."

Cesar smoked in silence for a few moments. "When they're discovered," he said deliberately, "they'll get shot back into the water."

"I'm not so sure," Joseph replied. "Some more wine?" Cesar nodded agreement. Joseph rose and walked to the cupboard, rummaged through it, and returned with an unopened bottle. Uncorking it, he filled the two glasses already on the table. Joseph sat down again and continued. "The Americans landed about a week ago. Pitched their camp in the hills. Well concealed—camouflaged. At first they worked only at night. Now they work during the day."

"They must be very sure of themselves. General Magli has at least fifty thousand Italians. And how many Germans? Fifteen thousand, anyway."

Joseph laughed. "I suppose the Americans have their reasons." He took a sip of wine, then rested his elbows on the table. "I've talked to some of their officers who speak French." His lips twisted in a wry smile. "Atrocious French. I'm also beginning to understand a little English, although I make sure they don't know it. Anyhow, I've picked up a few pieces of information."

The young men had lowered their guard of restraint and were speaking freely now. "Such as . . .?" Cesar asked.

"Well, you know the Germans and Italians have always stayed in the cities—Ajaccio, Calvi, Bastia, Porto-Vecchio, and so on. They're never gone into the countryside . . . the mountains."

"Because they can't move their equipment. There are no roads to take their tanks and trucks." Cesar's eyes were blank, dark pools. "Germans on foot in the mountains are better hunting than wild boars."

"Exactly," agreed Joseph. He slanted in his chair, draping an arm over its back. "The Americans believe the Axis is planning to evacuate, possibly to Elba. At least closer to Italy, where they expect the Americans and British to invade next."

"They believe this? That the Germans are getting out of here?"

"Yes. The Americans don't want to lose men unnecessarily, so they don't interfere with the Germans leaving. And the Germans, on their part, see no particular point in trying to launch an attack on Ghisonacia."

8

"Then why do the Americans bother to build a landing strip? They can take over the German fields when they leave."

Joseph shook his head. "I've tried to figure it out. The Germans, naturally, will destroy all their fields when they pull out. It'll take time . . . possibly weeks . . . to repair them. The American planes, I've heard, have only about forty-five minutes of flying time under fighting conditions. They'll need a field as close to Italy as they can get. One that's ready for operation. They'll have it here."

Cesar nodded thoughtfully. "What do you think of the Americans?"

Joseph smiled and shrugged. "They brought plenty of supplies. Some of the stuff has already found its way into Ghisonacia. You saw what I brought today." Reaching into his pocket he pulled out two paper bills and spread them on the table. "Look at these. They've come prepared with their own money."

Cesar studied the money. "Where'd you get them?"

"From a supply officer." Joseph glanced blandly at Cesar. "Requisitioned them, as the Americans say, for my own use." He paused, then asked, "Notice any difference between them?"

Again Cesar examined the five-dollar bills. "They're identical . . . except for the small seal. On this one, the seal is blue. This other, it's gold."

"A most *important* difference," Joseph agreed. "The gold seal means it's good only here in Corsica, in France, and in other parts of Europe." He spoke quietly, earnestly. "But the *blue* seal is good in the United States. If it's good there, it's good anywhere in the world!"

Cesar refilled his glass with wine. His voice and face betrayed nothing of his feeling of excitement. "It'd be pleasant to have enough of the blue-seal bills."

"Wouldn't it!"

The two men exchanged glances. Cesar waited for Joseph to continue. "I've thought about this," Tasera went on, "and I've decided that the blue seals are important only because through them, one can get many, *many* gold seals. And with enough gold seals! Ahhh!" Joseph's voice faded away.

Cesar's fathomless gaze was fixed on his cousin's face. "You know about such things, possibly. I don't."

"In my studies . . . I enjoyed mathematics," Joseph said modestly.

Cesar, who had stopped attending the small parochial school in Col Pieto after laboriously learning to read and write, and who had barely absorbed the bare rudiments of arithmetic, did not reply directly. Instead, he said, "Suppose I arrange that we get some—many, perhaps—of the blue-seal bills. Then what?"

"How will you get them?"

"I don't know yet. There's time to think and make plans."

"Where will you start?"

"First, you must point out to me the supply officer who has all these bills. What's his name?"

"James Hegan. He's a captain. We'll go to the strip. He'll be there and I'll show him to you."

Captain James Hegan, 15th Air Force, 55th Wing, standing on the beach that day, did not know that he had traveled from Des Moines, Iowa, to Ghisonacia, Corsica, because Fate had decreed that he was to be pointed out to Cesar Satisanni by his cousin, Joseph Tasera. As a result, Hegan would ultimately be responsible for the change of many things in a constantly changing world.

Chapter 2

From Ghisonacia to Col Pieto is sixty kilometers, as the crow flies, through some of the most beautiful and lonesome country in the world. The few roads in Corsica, in 1943, were mostly confined to short stretches along the coasts, and were usually poor. In the mountainous interior, practically no roads existed at all. Not even the Romans, the ancient world's most industrious highway constructors, built roads through the incredibly rugged island. But from time immemorial—back before the Greeks, who preceded the Carthaginians and Romans—the men inhabiting Corsica had developed lines of communication. These consisted of paths and trails in a maze, a labyrinth, which covered the wild tors in a tangled skein. The paths—some nearly invisible, others worn deep through the centuries—wound, looped, cut back, hung, and clung to the sides of dizzy heights. The trails squeezed between crags and ledges, scrambled up the snow-covered peaks and pikes, dropped from crests to the rugged gorges, rocky canyons, and green valleys below.

All was up; all was vertical. Above there was only the depthless sky and the bright Mediterranean sun. Everywhere stretched the forest, up—up! to the snow lines, in great green stands of pine, oak, and cedar; fold after fold after fold. And where the huge, bare boulders of crumbling granite and eroded breccia fell like frozen waterfalls down

11

the sides, purple-green *maquis,* arbutus, and myrtle covered the wounds of the tortured mountains.

Men moved in solitude through the mountains, with nothing to hear except silence itself. For days they might travel the paths without meeting another human. At long intervals—far in the distance across a yawning chasm—perhaps a cluster of tiny buildings like a wasp's nest might be seen clinging to the vertical slope of a neighboring mountain. No farms could exist above the valleys and foothills. But foliage was plentiful, even on steepest inclines, so travelers sometimes came across tiny stone huts of shepherds—isolated, alone, with small flocks of goats and sheep.

But usually there was nothing except the mountains.

Cesar Satisanni followed the trails through the mountain folds between Ghisonacia and Col Pieto with ease. Although it was sixty kilometers on a straight line, the distance he traveled was three, possibly four times greater. He carried no map; he had never seen one of Corsica except for an old reproduction in a geography book owned by the Fathers in the school at Col Pieto. A homing instinct guided him along wild leafy paths toward his goal.

Cesar's mind was lulled into a limbo that erased the monotony of time. His muscled legs moved independently of his body; his eyes and ears automatically registered the sights and sounds around him—the faint trickle of a mountain stream, the flash of a deer, the rooting of a wild pig. Cheese and a chunk of bread, which Joseph had given him when they parted in Ghisonacia, hung in a pouch at his belt. He had spent two of his bullets on a brace of hares and had robbed a game-bird's nest of eggs to roast over a fire. Water could be found for the listening. Cesar was content.

He was always content when alone in the mountains. Only when he was with others did he find himself restless. It was more than restlessness, it was aggressiveness—a competitive drive for domination which seized him. He was given to introspection only on rare occasions, and consequently was unaware of his reactions to the society around him.

Corsican men inherited a legacy of unrestrained, often cruel independence. They courted respect among their peers. Loyalty and allegiance were not matters of morals and ethics, but were determined by each man individually—excepting, of course, the bloodlines of his family, which were unbreakable. The days of savage feuds and vendettas were past, set to rest for nearly a generation. However, old hatreds and mistrust still remained. Ancient grievances—real or imagined—were not entirely forgotten. Families still refused to do business with certain others; marriages were sometimes forbidden; suspicion of strangers was yet strong.

In the family hierarchy women played an important, although concealed, part. Their bloodlines counted, their small dowries and inheritances were matters of consequence. However, they were completely dominated by their fathers, then their husbands, and finally their sons.

Aristocracy, such as it was, depended on tradition from the old Genoese families who settled the island when it was given to Genoa for administration by the Pope in the Middle Ages. The Genoese brought with them the traditional Italian love and respect for land. Since only about five percent of the entire island was cultivable, the families that managed to get land first never relinquished it. They became a society of landed gentry of primitive position. In the following generations those without land became fisherman, shepherds, sailors, smugglers, adventurers, mercenary soldiers, traders, robbers, bandits, and—often enough—pirates. Many migrated back to Italy or, after Corsica became a French possession, to France.

The Satisanni were landlords of fifteen hectometers of earth, a little over thirty-one acres, at the foot of Mount Pieto. A diminutive village lay just below the pass and was named for it, Col Pieto. A kilometer and a half down from the pass was the small green valley owned entirely by Victore Satisanni. The valley, too, was called Valle Satisanni.

After reaching Col Pieto, Cesar followed a wider path—actually a narrow dirt road—that dropped from the pass, wound past the valley, and continued toward Piana. He walked neither faster nor slower than when he had left Ghisonacia five days earlier. Through long familiarity he approached the huge, square, ugly four-storey house with indifference. Made of fieldstones picked from the ground and roughly smoothed, cemented with grainy mortar, and supporting a heavy tile roof, the house was completely without ornament. Windows were narrow and few on each storey; all were protected by heavy wooden shutters. The two doors to the house, front and rear,

13

were solid planks of oak hung from iron hinges. Both were equipped with heavy bolts. The house, which stood on a slight rise of land beside a narrow clear-running stream, had been fortified over the centuries to withstand siege and assault like a fortress.

A short distance to one side of the house stood a shoulder-high, oblong enclosure also constructed of stone. At one end it developed into a shed, open on one side to face the corral. During the lambing season the flocks of sheep were brought there; too, it was used for shearing and, occasionally, for slaughter. Dusty brown chickens stalked around the house and enclosure, ignoring the partly tame cats. Half a dozen little donkeys waited in positions of resignation around the farmyard and a scattering of outbuildings.

The ascending mountainsides surrounding Valle Satisanni held it as if it were a cup. Although the land was fertile, and there was plenty of water to raise crops, the valley never received complete sunlight except at high noon. The crops of corn, beans, pimientos, tomatoes, and potatoes were scanty and stunted. The Satisanni were indolent farmers; so long as the vegetables were edible, they were eaten. Little effort was made to sell or trade the produce. What cash the family received, before the war, came from the sale of ewes' milk for Camembert and *broccio* from goats' milk for Roquefort cheese, which were exported to France.

Near the center of the valley, against the west walls of the mountain, rose a series of small, rock reinforced terraces. These ascended like narrow steps and supported a vineyard. They had always been there—built by some long-forgotten Satisanni. From the grapes the family made a strong but not unpleasant wine, which they sold in Col Pieto and sometimes as far away as Piana.

A pack of dogs came rushing out to greet Cesar—yelping, snarling, baring their teeth, yet wagging their tails. They were hunting dogs, of a kind, marked with deep russet and vaguely resembling hounds. The more gentle, longer-haired dogs were used by the herders, high in the hills, to guard the sheep. Cesar had no words for the dogs meeting him; he ignored them, accepting them with neither like nor dislike.

He walked up the three heavy wooden steps. The door was unprotected and unadorned by any kind of a porch or decoration. It led directly into the main reception room of the house. He opened the door and entered.

Generations of Satisanni brides had brought furniture among their dowries. French gilded chairs, Spanish marble-topped tables, Italian carved wooden chests, painted leather trunks, English horsehair settees, Moroccan tapestry-covered ottomans, heavy handmade benches, drum-shaped taborets, massively ornamented provincial pieces, and leather slung chairs crowded the tile floor of the large room. Nothing was ever discarded from the halls of the Satisanni. Ancient aquatints of the Bay of Naples, the Champs Élysées, St. Peters, the Colosseum, Emperor Napoleon I, and the Arc de Triomphe brought touches of faded color lost in the wide expanse of whitewashed walls. Pale daguerreotypes, dimming tintypes, and discolored yellowing photographs of bridal parties, funerals, christenings, family, and relatives littered the room like fallen leaves. Angled across one corner of the floor squatted a stone fireplace large enough to burn long lengths of heavy logs supported on massive hand-forged fire dogs.

The great, cold drawing room was seldom used by the family. The stark, narrow, shuttered windows set in the thick walls were without drapes; the chill tile floor was bare of rugs and carpets; no chandelier of candles hung from the low-raftered ceiling. Decade after decade, generation after generation, the room had become more cluttered, the furnishings deteriorating, a relic of the past. It was maintained —in its rough provincial grandeur—because it represented the prestige, the facade of dignity, and the power of the Satisanni. There was no other room like it between Col Pieto and Piana.

At six in the summer evening the house was already filled with shadows, the bright light cut off by the surrounding mountains. However, the ancient manse teemed with invisible life. In the rear of the house, in a huge crude kitchen, women of the family were preparing supper; upstairs, children and babies were being tended. Soon the men would come in from their day's activities in the fields, from handling the livestock, from hunting and fishing, from drinking with friends in Col Pieto, or from errands and jobs assigned to them by Victore Satisanni. The house was always filled with relatives— men, women, children, and babies—who lived on the bounty of the family. In return, they offered their services and loyalty to Victore.

15

Often there were twenty or so relatives, of varying degrees of blood closeness, living in the house; occasionally there were more. Some stayed only a short time, others remained for years; a few lived out their lives in the Valle Satisanni. No relative, no matter how distant, was ever turned away.

Cesar, the only son, was heir apparent to this tight, introverted domain. His male relatives treated him with respect. His mother, sisters, and all other household females accepted his commands and served his wishes as readily as they served his father. In one way only, perhaps, had Cesar's boyhood and youth differed from his contemporaries in other very old Corsican families. With few exceptions there was little family wealth on the island. Wealth was replaced with pride. As a matter of prestige the oldest son was educated abroad, preferably in Paris or Marseilles. If he were not sent to France, he attended the local schools, and after graduation his family often went into debt to arrange a life of ease for him in Ajaccio, the capital. There he spent his days dressed in the height of fashion, lounging in the cafés. His nights were spent drinking and gambling. He followed no profession and accepted no career. Eventually he hoped to make a suitable marriage and return to take over his family lands and holdings. Thus he became a symbol of pride for his aristocratic family; his disdain of money and job shown brightly on his family's escutcheon.

As a younger second son, Victore Satisanni had received only an elementary education. He held the scholarly priests of Col Pieto in low esteem. Other more distant schools he regarded even more bleakly. When Cesar dropped out of his classes, Victore did not challenge him. Instead, Victore was content that Cesar spend his days learning to supervise the family property and hunting in the mountains. The boy showed little interest in the land, but he became an expert shot and hunter.

At that time an elderly distant cousin of Victore, Raphael, was living in the house. Raphael had become too old to follow the sea, where he had spent his life. Before retiring he had fought in most of the bars, bistros, saloons, and whorehouses between Marseilles and Madras. Raphael had survived, not without scars, through the judicious and expert use of his knife. This skill he conscientiously and laboriously passed on to young Cesar—as a fencing master might instruct a favorite pupil. The youth became so adept that he could hunt successfully with his blade, throwing it with deadly accuracy at prey up to distances of fifteen feet. This also pleased Victore, for it saved on ammunition expended by Cesar, although the spent brass cartridge shells were kept to be reloaded for additional service. But powder, primer, and lead cost money—cash money—a commodity Victore always found in short supply.

Cesar crossed the tile floor of the empty drawing room to a heavy door leading to an interior hall. Rough, uncarpeted steps led to the upper floors. In the hall he met his father. Victore did not appear surprised by the unheralded appearance of his son, whom he had last seen nearly two weeks earlier.

Victore, a man going to fat, wore an untrimmed, roughly square beard that fell below his neck to his chest. It was white, as was his thick hair hanging to his collar, and they contrived to make him appear older than his fifty-some years. His baggy dark trousers ballooned below the knees where they were tucked into high black boots. A black cummerbund around his belly was worn for warmth against the evening chill of the house. Victore Satisanni belonged to the generation of a dying tradition. As if continuing a recent conversation, he asked, "What did you find out?"

"I'm not joining the underground."

The interior hall was dusky with shadow, and it was difficult for Victore to see his son's face clearly. "Why not?"

Cesar shrugged. "I may have better things to do."

"Did you talk to them?"

"To several *maquis* bands between here and the coast to the east." Cesar paused, then added, "I heard the Germans will soon be gone. When they leave the Italians will go, too."

Victore was surprised. "Without a fight?"

"Possibly. They're moving their strength closer to Italy."

Victore shook his head, puzzled. "What then?"

"The Americans will come. So will the British and the Free French. Things will be different."

"I hope so! Pasta . . . rice . . . olive oil . . ." Victore's voice held both anger and longing. These food items were imported into Corsica, and had been unavailable under the occupation. Victore missed them sorely. "What made you change your mind? You've talked of nothing but the *maquis*. You are content now to stay?"

"I have new things to think about." Cesar moved past his father and started up the stairs. Somewhere on the second floor a door closed, shutting off the cries of a baby.

"I'm glad you're home. Your mother has missed you," Victore said.

The musty damp smell of age, the massive thick walls, the somber deepening shadows, the sense of forever being pinned to the stairs on which he was standing grasped Cesar by the throat. Words, even the lying amenity of 'I'm glad to be home again' which his father waited to hear, refused to pass his lips. Instead he replied, "Nothing has changed."

Cesar climbed the stairs to the third storey and entered his room, a bare, cheerless chamber with planked floor and a large crucifix on the wall. The few essentials crowded it—a heavy wooden bed, a scarred armoire to hold his clothes, and a small table supporting a washbasin and a pitcher of water. Placing his rifle on top of the armoire, and tossing his knife on the bed, Cesar walked to the narrow window. He stood before it for some time. The hot, spicy scent of eucalyptus mingled with the sweetness of oleander in his nostrils. Higher up the mountain, from a stand of holm oak, came the unexpected barking of a fox. From the farmyard the dogs angrily replied.

His hands clenched the windowsill and he leaned out. A sense of frustration so deep as to make him dizzy welled within him. Then it drained away, leaving his spirit heavy and leaden. His lips parted and he spit into the dusk. "I heard you'd returned," a voice said from the doorway.

Cesar slowly turned around to stare at the loutish face of his distant kinsman, Giotto. Although a year younger than Cesar, Giotto loomed above him—a hulking figure of great strength. Slow of wit, and of a surly manner, Giotto had devotedly trailed and served Cesar since they were two tiny naked males playing in the stream where the women washed the clothes. Cesar's expression did not betray his irritation. "Don't sneak up on me that way!"

Gio's heavy features broke into a grin. "Did I surprise you, Cesar?" Cesar shrugged, and Gio sat down heavily on the side of the bed. "Where'd you go?"

"Places."

"Are you going back?"

Cesar closed the shutters. The room was dim. There was no electricity. Cesar made no move to light a candle. "Possibly."

"What are you going to do?"

"I don't know for sure."

"Will you take me?"

"Perhaps."

"When, Cesar?" Gio's heavy face filled with childlike anticipation. He had never been farther away from the valley than Col Pieto, except once when Victore took him and Cesar to Cargese, a small costal village.

Cesar's words were coldly formal. "I'll go when I decide the time is right."

Gio's face fell before the tone of Cesar's voice. "But I can go with you, can't I?"

Cesar poured water from the pitcher into the basin. He began to wash the dust from his face. "You're a pain in the ass, Gio," Cesar remarked dispassionately. "I'll have more important things to do than to take care of you."

"No!" Gio protested. "I'll help you. I'll do anything you say!"

Chapter 3

Excitement ran high along the short length of the steep main street in Col Pieto. Benozzo Florus, proprietor of the only tavern-café and owner of the village's single radio, picked up a very weak BBC broadcast announcing Italy's capitulation on September 8, 1943. The Corsican *maquis* began harassing the German troops in Ajaccio, while the Italian garrisons remained neutral.

"Now we rise up! We'll kill every Nazi bastard on our land!" Benozzo shouted. The tavern keeper's face was red with aroused patriotism mixed with wine.

Many of the shop's patrons loudly agreed.

Aging Father Massafra preferred to leave further developments in the hands of the Diety whom he had served for more than forty years. Smoothing out his loose-fitting black cassock, the priest said, "It is the will of God. In His fury He may strike them all dead. That is . . . if He so desires. Meanwhile we'll pray for all souls, friends and enemy alike."

Victore Satisanni, as the largest landowner and the person who numbered more relatives, direct and indirect, than any other man in the area of Col Pieto, was often awarded the honorary title of *cavaliere*. "Cavaliere Victore," Benozzo addressed him, "what are your thoughts on this matter? Shall we join in driving them out?"

Victore carefully poured another glass of wine before

21

answering. When a young man, thirty years before, during the feuds between the families Satisanni and the Basantelli, he had killed a few men himself. It seemed so long ago that he had difficulty recalling their faces, although he still remembered their names. His older brother, Antonio, had been killed in the vendetta; that was why Victore had inherited the land in the valley. With alarm, he thought of Cesar. If anything happened to his son, he would have no heir. After nearly four hundred years, a Satisanni would not own Valle Satisanni. But the fires of a man's youth become banked in the ashes of his years, and Victore no longer had a taste for violence. He had no desire to become a *caporale*—the leader of a group of men in the maquis. Running his fingers through his beard, he said, "Each man must do as he believes he must. I'll leave the fighting to soldiers who are paid for their services."

A murmur of approval came from the older men. The younger ones shifted uneasily. "How about Cesar?" asked Benozzo.

"He can answer for himself." Victore glanced at his son.

Cesar leaned back in his chair at the small circular table and fingered the narrow scarf tied around his neck. "The Germans and Italians will get out—without our help. I . . . or you . . . or a few more men will make no difference. I'll be busy with other matters."

"You won't be with maquis?" Benozzo asked.

Cesar smiled coldly. "I'll be by myself."

"What can one man accomplish?"

"That depends on what he wants to do."

The men sipped their wine in silence, thinking about it. Father Massafra finally said, "After the war is over, many young men will leave their villages. That is the history and tragedy of our land. Too few remain."

"Remain to do what?" Cesar stared across the narrow street that fronted the tavern. The few shops and houses were built along only one side of the street; the opposite side supported a low stone wall, and beyond the wall was nothing but a precipice dropping a thousand feet. His eyes scaled the void to a neighboring peak. It had always seemed to Cesar that the village faced nothingness. It was empty, as all their lives were empty. "Anyhow, the war will not be over quickly," he said to the priest.

"Italy has already fallen. Germany will be brought to its knees!" Benozzo exclaimed.

"But not too soon." Cesar dropped his eyes and studied his wine, swirling it gently as if to read the glass.

"What do you mean? Do you want this war to continue?"

"Did I say that?"

"If he wishes to take part, in his own way, that's his privilege," Victore said heavily. "He'll return to Col Pieto when he's had enough." He glanced at his son.

But Cesar did not reply.

Later they returned side by side down the mountain road to the valley. The fumes from too many glasses of wine gently clouded Victore's thoughts. He puzzled over Cesar: He had been a good son, posing no problems to his family. Yet Victore had never felt close to him. He remembered how Angela Andrea, Cesar's mother, had often complained of Cesar when he had been little more than a toddler. "Your son doesn't love me," the mother had fretted. Assurances from Victore that Cesar did indeed love her brought only additional protests. "He doesn't want me to hold him. He avoids my arms and caresses!" In a society where children are completely spoiled by their mothers, Angela Andrea's complaint was grounds for maternal unhappiness.

It seemed, Victore reluctantly admitted to himself, that Cesar lived in a world removed from Valle Satisanni. Victore agreed that it is good for a man to be reliant and contained within, but Cesar apparently needed *no one*. Further, he had the disconcerting manner of looking at a person as if through an opaque curtain. Victore wondered about that curtain. What was it made of . . . blankness? Coolness? Self-sufficiency? Perhaps all of these—and more, which Victore could not define. It was indeed as his wife had complained; when he, too, had reached out to the small boy with affection, the father's advances had been accepted without response. Did the boy think it was his *due?* That he was really *Caesar!*

As father and son they had joined in little, except a common table. They had shared no confidences. Cesar had never asked for help or aid from his father. Yet the son obeyed the family head in all things and without complaint. Sometimes as his son grew older, Victore had thought that Cesar was biding his time—like a young bull waiting for the older, stronger one to weaken enough to be challenged successfully. However, this was not true either. Perhaps it was *indifference* to the old family ties of warmth, duty, and affection that pained Victore so deeply.

"When you leave . . . for whatever you're planning . . . you'll come back?" Victore asked, pausing on the steep road.

"I'll keep in touch with you." Cesar evaded a direct reply. Yet, so far as Victore knew, his son had never lied to him.

"What do you wish to do?"

Cesar turned away from his father. "Everything I can't do here."

"What is it you want? We have land . . . and respect. We don't go hungry. It's here that we have our family and friends." Victore shook his head, baffled. "What more do you need?"

Cesar shifted his eyes to look over Victore's shoulder—up the mountain to the thin moonlit clouds far above. He shrugged, but did not reply.

"Soon I'll need your help," Victore continued.

"You'll have it," Cesar replied obliquely.

Victore took off his black corduroy jacket, slung it over his shoulder, and continued down the road.

The radio in Benozzo's tavern brought additional news in the following weeks. On September 20 the Free French forces joined the maquis resistance.

Cesar continued to wait in the valley.

By October 4 the Germans had retreated from the island, departing through Bastia. The Italians retired to Sardinia over the Strait of Bonifacio. The Corsicans set up Committees of Public Safety in Ajaccio, Corte, Calvi, Bonifacio, and Bastia.

On November 1 Cesar, accompanied by Gio, left for Ghisonacia. Cesar carried with him a small hoard of silver franc coins that he had saved from boyhood, his knife, and a single small-bore shotgun. Gio was porter to a pack of Cesar's clothes, a skin of wine, and a supply of food. The two men slipped out of the house before dawn to avoid explanations and goodbyes.

Five days later, from high in the mountains, they saw the landing strip at Ghisonacia astir with military activity—a depot with dumps of fuel, ammunition, and supplies which supported the fighter planes that landed and took off again for action further east in Italy. Temporary barracks for maintenance and support crews dotted the end of the field like metal mushrooms. Before withdrawing from Bastia, the German forces had blown up all the ancient, narrow stone bridges on the eastern side of the island. Transportation was difficult. Practically all communications were conducted by field radio.

Cesar displayed little interest in the American airfield and the war effort. Instead, he and Gio headed straight for Marc's house, where they met Joseph. Because of Cesar, Joseph and Gio accepted each other without hesitation when they were introduced. Gio was silent, withdrawn, and surly; Joseph was alert and outgoing.

Cesar asked Joseph, "Where is Captain Hegan?"

"In Ajaccio. He was transferred."

"Does the captain still pay for supplies?"

"As far as I know, his duties remain the same."

"Did you get to know him well?"

Joseph shrugged. "The Americans have orders to stay away from the village. Sometimes there are opportunities to sell them things. Fish, langouste, fresh eggs . . . you know. And the enlisted men— they'll trade cigarettes and sweets for wine and brandy. That's how well I know Captain Hegan."

"That's not much."

"Well, I've told you."

"I want to know his habits. Did he drink . . . get drunk? Did he try to take the village girls? Was he *formidable?*"

"He wasn't any better or worse than other officers. He kept lists and accounts."

"That tells me nothing."

"Why are you so interested in this Captain Hegan? There are other officers more important."

"With a great supply of blue- and gold-seal dollars?"

Joseph was silent for a moment. Finally he admitted, "No . . . I don't know any others."

"That's why I'm interested in *him.*" Cesar helped himself to one of Joseph's Lucky Strikes. Gio leaned forward and struck a wooden match for him. "You told me," Cesar continued, "that if we had those bills you knew how we could become rich."

"Yes, that's so," Joseph said.

"You still believe it?"

"America is the richest country in the world. If it's so rich, then its money must be better than any other. The bills with the blue seal will be good *anywhere*. Everyone will want them!" Joseph gestured for emphasis. "But it's through the gold-seal bills, the ones to be spent only here and on the mainland, by which a fortune will be made. Do you understand?"

"No," Cesar told him bluntly. "But then such details don't interest me. What matters is that *you* understand them." His stare fixed on Joseph. "Do you assure me that if I get those bills you know what to do with them?"

Joseph moved uneasily beneath the dark scrutiny, but his voice held assurance. "I know exactly what to do with them."

The old housekeeper shuffled into the room in her dusty black dress. She placed two open cans of Spam, peanut butter, and a heap of crackers on the table. Cesar looked at the food. "Yes, it's American," Joseph said. He spread a cracker and ate it. Cesar followed. His face reflected no reaction, but he did not take a second. He gestured to Gio. "Help yourself." Gio fell on the food.

Cesar resumed the conversation. "All right. I'll get the money."

Joseph looked at his distant cousin, his sensitive face thoughtful. "Why are you so single-minded? Does Signore Victore need money to save his land? Or do your sisters need money to get married?" When Cesar did not reply, Joseph continued, "I don't know how you intend to do it. But it is dangerous . . . he who runs with dogs is bitten by dogs. The army—American, German, Italian—it makes no difference. The officers in them, in uniform, are dangerous. It's one thing to steal a bit of food here, a little money there. That is to be expected. But . . ." Joseph's voice trailed away.

Cesar sat motionless, his face impassive. Then, slowly, he turned his head to look at Gio, who was eating a tin of Spam. Gio stopped. Cesar returned his gaze to Joseph, but it included Gio as well. "At home, in the mountains, when I look up all I see above is part of the sky. Here at Ghisonacia, looking over the sea, I can see more sky. The sky covers the entire world, and I want to see *all* of it."

Cesar's two companions stared at him in silence.

"I want money," Cesar continued, his voice flat, "because money is power. And with enough power I can own the clouds in the sky —if that is what I want! Do I make myself clear?" He waited for their reply. They nodded. "We have found this Captain Hegan. His money was too well protected here in Ghisonacia—where trouble might be expected. But in Ajaccio in may be different. Anyhow, I'll not lose this opportunity to try. If you don't want to join me, I'll find others." His voice hardened. "Do you?"

Joseph was first to break the silence. "Yes. I'll do my part."

Gio's heavy face was earnest. "Whatever you say, Cesar."

Cesar pushed aside the food and rested his forearms on the table. "I don't know how much money I'll need in Ajaccio before I find Hegan—and conclude my business with him. How much money do you have, Joseph?"

Joseph took a small roll of bills from his pocket and tossed it on the table in front of Cesar. "Fifty-seven dollars. American. Both blue and gold."

Cesar picked up the bills and, without counting them, removed a five-dollar bill and handed it back to Joseph. The remaining bills he tucked in a pocket beneath his belt. "These will do along with what I have unless it takes more time than I expect. Gio and I will go to Ajaccio. When I'm ready, I'll send for you."

"When the time comes, I'll be there," Joseph said.

Chapter 4

Freighters, supply ships, tenders, and support craft filled the Bay of Ajaccio. Gray destroyers, swifts escorts, and transports arrived and departed on their hurried and mysterious ways. Quays and piers were piled high with matériel. Behind the now busy port lay the once quiet small city and capital of the island, Ajaccio. Its twenty-five thousand inhabitants were caught in the victorious hustle of the Allies. Foreign uniforms—American, British, Free French —filled the streets, as well as Algerian troops with black faces wearing colorful and exotic Zouave regimentals.

For centuries Ajaccio had watched other armies arrive and leave. The city's tall, plaster-finished white and yellow buildings with their tile roofs and painted shutters tried to remain aloof from the strangers. Ajaccio lay scattered in a dogleg pattern along the port, squeezed between the bay in front and the seared *maquis*-covered foothills behind, but it had seen war too many times before to be impressed. After the Romans had come the Vandals; then for three hundred years the Saracens; next the Genoese; and finally the French. In time the Allies would go, too, as had the Italians and Germans. The townspeople spoke French to the French and made little effort to learn English. Among themselves they continued to use their own Corsican.

Cesar Satisanni managed to find lodging for himself and Gio in the crowded city. Their room was located on a

29

narrow, damp street of arched, twisted passageways and decaying houses of peeling plaster. It offered little more than privacy and protection against the chill of night. An outside flight of stone stairs contained by a rusted metal railing led to their door on the second floor. Three families occupied the rest of the house—families with their usual quota of relatives and innumerable children. Clotheslines, sagging with damp wash, stretched from storey to storey and balcony to balcony. The house was permeated with layers of odors from generations of cooking oil, fish, sour wine, urine, and mold.

Cesar was indifferent to the squalor of their room. Not so Gio. "We are fortunate to find it," Cesar said.

"It stinks!"

"Since when has your nose become so delicate?"

"I don't see why we can't find one that's better."

"You'll get used to it," Cesar pronounced flatly. "Unless you prefer to return to the fresh air in Col Pieto." Gio shook his head in sullen acceptance. Cesar relented slightly. "In this miserable place no one can find us. We've disappeared like rabbits in a hole. We'll move later."

Gio began to unpack Cesar's clothes, which he had carried on his back all the way from Valle Satisanni. Taking off his rough mountain clothes, Cesar put on his best—a red shirt, dark alpaca jacket with silver buttons, and fawn-colored trousers. His shoes were French and pointed. Finally he tied a black silk scarf around his throat beneath the open neck of his shirt.

"A *cavaliere!*" Gio stared at him in open admiration.

"It wouldn't hurt you to look less like a peasant," Cesar said.

"I haven't any other clothes."

"I'll get you some."

"You will, Cesar?"

"Yes." Cesar transferred his sheathed knife to the back of his belt, where it was concealed by his jacket.

Before leaving the room, Cesar hid the shotgun beneath the lumpy mattress on the bed. The gun had been brought into the room wrapped in the bundle of clothes.

They strolled down the Cours Napoleon, a main street running parallel for some distance along the harbor. The street was lined with small bars, cafés, and shops filled with sailors, merchant seamen, and soldiers. Military trucks and jeeps fought among themselves for right-of-way in the heavy traffic. At one of the small street cafés Cesar seated himself at a tiny empty table. Gio jammed his bulk into a second chair and pulled it up beside him. Cesar casually signaled a waiter for two glasses of wine. "What do we do now?" Gio asked.

"We listen," Cesar said.

Two days, two nights, and a score of bars later, Cesar heard a French soldier speaking fluent English with two American sailors. The three were slightly drunk and cursing the lack of available girls. While Gio figeted, Cesar waited patiently, his attention riveted on the Frenchman. Eventually the two Americans—weaving slightly— headed for the street. The French soldier looked around the bar and sighed. At that moment Cesar caught his eye and nodded. "A drink?" he called.

The Frenchman moved away from the bar and stood looking down at Cesar. "I'm broke," he said thickly.

"Sit down, I'll buy."

The soldier drew up a chair. Seating himself heavily he said, "A pig can't buy slop on my filthy pay." He stared with belligerency at Cesar. "I won't buy you one back," he warned.

Cesar shrugged. "What does it matter?" He ordered a brandy from the waiter who placed it in front of the Frenchman.

The soldier held his glass and looked with suspicion at his host. "How come you fellows aren't in the service?"

"We're with the maquis," Cesar said easily. "Down from Bastia for a few days." The soldier nodded and pulled out a pack of Gauloises. He passed it to Cesar, then to Gio. They lit up. "I heard you talking to the Americans," Cesar continued. "I'd guess you speak English very well."

"I sure as hell do," the soldier agreed. "I learned it the hard way."

"How's that?"

"Before this shitty war, I was a waiter in Paris. At the Hôtel des Fleurs. You ever hear of it?"

"No."

"The Limeys used to come there on vacation. Most of them couldn't speak a word of French, and those that tried you couldn't understand anyway." He looked bitterly at his glass. " 'Louis get me this . . . Louis do that,' " he mimicked. "If you didn't know what they were saying, you didn't get a tip." Louis took a sip of brandy. "They were all miserly tippers anyway," he added.

"Oh, well, you survived." Cesar was dispassionate.

"And you speak with a Midi accent thick enough to spread for manure," Louis accused, still angry.

"We seldom get a chance to hear a correct Parisian accent. Maybe because of the war, we'll improve." Cesar's irony was lost on Louis. He glanced at Louis' empty glass and ordered another drink for his guest. "Perhaps you might do me a favor," he remarked casually.

"I might," said Louis, "but I doubt it. I can't do myself a favor let alone anybody else. If I could do myself any good, I wouldn't be here."

"How about some money to carry you to next payday?"

"Black market! I knew there was a catch to this. But I don't have anything to sell."

"No, you have me wrong," Cesar told him. "My pal and I are strangers here. We have an old friend somewhere in town. Knew him in Ghisonacia. We'd like to get in touch with him."

"Who is he?"

"James Hegan. He's a captain with the American 15th Air Force . . . 55th Wing."

"Ask at American HQ."

"How? We don't speak English, but you do. The captain might not like us walking around asking questions through interpreters." Cesar's voice held a delicate, knowing edge.

"Oh, it's like that, eh?"

"We did him some favors. He did us some."

"What do you want to know? Where he's bivouacked?"

"That'll do."

"I drive for this colonel. Talmant! He's a bastard, but he gets around. Long as I have to haul his ass, I can ask at the places where we go." Louis scratched his chin. "If I locate Hegan, what's in it for me?"

"Ten dollars American," Cesar said promptly. The sum was a substantial amount of Louis' monthly pay.

"It might take time and a lot of effort. It's worth more . . ."

"Ten dollars," Cesar repeated flatly. "You get five dollars now and five more when you locate Hegan."

"He'll screw you out of your money," Gio warned. "You won't hear from him again."

"Then I'll lose five . . . and he'll lose five." Cesar looked at Louis. "How about it?"

Louis held out his hand. Cesar handed him a five-dollar bill. "Where'll I get in touch with you?" the Frenchman asked.

"We'll be here at Le Bélier every night," Cesar said.

"All right." Louis stood up at the table. He paused. "What the devil are your names?"

"Xavier," Cesar replied, unblinking. "My pal is Roger."

"*À bientôt . . .*" Louis pushed his way through the door and disappeared in the crowd on the street.

"He'll get so drunk tonight he won't remember in the morning," Gio said.

"He won't forget he has another five dollars coming," Cesar assured him as they paid the waiter and left The Ram bar.

On a side street between the Cours Napoleon and the Rue Fesch, Cesar paused before a small shop and stared in the window. It was filled with secondhand suits and clothing. Nodding to Gio to follow, Cesar entered the store. In the musty interior the owner glanced up, without interest, from a seat behind a low counter. "He needs some clothes," Cesar said. "Do you have something that'll fit him?"

"Look around," the man said with indifference.

Gio foraged through the piles of clothing while Cesar leaned casually against a wall. Nothing was said; the silence was broken only by Gio's heavy breathing. "Look," Gio announced after some minutes, holding up a pair of shiny, well-worn blue pants and a black-and-white striped shirt. "These'll do."

"Get a jacket and shoes while you're at it," Cesar said.

Gio returned to rummage through the used clothes. Eventually he found a reddish-brown and white houndstooth check jacket. It was an astounding item to be found in Ajaccio and had been pawned, probably, by a hard-up American seaman. The jacket fit Gio, although it was slightly tight across the shoulders. His broad flat feet fit none of the shoes, so he settled for a pair of heavy leather, strapped sandals. He placed the clothes on the counter.

"How much?" Cesar asked.

The shopkeeper sized up Cesar's rather foppish appearance and considered Gio's obvious country clothing. "Sixteen hundred and fifty francs for the pants," he replied, squinting shrewd, dark eyes down his long nose. "One thousand-fifty for the shirt. Coat twenty-two hundred and sixty. Sandals, fourteen hundred."

"That comes to what?"

"An even six thousand five hundred francs." The shopkeeper had added an additional hundred and forty francs to the total, rounding it out, figuring that his customers would not know the difference. At the prevailing rate of exchange, the bill was approximately twenty dollars.

"You take us for fools," Cesar said softly.

"Those are fine clothes! With this war, good clothes are hard to get!" The man rose from his chair.

"You ask too much. A man is entitled to a profit, but they're not worth half of what you're asking." Cesar stared at the shopkeeper, who placed his hands on top of Gio's assortment. "I'll give you four thousand francs for them."

The man gave a short, harsh laugh. "Don't waste my time. If you don't like the price, get out!" he snarled.

"You're *ordering* me?" Cesar appeared surprised.

"You heard me!"

"Put them on," Cesar ordered Gio.

"But . . ." Gio looked at Cesar, confused.

"Do it!" Cesar snapped. "Change in the corner."

The shopkeeper charged around the end of the counter, his face twisted with anger. "I'm calling the *flics!*" he threatened.

Cesar's knife suddenly pressed against the man's belly, stopping him in his tracks. "While we wait," Cesar said, his voice flat, "you will make out a receipt. You'll list all the items—and mark them as sold for *three* thousand francs." He twitched the knife slightly, the point gently pricking. "And paid in full!" The shopkeeper retreated behind the counter. "We don't have all day," Cesar warned. Hurriedly the man began to scribble with a pencil on a piece of paper.

Gio came out of the corner wearing his new outfit. He was pleased. Never before had he worn such fancy clothes. His old ones he tossed on the counter. "Take them with you," Cesar said.

"I won't need them."

"Roll them up and take them!" Cesar leaned over the counter and picked up the paper. He slowly read the scrawled receipt. "Sign it!" The shopkeeper hastily complied.

Cesar folded the receipt and placed it in his pocket. He took out a thin roll of paper francs and counted out three one-thousand notes. Placing them on the counter, he deliberately returned his knife to its sheath in the back of his belt. He stared at the shopkeeper. "Now you can call the *flics,*" he said. The man said nothing.

"Let's go," Gio urged.

Cesar shook his head, his eyes still riveted on the man before him. "You're stupid," he said, his voice emotionless, "because you tried to cheat me out of a few thousand francs. Furthermore, I don't like your manners. I've put up with you because *I* had a reason. Otherwise . . ." Cesar's fingers snapped as if breaking a twig. He glanced at the silent Gio. "Come on."

The shopkeeper, gray-faced, stared at the empty doorway long after his two customers had gone.

Chapter 5

The pair of Zouaves stood back to back by the bar, their teeth gleaming white between drawnback lips. Long, wicked knives glinted in their hands. Their uniforms of full harem-cut blue trousers, yellow blouses, green vests, and crimson sashes were showy blooms of color in the surrounding crowd of drab olives and navy blues.

"Those are the two black sons of bitches who robbed me the other night!" a sailor continued, pointing an accusing finger. Half a dozen of his companions gathered in an ominous group behind him.

Voices died away. The scuffling of feet, the clink of glasses, the scraping of bottles were silenced. It was very quiet. The dimly lit bar drew itself together waiting for the full fury of violence to strike. Knives appeared in the hands of some of the sailors; others grasped the necks of heavy wine bottles. "You sure?" one of the sailors asked.

"Goddamn right I'm sure!" the accuser shouted. His head was bandaged.

"All those ugly monkeys look alike."

"That one! Him with half an ear! I'd recognize him anyplace!"

The accused Algerian, actually a Moroccan enlisted in an Algerian unit, licked his heavy lips but said nothing.

Behind the bar, the owner of Le Bélier cautiously moved aside, his eyes helplessly looking to the door for aid. The bistro was long and narrow, the slate-covered bar running almost the entire length of one side. Against the opposite wall was set a line of tables and flimsy chairs beneath a series of dusty mirrors. At the far end perched a battered machine used to make coffee and hot chocolate—which sometimes were available on the black market. The fourth side completely opened on the street and offered four additional tables for the sidewalk trade. During the few hours when the bar was closed, a metal grill was stretched across the front and padlocked. It was not an attractive pothouse; soon it would be a shambles.

A Free French soldier joined the group of sailors. His blouse concealed a .25-caliber MAB. He took it out and waved it, drunk with hatred. "Shoot 'em!" he yelled. "Don't get too close or they'll slit your frigging throats!"

Cesar, seated at a table, inched out his foot. Leaning back, relaxed, he appeared an uninvolved observer interested in the drama playing before him. The toe of his shoe hooked around the leg of an empty chair. The muscles of his leg tightened. His ankle jerked.

The chair skittered across the floor and crashed behind the knees of the soldier. His knees buckled, and he fell forward into the group of sailors.

In the moment of confusion, the two Zouaves leaped forward and raced for the door. The small, bloodshot eyes of the Algerian with the mutilated ear flicked at Cesar in passing. Then they were gone.

A roar of shouts and curses filled the bar, but no one went out into the night after the fleeing blacks. Cesar calmly sipped his wine. Only Gio had noted Cesar's part in breaking up the fight.

"Why?" Gio asked. "It was none of your business."

"Lower your voice. You want those sailors on us?"

"All right." Gio replied in a whisper. "But why?"

"A shooting . . . the M.P.'s and gendarmerie would be here on the run. Questions! ID's! We don't need that."

Louis entered and looked around. Spotting Cesar, he made his way to the table through the press of loud, arguing customers. "What happened?" he asked.

"Nothing." Cesar shrugged. "Missed a near fight."

Louis pulled up a chair and sat down. He looked for the waiter, failed to see him, got up and walked to the bar. Returning with a brandy, he seated himself again. "I've located Captain Hegan," he said.

"Good."

"A lot of American officers are billeted at the Grande. So's Hegan. Know where it is?"

"I'll find it."

"It's over near the Cours Grandval."

Cesar nodded and handed Louis the additional five dollars. "We're even," he told the soldier.

Louis put the bill in his pocket. "You're a strange fellow . . ."

"You think so?"

"Yes. Sometimes it's like you're wearing dark glasses."

"I don't wear them," Cesar said.

"True. But just the same it's hard to read your eyes."

"If you did, maybe you wouldn't like the color."

Louis laughed. "I like the color of your money." He drained his brandy.

"Perhaps there'll be more."

"I thought you were only staying a few days."

"That depends."

"In that case, if you should need me again . . ."

Cesar stood up and gave a slight gesture to Gio, who lumbered to his feet. "If I do, I'll leave a message for you."

"Where?"

"On the cornerstone of Saint Roche. The church. I'll leave a mark." Cesar smiled slightly. "An *X*—for Xavier. That'll mean to meet me here."

In peace, the streets of Ajaccio were dimly lit at night. With the war and its new demands on power, except for the few main boulevards, the streets were black pools of shadows and darkness. Returning to their room, Cesar and Gio walked down the center of the cobbled, winding side streets to avoid the deep doorways and arches in which thugs and robbers often waited for the unwary. After some distance Cesar stopped between the rows of night-mantled, shuttered houses to listen. "We're being followed," he said. Gio's foot explored the darkness until it located a heavy stone. He picked it up and carried it in his hand as they continued on their way.

Climbing the outside stairs, they reached their room. Inside, Cesar lit an oil lamp and placed it on a wooden table by the door. He removed the shotgun from beneath his mattress and loaded it with heavy shot, then sat down on the bed. "I'll bolt the door," Gio said.

"No. Leave it unlatched."

"But if someone's trying to rob us . . ."

"It's better to know who your enemy is. Shut up and sit over by the window—out of the way."

Gio obeyed, hunkering down on his haunches. Both young men kept their eyes riveted on the door. It moved very slightly. Gio started. Cesar motioned with his head for him to remain quiet. The door inched inward. "Come in!" Cesar said. The door swung open.

In the doorway stood the Algerian Zouave with the half ear.

Cesar's shotgun was pointed at the black's belly.

Cesar said nothing—waiting. "I followed you," the Algerian said. He spread his hands to show they were empty, but his long, wicked knife was tucked in his sash.

"That's obvious," Cesar said.

"I want to talk to you."

"You're here. Talk."

The Zouave nodded toward the lamp. "The light. I can be seen from the street."

"Come in." Cesar shifted his position on the bed, placing the shotgun beside him on the blanket.

The black stepped inside and kicked the door closed behind him. His hands went to his vest as if to pull it down. Cesar's knife flashed through the air to bury itself in the door only inches from the Algerian's throat. "I could've put it through your neck," Cesar said calmly.

The startled look faded from the black's face. "I wasn't going for my knife," he said.

"Gio, get mine," Cesar snapped.

Gio stood up, walked to the door, and pulled the knife from the wood. Handing it to Cesar, he returned to his place by the window.

"I don't need a shotgun to kill you," Cesar said. The black nodded. "What's your name?"

"Anse," the Algerian replied, pointing to his mutilated ear standing out like the broken handle of a pot—for which he was nicknamed.

"All right, Anse. You want something. What?"

The man's bloodshot eyes peered through the yellowish light at Cesar. "Tonight in the bar you saved me from getting killed. You don't owe me nothing. Why'd you kick that chair?"

"Bored," Cesar replied lazily. "I didn't care if they punctured your black hide."

"No, it wasn't that!" Anse said. "You got reasons of your own." His voice dropped slyly. "Maybe you don't like the *miléteri* or *flics* poking around?"

"That's my concern."

"Maybe mine, too. I want to get the hell out. Desert. What chance I got on a flea-bitten island? No friends or money. Where'll I hide?" Anse grimaced. "With this face of mine, they catch me pretty quick."

"So?"

"Maybe you got connections. Maybe you help me? I'm handy to have around. No scruples about nothing."

Cesar stared thoughtfully at the intense black face. Despite the coolness of the night, sweat ran from beneath Anse's red fez and gleamed on his forehead. "Perhaps," Cesar said finally. "In a few days I may be able to use you. But not now. If you want to come with me, you have to do something first."

"What?"

"I need four automatic revolvers. And plenty of rounds for them."

"You can find them in the black market."

"I don't intend to buy them," Cesar's voice was cold, "when you can steal them."

"Each gun's checked out and a man's responsible for it. Once I grab them, I've gotta run."

Cesar nodded. "Go back to your company. Line up the guns so you'll be ready when I tell you." He nodded toward Gio. "When you see him outside your barracks, you'll know it's time to move."

"Agreed."

"You're broke, of course?"

"Naturally."

Cesar jingled some silver francs, then handed them to Anse. The black accepted the money without change of expression. "The next time I see you, you'll have four revolvers and ammo. In return I'll give you money, a place to hide, and arrange that you aren't caught.

41

I'll protect you." Cesar indicated the door. "Now it's time for you to get going."

After Anse left, Gio bolted the door. "The way you pass around money! Louis, now Anse. One would think you were a *grand signor*." Gio shook his head.

Cesar unloosened the silk scarf at his neck. "Once a man takes my money, then he's *my* man."

"He might sell you out!"

"No one had better sell me out," Cesar said.

In the morning they arose early and walked to the Grande Hôtel. Gio was back in his rough country clothes. The two sat on a bench in a small park directly across from the entrance of the hotel. They shared breakfast while Gio grumbled, "The bread has no taste. The wine's bitter . . ."

Cesar ignored him. His eyes were fixed on the wide doors beneath the hotel's old marquee. Already American noncoms and enlisted men were arriving and departing, carrying briefcases, packages, gear, and equipment. Gio ate the last crumb of the thick-crusted bread and drained the final drop of wine. Then officers began to appear. Pedestrian traffic past the hotel became heavy. Messengers and couriers gunned their motorcycles, filling the street with shocks of reverberations.

Captain James Hegan came out of the doors and stood by the curb, looking down the street to a line of parked jeeps with drivers. "There!" Cesar said. "That's Hegan. Look at him so you'll recognize him!"

Gio stared at the officer who walked briskly down the street. He was a slender man, in his early thirties, with pale skin and sandy red hair, and he carried himself with a slight stoop in his shoulders. Hegan stepped into a jeep, settling down beside the driver, and the machine pulled away from the curb.

"Would you know him again?" Cesar asked.

"Yes."

"Then go to the hotel and hang around. Offer to run errands and make yourself useful. Fetch and carry, and be grateful for small tips."

Gio sullenly threw the empty bottle under the bench. "I'm not a servant . . ."

"You are if I say so!" The grim lines on Cesar's face softened. "No," he assured Gio, "you're not a servant. You're doing something important . . . something that must be done so I can make my plans. Don't ask questions at the hotel, but keep your eyes open. Find the room where Hegan is staying. Look inside it—if you can. Find out how many guards they have, and where they are. I depend on you to tell me what you've seen."

"I'm not clever at such things," Gio muttered.

"I know that. But it's better that you be remembered, later, instead of me."

Gio rose reluctantly to his feet. "If they speak no French, what do I do?"

"You act the part of a country fool—which you are!" Cesar was irritated. "But be pleasant, and the chances are that no one will pay attention to you." He added, his voice holding an edge of warning, "It won't take too long!"

"How long is that?"

Cesar's eyes bored into Gio. Gio squirmed. "You decide." Cesar turned on his heel and started for the corner while Gio slowly crossed the street to the Grande.

Young Satisanni walked rapidly for a few minutes, stifling his anger against the stupidity of Gio. On the Avenue de Paris he approached a wide paved square. Recognizing the massive bronze statue of Napoleon, he stopped. Empty fountains, not in use, surrounded the heroic figure of the emperor seated on a spirited warhorse. He crossed the plaza to stare up at the face of the famous equestrian.

"You were born here," Cesar silently addressed Corsica's greatest son. "When, first, did this island become too small for you? What made you an emperor? You were short and fat . . . and too often ill! What was your genius the old men talk about? That you understood artillery? That is one way to power, and you got what you wanted —an empire! Well, I'll find other ways to get what I want." He turned away, paused, then swung around again. He smiled coldly. "And I'll not be dragged down by my enemies—as you were!"

Cesar walked away from the statue without a backward glance. He returned to his room, threw himself on the bed, and promptly fell asleep. Awakening at noon, he sauntered downtown again and ate lunch in a small brasserie. Nearby, overlooking the Boulevard Sampiero, an outdoor flea market was operating from flimsy temporary booths. Rough tables and partitions were set up in an open area beneath a stand of trees. Selling was conducted by old women and mothers with babies.

Cesar looked through the offerings of freshly caught fish, roasted chestnuts, black-market cigarettes, old clothing, and odds and ends of used household items. He selected a pair of mechanic's coveralls and a seaman's knitted cap. And, finally, he found a package of black tea. Disdaining to haggle, Cesar paid the few francs asking price to a white-haired crone and carried his purchases back to his room.

He waited patiently for his cousin's return. It was long after dark when Gio entered and kicked the door shut in sullen anger. "Did you locate Hegan's room?" Cesar asked quietly.

"If you knew what I went through to do it. If . . ."

"I'm not interested in a long story," Cesar interrupted.

"A dozen times today they chased my ass around . . ."

"What's his room number?"

"Christ! Those Americans! You'd think . . ."

"The number!" Cesar raised his voice.

Gio's heavy features sagged. "The number is 318 . . . and 320. At the end of a hall."

"Two rooms? What is he, a general?"

"One room is an office. Next to it is the captain's bedroom. There's a door between. All day long a sergeant sits at a desk in the office."

"An office?"

"The Americans have taken over the whole building. Some of the rooms are used for offices, too."

Cesar flipped a hundred-franc piece to Gio. "If you're hungry, get yourself some supper."

"Aren't you going to eat, too?" Gio asked. Cesar shook his head. "I . . . I saw a lot of other things. Don't you want to know about them?"

"I'll ask you questions when you come back." Cesar folded his hands behind his head and leaned back on the bed. He was deep in his plans when Gio clomped down the outside stairs to the street.

Chapter 6

"I saw your mark," Louis said.

Cesar was seated at the table that was becoming his regular place in Le Bélier. He gestured to the soldier to sit down and ordered a brandy for him. "How many uniforms do you own?" he asked.

"Two. My dress and fatigues."

"I want to rent one. I don't care which."

"My dress is worn only for inspections . . . and special duty."

"Then that will do."

Louis hesitated. "What do you want it for?"

Cesar disregarded Louis' question. "I'll need it for twenty-four hours. It'll be returned."

"Suppose something comes up and I need it? That Talmant is one tough bastard."

"That's your problem."

"I could put in for sick bay maybe . . ." Louis was uneasy.

"You'll get another ten dollars when you deliver the uniform and a dispatch case."

"Dispatch case? I don't have one!"

"Your colonel has."

Louis nodded slowly. "He's got a couple . . ."

"I only want one. Empty. A simple request. You'll get it back with the uniform."

"When do you want them?"

"Today."

"Here?" Louis was surprised.

Cesar shook his head. "Contact us here, but leave the stuff in your jeep. We'll pick it up someplace else."

"Another drink'll help me decide." Louis eyed his empty glass.

"All right," agreed Cesar, "but you've already decided."

Gio entered the bar, crossed the floor, and sat down at the table. He looked cautiously at Louis. "He's on his way after he finishes his drink," Cesar said. Gio nodded and sat back, his big hands resting on the table. Confronted with the Corsicans' cold patience, Louis hurriedly gulped his brandy and went on his way. Cesar turned to Gio. "Did you see Anse?"

"Yes. From a distance. And he saw me—no question about it."

Cesar took ten dollars from his pocket and handed it to Gio. "When Louis comes back, he'll have a uniform and a dispatch case in his jeep. Get him to drive you where you won't be seen. Take the stuff from him and give him his money. Then go back to the room and wait."

From Le Bélier Cesar went directly to the Grande Hôtel. Behind it, as described by Gio, ran a narrow, damp alley. The hotel's large service door was partly blocked by cartons and crates of refuse, and cans of trash. Cesar strolled down the alley once; turning, he retraced his steps, absorbing the details of the scene in his mind. Assuming an air of assurance, he pushed open the heavy swinging door and stepped inside the rear of the hotel.

The back hall was dark; at one end he saw white-clad figures working in a kitchen. At the other end of the corridor a steep stairway ascended. Gio had not been sure that the stairs retained their position in the upper storeys of the building, so Cesar dismissed them from his calculations. Supposedly a guard was on station beside the back door, but Cesar did not see one. Facing him, across the hall from the back door, was the service elevator—old, decrepit, little more than a metal cage. The lift was stopped somewhere on the floors above.

Cesar turned at the sound of heavy feet descending the service stairs. He stepped quickly across the hall and pressed the elevator button. Overhead, the ancient machinery came slowly to life. Satisfied that the elevator was in running order, Cesar turned and moved

46

swiftly to the door, but he was stopped by a loud command. "Hey, you! What you want?"

The missing guard, in American uniform, strode quickly down the hall from the stairs. A .45 was holstered at his belt.

Cesar spoke rapidly in a flow of French.

The American, who understood nothing of the language, stared in bafflement at Cesar. "ID. ID. Carte ID!" The guard held out his hand.

Although the American's meaning was clear, Cesar ignored it, pretending not to understand. Instead, he pointed through the door at the collection of trash and broke into another rush of French. Then he pushed open the door and stepped outside. The guard followed him. Cesar picked up a carton as if to take it away; he set it down again. Kicking a crate, he made the motions of pushing it down the alley. Cesar looked at the guard as if in expectation. Slowly the guard seemed to understand. "You want to salvage that junk?"

Cesar launched into another session of unintelligible French.

The American gave up. "Beat it!" he ordered, jerking his thumb toward the end of the alley. "Move!"

This time Cesar was pleased to comply. He started down the alley away from the hotel. His face was impassive, but he enjoyed the ease with which he had evaded the guard.

The Mediterranean dusk fell early in the winter months. It was well after dark when Anse knocked lightly at the door. Gio unbolted the lock and the black stepped inside. He was bareheaded and wore a long, dark raincoat to conceal his Zouave uniform. In his hand he carried a small duffel bag. Without a word he crossed the room to the bed and emptied it. Four automatic revolvers and a dozen boxes of bullets tumbled out. Anse looked at Cesar and smiled.

Cesar nodded, pleased. "Good, Anse." For a moment a tiny flame seemed to flicker in his eyes. "Now get out of that uniform."

As Anse stripped off his clothes, Gio put them on. Although the Algerian was a big man, Gio was larger. Fortunately the loose, baggy cut of the Zouave design enabled Gio to wear the uniform. Cesar tossed the coveralls and knitted cap to Anse. "Put them on—and wear the cap all the time. Keep it pulled down over that hacked-up ear of yours!"

A discarded can stood on the table. In it Cesar had boiled down strong black tea mixed with walnut stain scraped from the headboard of the old bed. He applied the makeup to Gio's face, neck, and hands.

Anse watched. "Never going to make him look black," he warned.

Gio's tanned, olive skin had turned several shades deeper. "Maybe not, but I can make him look like a half-breed," Cesar told Anse bluntly.

The Algerian shrugged, taking no offense. "We got couple or three in our company, but they don't look like him."

"Put it on! All of it! Rub it in," Cesar ordered Gio, "while I get ready."

Cesar began donning Louis' Free French uniform. When he was dressed he loaded a .45 with a full clip. He hefted the gun in his hand, then wadded up Anse's raincoat, folded a sheet of paper on which he had laboriously written a receipt, and put the items in a dispatch case. "How do you look?" he asked. Gio straightened in his Zouave uniform, his heavy face a deep chocolate brown. Cesar inspected him carefully. "Your hair won't fool anyone!" He turned to Anse. "Where's your fez?"

"Pocket of the raincoat."

Cesar opened the dispatch case, located the fez, and gave it to Gio, who put it on. "Better . . ." Cesar regarded the change. "Think he'll do?"

"If nobody don't look too close," Anse grunted.

"Stay here," Cesar told the Algerian. "Don't go out. Let no one in." He picked up the dispatch case. Gio lifted a heavy case of wine to his shoulder. They walked to the door. "Lock it when we leave," Cesar ordered Anse.

On the balcony outside the door, Cesar paused. The houses were shuttered for the night; the street was silent and empty. Behind him, he heard Anse shoot the bolt in place. The two started for the hotel.

Across from the Grande, Gio lowered the case to the ground. He rubbed his weary shoulder. "Suppose he isn't in?" he panted.

"Then we'll come back later." Cesar reached into his dispatch case and released the safety on the automatic. He gave last-minute instructions to Gio. "*You* say nothing. Keep your head down—look at the floor. Hide your face behind the wine case."

"All right," Gio agreed. He again hoisted the weighty case to his shoulder and they crossed the street.

Two M.P.'s looked up when they entered the Grande. Carpeting had been stripped from the floor of the lobby, leaving only the hardwood floors scarred by army boots. A high chandelier cast a feeble glow over a scattering of wooden tables strewn with old newspapers and magazines. Bulbous ashtrays stood beside worn brown davenports and leather chairs. The old, once elegant room bore the irremediable stamp of the military.

A sergeant lounged behind the chipped marble of the registration desk. Cesar marched, eyes straight ahead, through the narrow lobby toward the single elevator at the far end. Gio followed closely at his heels carrying the wine. An M.P. called, "Where you going?"

Cesar stopped. "*Le capitaine* . . . James Hegan." He pointed to the wine.

The sergeant recognized the name of Hegan. "Leave it here." He motioned to Gio to bring the case to the desk.

Cesar did not move away from the elevator. He opened his dispatch case, removed the sheet of paper, and held it up.

"Okay, I'll sign for it," the sergeant said.

Cesar shook the paper. "No!" he protested. "Le Capitaine Hegan must sign. Personally. This is a gift from Colonel Talmant. I am not to be responsible for leaving it otherwise!"

The second M.P. stood up lazily from a sagging leather chair. He sauntered over to the sergeant. "I thing what he's saying is—the juice is from his colonel and the captain's got to cut a receipt for it."

The sergeant hesitated, then turned to a switchboard. He plugged in and rang a room. After a moment he said, "Captain Hegan? Sergeant Willard, desk duty. Couple Frenchies down here. Something about a case of wine."

"I didn't order any," Hegan's voice replied.

"It's a gift . . . from some colonel."

"Then send it up."

"They want a personal receipt for it."

"Okay. Cut the crap, Sergeant. Have 'em bring it up and I'll sign for it."

"Yes, sir." The sergeant disconnected and faced around. "Go ahead," he said to Cesar, and waved a hand toward the elevator. Cesar immediately stepped inside, followed by Gio. "Wait a minute!" the sergeant called. "One of the M.P.'s will take you up."

But Cesar had already pulled the cord and the elevator was slowly ascending.

The two Corsicans walked with unhurried steps down the third-floor hallway. "No second chance," Cesar warned. "Watch me close. I'll tell you when." Gio nodded and led the way to room 318. The door was closed. "Is this the office?" Cesar asked.

"Yes."

"He'll be in his bedroom this time of night." They started to the next room when the door of 320 opened. Hegan looked out from behind the door. "You're the men with the wine," he said in stiff college French.

"Yes, sir. Where'll we put it?"

"In here." Hegan opened the door wider. He was wearing shorts, socks, and bathrobe. Close up, Cesar thought, he looked more like an accountant than a soldier. "Who sent this?" Hegan asked.

"Colonel Talmant, sir." Cesar entered the bedroom and motioned to Gio to set down the heavy case in the middle of the floor.

"Colonel Talmant . . .?" Hegan shook his head. "I can't place him."

Cesar opened his dispatch case and again took out the sheet of paper. "Will you sign this please, sir?"

Hegan regarded the paper in Cesar's hand with suspicion. "I'm not signing anything until I get this straight. Who in hell is Colonel Talmant?"

"My commanding officer, sir. Read this. Perhaps you'll remember . . ." Cesar moved nearer to the American and glanced at Gio. Gio stepped up beside Hegan as Cesar handed him the paper.

Hegan reached for the paper. Cesar stomped his shoe down hard on the American's unprotected toes.

"Jeezus!" Hegan bent forward under the excruciating pain.

"Now!" said Cesar.

Gio's massive fist crashed on the back of Hegan's neck. Hegan dropped as if felled by a poleax.

The Corsicans stared at the quiet figure. Cesar hunkered down and turned Hegan over. The American's eyes were rolled up in their sockets and his head angled oddly. A drool of slime edged from his mouth. "You broke his neck!" Cesar said.

Gio unclenched his fist. "I didn't mean to . . ."

"You're a fool!" Cesar's face was white with anger.

"But . . . you said . . ." Gio looked bewildered.

"I said knock him out with the first blow. Not kill him! Now they'll really be after us!" Cesar stood up. He had regained his composure. "Is that the door to the office?"

"Yes." Gio hurried to make amends. He swung open a door leading to the adjoining room.

The office consisted of two metal desks, two chairs, three banks of filing cabinets, a typewriter, an adding machine, a metal typing stand, and a large wall calendar. Cesar switched on a light and walked to the larger of the two desks, bearing a sign that read: Capt. J. Hegan. The lower double drawer to the desk was locked. "Hurry!" Cesar snapped. "Find his keys. Look in his pockets." While Gio returned to the bedroom to search Hegan's uniforms, Cesar attempted to pry the lock with his knife. The metal withstood the blade.

Gio returned with a ring of keys. Cesar quickly opened the drawer. Within it nested a heavy fireproof box. Cesar looked over the keys, selected one, and inserted it. The lock turned; he lifted the lid.

The strongbox was filled with stacks of neatly taped United States bills.

Cesar opened the dispatch case and stuffed the money in it. He tossed the crumpled raincoat to Gio, then tucked the .45 beneath his belt. Moving quickly, he crossed the room and switched off the light.

In the bedroom he opened a bureau drawer and took out a white shirt belonging to Hegan. Glancing around, he saw several civvy jackets hanging in an open wardrobe. He grabbed a worn flannel. "Come on!" he urged Gio. Cesar cautiously cracked the door. Two army officers walked down the hall, deep in conversation. When they had disappeared in the elevator, Cesar moved into the corridor. Gio followed him. The door was pulled shut. "Is it locked?"

Gio tried the handle. "Yes."

Cesar casually carried the dispatch case. Draped over Gio's arm were the raincoat, shirt, and jacket. Cesar moved through the hallways to reach the rear of the building. He stopped in front of the service elevator. Without hesitation he pushed the button. He heard the old cage start to rise. "Listen," he said to Gio, "there'll be a guard by the back door. I'll take care of him."

The lift descended slowly, giving Cesar plenty of time to examine the back hall as the elevator came to rest on the ground floor. The service doors to the alley were closed and bolted. Beside them, tilted in a chair, a guard was reading a tattered magazine. He raised his eyes to observe the two French soldiers. Puzzled, he put aside his reading and stood up.

Cesar opened the latticed metalwork of the elevator door and stepped out, holding his dispatch case close to his belly, hiding his automatic. A glance told Cesar that the kitchen down the hall was closed for the night—as he had expected.

Smiling, Cesar walked up to the sentry. *"Bonsoir,"* he said, and suddenly shoved the dispatch case into the hands of the guard. The American's hands automatically closed on the case. Before he could duck, Cesar laid the .45 against the side of his head.

With a sigh, the American slumped forward. The dispatch case fell to the floor.

Cesar caught the guard and propped him back in the chair. Picking up the fallen case, Cesar nodded to Gio standing by the elevator. In another moment they were hidden in the safety of the pitch black alley. They walked quickly to its end near the street.

"Put on the raincoat," Cesar told Gio, while he shucked off Louis' military blouse. He quickly put on Hegan's white shirt and jacket. "Carry Louis' uniform coat under your raincoat—and take off that fez."

"Yes, Cesar."

"In case they find Hegan or the guard too quickly and send out an alarm for two men, we split up here. I'll meet you back at the room. Stay to the side streets. Don't stop. And don't talk!"

Cesar, a shadowy, unmilitary figure in sports jacket carrying a briefcase, faded into the darkness. Then Gio, a bulky half-caste in a long raincoat, disappeared in the night.

Anse opened the door at the sound of Cesar's low, identifying whisper. Cesar looked around. "Where's Gio?"

"Not here."

"The stupid peasant! Hope I don't have to go look for him . . ." Cesar sat down on the bed and opened the case. At the sight of the money, Anse grinned broadly.

"What a haul!"

52

Cesar nodded and shut the case again.

"How much?" Anse asked.

Cesar appeared indifferent. "I'll count it later." He poured himself a glass of wine, then lifted his head, listening. Moving swiftly he crossed to the door. A slight scraping sounded outside. "Gio?"

"Yes."

Cesar opened the door and Gio lumbered into the room. "Any trouble?" Cesar asked, locking the door again.

"No. I was careful like you said." Gio's anticipation was obvious. "How much did we get, Cesar?"

"You'll know later. Now get some sleep. Tomorrow you take a trip."

Gio's face was sullen. "Why?"

"You killed an officer. You'd better get out of town until that stain wears off. And . . ."

"And what?"

"You're going to Ghisonacia to see Joseph. Tell him it's time to join us."

Chapter 7

Louis sat down beside Cesar in Le Bélier. "Where's your *pote*, Roger?" he asked.

"Why?"

"Usually he's sitting beside you grinning like a gargoyle."

"He went to Bastia. He'll be back." Cesar ordered a brandy for the Frenchman.

Louis sipped his drink. "I need my uniform," he said.

"You'll get it."

"When? It's been three days. I can get my ass in a lot of trouble." Louis looked around the crowded bar. "Lucky for me that bastard Talmant's too busy to think up special duty ..." He returned his attention to Cesar. "If he does, though, I'm in for it unless I get back my uniform."

"He won't have you shot."

"Maybe not, but he's in a foul temper." Louis moved the brandy glass back and forth on the table. "Ever since some kind of a brouhaha at the Grande." He avoided Cesar's eyes.

Cesar lit a black-market Lucky Strike. His voice was casual. "What about it?"

"You didn't hear?" Louis looked at the pack of cigarettes. "Can I?" Cesar gestured slightly and Louis took one. "Course, the gold-braid are keeping it top secret."

"You're being a commere."

"No, I'm not gossiping." Louis lit the cigarette, then

sipped his brandy. His voice was nonchalant. "Seen your friend—what's his name?—Captain Hegan, yet?"

"I'll get around to it."

"Don't hurry. You've already missed his funeral."

Cesar lifted his brows. "He's dead?"

Louis gulped the last of his brandy. "Talking makes me thirsty." After Louis sampled his second drink, he continued. "Too bad . . . all the trouble you went to, then not get to see him."

"What happened?"

"Two soldiers—a Free French and a Zouave—delivered a case of wine to him. And Hegan got a broken neck. Can you figure that one out?"

"No."

"The men said the wine was a present from Talmant. Hah!" Louis snorted. "That swine wouldn't give away a hair from his hairy ears! Now all the brass is climbing on his back and asking questions."

"Why'd anyone want to kill Hegan?"

"*Le blé.*" Louis rolled his fingers. "His office was robbed."

"Who pulled it?"

Louis laughed. "Three Americans in the lobby and another in the back all disagree. According to them the Free French was short and stocky as well as tall and lean. The Zouave was blacker than the balls on a crow while at the same time he was the color of milk chocolate, but he was a *big* son of a bitch." Louis blew a cloud of smoke and, with a cynical regard, watched it dissolve.

"How about fingerprints?"

"Eighty thousand of 'em in the hotel. No way of figuring *what* belongs to *who.*" Louis glanced at Cesar. "Without a tip. . . . something solid to go on . . . they're wasting their time."

"About your uniform . . ." Cesar said. "My fault for keeping it so long. Get yourself another, to be safe." He handed Louis one hundred dollars. "Fifty will get you one in the black market. Keep the rest."

"I'm not turning this down," Louis said, tucking the money in the pocket of his blouse. "But why not give mine back?"

"How about making a lot of money?" Cesar asked, as if not hearing Louis' question. "Two or three hundred dollars. Interested?"

"Sooner the better!"

"I'll leave a mark for you again at the church."

"When?"

"Not long." Cesar's voice was vague.

"Don't string me along. I've got better things to do than wait."

"You'll hear from me." Cesar was definite now.

Louis finished his drink, helped himself to another cigarette, and stood up. As he slouched away from the bar, he was unaware of Cesar's cold, piercing stare fixed on his back.

Clemente Valdo, owner and barkeep of Le Bélier, looked at his watch and sighed. The hour was after midnight and trade was slackening off. The servicemen had staggered back to their quarters to meet the curfew. Only a few merchant seamen and elderly civilians remained hunched over lonesome, solitary glasses. Valdo, a tough Spaniard from Barcelona, had jumped ship years before in Ajaccio. The war had been his salvation; it had lifted Le Bélier from beneath the constant threat of bankruptcy to the position of a profitable bistro.

At Cesar's invitation, Valdo poured himself a glass of red wine and joined him at his table. "*Salud!*" the Spaniard said.

"You keep a good place," Cesar remarked.

Valdo shrugged. His pockmarked face looked gritty in the uncertain light. "It'll do."

"I've spent a lot of time here in the last few weeks."

"You haven't spent much money," Valdo said. "On the other hand, you haven't caused any trouble."

"I'll spend more, don't worry. So will my friends. Others will come to see us—and that means more business, too."

Valdo wiped a hand across his blue-veined nose. "What are you getting at?"

"I always sit at this table—here, near the door. One of the best in the place." Cesar motioned with his head toward the back of the room. "That last table, against the wall. I like it, too."

"If you want it, take it."

"Reserve it for me—and my friends. Permanent. From the time you open to the time you close."

"If you're not here and somebody else wants it, what am I supposed to do? Kick 'em out?"

"I'm not asking you for a favor. That back table is the poorest one you have. I'll guarantee to pay you twice what you take in on the *best* table in the bar. But no one ever sits there except me . . . or whoever I say."

"Twice, huh?" Valdo's eyes glinted. "I could say it was my own private table . . ." he said slowly.

"I don't care what you say. Starting tomorrow, is the table mine?"

"Double whatever I get from *any* other table?"

"Double." Cesar nodded.

Valdo started to speak, changed his mind, took a drink of wine. "You're not paying for that table for no reason at all." He regarded Cesar with cunning. "I've been in Ajaccio for twenty years, but the *poulaille* . . . the cops . . . still consider me a stranger. I don't want any trouble with 'em."

"No trouble. My friends and I like to talk to people." Cesar smiled slightly. "We want people to know where they can always find us."

"We'll try it," Valdo agreed after another moment of calculation. "If I don't like it, I'll change my mind." He hooked a thick finger into the collar of his open shirt and scratched his chest. Beneath the curled gray hairs was a green tattoo of a mermaid.

Cesar nodded. "You can always do that."

Two days later, slightly before noon, Cesar climbed one of the foothills about nine kilometers north and east from Ajaccio. He was again wearing his rough country clothes. Near the rounded crest of the hill a shepherd, with a small flock of sheep, watched him approach. A short distance below the shepherd, a crude corral leaned against a small stone hut. Nearby a tiny spring trickled between a ledge of rocks and supported a few stunted trees growing on the *maquis*-covered hill.

The shepherd was Salvatore Vallica, a thick, sturdy man in his late thirties, of a family distantly related to the Satisanni through marriage. Cesar established his credentials and Vallica accepted them. The two men sat down on the hillside. Vallica waited politely for Cesar to bring up the reason for his visit.

"You have few visitors," Cesar said, finally.

"None. Which is good as my flock isn't disturbed."

Cesar pointed to a narrow dirt track winding through the foothills, which missed the corral by about a kilometer. "Is that the only way to get here?"

"Yes. There's no other road."

They again lapsed into silence. Salvatore kept an eye on his flock, which was under the watchful supervision of a dog with a long matted coat. Cesar, thoughtful, gazed into the distance. After some time had passed, Cesar said, "I'm engaged in several small matters in Ajaccio. A friend of mine needs to remain out of sight. If he stayed in your hut, and kept certain other . . . uh, items . . . out here, it would be worth your while."

Salvatore nodded. "A man makes little money on the side of a hill."

"Supplies will be brought to him. You'll share them and it'll cost you nothing. And, of course, you'll receive *rent.*"

"Who is your friend?"

"A black. His name is Anse."

Salvatore took off his flat, stiff-brimmed hat, and wiped off the sweatband. His face and the back of his neck, tanned from the sun and wind, were furrowed with white lines. He put on his hat again.

Salvatore Vallica understood that Cesar's "small matters" were unlawful ones. Many of his closer relatives, as well as his few friends, were engaged in dubious activities also. Such efforts were means of survival, and Salvatore was not against staying alive. Lying, cowardly murder, rape, and thieving from a man's own family were about the only acts that Salvatore considered to be crimes.

What concerned Salvatore was Anse.

Since the centuries-gone period of the Saracen occupation, Corsicans had lumped all Arabs and blacks as "Moors." Ignorant and superstitious, Salvatore disliked all Moors in general, although he had never met one.

Cesar correctly read Salvatore's hesitation. "You can trust him," he told the shepherd. "The army's looking for him, so he won't cause trouble. He minds his own business and he won't talk you to death."

Salvatore considered the idea of free provisions and extra francs. He found it inviting; it was the only offer in his hard life that required nothing from him in return. In addition, regardless of how distant, Cesar was "family," so Salvatore could put faith in his words. And it would be a good investment for the future to have the Satisanni obligated to him. "Agreed," Salvatore said.

"Not a word to anyone."

"Who would I tell—the sheep?"

"Not even the sheep," Cesar smiled. His knowledge of human nature was growing. Instead of offering Salvatore paper francs, Cesar gave him a few of his silver pieces. The shepherd would appreciate the silver more—hard, precious metal that jingled a lovely sound to peasant ears. "When I return, another payment," Cesar promised.

"When do I expect the Moor?"

"When you see him."

Cesar arose, dusted himself, and started down the hillside on his long walk back to the city. He enjoyed the freedom of striding along the slopes, the scent of *maquis* around him. Ajaccio seemed far away; James Hegan had never existed. The reckless urgings, the abandoned fierceness that he held forcibly under control in Le Bélier, dissolved into a calm acceptance of the moment. And for the moment a small, quiet wind was coming in from the sea and blowing gently over the hillside. The enchantress' kiss.

That night Gio returned with Joseph from Ghisoncia. The presence of four men cramped the damp, musty room of their lodging place. Much of the stain was gone from Gio's face, removed through the application of milk and alcohol. Joseph had managed to get a handful of chlorine tablets, used to purify water at the airfield in Ghisonacia, and the chlorine had helped to bleach Gio to a shade not much deeper than his own. They sat on the floor drinking wine and conversing in low tones so as not to arouse the curiosity of the other tenants in the old house.

"Twenty-eight thousand dollars," Joseph repeated for the second time since Cesar had opened the dispatch case and placed it in the center of their circle.

"Is it enough to start?" Cesar asked.

"Sufficient. Money is *numbers*. A man who knows numbers can make them do *anything*."

"Make them get me out of this damned room," Anse said. "It's driving me *con!*"

"Soon enough," Cesar assured Anse. He looked at the faces that watched him. "We can't all stay in this one room. People around here are going to start asking questions. We'll find another place as quickly as we can."

"You said you had an office. Where?" Joseph asked.

"In Le Bélier."

"A bar?"

"What could be better?" Cesar yawned. "A crowd going in and out all day—and night. Who's to get nosey?"

"Not a bad idea," Joseph agreed. "What about the owner? Is he in on it?"

"Valdo? No."

"When he finds out . . .?"

"I'll take care of him," Cesar replied lazily. "Hey, Gio! are you sober?" Gio nodded. "I want you to go down to the church and leave another mark for Louis."

"It's late. I'm tired," Gio protested.

"It's late . . . and it's dark . . . and no one will see you."

"Merde!"

"Tonight!"

Grumbling, Gio stood up and stretched. Walking toward the door, he paused to glower into the night. Then he left for Saint Roche.

Chapter 8

Joseph and Gio sat at the table against the far back wall in Le Bélier. Gio's face was screwed in a scowl of concentration while the two men played *belote*. Joseph smiled. "Win," he announced.

"Damn! Not again!" Gio protested. His big fist thumped the table.

"Again."

"I haven't won a game!" Gio scattered the cards in anger. "No sport if I never win." Joseph did not bother with the score. Picking up the cards, he shuffled them. "I've had enough!" Gio said.

"Keep playing," Joseph advised quietly. "If you don't, Cesar'll give you hell."

"I don't see why we keep on with this lousy game."

"We can't sit here all day doing nothing." Joseph dealt the cards. "And *belote*'s all you know how to play."

"I'll learn something else."

"What? I'm willing to teach you."

Gio stared at the cards, his forehead wrinkling, as he attempted to think of another game. He gave up in despair. "What the devil!" he growled. "I'll play this crap."

Near the door, Cesar sat aloof and alone at the table he usually occupied. Before him was a glass of wine. Composed, quiet, he seemed unaware and dissociated from Joseph and Gio at the back of the barroom. Concealed by his jacket, his knife rested in its sheath.

An American corporal entered and bellied up to the bar. He ordered a whiskey. Valdo had none and shoved him a glass of brandy. Lounging against the bar, the American looked over the room until he spotted the table with Joseph and Gio. Carrying his drink, he walked over to them. He watched for a moment while they continued to play cards. "You guys the ones who change money?" he asked.

Joseph looked up. "Sometimes . . . *caporale,*" he replied to the corporal.

"I got these gold seals and I wanta send some money home."

"How much . . . do . . . you have?" Joseph spoke in slow, careful English.

"Hundred bucks. What'll you give me?"

"Four to one," Joseph said, pronouncing each word separately. He had driven himself hard to learn English from the Americans in Ghisonacia.

"Four to one!" The corporal exploded in pretended outrage. "I can buy blue seals . . . two to one! . . . lotta places!"

The American was bluffing. Joseph was well aware of the going black-market rate of exchange. However, in the few days that he had operated in Le Bélier, Joseph had offered better rates than his competitors—most of whom had only small amounts of capital. He was not doing this from generosity, but because he believed in the adage that good news travels fast. His customers bragged about beating down his rates; this brought him new business. Once he was firmly established, he would adjust his rates to every cent the traffic would bear. Joseph reasoned that he was not losing money, merely lowering his margin of profit in return for publicity—although the word "publicity" was not yet in Joseph's vocabulary.

"Three and a half," Joseph said.

"Three!" The corporal gulped his drink. "Or I'm heading someplace else."

Joseph shrugged as if in resignation. "Agreed." Three to one was the exchange he had in mind originally. He looked at Gio and nodded. Gio took out a large black billfold from under the cushion on which his heavy buttocks rested. He handed the money to Joseph. Joseph carefully counted out thirty-three blue-seal dollars for the American.

"I got thirty-three cents coming," the corporal said.

Joseph shook his head as he stuffed the hundred gold-seal dollars into the billfold and returned it to Gio. Gio put it back beneath the cushion and sat on it firmly.

"Look!" the corporal persisted, "how about my change?"

"Off the top," Joseph said. Gio hunched his shoulders and stared with menace from beneath lowered brows. The American folded the money and tucked it in his pocket.

"Shove it up your ass, greaseball," the corporal said as he turned away. Fortunately Joseph was not yet proficient in American slang and could make no translation.

A Free French private nearly bumped into the American. He stopped at the table and looked down at Joseph. "I'm shipping out this afternoon," the Frenchman said. "I have some francs."

"What kind?"

"Tresdors." The "tresdors" were occupation francs good only in Corsica and certain areas of Free French possessions.

Joseph said nothing, but his face reflected his distaste.

"Listen," the private urged, "who knows where I'm going? Wherever the hell it is, maybe I won't be able to use 'em." He leaned over the table. "What'll you give me?"

In theory, the legal rate of exchange was around three hundred and fifty francs to the dollar. The black-market rate fluctuated between six hundred to seven hundred. And tresdors had half the value of regular francs. "I don't want them," Joseph said.

"I want some blue seals," the Frenchman pressed, his tone almost pleading. "Come on . . . you know. Some *blé* I can spend wherever I end up. How much?"

"Fifteen hundred to one," Joseph said calmly.

The private paused, then slowly removed a large wad of small franc notes and began to count them.

Louis stopped at Cesar's table. "Don't sit down," Cesar told him. "I'll meet you outside." A moment or two after Louis left, Cesar followed him. They walked to a corner of Cours Napoleon and turned down a side street. "It took you long enough to get my message," Cesar said.

"I've had to pretend to be on sick roll because of that damned uniform."

"Did you get another?"

"Finally."

Cesar stopped beside a faded, mustard-colored plaster wall. He lit a cigarette. "That money I mentioned to you . . ." His voice was casual.

"Don't think I've forgotten it."

"Teach me to drive your jeep." Cesar adjusted his alpaca jacket.

"You're crazy!"

"Two hundred and fifty dollars isn't crazy."

"You said—three hundred."

"I know what I said. But I'll *make* it three hundred."

Louis thought about it, hesitating, and finally shook his head. "Christ! . . . I hate to think what'd happen if it got back to Talmant I was teaching a civilian to drive his jeep."

"I'll wear your old uniform," Cesar said calmly.

"So that's it! You never intended to return it. You had this in mind!"

Cesar looked past Louis' shoulder, his eyes climbing to the roofs of the old buildings lining the narrow street. His voice was impassive. "There are some roads behind town. The military never uses them. A good place to practice."

"I don't know . . ." Louis rubbed his knuckles along the side of his jaw. "I could use the *fric* . . ."

"Three hundred dollars," Cesar said, as if addressing a rooftop. He dropped his cigarette and ground it out. "*À bientôt,*" as he started to turn away.

"Wait," Louis said. He shrugged, then slightly spread his hands. "*Au diable* to Talmant."

Although Cesar had never driven a car or operated a piece of machinery, he learned quickly. Discipline was somewhat lax among the small garrisons stationed in Ajaccio, and Louis was able to snatch an occasional afternoon hour to instruct his pupil.

When Cesar was satisfied that he drove the jeep with sufficient skill, he paid Louis the final one hundred dollars due him. Louis accepted the money without apparent enthusiasm. He shoved it in a pocket of his tunic with indifference. "I've run a lot of risk doing this."

"You've been paid," Cesar replied.

"I can't figure what the hell good it'll do you—learning to drive this junk. You're not in the army." The two men were seated in the vehicle, pulled off to the side of a rough country road. The jeep was parked in the shade of a huge roadside boulder. Louis switched a quick glance at Cesar. "I'm not stupid, you know."

"I hadn't noticed."

"That *copain* of yours, Roger, he's back with another *mec*. They're doing pretty good in Le Bélier."

"Meaning what?" Cesar asked.

"I haven't forgotten you and Roger were looking for Hegan. You always have plenty *fric*. Maybe I can guess what happened."

"You're keeping your guesses to yourself? People might get the wrong idea."

Louis laughed. "I'm no squealer. Certainly not yet. You're an understanding fellow, Xavier. Get what I mean when I say I appreciate the little handouts so far . . . *but?*" He shifted in the seat behind the wheel. "*But* . . . I like money as well as you do."

Cesar nodded, his face grave. "Naturally."

Louis' finger tapped the money in his pocket. "Nice, and more wouldn't hurt."

"I see . . ." Cesar's eyes were dark holes as they burned into Louis, partly turned toward him in the seat. "Would, say, a thousand dollars help make you more satisfied?"

"Now you're talking!" Louis grinned.

"I don't give away money," Cesar said. "In return for a little job, I'll pay you the thousand."

"Doing what? You must realize I'm willing to keep my mouth shut, but I'm not willing to get my ass in a jam."

"Drive a friend of mine to a sheep corral up there." Cesar motioned with his head toward the foothills behind them. "It'll take you an hour at the most."

"What's the deal?"

"The army's looking for him. He needs a place to lay low."

Louis pursed his lips and stared at Cesar. "He's not a Zouave by any chance?"

"You *are* a clever fellow," Cesar said.

"He's the one who helped you heist Hegan!" Louis chuckled. "I knew you were in it. That little business means the firing squad."

"Can you get away tomorrow just before dark?"

"I think so. Talmant's usually at the Officer's Club swilling around that time."

Cesar gave Louis a thick roll of francs. "Load up with supplies. My friend's got to eat while he's up there."

"All right." Louis spoke with a new assurance bordering on arrogance. "You understand you're not kissing me off after this job. I won't settle for a few lousy 'tips.' After all, I located Hegan for you, and I got you that uniform. I've had my suspicions, but I've said nothing. Now I'm helping your *copain* make his getaway." He started the motor in the jeep. "I expect a hell of a lot more."

"You'll get it," Cesar assured him.

That night when the four members of the group were gathered in their quarters, Cesar explained to them. "Anse has stayed here in the room, but he hasn't liked it. He's done it to save his black hide, but at the same time he's guarded the money. The big share of it is in the dispatch case and so far we've been lucky. If the *flics* had been tipped off, they'd have nabbed him and the money, too. Gio has guarded Joseph at Le Bélier. Joseph's never carried more than a thousand dollars at any time. If he and Gio get robbed, we can afford that loss."

"Nobody's going to rob us when I'm around," Gio said.

"Every day we get more money," Cesar continued. "We can't keep all of it here forever. Tomorrow Anse takes the *blé* and moves to the hills with Salvatore Vallica. He and the money will be safe there."

"With my *flingue*?" Anse asked.

"Yes, take your gun. At dusk, Louis will pick you up on the edge of town and drive you."

"Can't we wait until after dark?" Anse was uneasy.

"The way will be rough even for a jeep. I'll go with you to meet Louis and make sure he picks up you and the money."

"*Merde!* I don't trust that Louis," Gio said.

"I prefer to do business with a man I can trust," Cesar said. "But right now it's convenient to do business with Louis."

"No harm must come to Salvatore," Joseph said to Anse. "He's a member of our family."

"You heard that?" Cesar asked Anse. Anse nodded. "Salvatore's not a man of the world. He dislikes Moors. However, he won't insult you. If he's distant and silent, you will put up with it because there's nothing else you can do."

"Your job is to guard our capital and keep it safe," Joseph added.

"Somebody try . . . to lift a sou?" Anse patted his gun. "Huh!"

"I'm not worrying," Joseph told him, then glanced toward Cesar. "I've a hunch, though," he continued to Anse, "that it wouldn't be a good idea to start Cesar worrying about it either." He didn't amplify his statement.

"Once a week I'll come out with supplies and the extra profits," Cesar said.

"Even living with a bunch of sheep is better'n this room," Anse told him.

The late afternoon dusk was falling when Cesar and Anse stood by the fork of the Avenue Beverini on the outskirts of Ajaccio. The pavement ended near where they were waiting, and a dusty road continued into the foothills behind the town. "You know what you're to do?" Cesar asked.

"Perfectly," Anse told him. The Algerian was dressed in his coveralls and wore his knitted cap.

Louis arrived in his jeep and jammed on the brakes. "Hurry up," he said, "I had a hell of a time getting away. I got to get back fast!"

Anse, carrying the dispatch case, climbed into the jumpseat and sat down behind Louis. Cesar handed the soldier a pack of American bills. "Here's five hundred. Anse'll give you the rest of what you have coming when you get there."

"Where's *there*?"

Cesar gave Louis a crude hand-drawn map. "Follow it. Simple enough."

"If I'm able to read it," Louis grumbled. "It's getting dark fast."

"Don't use your lights on the hill," Cesar cautioned. "They can be seen from too far off." Louis nodded. Cesar stepped back. "On your way!" Louis shoved the jeep into gear and roared down the dusty road.

Fifteen minutes later Louis turned the jeep off the narrow road in the foothills and cut cross-country heading for the corral. He was forced to drive in low gear, crawling along the sloping hillside to avoid occasional boulders, gullies, and outcroppings. A damp sea breeze, touched with streamers of fog, helped deaden the sounds of scraping metal and the laboring motor of the machine. The dusk had deepened into darkness, although it was not yet night. Ahead, Louis saw a small flickering light—a lamp beside the corral, or the shepherd's hut. He fought the steering wheel of the jeep to keep it headed in the direction of the light while the vehicle ground its way over the rough terrain.

"Son of a bitch!" he shouted to Anse. "You should've hired a plane!"

Anse, with difficulty, remained in the back of the jeep, bouncing and jolting. One hand clutched the dispatch case while his other grasped the back of Louis' seat.

"*Foutre!*" Louis yelled over his shoulder. "I got to have some light! To hell with anybody seeing them!" He switched on his headlights. The low outline of the corral leaped into their beams.

"Stop here!" Anse shouted. "Turn off them lights! I'll walk the rest of the way!"

Louis halted the jeep. "I can't get out of here without the heads."

"You won't need 'em," Anse said, wrapping an arm around Louis' neck from behind.

The knife sliced Louis' throat from ear to ear in one deft stroke.

Before morning, the jeep was carefully concealed beneath a stack of shrub, brush, and *maquis*—just another brown, unidentified mound on the hillside.

And Louis was buried deep in the dusty earth nearby.

Chapter 9

Valdo said, "I want to talk to you."

Cesar, elegant in a maroon velveteen jacket, gray silk shirt, and gray flannel slacks, was seated at his table near the door. Only minutes before, Le Bélier had opened for the day. Gio and Joseph were starting their endless games of *belote* in the rear of the room while waiting for business. "Is that coffee machine fixed?" Cesar asked Valdo.

"No," the bartender said, "and if it was, I don't have coffee for it. But that's not what I want to talk to you about."

"Bring me a glass of wine and a roll. It's too early to talk."

"Not for me it isn't. Besides, I want to get this off my mind before I get busy." Nevertheless, Valdo poured out a glass of wine and placed it together with a grainy, hard-crusted roll on the table in front of Cesar. Valdo wiped his hands on the legs of his pants. "It's about this business you're pulling in my place," he said, his voice belligerent.

Cesar broke the roll and ate a small piece of it, washing it down with a mouthful of tart red wine. "Yes?"

"I've been watching what's going on these last couple of weeks. You and those *mecs* of yours are getting rich."

"Not rich." Cesar said, calmly continuing to eat.

"You're making *plenty*—tying up two of my tables for the crappy price of a few francs!" The Spaniard turned a

71

calloused palm upward and wiggled his fingers. "I'm changing my mind unless . . ." Valdo's voice trailed away.

"You've made more off those tables than you ever have," Cesar said in a reasonable tone. "Everyone coming in to see us buys a drink. Why're you complaining?"

"I deserve more."

"How much more?" Cesar's impassive face held no expression as he regarded Valdo.

Valdo shifted uncomfortably. "I haven't decided."

"A partnership perhaps?"

"Yes. Something like that." The Spaniard's voice resumed its normal gritty quality. "What's fair is fair."

"A partnership works both ways." Cesar finished his roll.

Valdo misinterpreted Cesar's meaning. "I've got friends," he threatened. "A word in the right places . . . maybe you wouldn't find it so easy."

"I'm sure I wouldn't," Cesar agreed. "I'll think about it."

Valdo stood up. "Think all you want. I've made up my mind!" He returned to the bar, then froze as two policemen in dark blue uniforms piped with white entered the door. They paused for only a moment before crossing to Cesar's table. "Let's see your papers," one of them said.

Cesar silently presented his *carte nationale d'identité*. The older policeman glanced at it, then said, "Come on."

"Why?" Cesar made no effort to move, but he shot a glance down the room to Gio, seated beside Joseph. Gio lumbered to his feet.

"Because you were told to!" The *poulet* shoved a nightstick into Cesar's belly. The blow winded him, and he gasped. Shoving back the table, he fumbled momentarily with his chair before slowly rising to his feet as Gio came up to join him. Gio's big bulk temporarily stood between Cesar and the *poulaille*.

"Sit down and wait for me!" Cesar ordered in a sharp tone.

Gio sat on Cesar's vacant chair, covering the knife that Cesar had dropped when standing up.

"Who're you?" the older *poulet* demanded of Gio.

"He works on my land," Cesar said. "I want to talk to him before he leaves."

Both police laughed, although there was little amusement in their

72

dark, hard faces. "He may have quite a wait." The older gendarme grasped Cesar by an arm. "Let's go."

"Am I under arrest?"

"Maybe."

"Where are you taking me? *Le frigo* . . . jail?"

"That depends." With a shove, Cesar was started on his way to an elderly Peugeot parked in front of the bar.

Colonel Paul Talmant was long soured on his life—and career. Tall, balding, with a large beak of a nose, he lived in a world of dour irritation. His bleak office was located in a series of nearly identical municipal buildings near the Avenue Marshal Foch. Cesar, shoved without ceremony into the colonel's presence by the two gendarmes, stood quietly before Talmant's desk. The colonel examined him, as a specimen, from pale blue eyes.

"What do you know about Louis Baccard?" Talmant shot the question.

"Never heard of him." Cesar steadily returned the colonel's baleful stare.

"You're lying!"

Cesar shrugged. A sharp jab between his shoulders from the nightstick brought him to attention. "Who is this man . . . Louis Baccard? How would I know him?"

"I'm asking *you!*"

"I know nothing."

Talmant stood up behind his desk and leaned forward. "You're Xavier?"

"*I'm* Cesar Satisanni."

The colonel slapped the top of his desk in anger. "Names mean nothing!" Talmant walked to the window, then swung around quickly. "Men in Baccard's company tell me he knew a man named Xavier in Le Bélier. *Un filou!* . . . a sharp operator with plenty of money. Apparently you're the only one who hangs around that bistro with two sous to rub together!"

"My home is Col Pieto. My family owns land there. We have money."

"Hah!" Talmant snorted. He returned to his desk but did not sit down. Cesar sensed a slight uncertainty edging into the colonel's manner. "This is a military matter, although the police are cooperating with us. The whole affair is more than a coincidence!"

"What is?" Cesar asked, then politely added, "sir."

Talmant sat down again behind his desk. "Baccard is . . . *was* . . . my driver. He's disappeared. My jeep, too! I can assume two possibilities: he has gone AWOL and taken my jeep, or he is dead and the jeep stolen." The colonel's pale blue eyes stared at Cesar from beneath bushy brows. "For the last time—what do you know about it?"

"Nothing."

Talmant sucked on his lower lip. "A short time back there was a murder and a robbery in which my name was used. Now Baccard is missing. Does that suggest anything to you?"

"Only that Baccard committed the crimes—and has taken a *cavale.*"

"Why should he scram?" Talmant shot back. "He was free of suspicion, so why take off and point a finger at himself?" The colonel shook his head. "You're trying to cover up something. You're not answering questions. And you're not pulling the wool over my eyes for a minute! I've given you every chance. Now you can face them!" Talmant nodded to the gendarmes. "Have them come in."

Cesar restrained his surprise when two M.P.'s and a sergeant, the Americans on duty in the lobby of the *Grande,* walked into the office. He glanced at them without a flicker of recognition.

Talmant spoke to the Americans in English. The three soldiers slowly walked around Cesar, inspecting him closely. Cesar, standing in the flat light of day and wearing expensive, well-cut clothes, bore little resemblance to the harassed Free French soldier, in ill-fitting uniform, beneath the weak light of the *Grande's* lobby. Standing at ease, he suffered their examination with indifference. The sergeant spoke to the colonel.

Talmant said to Cesar, "Say something. They want to hear your voice."

Cesar began to recite the names of mountains and villages in the area of Col Pieto. "Dammit!" Talmant ordered. "Call me by name!"

"Yes, sir. Colonel Talmant . . . Colonel Talmant . . . Colonel Talmant." The repetition brought a parrotlike quality into Cesar's voice.

"Now say Captain Hegan!"

Cesar did not use the French form of *capitaine,* which he had spoken the night of the robbery. Instead, he repeated, "Captain Hegan . . . Captain Hegan."

The Americans conversed between themselves in a corner of the office for a few minutes. "What's this all about?" Cesar asked Talmant.

"Shut up!"

The American sergeant stepped forward and addressed the colonel. After a somewhat lengthy exchange, the three soldiers left the room. Cesar, the gendarmes, and Talmant remained in silence.

Finally Talmant said, "*I* think you're a lucky son of a bitch. The Americans can't make a positive identification. You're about the same height and build—with a possible resemblance. But they're not sure!"

"They're absolutely right. How can they identify me when I haven't done anything?" Cesar replied.

"Do you want *us* to question him in private?" The older gendarme's voice held the tone of a gentle executioner.

"I doubt it would help," Talmant replied. "His room has been searched—there's nothing to go on."

"You've searched my room?"

Talmant mistook Cesar's surprise for annoyance—which the colonel enjoyed. "This morning after you and your friends left your pigpen. Fortunate for you, your neighbors deny seeing a soldier of Baccard's description, or a black Algerian we're looking for, around your place."

Cesar took an instant to congratulate himself that Anse, their capital, arsenal, uniforms, and jeep were all cached with Salvatore. Also realizing that the best defense is a good offense, Cesar demanded, "Did you take my shotgun?"

Talmant looked at the gendarmes. The gendarmes looked at each other and shrugged. Talmant said, "I don't know if the police or my men took it."

"I want it back," Cesar said. "I use it for hunting."

"To hell with it!" Talmant was losing his temper.

"It belonged to my father," Cesar pressed firmly.

"Take him out!" Talmant took a deep, angry breath and leaned back in his chair.

The gendarmes opened the door. Again the older one took Cesar's arm. "Shall we release him?"

"Hell, yes!" The colonel partly closed his eyes as the door shut. "That bastard," he thought. "There's something about him. He'd probably make a damned good soldier." Then Talmant put the thought aside. He had other things to do.

The three men walked in silence down the echoing corridor outside Talmant's office. Cesar had been searched for weapons after being taken in Le Bélier, but his personal items and money had not been touched as yet. He paused and looked at the two gendarmes. They regarded him with stony eyes. "*M'sieurs,*" Cesar said, "I hope there are no hard feelings."

"None," said the older, without inflection.

"It was a mistake . . ." The *poulaille* made no reply. Cesar continued, ". . . you were merely doing your duty. Right?"

The two gendarmes waited quietly, eyes alert.

"If you felt like it . . . held a grudge . . . you could make the rest of my stay in Ajaccio difficult. Unpleasant. I hope that won't happen." Cesar took out a roll of tresdor francs from his pocket, totaling slightly better than a hundred dollars. While the gendarmes pretended not to watch, he divided it into two equal packets and concealed one in each hand. "It would appear that I've forgotten my money," Cesar continued in a conversational way, "and it's a long walk back to Le Bélier."

The older one said, "It's always more agreeable to ride." They went down the hall and out the door. The three climbed into the Peugeot. In the privacy of the police car, Cesar passed a packet of francs to each. "Buy yourselves a drink when you're off duty," he said.

"To your health." The older gendarme put the money in his pocket. His companion did the same.

"I'd drink to yours—if I knew your names," Cesar said.

"I'm Loubet," the older *poulet* replied. "He's Cordeau."

When the police car drew up in front of Le Bélier, Cesar started to get out. "Wait," Loubet said. "We'll probably see you again." His

eyes stared straight ahead through the windshield. "Once a week."
Cordeau nodded agreement.

"That's to be expected," Cesar said quietly.

"A word. Take it as you like. There are others in this town with
powerful yet very tender toes. Don't step on them."

"I'll give the authorities no trouble."

Loubet glanced at Cordeau. They seemed amused at a silent joke
between them. "I'm not talking about the *flics* or the military,"
Loubet said.

"Then who do you mean?" Cesar was puzzled.

"Sometimes a man doesn't go around dropping names," Loubet
replied.

A thought flashed into Cesar's mind: Unione! Even in the isolation
of Col Pieto, its power and wealth were discussed in muted conversations around the tiny tables of Benozzo Florus' tavern.

Loubet swung an arm over the seat, reaching back, and opened the
car door. Cesar got out and waved an easy hand at the two police
inside. "*À bientôt . . . !*"

Loubet nodded, smiled, and the Peugeot drove off.

Inside the bar, Gio had returned to the back table with Joseph.
Ignoring the curious stare of Valdo, Cesar walked the length of the
room and sat down beside his two friends. Gio returned the knife
under the table. "What happened?" Joseph asked.

"Some men are born with big mouths. Some are greedy. Some
don't know when they're well off." Cesar sighed. For a moment he
stared through the distant open door into the sunny street. He turned
toward Gio. "We have some urgent business. Give me about five
minutes in the back room, then come in." Gio nodded. Cesar got up
and walked to the bar.

Valdo said in a strained voice, "What'd the *flics* want? I don't
want to get mixed up with 'em!"

A thin smile touched Cesar's lips. "Turned out they were friends
of mine. Let's talk about that partnership." He motioned with his
head toward a door at the end of the bar that led to a room in the
back.

"Can't leave the bar now," Valdo said uneasily. He picked up
several dirty glasses and dipped them in a pan of water.

Cesar gestured to Gio. "Come over here. Take care of the bar."

Gio lumbered to the bar and nudged Valdo out of the way. With reluctance the Spaniard followed Cesar into the back room. It contained a cot, sometimes used by Valdo when he slept in the bar overnight, and was partly filled with casks of wine and beer. A small window with dirty panes of glass let smoke-colored streaks of light from the alley filter into the room. Cesar closed the door behind them. "I understand the *flics* have been around asking questions."

"*Flics?*" Valdo appeared surprised.

"If not *flics*, then the military. You tell me which."

Valdo hesitated. Finally, "It didn't concern you."

"Who did it concern?"

"A Frenchman. A deserter."

"And his name was Louis Baccard? You told M.I. you'd seen him talking to me." Cesar was apparently unconcerned.

"They described him. I thought he might've been the one I saw you buy some drinks for."

"And perhaps . . . I might have some money?"

Valdo did not reply. He glanced uneasily at the closed door. "I got to get back to the bar."

"Don't you want to discuss our partnership?" Cesar unbuttoned his jacket and hooked a thumb over the band of his slacks. "Isn't it possible you figured if the *militaire* took care of me, you might take over the little business at the back table? A fine partnership . . . all for you and none for me." Cesar's voice was very soft.

"Get out! You and the lousy *mecs* with you! I don't need your business!" Valdo stormed toward the door. Pulling it open, he ran face to face into Gio. Gio shoved the Spaniard in the chest, forcing him back in the room. "Shitheads!" Valdo shouted, furious, but with rising fear.

Gio looked at Cesar. Cesar nodded.

Gio slugged Valdo full in the face and knocked the Spaniard back over a case of wine into a stand of empty bottles.

Valdo went down, sprawling on his back. In an instant he was up. Eyes squinted in hatred, his hand clutched a jagged broken bottle. In a low crouch he started for Gio.

The knife flashed in Cesar's hand.

78

Valdo screamed, then stared stupidly at the blood spurting from his right hand.

The bottle fell from it—along with two severed fingers.

Cesar wiped the blade of the knife on the back of Valdo's shirt. The Spaniard, unheeding, continued to regard his hand with fixed attention. Dazed, he offered no objection when Cesar wound a short length of dirty cord around his wrist and pulled it tightly in a tourniquet.

Valdo slumped down on the foot of the cot. Gio knocked off the head of a bottle of wine and gave it to Cesar. Cesar offered it to the Spaniard, who took a long, deep pull. Valdo was still confused. "Do you have a family?" Cesar asked.

"Yes."

"You're married?"

Valdo nodded. "And two kids."

"How many relatives?"

"None. My wife and I are from Barcelona."

"That's unfortunate."

"Why do you say that?" Valdo looked at his two fingers lying on the floor near his feet and shivered.

"I have many relatives," Cesar stated flatly. "So many that I have never counted them." He was not boasting. "Each of them might call on you sometime. In the day. In the night." He shrugged. "Who knows?"

"There's no need for that!" Valdo's face twisted with fear as he clutched the tight cord around his wrist.

"No need . . ." Cesar agreed, "now that we are partners. You trust me not to kill you, and I trust you never to speak to *anyone* about me again. Agreed?"

"Yes."

"One more thing," Cesar added almost with indifference. "We'll keep our tables. Each night you'll give me a quarter of the money you take in. I don't ask for half of it, although we are partners. In return, Gio will see that no one makes jokes about your missing fingers." Cesar smiled thinly and shook his head. "Jokes about them are in bad taste—especially as you might've lost your head instead."

Chapter 10

The Cours Jean Nicoli extends south from Cours Napoleon and runs along the Bay of Ajaccio, angling slightly to the west. The end of it tying to the Cours Napoleon is two or three kilometers distant from the downtown section of the city. In the days of World War II, the area served by Cours Jean Nicoli was not so densely built up as other sections and was comprised of shabby, but not too decrepit, private houses and a scattering of small shops. Many of the dwellings had plots of dusty gardens in which equally dusty chickens scratched out an existence; some families kept a goat for milk. The only beauty in the neighborhood lay in a magnificent view of the bay.

One of the houses was owned by a middle-aged, childless widow, Maria Proto. Carlo Proto, before his death, had owned an interest in a small fishing boat, of which fishing had been only part of its activities. His death at sea was considered a tragedy by his widow, but not by many others. According to custom, Maria Proto put on her black widow's clothes and never dressed in anything else the rest of her life. Carlo Proto left Maria very little other than the house, his share in the boat (which was bought out promptly by the surviving crew members), and numerous contacts among the local seamen and longshoremen of the waterfront.

Maria was starving to death, slowly and with silent dignity, when Cesar offered to rent her house and retain her as housekeeper. The widow was as impressed by Cesar's "quality" as by the money he offered. It was apparent to her that he was gentry . . . a *cavaliere* . . . and his presence in her home would lift her several degrees socially above her neighbors. Her opinion of Gio was considerably less, and she ignored almost completely the quiet, self-effacing Joseph when Cesar was present. She understood that Cesar had use for them—all the big *signores* had servants—and she accepted them on that basis. Cesar, recognizing Maria's typical peasant's awe and respect, treated her with great courtesy. The poor, dazzled widow became his loyal subject.

The Proto house was small, and poor by any standards, but it was an improvement over the miserable room the three men had shared in the cul-de-sac. The widow's place was narrow and three storeys high. A combination kitchen and dining room covered the entire first floor; the second storey included a tiny parlor and a bedroom; on the third floor were two additional bed chambers. An unpainted outdoor privy, behind the house, stood next to a peeling wooden shed with a wide, sagging door. Neighboring houses were not too close, giving some degree of privacy.

Cesar rented the house after due consideration and some wrestling of conscience. Following the army's search of his old room, he realized it had lost its value as a *gourbi* . . . a hideout. Not only would the neighbors now be interested, but the police might search it again at any time. Although Loubet and Cordeau had been bought off, other police, under pressure from Talmant, might continue the harassing. If Joseph and Gio were picked up, the "operating money" they carried would be difficult to explain—especially the blue-seal dollars.

Cesar realized that he, himself, headed the authorities list of suspects. Common sense told him that he should rent two places—one for himself, another for Joseph and Gio. Their domiciles should be separate and apart, distant from each other. Perhaps Joseph and Gio might escape surveillance altogether.

But through tradition Cesar had inherited a deep sense of paternalism. He *was* the center of his family, although, for the present, it consisted only of Joseph and Gio. Seemingly aloof and self-sufficient, his ingrained clannishness demanded that his family be around him.

While Cesar had never analyzed these feelings, he knew simply that where he was, there must Joseph and Gio be, too.

Maria Proto's house partly solved these problems. The police could not visit the house, or search it, without the widow knowing of it. And Maria's typical Corsican aversion to all authority, as well as her personal devotion to Cesar, would prevent her from answering their questions—at least truthfully. Sufficient space in the house and yard provided excellent places to hide the amount of money accumulated during the week, and the shed offered temporary concealment for the jeep, which Cesar brought back to town after the first furor had subsided.

Once a week, Cesar drove the jeep into the foothills to deliver supplies to Anse and Salvatore, and add the profits from Joseph's manipulations to the growing hoard of capital. The jeep was not used for any other purpose. The military identification numbers were changed on the machine, and Cesar wore Louis' old uniform when driving. He had not yet been stopped, but eventually—he knew—he would be apprehended.

Through Joseph's contacts in Ghisonacia, which extended to the thriving black market in Bastia, Cesar traded the jeep for an aged and decrepit Citroën. The jeep was in good operating condition, but the Citroën was in a deplorable state barely able to achieve forty kilometers per hour under its own power. However, the old car could haul supplies, and it offered protection to Cesar while transferring the money. In exchange for the jeep, Cesar received the Citroën and fifteen hundred blue-seal dollars. He stoically accepted the bad end of the bargain, which he considered justified because he could drive the Citroën with comparative safety. Under normal conditions, automobiles were few in Corsica; during the war they were unavailable at any price. The Citroën came with a set of papers, probably forged, but at least the authorities were not searching for it. The new owner of the jeep, in Bastia, planned to disassemble it and smuggle it out of the island piece by piece. Where it would eventually be sold was his business.

The aged Citroën could not navigate the steep slopes between the dirt road and the corral, so Anse and Salvatore carried the supplies from the parked car to the shepherd's hut. The Algerian and Corsican, both silent men, had reached an unspoken agreement and lived together, in a vacuum of solitude, without friction. During the day, Salvatore remained away from the hut with his flock. When he returned at dark, Anse had eaten his supper and was already rolled up in a blanket. The dispatch case no longer could hold all the money. It had been replaced by a large leather suitcase carefully wrapped in Anse's old raincoat. The hoard remained buried, between Cesar's weekly calls, beneath the ruins of a stone oven in the hut.

Anse accepted his life on the lonely hillside without comment. Only once did he bring up the subject of money. "Someday," he said to Cesar, "we're gonna spend that money, huh? Plenty fine clothes and fine women. All we can eat an' drink. People saying, 'Look at Anse! Bigger'n a sultan!' "

"When the war's over," Cesar assured him. "Unless you want to try it now—and end up in front of a wall."

"Not me!" Anse's teeth gleamed and he shook his head. "I can wait!"

Cesar turned away, but a question returned to his mind: what would he do when the war was over? He had no desire to return to Col Pieto. Fine clothes and fancy girls might satisfy Anse and Gio; Joseph was content with playing with his "numbers." Any man with sufficient silver in his pocket could always find what he wanted to eat and drink. No, there was more to life than that—it was something that had driven the Genoese and Venetians into the distant corners of the world's oceans. It was beyond avarice and plunder. Cesar was not yet sure what it was, but he had the restless drive to discover it for himself. With money turned into the alchemy of power, he would find it. In time.

Since Cesar had assumed partnership with Valdo, the bar had prospered even more. Le Bélier was one of the established black-market money exchanges in the capital. Cesar used his participation in the bar to explain his presence in Ajaccio. He needed a front, although Loubet and Cordeau stopped regularly for their weekly payoff. Valdo, even with a quarter of his profits going to Cesar, made more money than before. His one grim experience with Cesar and Gio remained fresh in his memory; he had no desire to repeat it.

Maria Proto had been told by Cesar that he had an "interest" in Le Bélier. Consequently, she was waiting up late one night when

Cesar and his two companions returned from the bar. The fire in the stove had been banked for the night, but the widow had not gone to her bedroom on the second floor.

"*Signor* Cesar," she said, seated on a wooden chair by the stove, "you are a busy gentleman. But maybe you'll want to hear what I have to say?"

Cesar bowed very slightly. "I'm never too busy to listen to you, signora."

"It is about this bar you have . . ."

Cesar nodded. "Le Bélier."

"A man my husband used to know, he came to see me today. He has heard that a rich *signore* is staying here."

Cesar's lips tightened. "I hope your neighbors have not been gossiping."

"I've said nothing," Maria apologized. "Believe me, *signor.*"

"What did this fellow want?"

"He asked if you'd be interested in buying some whiskey."

Cesar switched a glance at Joseph. "I don't drink whiskey," he told Maria.

"It is for your bar."

"How much does he have to sell?"

"He didn't say. But his name is Joseph, too, and he is called Jojo. If you want to talk to him, you'll find him around the *gare* . . . the railroad station."

"Thank you, *signora*. I'll think about it."

Cesar, followed by his two companions, climbed the narrow, uncarpeted stairs to the third storey, where Joseph and Gio shared one room while Cesar occupied the other. Each night before retiring, Gio concealed their thick wallet of money beneath a window-sill he had worked loose from its frame. Deposited in the wall of the house, with the sill returned to position, the money was well hidden.

Pausing before the door to his room, Cesar asked Joseph, "What do you think?"

"The whiskey? At the right price it can sell for a good profit in Le Bélier."

"I think so, too. Valdo buys it at twenty dollars a bottle. Even watered down, you can't turn a sou at that cost. If we can buy it cheaper . . . ah!"

"That's up to you. I'd be careful, though." Joseph's face was thoughtful.

"Why? If it's a bargain?"

"Jojo looked you up. He must know plenty of other buyers. Why go out of his way to find you?"

"I'll talk to him in the morning. And find out."

The *gare,* which Cesar had passed often but never visited, was a small brick building located at the corner of a short street, Avenue de la Gare. Behind the station, two little engines and numerous stubby freight cars operated in a cluttered, disorganized switchyard. The railroad ran less than three hundred kilometers of track in all of Corsica. The yard was separated from the Cours Napoleon by a low stone wall topped with a rusty spiked fence. The other side of the small terminal opened on piers and docks.

Jojo was more than willing to talk when Cesar finally located him in the turmoil of the yards. "Fifty cases of whiskey . . . of what the Americans call 'fifths.' Twelve bottles to the case."

"How much?"

"A hundred and seventy-five dollars per case. You got to take all of it or nothin'."

Cesar sized up the seller—dressed in stained workman's clothes and wearing a black beret. Jojo grinned back at Cesar from around a burning cigarette; a front tooth was missing, and a stubble of beard blued his jaw. Cesar held no illusions where the whiskey came from: Jojo and friends had stolen it either from the railroad or the docks. However, the amount of money asked for the liquor was considerable. Cesar needed time to figure it out. "How about a drink?" he invited Jojo. "Le Bélier isn't far from here."

"Never turn down a free drink." Jojo gave his black grin.

Walking down the Cours Napoleon toward the bar, Cesar said, "I'm wondering why you looked me up. Am I the first buyer you've asked, or the last of others?"

Jojo shrugged. "I want to unload and get my money. No *foutre* around. Get rid of it all at one time . . . and that takes a lot of *pognon* . . . dough!"

"What makes you think I have that kind of money?"

Jojo glanced quickly from the corner of his eyes at Cesar, who was striding beside him. "I knew Carlo Proto. He was a clever one, though his old woman likes to make him out a saint. I figured Maria might still have connections."

"The kind you're looking for?"

"It takes all kinds to make the world," Jojo said ambiguously.

Arriving at Le Bélier, they seated themselves at Cesar's table. A brandy was placed before Jojo. He took a sip and sighed, as if with great pleasure, although the brandy was the rawest served in the bar. "Do you want some cigarettes?" he asked Cesar while blowing the fumes of the hot liquor through his nose.

"American?" Cesar asked. Jojo nodded. "How many and how much?"

"A hundred cartons. Mixed. Lucky's, Camels, and Phillip Morris. Five dollars a carton."

Cesar shifted in his chair and caught Joseph's eye. He motioned toward the back room. "Take your time with your drink. Have another if you want it. I'll be back." Cesar stood up and walked around the bar.

Within a few minutes Joseph joined him in the back room. Cesar explained the deal to him. Joseph replied promptly, "He's asking $14.58 a fifth. That amounts to $8,750 for fifty cases. It's a good buy —if you can believe him. That's better than five dollars per bottle you save under the going black-market rate. On the first hundred fifths, of the six hundred involved, you save enough to get the cigarettes for free."

Cesar returned to his table and sat down. "I'll take your stuff," he told Jojo, "on one condition. I want it delivered here to the back room."

Jojo gave his black grin. "Afraid it's bad?"

"It might be." Cesar stared flatly across the table.

"Well, the seals have never been broken."

"If they have, I won't take it."

"When do you want it?"

"Tonight. We'll close at twelve. You deliver it right after midnight."

"You'll have the *pognon?* Blue seal?"

"I'll have it."

Jojo finished his brandy. The overly pleased expression on Jojo's face, as he swaggered from the bar, disturbed Cesar. But he put his uneasiness aside.

Chapter 11

The whiskey and cigarettes were delivered by Jojo and two unidentified companions. They arrived in a U.S. Army truck that pulled up in the slimy, unswept, black alley behind Le Bélier. An American, in uniform, sat behind the wheel and made no effort to help unload. Jojo's other companion, a Corsican, wore workclothes similar to his own. The haul nearly filled the back room of the bar. Each case was examined carefully by Cesar for signs of tampering with the bottles, but the seals were unbroken.

Cesar paid Jojo the exact amount of money agreed upon. In the light of the single weak bulb in the back room, the stacked cases rose shoulder high around the walls. Jojo said, "Now you'll really get the Americans in! They're lousy with *pognon.* You won't have to cut the crap with so much water that they raise hell about it." The Corsican stuffed the thick wad of bills in his pocket and returned to the truck. Within moments it had disappeared into the darkness.

Earlier in the evening, Gio had installed a heavy wooden drop-bar on the inside of the door from the alley, and covered the narrow window with protective layers of wire mesh securely nailed in place. Cesar bolted the door and turned to Valdo. "You'll sleep here," he told the Spaniard.

Valdo eyed the canvas cot with distaste. "For how long?"

"While I decide if we keep the whiskey here or move it.

89

If the whiskey stays, so do you." Cesar gave the window another inspection. "Jojo knows the stuff is here. I wouldn't put it past him to try to hijack it back again." Cesar nodded to Gio, who handed Valdo a revolver. "Use it if you have to," Cesar said.

Valdo held the gun loose in his right held. His two missing fingers made it impossible for him to pull the trigger. "What do I do? Club 'em with it?"

"Use your left. Hold it against his head if you have to," Cesar told him coldly.

Valdo sat down on the cot. Without looking at Cesar, he said, "I don't like this . . ."

"You will when the money comes in." Cesar had earlier informed the Spaniard that with the purchase of the whiskey, he was now counting himself a full partner in Le Bélier. Valdo took a deep breath, but said nothing. "Don't be unappreciative," Cesar warned softly.

The next morning Cesar slept late. Joseph and Gio already had gone to Le Bélier when Cesar arose, shaved, and carefully dressed himself from his new black-market wardrobe. He strolled slowly from the widow Proto's house, taking in the scented salt-tinged sea breeze. At the corner of Cours Jean Nicoli he paused: the sparkling waters of the bay glittered beneath the whitening sun . . . tenders and small boats skittered like darting waterbugs between the anchored war craft in the harbor.

A feeling of exultation lifted within Cesar, a state approaching euphoria. By all the blessed saints and martyrs, it was good to be alive! Life was almost as good in the city as it was in the green beauty of the forests amid the falling mountain streams and the cathedral spires of the titanic colanthes.

The muzzle of a revolver shoved into Cesar's back.

A voice from close behind him said, "Don't move!" Cesar felt a hand slip beneath his jacket and remove his knife. A car, parked a short distance down the street, pulled up and stopped. "Get in by the driver!" Cesar entered the blue Renault and sat down. The gunman took the back seat behind him.

The Renault drove across town to the Boulevard Lantivy, which ran along the bay behind the Square of Napoleon. Then, after a short distance, the car turned off Lantivy and stopped before a gray stone townhouse with a mansard roof. The doors and shutters, were painted black as was the roof. Cesar and the man with the gun left the Renault and mounted a flight of three low steps to the mansion. At the distant ringing of a bell, the massive front door was opened by a burly, heavy-faced servant. The houseman recognized Cesar's escort and stood aside, permitting them to enter.

No words had been exchanged during the drive from the corner of Cours Jean Nicoli and the entry hall of the townhouse. Still no words were spoken. At a gesture from the gunman, Cesar continued down the hall to a room in the back. Another affirming nod from his escort and Cesar opened a door and stepped inside.

A gray-haired man, with a sagging, sallow, aging face, was seated in a deep leather chair. Beside him a leaded window looked out over a small well-kept garden. The paneled room was lined with books. "Sit down, Satisanni," he said, gesturing to a chair facing him. The armed escort remained standing by the door.

Cesar took the seat. "You know my name. I don't know yours."

"Vito Nastacio," the gray-haired man told him.

"*Le Patriarche,*" the man said from the door, his voice a warning to Cesar.

"Tell your *casseur* to put away his gun," Cesar said, referring to the strong-arm.

"You won't need it, Cuomo," Nastacio told the gunman. He selected a thin Cuban cigar and waited while Cuomo crossed the room to light it for him. The *casseur's* revolver was tucked in the front of his belt, quickly accessible.

Cesar silently observed *Le Patriarche*—obviously a man of wealth, power, and command. The use of the term "patriarch" carried a meaning beyond the biblical connotation of head of a family or tribe and usually indicating great age. As used by Cuomo it was a princely title, the ruler of a state. Cesar's own father, Victore, although the head of a large and powerful family and often addressed as *Signore* or *Cavaliere,* was never called *Le Patriarche. Le Patriarche* was an archaic title, honorary to the fullest degree. It had nothing to do with a family. It indicated one thing . . . a state of power.

Cesar remained silent, waiting for Nastacio to begin. After his cigar was pulling well and to his satisfaction, Nastacio said, "Ordinarily I would've permitted Cuomo, or another captain, to take

91

care of this matter. But I've followed reports of your activities with interest and decided I'd like to see you myself." *Le Patriarche's* shrewd black eyes regarded Cesar from behind a thin veil of smoke.

"What matter?" Cesar asked.

Nastacio lifted his eyebrows in simulated and exaggerated surprise. He looked at Cuomo. "Is it possible that our friend is ignorant of the correct procedure? Perhaps you should explain to him." With a bored expression he leaned back in his chair and crossed his hands.

"The Unione sets the price of liquor and tobacco. We buy it at ten dollars a case and sell it to you . . . or anyone else . . . at twenty." Cuomo's voice was flat and hard. "You owe the Unione twenty-five hundred more for the whiskey delivered to Le Bélier last night. And another five hundred for the cigarettes."

Cesar's cool exterior did not betray the apprehension that had gripped him at hearing the name of the Unione. *"Le Patriarche"* had prepared him.

"You see," Nastacio's slightly patronizing voice explained, "your connection took advantage of you. By evading us, and going directly to you, he *thought* he could get fifteen dollars a case." He paused, a brief instant tinged with significance, then added, "On second thought, Jojo has since turned over *all* the money to Cuomo. In full repentance."

"Now come up with your balance. You're getting off easy," Cuomo said.

Cesar examined the brightly shined tips of his shoes in a cursory manner. "I've never had the pleasure of meeting the Unione Corse before." He looked up and met the stare of *Le Patriarche*.

Nastacio smiled. "We're simply businessmen—as you are. For instance, we have not interfered with your money changing. We permitted you to develop a business. In its small way, it didn't interfere with *our* business. You must understand, of course, that it was only because of us that *our* friends . . . in the *préfecture* . . . allowed you to operate. Their friendship costs us money. It's time now that you share our expenses."

"How much?" asked Cesar.

"A customary one third of your profits." Nastacio gently tipped the ash from his cigar. "That includes both the exchange and bar."

"I hadn't planned on additional partners."

Cuomo said, "We don't have to argue with you. Maybe you and your *copains* need to have your bar burn down. Or would you like a fatal accident or two? The two *flics* you're paying off won't hesitate long enough to pee when they get their orders to slam you in *le frigo!*"

Cesar's pride was a sour, bitter taste in his mouth. He swallowed it. Summoning up the resources at his control, he thought: "Joseph —no man of violence, of little use in a fight. Valdo will sell me out with pleasure. Anse? If I bring him back the army will get him before the Unione does. That leaves Gio—and me. We're outmanned, out-gunned. We won't have a chance." Cesar accepted the stark reality; before the hidden might of the Unione Corse, he was helpless. At least for the present.

But he also realized that even with turning over a third share to the Unione he still would be making a tremendous profit. Cesar was not so foolish as to jeopardize what he already had.

"In addition," Nastacio said as if following Cesar's thoughts, "you'll undoubtedly make some very useful friends through our association. You are a young man with a future. You'll go far." Cesar stared at him with opaque eyes. Nastacio went on. "I know of the Satisanni—and respect them. We do not go out of our way to make enemies. The less trouble for all of us, the better."

"You receive a third of what I make. What do I get in return?"

Nastacio nodded toward Cuomo. "Protection from what he said. But there's more. You're not a member of the maquis, but many of our people are. After the war is over, you may need them."

Cesar was not quite ready to capitulate. "This Jojo," he asked, "is he under your protection?"

Cuomo laughed. "That small-time thief! He's useful only on the docks. A handful of centimes will buy a dozen like him."

Cesar nodded. He looked at Nastacio lounging in his comfortable chair. "All right, *Patriarche,*" he said. "I agree."

Nastacio smiled. "I've always considered myself a man of some discernment. I depended on your good judgment." Older and wiser, he sensed Cesar's pride and shrewdly placated it, giving him a title of respect. "Signor Cesar, if you have any problems, Cuomo will take care of them."

"I can take care of my own, but I thank you."

"Good!" Nastacio nodded a dismissal.

"Where are the three thousand dollars?" Cuomo asked promptly.

"We'll get them," Cesar told him.

Late that afternoon, Cesar stood up from his table in the Le Bélier. American servicemen, sailors, and seamen thronged the bar to pay outrageous prices for the watered-down whiskey Valdo poured in a constant stream. Without comment, Joseph had given Cesar the money owed the Unione. After Cuomo had left, Cesar explained the situation to his friend. Joseph shrugged. "It was too good to be true, so now we pay for it," he told Cesar.

"When there are few choices, I prefer the better," Cesar said.

Joseph agreed. "We can always raise the prices." His face was thoughtful.

Now, some hours later, Cesar returned to Joseph's table. "Close up for a while. Gio's coming with me." Joseph took the heavy wallet of money and moved into the back room.

Cesar and Gio searched the *gare* and the yards and the docks around it. Dusk was falling when they found Jojo as he started down the Boulevard Sampiero toward a small, grimy café near the foot of the street by the station. They fell in stride on each side of him.

Jojo glanced at their expressionless faces and walked faster.

Gio grabbed him by the shoulder and shoved him hard against the retaining wall that supported the Avenue de la Gare above them. Few pedestrians were in the area at that time of evening. Jojo's beret was knocked askew. He tugged it back on his head. "Look," he protested, "you can't blame me!" Both Cesar and Gio regarded him silently. "It was a bargain. You were glad to get it!" His words tumbled out.

"At fifteen a case, yes. Twenty, no!" Cesar said. Gio's massive hands bounced Jojo's head against the wall. "Why didn't you tell me you were double-crossing the Unione?"

"You didn't ask!" Jojo's tongue nervously explored the space of his missing tooth. His rapid, frightened breathing was distinct in the silence. "I didn't make a sou . . . they took it . . . already have it! I don't have nothing left . . ."

Cesar nodded and Gio slammed his big fist in Jojo's belly. He gasped and cramped forward fighting for breath. Gio's next blow caught him solidly on the side of his face. Jojo was spun around and hurled back against the wall. Gio caught him and held him erect.

"I don't like to be played for a fool," Cesar said.

Gio hit Jojo again. The man whimpered and tried to pull away. With the heel of the palm of his hand, Gio mashed Jojo's nose upward until the skin tore away from the nostrils. Jojo screamed. Gio knocked him flat on the pavement.

"From now on," Cesar said without raising his voice, "each day you will pay me half of what you steal—until you have repaid me three thousand dollars."

Jojo lay sobbing on the bricks. Gio's heavy foot caught him in the ribs. "You heard the boss!"

Jojo's breath burst out in a clap; he rolled over. Gio's foot caught him again. "For the love of God . . .!" Jojo lifted himself to his hands and knees. Gio's kick sent him sprawling again.

"Do you hear me?" Cesar asked.

"I hear!" Jojo panted. Gio lifted him to his feet, propped him against the wall, and backhanded him across the face.

"If you miss one day," Cesar continued inexorably, "we'll look for you. Remember—wherever you try to hide, anywhere in Corsica, I'll find you."

"Yes . . . yes . . ." Jojo's feet slowly sprawled out as he sank to the ground, his back still against the wall.

With a nod to Gio, Cesar turned and walked back toward Le Bélier.

Part
Two

Chapter 12

Marseilles, founded by the Greeks about 600 B.C., is the oldest city in France. The greatest port on the Mediterranean, and one of the busiest on any ocean or sea, it lies approximately 175 miles north and west of Ajaccio. The French Third Infantry, in August 1944, lifted the city from a German occupation that had existed since November 1942. Under the command of General Hoislard de Montsabert, Marseilles was besieged, without bombing, in order to prevent complete destruction of the city. But the Germans, in their withdrawal, destroyed the port's facilities, leaving it in shambles for the Allies.

And the harbor installations were not all that were ruined. Marseilles suffered badly in the war. Twice the people of the city rose up and fought the Germans between 1942 and 1944. In retaliation, Old Town, a labyrinth of steep, dark, narrow streets inhabited by a seafaring population, was completely leveled, blown up, by the Germans in 1943.

The busy port, which before the war had a population of nearly one million persons, by war's end had lost from a third to a half of it.

In its almost two thousand six hundred years, Marseilles has survived many wars, many kings, many empires. It has been invaded, fought over, destroyed, and rebuilt so many times that very few ruins remain from its hoary past. Only a few crumbling bricks here and there tell the lost glories of its pride beneath the Greeks and Romans. There is little to show of its centuries as a medieval capital of scholars, poets, and princes. Where other cities of Europe point to their great and graceful cathedrals and palaces, Marseilles can recall only its memories of what has been. Most of the city that now stands dates back to the eighteenth and nineteenth centuries.

At the end of World War II, Marseilles was a city in turmoil, scarred with destruction and filled with hatred of its late occupiers —the Germans and their collaborators.

When Cesar arrived in the city, after VE Day, he carried one hundred and three thousand dollars in American currency, and was accompanied by Joseph, Gio, and Anse. The four Corsicans sailed aboard the *Dega,* a small fishing boat bound from Ajaccio to Marseilles with a smuggled load of black-market medical drugs and supplies. The supplies had been stolen from the British in North Africa and would bring exorbitant prices on the mainland of Europe, where hundreds of thousands were suffering from infection, malnutrition, and exposure. Cesar owned no part of the cargo. He had paid fares for himself and his companions.

The *Dega* eliminated the customs, declarations, and inspections that a more orthodox means of transportation would require. The boat carried a captain and crew of four, solving any problem of the seamen attempting to rob Cesar of his money—their forces were equal. In addition, either Gio or Anse sat with a loaded .45 by the side of the old leather suitcase during the boat's two-day run.

It was after dark when the *Dega* slipped out of the Bay of Ajaccio and set its course north by north-northwest to Marseilles. Cesar and Joseph stood in the stern of the boat as it plowed through the lifting waters stirred by the night breeze. To starboard, the lights of Ajaccio faded in the distance. The mass of the island was a block of black against a backdrop of darkness. A quartered slice of late rising moon had not lifted high enough in the sky to silver the night. The slap-slap-slap of water beneath the bow of the *Dega* and the brushings of invisible spray in their faces sped the two men on their course. Neither had ever before been off the island.

"So," Joseph said slowly, "we are on our way."

"You're surprised?" Cesar asked.

"No, but I've wondered. Often a man'll talk of plans but'll never carry them through." Joseph paused, his eyes fixed on a few remaining golden points of light in Ajaccio. "Haven't you any doubts?"

Cesar laughed. "Remember the saying: 'In trouble have a Corsican man by your side; in marriage have a Corsican woman!' I have three men by my side."

"And the woman?"

"She'll come later."

The old engine of the *Dega* throbbed, pounding the timbers of her hull through the limbo of water and night. "You have enough money to be a man of importance at home," Joseph said. "In Marseilles? . . . In France? What?"

"Back in Col Pieto—a *signore*? . . . I won't settle for that!" Cesar's voice was fierce. "When I was a boy, in the mountains with my gun and knife, sometimes I pretended I was a general and I led an army. Or I was an admiral with a fleet . . . like Genoa!" Cesar stopped abruptly as if embarrassed by his sudden confiding to Joseph.

"The days of the generals and admirals have past," Joseph replied.

Cesar was more composed when he continued. "The ones with horses and uniforms . . . and bands, yes. But the *private* armies, the underground ones . . .!" Cesar sighed. "The invisible way! That's the way to power."

In the darkness Joseph could not see Cesar's face, but he did not need to see to understand. He was able to sense and perceive many of Cesar's thoughts, and he often listened with an inner ear to his cousin's unvoiced words. "The maquis?" Joseph asked. "Soon the Underground will be only a word in history books. Besides, you were never part of it."

"I don't have to be," Cesar said.

"The Unione, then?" When Cesar made no reply, Joseph continued. "It's old . . . older even than the Mafia in Sicily. Two hundred years it's been the knife that bites most deeply. You've seen this for yourself. You've accepted it because you can't fight it."

"I don't intend to fight it."

"Cesar . . ." Joseph's voice was earnest. "Listen! If you must continue to pay dues, pay them. If you have to do business with the Unione, do your business, but mind your own. Let it use you to its benefit, but be happy that it leaves you alone!"

"I'll use it to *my* benefit," Cesar said.

Joseph lifted a hand to wipe the spray from his face. "With three men and a sum of money that isn't a *dot* in the eyes of *Les Patriarches* in Bastia . . . or Calenzana . . . or Ajaccio?"

"In Marseilles it will be different," Cesar replied firmly.

"How? Why will it be different? There you'll find the Volanti and the Rampini, Families as powerful as Nastacio."

"Only what is left of them. The Nazi bastards did a good job of wiping them out." Cesar stood in the lee of the small cabin and cupped his hands to light a cigarette. The flare of his lighter momentarily illuminated his face. "The Families will have to rebuild," he continued. "That'll take time. There'll be opportunities—for all of us!"

"Opportunities? For what, Cesar? I'm not sure I want to lose my head to the guillotine."

"You won't. Not if I'm strong enough . . . not if *we* have the power."

Joseph shook his head. In the darkness Cesar did not see the gesture. "This power . . . what's it for, Cesar? You talk about it, you want it, you're willing perhaps to die trying for it. But how will you use it?"

Cesar was silent, searching for words to explain what he himself did not understand. It was not a moment of truth that he was attempting to discover, but an argument to hold Joseph to him. He needed his cousin, with his facile mathematical mind, to help him. Cesar realized that Joseph was the essential missing part of his own character and ability. So far Joseph had been content to play his "games" with money; remote and removed from the violence of Cesar, Gio, and Anse, he had remained in the background. Joseph had offered quiet advice and Cesar had listened. But in the future, for how long would Joseph be satisfied to continue this role?

"Power," Cesar said finally, "exists in itself. It *is* . . . that's all. More than money—gold in vaults, land, fine cars, mansions, servants. There are millionaires who have all this and they are . . . *merde!* Power is a matter of life and death to hundreds . . . thousands . . . millions . . . who've never seen you and, maybe, never heard of you. But when you say 'yes' in Paris, they hear it in London, New York, and Bangkok. And when you shake your head, then Hong

Kong, Buenos Aires, and Geneva know it, too!"

"Dreams, Cesar!"

"How about Bonaparte? It took him from our island to the throne of France."

"Other days. Another age! Times are different now. Hitler had such a dream, too. He failed . . . and so will you!"

"No," said Cesar, "but I agree I must do it differently. How? I don't know. But somewhere there's a key, and I'll find it!" Cesar's voice softened. "And you, Joseph? How'd you like to rub shoulders with fat bankers in Berne, Geneva, Paris, London, New York? That back table in *Le Bélier* will seem far away from your big desk—with telephones and accountants all around you. You'll have your own teletype to print the latest reports from all the stock exchanges around the world." Cesar laughed. "Hell! There'll be banks of them in just one corner of your office. And every time you go to the can, it'll make the franc fall . . . so you must learn to control your bladder."

Anse stepped out of the low cabin. He glanced at the faint figures of Cesar and Joseph in the darkness, then spit over the side of the boat. "We'd make faster time on a camel."

"You ever been on one?" Cesar asked.

"No." Anse yawned. "Never been on a boat, either—except the transport that hauled my ass to Corsica. When do we hit Marseilles?"

"One more night," Cesar told him.

"This is Tuesday?" Anse squatted on his haunches, rolling with the lightly pitching deck like a built-in stanchion. "Things always happen on Tuesday." The whites of his eyes flicked briefly, then were gone. "Morocco. Put a knife in this *mec* on a Tuesday. Don't even remember what it was all about. We been drinking." He paused, trying to remember. "He just laying there and bleeding. I lit out."

"You have a family in Morocco?" Joseph asked. Although Anse had been with them for months, the black never spoke of his past. Following their code toward strangers, the Corsicans had not questioned him. This night, on a cork of life bobbing in the dark waters of the Mediterranean, their lives were wound inevitably. Anse was part of them, one of their own.

"Don't know if I do or don't," Anse said. "My mother, she didn't live with my father. He lit out 'fore I was born. Didn't know she was carrying nothing till it was too late." Anse's low chuckle rumbled in the darkness. "Lucky for me, or I wouldn't be here." There was a moment of silence, then he added, "Ain't seen her since I was seven. Ran away then."

Through the marketplaces of North Africa, through the *souks* and bazaars, through filth, disease, and starvation, ran the ghost of a seven-year-old black boy. A youth with a knife—a blade with no handle; a youth with thieving fingers, lies on his tongue, and hatred in his heart, who stayed alive. The boy became a man. A man on hash and cheap wine; a barroom brawl—many of them. Then one too many.

"You took a *cavale* to Algiers?" Cesar said.

"Yeah. When I left Morocco, I went to Algiers. Figured I'd eat regular enough in a fancy uniform. Then's when I joined up. Damned fool!" Anse stood and stretched. "Guess maybe I'll go in and spell-off Gio," he said.

Thursday morning, 2:00 A.M., the *Dega* warped gently against a pier somewhere below Marseilles. Above was Vieux Port—Old Harbor—its entrance guarded by archaic Fort St. Jean to the north and Fort St. Nicholas to the south. Silently, and without farewells, the Corsicans climbed to the pier. The *Dega* backed off, then swung north again toward its own mysterious destination.

Gio, loaded like a giant pack animal, labored under an assortment of suitcases, duffel bags, and footlockers. The overflow was carried by Anse. Cesar, in charge of the money, led the party from the pier to shore. The band walked along an area of abandoned warehouses and leaning storage shacks, the silence broken only by their footsteps. After some minutes, Cesar halted and motioned to a loading dock, with rotting boards on top and its three sides unenclosed. "Store the stuff there," he said. "We'll wait here until morning."

Gio tumbled his load to the ground and shoved the assorted pieces beneath the dock. Kicking it, he grumbled, "Look at it! Even the rats don't like it."

"Better than the *taule*. First *poulet* we meet will stop us," Cesar said. "In the morning I'll go to the city and bring a car to take us back."

"Meantime we stay here." Gio sat down on a footlocker.

"Exactly!"

Anse stretched out on the ground, propping his head on a duffel bag. "Not too bad," he said. "Seen worse."

Joseph walked slowly up a sagging board to the top of the dock. The abandoned, rotting buildings were scabs of past labor and lost hopes. "Once somebody—people—poured money into this," he said to Cesar. "What's it worth now? Whoever built it might've had dreams of power, too."

Cesar lifted his head to speak to Joseph standing above him. His upturned face was stone polished in the silver haze of the descending moon. Momentarily his features assumed a fleeting resemblance of those carved on the triumphant arches of the old Romans. "Power's where you find it," he said. A cloud dimmed the luster of the night, and Cesar's features faded. "You're our scholar, Joseph. In the old days, didn't people believe there was a magic thing . . ." he searched for words, "a charm? It could change one thing to another. Even the Church and kings believed it?"

"Yes," Joseph said. "The Philosopher's Stone. It was supposed to change lead into gold." He stared down at Cesar. "But no one ever found it."

"I'll find one . . . *make* one! . . . that can change this," Cesar gestured toward the shamble of decay around them, "or anything else I want. When I find that stone, I'll use it, Joseph!"

"Everybody's talking crazy," Gio grunted.

"Maybe," Anse told him, rolling over on his side, "but I heard of amulets with lucky stones in 'em."

Joseph smiled and walked down from the dock. "Want me to watch the money while you sleep?" he asked Cesar.

"I'll stay awake for a while. Rest of you turn in. You'll all have to guard it in the morning while I'm gone."

Late that afternoon an old taxi crept along a narrow, tortuous street in Vieux Port. Transportation was still difficult to find in Marseilles—tires, parts, and gasoline were almost impossible to buy. Only after extended haggling and being forced to settle at an outrageous price and a huge tip, was Cesar able to hire the vintage vehicle to make the extended trip. The cab pulled up to a stop before a disreputable four-storey building, Hôtel Le Marin.

Le Marin, The Mariner, constructed of brick sometime in the 1880's, presented a sandstone front to an indifferent world. The original beige-tone facade had accumulated layers of grime until it was the color of the scruffy, dark gray alley cats that swarmed the area. The small hotel stood on a dank, crooked street lined with similar buildings housing other cheap transient lodgings, sleazy bars, poisonous cafés, and discreditable shops. However, if transportation were difficult to come by, housing was even more of a problem to find in the immediate postwar months. Cesar again paid dearly for the four rooms he rented in Le Marin.

Cesar stood in the dark, narrow lobby surrounded by his companions and their luggage. A battered counter serving as a desk ran the length of the room, with a rack for mail and keys behind it. Across from the desk a long wooden bench extended against the opposite wall, stopping short at a door that opened to the hotel's adjoining café-bar. The serving bar was little more than a heavy table encased in linoleum; it stood in front of grimy glass shelves holding an assortment of cheap wines and brandies. A bell on the bar brought reluctant service. The menu, chalked on slate, listed coffee, hot chocolate—when available—café au lait, doughy *croissants* with imitation grape jelly, and hard rolls. Half a dozen round tables, surrounded by miscellaneous wood and metal chairs, filled the dreary room. A solitary decoration brightened its streaked and sooty walls —a yellowing poster extolling the prewar virtues of a cruise aboard the *Ile de France.*

At the far end of the hotel lobby, a narrow stairway ascended to the three upper floors. Each floor contained rooms and one frantically flushing toilet. Hallways were uncarpeted as well as unmopped.

The owner and proprietor of Le Marin was a middle-aged man with spiky hair, a cautious and taciturn manner, a protruding belly, and heavily bagged eyes. M. Prosper Flot had achieved possession of Le Marin through the inheritance of his wife, Madame Flot. Before becoming an innkeeper, Flot sweat out his life as an oiler on tramp freighters. He developed little taste for work of any kind, and despised hard work in particular. Early in life, Prosper had taken to the sea through necessity and not desire, and he had retired to the hotel with no regret.

The hotel, already in neglect and disrepair some ten years earlier when Madame Flot unexpectedly inherited it, had deteriorated to a state of mean shabbiness under Flot's slothful indifference. Oddly enough, it seldom lacked guests from the faceless wanderers, seamen, refugees, and petty criminals of the old port. Accompanied by little luggage and lean purses, the unobtrusive lodgers remained for a night or two, then abruptly departed as suddenly as they arrived.

Flot handed Cesar four keys and nodded toward the stairway. "You can find your way," he wheezed. The Corsicans carried their luggage up the steep stairs.

"All the way to the top?" Gio was unhappy. "Why didn't you take the second floor?"

"With strangers wandering the hall outside our doors?" Cesar continued to climb. On the fourth floor he passed out the keys, retaining the two rooms fronting the street for himself and Joseph.

Cesar let himself into the cheerless room. He crossed the bare floor to a high, narrow window barred with a heavy, peeling shutter. Throwing it open, he looked into the shadowed street below, then up the buildings opposite and over their roofs. He could not see the harbor. Vieux Port runs west to east, and its narrow streets ascend slightly to form an amphitheater facing south. Across this expanse of great colosseum stalked the specter of violence and death in one of the toughest cities in the world.

Although Cesar did not see the specter, he was soon to know it well.

Chapter 13

"Call me Heloise," she said, "and it's none of your god-damned business if it's my name or not." The hollow-faced girl with thin shoulders and large, drooping breasts stared angrily at the drunken, grinning Gio. The massive figure of the Corsican dwarfed the spindling figure of the prostitute seated with him at a table in the bar of Le Marin. Gio stood up unsteadily and took a few steps; his finger punched heavily at the bell on the bar. In response to its surprisingly gentle tinkle, a small, gnomelike young man with a wide flat face appeared through a door beside the coffee machine. Scurrying behind the bar, he wiped his stubby fingers anxiously on a dirty apron.

"Two more brandies, Jean," Gio said. Returning to the table, he sat down and planted his great forearms on its top, tipping it. Their empty glasses rattled. Gio quickly withdrew his weight and grinned an apology. Jean delivered the brandies and disappeared again. No other customers patronized the cheerless bar.

"I can't sit here drinking," Heloise said. "There's this whole night ahead of me. Make up your mind."

Gio's good humor evaporated with the fumes in his glass. *"Cette merde,"* he growled. "Cut it out. If you don't want the brandy, I'll drink it."

Under the stark, flat light the girl's face was pallid, her eyes hidden in dark shadows. The slash of crimson lipstick was worn thin to reveal her pale lips. She was young, not over twenty, but thin to the point of emaciation and looked older. Her surprisingly large bosom, mounted to such a small frame, seemed more than she should carry. Slowly she reached for the brandy. Her voice held indifference. "Never turn anything down that's free."

Gio glanced through the door into the lobby. Cesar was passing, headed toward the stairs. "Hey, come here," Gio called. Cesar turned and entered the bar. He approached the table, a question in his eyes, observing Gio and the girl. "I want you to meet this *poule,*" Gio said expansively. "Picked me up outside the hotel." He took a slug of his brandy, then added, "Her name's Heloise . . . least that's what she says." Gio laughed.

"Is this *mec* a friend of yours?" Heloise coldly asked Cesar.

Cesar regarded the girl carefully. "Yes," he replied. Prostitutes were a rarity in Corsica. Wayward girls and fallen women were not tolerated in the strict structure of the island's society. A seducer was sometimes offered the alternative of marriage, if he were not killed by the woman's family. Cesar had never met a prostitute. He was curious. "I'll get a drink," he said, and rang the bell for Jean.

"Why is it all you *mecs* will buy liquor and then squabble with a whore about her price?" Heloise asked.

"I'm getting a drink because I want it," Cesar replied. Seating himself on a chair at the table, his eyes took in the girl's cheap orange dress, her mended black hose and stilted platform shoes. A large, black, imitation leather handbag, with a long broken strap, rested in her lap.

"Your *copain's* trying to get me drunk so I'll give it to him for nothing." A sneer tinged Heloise's voice. "I drink more for breakfast than he can hold all day."

"*Merde!*" Gio said.

The girl turned on him. "Peasant! Couple glasses of cheap brandy . . . and you want to hear the story of my life. What difference does it make?" Her laugh was scornful. "You pay a few lousy francs for a *passe* . . . and that's what you get!"

Gio's heavy face turned red with anger. "Why'd you come in here?"

Heloise paused. "To get off the street." She took a drink of brandy and tossed her head, flinging the hair from her face. "You want a story, I'll give you one. Suppose I started whoring cause I got raped by a gang of Nazi bastards? Would you believe it?" She looked at the faces of the two men. "All right, let's try this one: I was fifteen and sicker'n a dog and didn't have enough to eat. Needed food and medicine. The German officers had a whorehouse, so I became one of the girls. How about that?" The Corsicans stared at her in silence. "Here's another. I'm a lazy slut and would rather wiggle my ass in bed than do an honest day's work in some goddamn factory. You don't like that either?" She paused, shrugged. "Hell," she said, "maybe the plain fact is I just like to screw." She drained her glass. "Take your pick."

Cesar took out a ten-dollar bill and passed it across the table to the girl. "Keep it," he said.

Heloise looked at the bill. Opening her handbag, she gave a surprised smile to Cesar. "Thanks. You're a real gentleman." She regarded him more carefully now, observing his expensive jacket and white silk shirt. "That ten dollars buys you a long time." She gathered her handbag together and arose, looking around. "Upstairs?"

"Sit down," Cesar told her. "Let's talk."

Heloise slowly took her chair again, her eyes fixed on Cesar. "Get us all another round," he said to Gio. "You came in here to get off the street. Why? Isn't that where you do your business?"

She nodded. "Certainly! But at night it's dangerous out there. Every thieving, cutthroat, perverted bastard in the world waiting to jump you! Beat you up, stick a knife in you, take your money soon as you turn a trick. All the whores are scared. Lot of 'em won't come out at night!"

"No protection?"

Heloise gave Cesar a tight smile. "A pimp's no good. If he tags along, it scares off trade." She shook her head. "A girl lines up a stunt . . . and the *mec's* afraid to go with her. Scared to go to her place because maybe he'll get robbed."

Gio returned with the drinks and sat down. "Rent a room in a hotel," he said.

"Try to find a fleabag at night in this town," Heloise said. "Most hotels are afraid of the new procuring law."

"What's that?" asked Cesar.

"Well, there's no law against whoring," Heloise replied, "but there

111

is one against operating a whorehouse. The *flic* sons of bitches can close down a hotel cause they claim renting out a room's same as procuring."

Cesar stared at his brandy, his face thoughtful. "Suppose there was a place you could go. Take your customer. Place where you'd be safe and nobody'd bother you . . ."

"Every whore around would use it," Heloise said.

"How many is that?"

Heloise shrugged. "Who can count 'em?"

"Twenty?"

The girl laughed. "I know twenty myself . . . maybe fifty. More'n a hundred . . . easily." Her face sobered. "A thousand, even. That's why hustling's so goddamned tough."

"A trick takes how long?"

"No longer than's necessary, believe me!" She opened her handbag and ran a comb through her hair. Her gaunt face held no expression. "Fifteen minutes, half an hour at the most. Some of the *mecs* try to get more time, but most of 'em are in a hurry, too. 'Specially when it's night and we're outside. Alley or a car . . . or something."

"How many tricks a night?"

Heloise turned her eyes to meet Cesar's. The flatness of her stare matched his. "You planning to turn pimp? All these questions?" Her expression softened. "You wouldn't do too bad," she added.

Cesar ignored her question. "How many tricks a night?" he repeated.

"Now? Two or three. Way things are, it takes awhile to convince 'em they're not going to get muscled. And then you got to find a place to do it. And if it's raining or cold, it's just no use."

"With a place all set up to go, you could do twice as much?"

"Certainly. On good nights a hell of a lot more!"

"How much do you charge?"

"She wanted a thousand francs," Gio said. Slightly less than three dollars.

"Could you charge fifteen hundred francs per trick, if you had a good place to go?" Cesar asked. Heloise nodded. "Would you be willing to pay half of it for a hotel room?"

The girl thought about it. Finally she said, "Yes, yes I would. 'Specially if I had a place I could depend on. You know, where I wouldn't get beat up or robbed . . ." Abruptly, a strained look spread over her face. Hastily she gulped her brandy. Her hand trembled as she placed the glass back down on the table. "It's getting cold in here," she said, wrapping her arms around herself as if for warmth. "You guys don't mind, I better be going . . ."

Cesar reached out and grasped her arm, pulling it away from her body. She resisted for only a moment, then let it lay limp on the table. Cesar pushed back the sleeve of her dress. The inside of her arm was covered with scabs and punctured with needle marks. Cesar's eyes asked her a question. "Course it's Horse," she said, her voice trembling and then filled with irritation. "Don't be a damned fool!"

"You need a fix," he said without expression.

"Damned right! And soon!" Heloise started up from the table.

"Ask around . . . next day or two. All the whores you know. About what we were discussing. Would they join you?" Cesar took out another ten-dollar bill and put it in her hand. "Come back and tell me what they think. No lies. No promises. Only the facts! There'll be more money waiting for you."

"Here?"

"Yes. At Le Marin."

"Don't worry, you'll see me." Heloise forced a smile, then turned and hurried toward the door to the lobby.

Cesar's eyes followed her, full of thought. "One thing she left out of her stories," he said to Gio, "was that she is hooked. Our little *poule* carries a monkey, and that costs money. And she's willing to work the rest of her life to support it."

"Who cares if that's why she's whoring?" Gio was indifferent.

Cesar finished his brandy and stood up. Leaving the bar, he climbed the stairs to the top floor. Joseph was lying on his bed, reading, when Cesar opened the door. Cesar entered his cousin's room and said abruptly, "We're paying Flot rent. High rent. And we get little in return."

Joseph put aside his book and hunched upward on the bed. "So?"

"How much would it cost to buy Le Marin?"

"That depends on Flot—how much he'll ask and if he wants to sell. Whatever it is, it's not worth the rent you save."

"We need a place. Own it."

"That's up to you. But Flot survives here because he puts nothing

113

into it, takes everything out—and still lives like a pig."

Cesar pulled up the single, rickety chair and sat down. He lit a cigarette. "I'm not good with figures, but I heard something tonight."

"Tell me." Joseph listened attentively while Cesar repeated his conversation with Heloise. When Cesar finished, Joseph sat upright on the bed. Swinging his feet to the floor, his mind busy, he said, "If we keep the top floor, that'd leave eight rooms."

"Right."

"Two half-hour tricks per room per hour . . ." Joseph calculated. "Eight rooms. Eight hours . . . or more . . . each night, seven nights a week. Seven hundred and fifty francs per trick . . ." He leaned forward. "That'll gross better than two thousand dollars a week. More if you want to keep open for longer hours."

"I had a hunch it would be a good deal."

"From your gross you'll have to pay costs and maintenance. And fix up this dive before it completely falls to pieces. You'll have to figure amortization of your capital investment. And police protection. Don't forget *that*. It'll cost you *plenty!*"

"But we'll still make money?"

Joseph slowly agreed. "Yes . . ." Then he qualified his approval. "If the Unione doesn't cut in for too large a share."

"It won't for a while," Cesar said quietly. "It's too busy with other things."

Joseph fell into thought. "That girl . . . Heloise? You can't take the word of a whore for anything. She may be telling you what she thinks you want to hear."

"She won't lie to me . . . not and get away with it. She takes my money, she's mine." Cesar pushed back the chair. "While I'm waiting to hear from her, talk to Flot. Find out what he wants."

"He's going to want more than it's worth," Joseph warned.

"If he does," Cesar said, "we'll convince him to lower his price."

Chapter 14

Prosper Flot wiped the back of his hand across his lips, then continued to spoon up the thick fish soup. "I don't trust those Corsican bastards," he told his wife. " 'Specially that big black. Son of a bitch would slit his own mother's throat."

Madame Flot pulled up a chair and placed fleshy, begrimed elbows on the kitchen table. "They're 'bout the only customers we got left," she said. "Long as they pay their rent, you better hold a civil tongue." Madame sighed, then pulled the print wrapper around her bulging figure.

"Can't figure it out," Flot said. "Last three weeks no business at all. No check-ins, 'cept maybe one or two during the day. Used to be, couldn't pack 'em in at night." Prosper paused, spoon in midair. "Funny thing about that . . ."

"About what?" Madame waggled her foot. The large bedroom slipper slapped loosely.

"That black . . . and that other one. The big bastard. Two of 'em go out every night soon as it's dark. Don't come back till morning." Prosper continued eating again. "Out every damned night . . ."

"None of your business what they're doing," Madame said.

"Maybe not," Flot agreed, "then again, maybe it is. The one they call Joseph . . . he's a sly, foxy one. Quiet, doesn't say much. Know what he said to me couple days ago?"

115

"What?" Madame's voice held indifference.

"He said, 'Why don't you sell this place? It's losing money.' "

"What'd you say?"

"I told him business would get better, what with all the rebuilding has to be done in the harbor. But then he gave this sort of . . ." Prosper reached for a word, "know-it-all smile. He said it took money to back a gamble like that."

Madame tucked loose hair into the bun at her neck and glanced at her husband's empty bowl. "More?" Prosper nodded. She padded to the stove and ladled soup from a heavy iron pot. Seating herself again, she asked, "*One* thing they got is money."

Flot's mind turned slowly. A memory returned sluggishly. "Jean!" he bawled. "Jean!" The gnomelike handyman slipped quickly into the kitchen. His flat face turned blankly to Flot. "What was you saying . . . them two Corsicans talking in the bar?"

"*M'sieur?*" Jean stuttered anxiously.

"What you heard them saying! What you told me! 'Bout buying property."

"Oh . . ." Jean's fingers rolled the end of his dirty apron. "M'sieur Cesar . . . when he was drinking with M'sieur Joseph?" Flot nodded. "Well, they were talking about buying a bar . . . or a hotel. Or something. The gentleman, he says to the quiet one, he doesn't like not having his money invested . . . just doing nothing. And the other one, he agrees, but says property round here's no good cause all the business is going to move toward the new port." Jean shifted nervously before his employers. "That's all I heard," he mumbled. "Maybe they heard me listening, cause then they stopped talking."

"All right," Flot said. "Mop up the bar."

Madame Flot twisted a strand of hair around her pudgy finger. "Maybe they're right, Prosper," she said, her face anxious. "Maybe now, with everything different, business won't ever be so good again . . ."

"Other places are doing all right," Flot told her, but his voice held a tinge of doubt.

"Maybe you just think so . . ." Madame replied. "Would you tell people your private business? Somebody ask you, you'd say it was good." She paused, her heavy eyes fixed on her husband. "Le Marin's all we got. Don't forget we're never going to have another . . ." Her voice dropped to a whine. "Hadn't been for my uncle, we wouldn't had this. You never earned enough to support a flea on a dog . . . 'fore he died . . ."

"Shut up!" Prosper scratched his spiky hair. His eyes squinted in thought beneath their puffy bags.

Cesar looked up at the sound of the light knock on his door. "Come in," he said.

Jean entered hurriedly, bobbing his head in deference. "M'sieur Flot. He and Madame, in the kitchen. I told 'em what you said to tell 'em."

"Good." Lazily Cesar handed Jean a five-dollar bill. When Jean departed, Cesar pounded the palm of his hand against the wall. Within moments, Joseph entered the room. "They're taking the bait," Cesar said. "Are Gio and Anse sleeping?"

"Yes."

Over the past weeks, from dusk to dawn, Gio and Anse had stationed themselves in the doorways of buildings flanking Le Marin. Prospective guests were urged, firmly, to seek other lodgings. None, after considering Gio's massive shoulders or Anse's glinting eyes, had remained to debate their advice. Consequently, only an occasional traveler, wandering into the lobby during the day, had run the blockade.

"Wake them up," Cesar said. While Joseph went to arouse the two sleeping men, Cesar lit a cigarette and waited patiently. When they were all assembled, Cesar explained. "Pick out a room on the third floor. Any one of them. They're all empty. Start a fire. Not a large one! Not one that'll catch the room and spread. We don't want to burn down this pigsty."

"A fire's a fire," said Gio.

"Enough to destroy the bed . . . the mattress and covers. Plenty of smoke and stink!" Cesar explained carefully. "A fire small enough that we can put it out ourselves—if necessary. Is that understood?"

"Yes," said Gio. Anse nodded.

"Joseph and I'll go downstairs to the bar. When the fire's smoking well, open the door to the room so the smoke can come down to the lobby. You remain up here and pretend to be asleep. I will give the alarm. Then you'll come down, half-dressed. Pretend to be confused

117

and anxious to get the hell out." Cesar looked at Gio, then at Anse. Both shrugged. "All right," Cesar said. He nodded to Joseph and walked out of the room.

In the bar Jean served the two men black coffee laced with brandy. At a question in Cesar's eyes, Jean motioned with his head toward the small, greasy kitchen where Flot and his wife were still at lunch. The handyman resumed swabbing the floor. Cesar and Joseph remained at their table.

When the first wisps of smoke floated through the barroom, Cesar glanced at his watch, then waited calmly. The acrid smell of smoke grew heavier. A gray mist filled the lobby and edged its way, in a thickening cloud, into the bar.

Cesar stood up and shouted, "Fire! Fire!" Followed by Joseph, he strode into the lobby as Flot and his wife hurried from the kitchen.

"My God!" Flot looked around, wracked by indecision. "Where?" He started to run for the stairs.

Cesar stepped quickly in front of him, blocking the way. "Call the fire department! Turn in the alarm! My friends are upstairs asleep. I'll awaken them. Hurry!"

Flot turned and ran to the street, heading for the public phone on the corner. "Fire!" he shouted. "Fire!"

Gio and Anse, wearing only their trousers, coughed their way down the stairs. Madame Flot wrung her hands, her eyes filled with tears. "We're ruined!" she cried. "Everything . . . our last sou . . ."

"Where's the fire located?" Cesar asked.

"Third floor!" Anse replied. "It's so thick . . . can't see through it!" He shook his head. "I'm getting out of here! Firetrap!"

Gio shouted, "Lousy old firetrap. Never should of stayed here!"

"Get some pots . . . pails!" Cesar ordered Madame. "Maybe we can contain it till the firemen get here!"

Madame, one bedroom slipper missing, hurried back to the kitchen.

"How goes it?" Cesar asked Anse in a low voice.

Anse's black face wrinkled in a grin. "Smell it for yourself."

"Much danger of it catching?"

"Not for a few minutes."

Madame Flot returned, panting, from the kitchen. Her arms were filled with pots, pans, and a pail. She dropped the utensils on the floor and buried her face in her hands. "Gone, everything gone," she sobbed.

The men picked up the pail and the larger pots and ran upstairs. The third-floor hall was filled with a dense cloud of smoke. Cesar turned on the tap in the bathroom and they filled the utensils. Coughing, eyes watering, they poured water on the burning mattress, making return trips between the bathroom and the bedroom next to it. The water began to smother the flames, but increased the smoke.

"Throw the damned thing out into the street," Gio gasped.

"No! The more smoke the better," Cesar told him. They continued until the mattress was completely doused with water. By then, Le Marin was filled with smoke throughout its entire aged structure.

A high, keening "weep-weep" heralded the approach of the fire truck, followed by the pounding of booted feet on the stairs. A captain, wearing a silver helmet, burst into the room, followed by several members of his crew and, finally, a frightened Prosper Flot.

The captain looked at the soot-streaked walls of the room. His foot kicked the sodden mess of mattress and bedding. He turned to Flot. "Who occupied this room?"

"It was empty."

"Someone was smoking in this bed," the captain stated.

"I assure you, no one has slept here," Flot replied.

The captain's face reddened with anger. "I've seen enough fires like this to know! It's obvious."

"It's equally obvious," Cesar spoke up, deliberately pushing the captain to a fury, "that a little authority has gone to your head. Take your men and go back to plucking chickens! *We* put the fire out. If we'd waited for you to do it, the place would've burned down!"

The captain's face flooded from red to purple. "Who're you?" he demanded. "Where'd you come from?"

"My friend and I were in the bar having coffee." Cesar indicated Joseph. "The barman was there, too. We smelled smoke coming down the stairs into the lobby."

"That's correct, M'sieur," Flot assured the captain anxiously. "And my wife and I were in the kitchen."

Cesar regarded the captain with disdain. "These two gentlemen," he gestured toward Gio and Anse, "were asleep. On the floor above.

119

They were awakened by my shouts and rushed down to the lobby partly dressed, as you see them now." Cesar laughed, a short, jeering note. "Perhaps a ghost was smoking in bed."

The captain turned his anger on Flot. "You're lucky this place didn't burn to the ground and take the entire block with it! I'm reporting your hotel, condemning it as unsafe!"

"M'sieur . . . M'sieur . . ." Flot clasped his hands together as if in prayer. "Don't . . . I assure you . . . please!"

"See what I mean?" Cesar remarked in a clear voice to Joseph. "A man who uses his small position to threaten. He has a big mouth. A bluff!"

The captain yanked off his heavy brass helmet and for a moment brandished it in Cesar's face. Cesar regarded him levelly, a slight sneer on his lips. Slowly, the man replaced the helmet on his head. His voice shook with anger. "Corsican swine!"

The room was silent, so silent that the heavy breathing of the captain could be heard. Cesar's face was impassive. "You've had many escapes in your career, Captain, but you've never had a closer one." Cesar's voice was calm. "Suppose you and I have a talk?"

The captain shifted nervously and glanced at his men standing in the room and in the doorway to the hall. He could not afford to lose face; he felt their curious stares. "What about?"

"You're no longer angry. I'm not angry. A few words in private?" Cesar looked at his three companions. "Out," he said, "and take M'sieur Flot with you." Joseph, Gio, and Anse started for the door, elbowing their way through the firemen. Slowly, Flot followed them. "Well?" asked Cesar.

"Wait for me," the captain told his men, when he dismissed them.

Cesar closed the door and turned to face the captain. "Sometimes words are spoken for a purpose. Am I not correct, M'sieur?" The captain waited. Cesar continued. "You're a brave man. I respect you. I'd not want a job like yours. You're entirely right about this fleabag. It is dangerous. And I urge you to write out a report condemning it."

Surprised, the captain nodded. "I intend to."

"But!" Cesar lit a cigarette and drew several slow and deliberate puffs. "Don't be in too much of a hurry to turn it in. Perhaps, for a while, it should remain securely in your drawer. M'sieur . . . ?"

"Zallu," the captain said.

"M'sieur Zallu. It's possible in a short time that Le Marin will have other owners. The new proprietor'll make necessary changes. But who wants complaints and too many fire inspectors poking around?" Cesar quietly folded five one-hundred dollar bills and placed them on the dresser. "Not, believe me, Captain Zallu, that M'sieur Flot should not be *told* that such papers will be filed. It's your duty to tell him. It's proper that after changes have been made, the papers should disappear, and perhaps be replaced by . . ." Cesar glanced at the bills on the dresser, "more of those."

Cesar turned, opened the door, and walked out into the hall. The firemen were clustered by the stairway. Cesar continued down the stairs to the lobby where Prosper Flot and Madame waited anxiously.

"Condemned!" Madame wailed. "We're ruined!"

Cesar leaned against the counter. "I tried to reason with the captain," he told the harassed couple, "but it's hopeless. The captain insists. Nothing short of rebuilding the hotel . . ." Cesar shrugged.

Flot's gaze was fixed on the stairs as if expecting the arrival of an executioner. The bags beneath his eyes were blue with despair. "A hard man . . ." he groaned, "but you made him impossible. If only you'd stayed out of it. Kept your mouth shut! You provoked him . . ."

"Me?" Cesar straightened. His brow arched slightly in surprise and affront. "You're blaming *me*? Because I stood up for you . . . refused to see you abused and humiliated?"

Flot's face sagged with misery. Outside in the street, a crowd was gathered around the fire truck. Faces filled with curiosity peered into the lobby. "It's too late," wailed Madame. "A fire . . . people will be afraid to stay here."

"You are right," agreed Cesar.

The booted feet of Captain Zallu appeared on the stairs. Flot clawed his ears in anguish. "What'll I do . . .?"

"Well," said Cesar, walking toward the bar, "you can grow cockroaches."

Three days later, Joseph arranged the purchase of Le Marin. At the beginning of negotiations, Prosper Flot had asked twenty-five thousand dollars. He settled, eventually, for six thousand and the privilege of taking what furniture and other items the couple needed. The cost of repairing, refurnishing, and decorating, because of the scarcity of materials, would run about ten thousand dollars. Joseph estimated the actual value of the property to be seventeen thousand five hundred dollars. Including the bribes to Captain Zallu, purchase price, and building costs, the transaction was a good one.

The transfer of title was recorded in the name of Giotto Archino. Joseph kept possession of a quitclaim deed, signed by Gio, which needed only the inclusion of a date to hand over Le Marin to Cesar.

After the Flots had departed, the hotel's occupants were the four men from Corsica and Jean, the handyman. Unemployment was high in Marseilles, carpenters and craftsmen were plentiful and cheap, so remodeling went ahead rapidly. The only delays were caused by occasional lack of materials.

One evening Gio entered the bar accompanied by Heloise. She sat down at the table next to Cesar. "You wanted to see me?" she asked.

Cesar nodded. "In another week we'll be through with the work here."

The girl looked over the room—freshly painted, with heavy new linoleum; a used wooden bar, but in good condition, with a large ornate mirror behind it; additional glass shelves lined with bottles of a wide assortment of liquor. The tables and chairs matched, although of a common design of wood and metal, and the seats were upholstered in imitation leather. Heloise nodded approval. "Not bad," she said. "I noticed you're fixing up the lobby, too."

"Upstairs," Cesar said, "the rooms are going to be clean. Comfortable. Toilets—they'll work and they won't stink." Cesar leaned back in his chair and stared at the prostitute. "You told me not once but three times that you talked to the girls before I bought this place."

"They need a joint like this. They'll bring all their stunts here."

"When we open, you're going to be in charge."

"What?" Heloise stared at Cesar. "Me . . . the Madam?"

Cesar shook his head and smiled. "Madams are illegal," he said. "You're going to be the, ah, madame concierge. Put another way, the desk clerk. The girls know you . . . trust you. You'll check them in and out—and collect the rent."

Heloise turned startled eyes to Joseph seated across the table.

Joseph nodded. She looked at Cesar. "You're serious!"

"We'll agree on a salary. In addition, you'll receive a percentage of the collections, which Joseph will figure out. The more business you bring in, the more money you'll make."

"How about a few stunts on my own?" Heloise asked.

Cesar shook his head. "Not here. You'll have to know what's going on every minute. Keep the stunts moving. Steer the *mecs* to the bar for drinks . . . if they have to wait. Or afterwards on their way out."

"There'll be drunks . . . and trouble," Heloise warned.

"Gio and Anse'll take care of it."

"A lot of them'll come back here looking for a girl."

"No soliciting in the lobby. Get that straight!"

"All right." Heloise smiled. "Sweet Jesus! Who'd of thought I'd end up a madam!"

"Madame concierge," Cesar corrected. He called to Jean behind the bar. "Open a bottle. Corsican! We'll drink to that."

Four guards dragged Gio down the stone corridor past eight cells to the one on the end. There was little that was modern about the *Conciergerie;* it resembled an eighteenth century prison more than a twentieth century jail. When one of the guards released his hold to open the cell door, Gio shook free long enough to swing at one of his tormentors and knocked him to the floor. The other three loosened their batons and swarmed over him. Blood spurted from the big man's nose and the sound of the sticks on Gio's skull echoed down the empty corridor.

"Bastards! Shitheads!" Gio yelled as he struggled against the hopeless odds.

The fight brought detective-inspector Jacques Roncin on the run from the office at the end of the corridor where he had been booking the complaint against Gio. Roncin arrived in time to see the fallen guard rise and club the prisoner senseless. The four men dragged the heavy body into the cell then locked the solid door.

"Tough son of a bitch," a guard observed to Roncin.

Roncin glanced at the locked cell. "He's not the one I really want, but he'll do to start," he said. Turning, the detective walked heavily, in a shambling gait, back up the corridor.

A few hours later, Cesar stood in the chambers of the *juge d'instruction*, a room in red—its rugs and draperies over the big windows the color of blood. Moments earlier, Cesar had left a heavy envelope on the magistrate's desk before the judge appeared; it was well filled with money.

"The prisoner's name?" the judge asked.

"Giotto Archino," Cesar said.

"Yes, here it is." The judge looked over the papers. Under French law his duty was to evaluate the evidence and determine if the accused was to be held for trial or released from jail. The French code of criminal law made no provision for bail or bond. "Archino is accused of operating a *maison de tolérance* (whorehouse), pimping and procuring." He glanced up to stare at Cesar. "Serious charges, M'sieur, with sworn statements by witnesses."

"If M'sieur *le Juge* pleases," Cesar said politely, his voice formal, "I am not an Advocate for M'sieur Archino, but merely his friend. I have known him for many years. He is a good man who has never been in prison . . . with no previous criminal record." Cesar paused to look frankly at the judge. The magistrate, a career judge, listened without trace of emotion and with an attitude of strict impartiality, but he was never entirely convinced of the sincerity, or honesty, of any of the accused, witnesses, or police who appeared before him. The judge cleared his throat, and removed his reading glasses—two half moons rimmed in silver, and nodded. Cesar continued. "M'sieur Archino is *petits bourgeois*, a little business man, as are so many others in our city. He invested a small inheritance in real estate . . . a building condemned by our efficient and upstanding fire department, a place unfit to live in, a danger to the neighborhood. He poured his few savings into Le Marin, the rat hole, and it is now Le Marin, a place of beauty. For this, may it please *le Juge*, he should be thanked, not persecuted." The judge returned the glasses to his nose and again looked at the papers before him.

"These complaints . . ." the judge said.

"Yes, the complaints," Cesar agreed. "But it must be understood that M'sieur Archino is a simple man. He retires early after a hard day's work. He does not preside at the desk, but has hired a young lady to do that job . . . to check in the guests. It is quite possible that she is not . . . uh, ah, so good a judge of character as others of a more worldly nature," Cesar smiled easily and went on. "Undoubtedly on a few occasions, women of dubious reputations may have slipped through to take shelter for the night, but that is not M'sieur Archino's fault who is sound asleep in bed at the time." Cesar paused to let the absurdity of the situation sink in, and then dismissed it with a slight gesture of his hand. "And in defense of the young lady, Mam'selle Heloise, it is only her own simplicity and goodness of heart that is questioned. And I assure *le Juge,* that she will be warned, most vigorously, not to repeat such mistakes in the future."

"I see," said the judge.

Cesar hurried down the steps of the *Palais de Justice,* caught a taxi, and drove to the jail. He presented the judge's signed order for the release of Gio to the head warden, then followed a turnkey to the cell. Before unlocking it, the jailer opened a small wicket in the door and looked in. Cesar peered over his shoulder to see Gio stretched out on a bunk, lying on his back, with a handkerchief over his eyes. Overhead, a bright light blazed down into the cell. At the sound of the key, Gio leaped to his feet, fists clenched, and a fierce scowl on his face. His features were a mass of red, blue, and purple bruises. Lumps sprouted from his head almost like small horns.

"Cesar!" Gio shouted and embraced his cousin in his massive arms. "I been waiting for you!!"

"Well, I'm here," Cesar said, freeing himself. "Now let's get the hell out."

As the two walked toward the door to the street, they passed the booking room at the end of the corridor. Gio stopped and nudged Cesar. "There's the son of a bitch who arrested me!" he said in a whisper.

Cesar turned to look at the detective. Their eyes met in a stony stare. Cesar was surprised by the heat of hatred transmitted by the inspector. "An honest man," Cesar thought, "and a dangerous one." He started walking again, Gio at his side, and asked in a low voice, "Who is he?"

"His name is Roncin," Gio said.

"I must remember him," Cesar replied.

Roncin watched them leave. He spit on the stone floor.

Chapter 15

Henri Gozy smiled expansively and waved toward a chair. "It's a pleasure to meet you, M'sieur Satisanni."

Cesar sized up the politician carefully—a slender, dapper man dressed in a double-breasted blue flannel suit, white shirt with a light gray tie knotted at the collar. Gozy's eyes were almost the color of his tie. Longish hair was combed back in a pompadour to cover the balding spot on the back of his head, and sideburns reached far down the cheeks of his face. "You were expecting me," Cesar said.

"Yes. For several days." With elaborate concern, Gozy removed a heavy wooden box from the drawer of his desk and opened it. "Have a cigar? Havana."

Cesar carefully unwrapped the cheroot, sniffed it, then struck a light. "You're fortunate to have these, *M'sieur,*" he thanked Gozy.

"Yes. They're difficult to come by." Gozy lounged comfortably in his big chair behind his desk. "How're our friends in Ajaccio?" he asked.

"You've talked to them since I have," Cesar said.

"Yes . . . quite right." Gozy laughed politely.

Cesar, a bit at a loss to evaluate the man, gained a few additional seconds by puffing on the cigar and studying its ash. Circumstances had forced him to ask the advice of *Le Patriarche* in Ajaccio. At the end of the singing, stuttering wire, Vito Nastacio's voice had been sympathetic. He had

127

inferred to Cesar that the Unione had a good friend in Henri Gozy. Nastacio was positive that M'sieur Gozy, residing in Marseilles, could be helpful.

Thanking Nastacio, Cesar had hung up. Reluctant to again become obligated to the Unione at this time, he had discussed the situation with Joseph. "If the arrests continue," Joseph said, "not only will the girls refuse to continue at the hotel, but the bribes are running higher than our business. And Gio . . ."

Gio, as registered owner of Le Marin, was the unfortunate arrested by the police, held, and released after stiff pay-offs. Although Gio had not as yet been tried, or sentenced, on charges of procuring, the threat hung over their heads.

"The bastards have been paid off," Cesar protested to Joseph. "All the way from the *flics* on the street to the commissaire in the arrondissement."

"That's why Gio hasn't been given a jolt," Joseph replied.

Before following Nastacio's advice, Cesar made inquiries concerning Gozy. Gozy was a rising politician. What kind of a politician—and exactly what his status, duties, and obligations were—no one was quite sure, except he was important. A former member of the maquis, he had risen, brilliant as a phoenix, after the war. Rumor said that Gozy held close connections in the National Assembly; it was clearly demonstrated that he had friends in the mayor's office, for he lunched with dignitaries, in public, on numerous occasions. Henri Gozy's own official position was unclear—as muddied as the waters of his past. But in the subsiding eddies in the aftermath of the war, other more powerful and prominent leaders were content to let the sediment settle and leave infamous pools unstirred.

Cesar raised his eyes from the tip of his cigar to look at Gozy. The politician wore a patient smile—waiting. "I'll play it the way he does," Cesar thought. "A friend of mine recently bought a hotel . . . Le Marin. He's being harassed by the police. Unnecessarily. He's invested a sizable amount of money. Before, it wasn't fit for roaches; now it's a decent enough place."

"A pity," Gozy said. "Sometimes the police become, ah, too officious." He paused and took a puff. "Although, usually, they've some basis for their zeal."

"You know what the situation is at Le Marin. I won't go into

128

details. My friend has paid off the *flics*—up and down the line. He has paid fines—for what? Because some girl and a man want to rent a room? Or would the authorities prefer they screw in the street like a couple of dogs and end up with broken heads as well?"

"I'll say your friend's actually performing a public service," Gozy murmured. "But the authorities may not agree with me."

"That's why I'm here. What does it take to make them agree?"

Gozy straightened in his chair. He looked thoughtfully at Cesar, then out the window. In the distance glistened the imposing columnar facade of the Palais de la Bourse. "A favor to one man is often a favor to another," he said, his voice suave. He returned his attention to Cesar. "Your friend is anxious to succeed in his . . . business?"

"Assuredly."

"Willing to . . . ah, *work* . . . very hard?"

"My friend's willing to work, but he doesn't want it to be wasted."

"Of course! The more difficult the job, the greater the return, eh?"

Cesar was silent for a moment. "Perhaps some work might be too difficult," he said finally.

"For some men," Gozy agreed. "For others, no. Especially when the returns would be so great . . ." He spread his hands helplessly.

"My friend'll like to hear about it," Cesar said.

Gozy nodded. "You understand, of course, I know nothing of the details. As a matter of fact, I don't even know what I've been talking about." He smiled. "Only . . . scraps and bits I've overheard here and there. This is absolutely confidential, but on the recommendation of our mutual *friend* whose judgment I trust implicitly, I've talked to you . . . generally. To discuss this in detail requires someone who has more knowledge than I have. Now, perhaps such a person may contact you at the hotel. Although I, personally, don't know such a fellow, possibly he'll have heard of you and will look you up."

Cesar stood. "I'll wait till he does." He started for the door.

Gozy stopped him. "One other point, *M'sieur*. There is no record —*anywhere*—that you have made a visit to my office."

Cesar smiled thinly. "Why should there be? It's such a fine day that I took a walk on La Canebiere." He closed the door behind him.

The following afternoon, a stranger entered the bar of Le Marin. He was a small man dressed completely in brown—a somewhat worn brown suit, tan shirt, brown and yellow foulard tie, brown ribbed

129

socks, and two-tone brown shoes. Sitting down beside Cesar, he introduced himself as *"La Passe"*—obviously a pseudonym since it meant "The Permit." Cesar's offer of brandy was accepted. "We're alone?" Passe asked.

"I'll see to it." Cesar ordered Jean to leave his post behind the bar and busy himself in the kitchen. Walking to the door of the lobby, he closed it. He returned to the table and sat down again.

Passe's size, personality, and appearance were so nondescript that his presence was ephemeral. He toyed with his brandy glass, his eyes carefully avoiding Cesar. When he spoke, his voice soft and ingratiating, it was as if he were making a recitation. "The government's proceeding to make up a list of the most notorious collaborators of the war. Frenchmen who sold out their country; traitors who licked the boots of the Nazi pigs; men who betrayed their friends, neighbors, and countrymen for money and prestige! They'll be brought to trial. Each'll get his just dessert. Death!"

Cesar said nothing. He waited.

"But arrests, hearings, and trials cost dearly—money ill-spent on such bastards," Passe continued. "Worse yet, it may take years before the authorities are finished with the lot of them. Much time, much effort, much money wasted, which might well be saved to be spent on the poor, hungry, and sick of our country—the miserable victims who have suffered at the hands of these same notorious collaborators." Passe paused, sipped his brandy, and flashed a sideways glance at Cesar.

Cesar examined his fingernails. His voice casual, he asked, "Isn't it also possible, Passe, when the collaborators are put on trial that they'll talk? *Mouchards!* Squeal pretty loud? Damned embarrassing . . . maybe . . . to government fat cats *now* in power?"

"How should I know what the criminals might do? Such men are liars."

"When a man faces death, he often tells the truth. But I don't want to argue . . ."

Passe nodded. "Now let's suppose . . . if *specific* collaborators— the worst ones who deserve death without question—happen to die before they're arrested and put on trial, wouldn't that benefit everyone?"

"It'd undoubtedly benefit certain politicians, you can be sure of that," Cesar said. He arose and walked to the bar. Returning to the table with a bottle of brandy and a glass, he refilled Passe's glass, then poured a drink for himself. "We'll continue," he said. "The politicians . . . in this thing . . . stand to make plenty. What happens to the *mecs* who save their asses?"

"There'll be expenses involved. Certainly. For each case disposed of, twenty-five hundred dollars, American, wouldn't be unreasonable. And, of course, the goodwill and friendship of very important men. They'd have obligations . . . to be filled when necessary." Passe sniffed his brandy. "In reality, it's a very patriotic act—for your country."

"Oh, I can see that," Cesar said.

"There are other Corsican patriots who agree with you." Passe ignored Cesar's cynicism.

Cesar sat quietly. "The Rampini?" he asked finally. "The Volanti?" Passe did not reply. Cesar went on. "They're able to handle all the contracts for you."

Passe said, "The list is long." He shrugged and sipped his brandy. "I was told to contact you. What more can I say?"

Cesar stared thoughtfully at the small, brown man. Passe avoided the opaque stare. Finally Cesar said, "I don't think that you'd sit there with a straight face and shove *merde* at me. If whoever sent you trusts *me,* then I have to trust *him.*"

"That's not unreasonable," Passe said.

"Before I prove myself to be a great patriot, two things must happen. First, the *flics* lay off Le Marin. Don't come inside the door, except once a month to collect their payoff. And tonight, an inspector will walk in here and buy me a drink at this goddamned bar! That's the first condition."

"The other?"

"Luigi Venito. I knew him in Ajaccio. He's a penman. If I go ahead, I'll need a good counterfeiter. Venito's in the *frigo,* here in Marseilles. When I see him in Le Marin, free, I'll believe you. Your boss! And la belle France!"

Passe nodded. Reaching inside his coat pocket, he took out a sheet of paper typed with a list of names. Placing it on the table beside his empty brandy glass, Passe said, "I'll leave these names. Ten of them. Quite interesting ones. They're in no particular order. You won't find them difficult to locate." He stood up and smoothed down his wrinkled brown jacket. "Thanks for the brandy," he said politely.

"It is nothing . . ." Cesar told him, equally polite.

He remained seated at the table for a long time thinking about Passe's proposition. He realized that some of the top politicians in power feared exposure from other former collaborators. In the atmosphere of a witch-hunt which then prevailed, at worst they also faced death or imprisonment, at best—their loss of position and power. Many of them in office had been forced during the war—in one way or another, at some time or other—to cooperate with the Germans. They could not afford to have this known to the public. Certain collaborators if brought to trial would speak up and involve them. The politicians could not afford to have this happen. Hence, the resolve to silence these potential threats in advance. If, as Passe had assured him, the authorities would not intervene (and it was in their interest not to) the contracts for the collaborators' deaths could be carried out with very little danger. Also, there was the prospect of earning twenty-five thousand dollars at small risk.

But, more important, Cesar thought, was the opportunity to gain the goodwill of the men in power. Gozy, and his bosses, would be indebted to him. Their political protection would give him, Cesar, freer rein to conduct his own business and take the heat off Le Marin —as well as any other future plans he might develop. This chance, opportunity was . . . *big!* How big it really was, he had no idea at that time. However, he was determined to grasp it if Gozy showed good faith in backing him up.

The remodeling of Le Marin included enlarging the ancient kitchen. A former ship's cook, known only as Gras (Greasy), was hired and placed in charge of it. Between bouts with the stove, Gras spent his hours stretched out on a cot in a narrow pantry adjoining the kitchen. His large, bulbous red nose, cross-thatched with blue veins, testified to his spare-time activities. Gras' talents would not have satisfied a gourmet, but he was fast. And under the adverse conditions of barely being able to stand before the stove, he turned out plain, digestible dishes.

Joseph had suggested to Cesar the idea of using the kitchen not only to feed them and the growing staff of employees at the hotel, but also to offer simple dishes in the café-bar. Many of the *tapineuses* and their companions had after-the-fact appetites. Gras' uncomplicated skills, amounting to a ridiculously low price since he quickly sank his salary in the bar, were a success. Each week, Le Marin's café-bar showed a rising profit.

At ten o'clock the night of Passe's afternoon visit, Cesar and Joseph were eating dinner. Jean, serving them, stiffened. His eyes switched to the door of the bar leading from the lobby. *"Vingt-deux, les flics,"* he muttered and moved away. Cesar looked up to see a heavy-faced man accompanied by a shorter, slighter companion approaching the table. The heavier of the two, dressed in a dark suit, with heavy shoes, wore a scowl on his face; the slighter looked around, wary and perplexed.

Cesar smiled. Placing down his knife and fork, he called, "Luigi! Welcome! You're just in time to join us for dinner."

Luigi Venito glanced nervously at the man beside him. Forcing a grin to his sallow face, he ran a finger around the open, soiled collar of his shirt. "Jesus," he said, "what's happening . . .?"

"Don't worry. Sit down. You know Joseph. You look like you could use a good meal!"

"That food . . . in the *cabane!*" Venito shook his head in disgust. *"Merde!* Gag a man to even smell it!"

The heavy-faced man spoke up. "You're Satisanni? I'm Inspecteur Roncin." The big detective's eyes blazed with anger. "Orders . . . turn over this thieving son of a bitch to you. Here he is!" The inspector stopped. He choked with frustration and fury. "I'm supposed to buy you a drink." Roncin took out a hundred-franc note and slapped it on the table. "That's for your drink!"

Cesar glanced at the note. "We don't serve cheap booze here, *Inspecteur.*"

"You don't know the difference!" Roncin turned and stalked back to the lobby, then out into the night.

Cesar smiled. He picked up the bill and folded it carefully. Putting it to one side of his wallet, he said, "This is a down payment. To own Marseilles!"

Chapter 16

At the foot of La Canebiere, a central boulevard lined with shops, office buildings, and restaurants, lies Le Quai des Belges. The quai, like a giant concrete horseshoe, encircles the eastern end of Le Vieux Port. Late in the afternoon a Monsieur Émile Heyries left one of the hotels facing the broad expanse of the quai and walked briskly toward the corner of La Canebiere. His soft figure supported a paunch; across his tightly buttoned vest was draped a heavy gold watch chain that swung slightly with each stride. A brisk breeze coming in across the port tugged at his dark homburg. Shortly before he reached the intersection, a four-door Renault sedan pulled to the curb ahead of him and a massive figure got out.

"M'sieur Heyries?"

Heyries paused to stare up into the face of Gio. Fear, which had been Heyries' constant companion for weeks, surfaced in his voice. "What do you want?"

"You are Émile Heyries?" Gio was insistent. The big man seemed even larger in his loosely cut blue serge suit.

"Yes . . ." Heyries replied uneasily.

"You'll come with me." Gio displayed a document. "It's a warrant for your arrest. You want to read it? Your privilege." The fake warrant had been carefully forged by Luigi Venito.

Heyries' eyes, unable to comprehend because of fear,

135

merely registered the official appearance of the document. "You're from the Sûreté?" he asked, his voice quaking.

"I got my credentials," Gio said, patting another pocket. "Get in the car." Gio grasped Heyries' pudgy arm and urged him into the back seat. Heyries climbed in. Gio seated himself beside him. "All right," Gio told Anse.

Anse, behind the wheel, pulled away from the curb. The car continued a short distance following the curve of Le Quai des Belges, then shot off into a narrow side street heading north.

Heyries sat slumped in deep dejection. The sedan threaded its way through bleak, winding side streets. After some time Heyries said, "It's warm in here . . ."

"Leave the windows up!" Gio told him.

Heyries wiped a plump hand across his sweat-beaded forehead beneath the homburg. "What're the charges against me, *M'sieur?*"

"You belonged to the Milice Française, collaborating with the Nazi turds tracking down the Resistance," Gio said. "Traitor!"

"Lies!" Heyries took off his dark hat and held it in his lap. "That isn't true!" Gio said nothing; he looked out the window. Heyries turned the hat over and over in his hands. Finally, with leaden voice, he said, "Everyone had to do *some* business with the Germans. There wasn't any other way . . . not and stay alive! I wasn't the only one. Believe me, I can tell you of others in the Milice. You'd be surprised!"

Anse continued to drive, more slowly now through the darkening streets. The occupants of the car were silent. "I tell you now!" Heyries said suddenly, loudly. "I'm not going to take the blame for everything! And you can tell your sanctimonious bosses in the Sûreté that I said so! Let them squirm, too!" He stared out the window for a minute, then stiffened. "Where're you taking me?"

"You'll find out," Gio said.

"This isn't the way!" Heyries protested. "You're heading for the country!"

"It's *our* way." Anse spoke up for the first time.

Heyries stared at the back of the black's neck. Abruptly he leaned forward, reaching for the door. "You're not the police!" he shouted. Gio stretched out an arm and knocked his hand away. Heyries continued to shout, "Let me go! Help! Get me out of here!" His cries were muffled within the sealed confines of the sedan. The streets were thinning out, with no passing traffic and few pedestrians to hear him. The collaborator's puffy face looked like a moist gray mushroom in the shadows of the car. His eyes were round circles of fear. "Bastards!" he screamed, clawing at the back of Anse's shoulders.

Gio's massive fist sledged against Heyries' jaw. Heyries slumped against the back of the seat, unconscious. Anse continued to drive.

The final outskirts of Marseilles were a twenty-minute drive behind when the car turned off the highway to enter a small country road. A few kilometers off the highway, the back road straightened and ran through an area of grazing land. Several weeks earlier this stretch had been selected by Cesar because of its complete isolation. No farms or houses adjoined it; no traffic of any kind moved on it at night.

Anse slowed the sedan to a stop. Heyries moaned and moved fitfully in the back seat. The section of road stretched ahead of them. The moon had not yet risen and the countryside was in darkness. Gio and Anse sat for a few minutes—watching, listening. Nothing moved on the road or stirred in the land around them. "Guess it's clear," Anse said finally.

Gio got out, then reached into the back seat and dragged Heyries after him. The cool night air cleared Heyries' benumbed mind. He struggled, panting, twisting in the hands of Gio. "No . . . no!" The man fought with surprising strength supported by terror. Gio, silent, held him by the throat and with his free hand again clubbed him unconscious. With both hands grasping Heyries' shoulders, Gio held him erect.

Anse drove the Renault several hundred meters down the road, turned the car around, and headed back toward Gio. The black's foot pressed hard on the gas. The Renault picked up speed, reaching one hundred kilometers per hour. At the last split second, Gio threw the unconscious Heyries in the path of the hurtling car.

A sound like a great water-filled bag falling from a far height split the night.

Anse braked gradually to a stop. Gio walked down the dark road to the car. "Christ!" he said, "you sure smashed up the grill." Anse got out of the machine, carrying a folded canvas tarpaulin. He opened it and spread it out on the road. The two men lifted the split,

137

shattered body of Heyries by its hands and feet and dumped it on the canvas. After rolling up the corpse in the tarp, they deposited it in the trunk of the car and climbed back into the Renault. The moon edged above the flatland, picking the gravel of the road with points of gilt. "Gotta be careful," Anse said, shifting the car into gear, "in case the *flics* stops us. This front end all banged up . . ."

"Not banged up bad as Heyries," Gio said.

Approximately half an hour later, the car stopped at an intersection of two small streets within the city in an area of decrepit shops, boarded and blind against the night. Anse turned off the single unbroken headlamp. He and Gio left the car. They stood on the curb, again waiting a few minutes to be certain that the narrow sidewalks and stone streets were empty. By mutual consent, both turned to the trunk. They deftly swung out the tarpaulin, unrolling it quickly to deposit the body in the street near the gutter. Heyries' sightless eyes stared at them through a mask of blood. After locking the bloody canvas back in the trunk, the two men leaped into the car and continued to drive toward the center of the city.

Although the evening was still early, Le Marin was gearing for a busy night. Business was good; it had been excellent since the night Roncin had left his money for a complimentary drink. Heloise was dressed in black, and her dark hair was piled in a high bouffant. She presided behind a pulpit-shaped desk in the narrow lobby carpeted in red. The former wooden bench, enameled white and covered with cream-colored cushions, matched the recently painted walls and stairs. Above the desk hung a large, leaded, stained-glass shade, shaped like a tulip, which cast multicolored facets of light around the lobby. The furnishings were all secondhand, selected and bought in the flea markets of the city. Assembled together, they gave a mixed air of tawdry elegance. To the streetwalkers, the wandering, harassed prostitutes of the port, Le Marin was a symbol of security and culture.

Gio and Anse concentrated on the list of names left by Passe; their activities left them little time to maintain peace in the hotel. Consequently, three new men, all Corsicans, had been added to Cesar's growing payroll. Watching the lobby and the bar was Galon—"Stripes"—so-called because of his penchant for horizontal striped, knitted shirts worn by sailors. Galon, a former middleweight boxer, was formidable in a barroom fight. Franco, a lean, wiry, tough ex-paratrooper expert with brass-toes shoes, was fully as awesome; his station was the second floor. The third floor came under Beni Turnella. Beni was hired under the high recommendation of Luigi Venito. The forger had known Turnella, a two-time murderer, in prison.

The café-bar was full. Jean's new assistant carried trays of drinks to the busy tables. Cesar and Joseph were seated at one of them when Gio and Anse returned from their trip with Heyries. The two sat down with Cesar and Joseph. Gio looked at Cesar and said, "Number four."

"No hitches?" Cesar asked.

"None," Gio replied. Anse confirmed it with a slight nod.

"The car?" Cesar asked.

"Ditched and stripped," Gio told him.

"Wiped clean?"

"Absolutely."

"The tarp?"

"Somewhere in the bay," Gio said.

Cesar was satisfied. He had worked out the plan carefully to murder the collaborators, and he insisted that it be carried out strictly: a stolen car, retouched license plates, false papers. The victim was always killed by the car on the preselected country road, then the body was returned to the city and left as if struck by a hit-and-run driver. The car was abandoned in another section of Marseilles.

Cesar realized that any intelligent detective would notice instantly the lack of blood at the supposed scene of the accident, but so long as no other evidence blatantly contradicted the theory of hit-and-run, the authorities would not pursue it further. Or if an investigator became too inquisitive, somewhere up the line of police command, the inquiry would be dropped quietly. So far, Cesar had been right. Despite the prominence of the victims, the newspapers had carried only brief notices of their accidental deaths.

Anse stood up and stretched. "I'm hungry," he said. "I'm gonna get drunk and get me a girl and take 'er to my room all night."

Gio yawned. "Who do we start on next?" he asked Cesar.

Cesar shrugged. "Take your pick." Preparations usually took part of a week—staking out the victim and learning enough of his habits to pick him up without commotion, at dusk; stealing a car, and having Luigi prepare new papers, documents, and plates.

Gio pushed back his chair and wandered out after Anse. Joseph sat in silence for a while watching the activity in the bar. "Did you ever study that list of names carefully?" he finally asked Cesar.

"No. They're all the same in the end," Cesar said with indifference.

"Have you ever heard of Jullien Durand? He's one of them," Joseph said.

"Perhaps. Sounds familiar."

"Durand's the major partner in the Crédit de Berre. Private bank."

Cesar turned his stare on his cousin. "You have an idea? Ransom?"

"Possibly. In a way . . ." Joseph's voice was very quiet.

Cesar shook his head. "Too dangerous! A doublecross and Gozy's people would hand our heads to the guillotine."

Instead of replying directly, Joseph answered as if speaking to himself. "What's honor among thieves? For one moment, if it served Gozy's purpose—or the higher-ups he represents—do you think he'd play straight with us? Are we naïve?" Joseph stared at the table. "Have you thought what it might mean—to own a bank?"

"No," Cesar said.

"If we must kill, why do it like an executioner to collect a fee and a pat on the back? We're whoremasters and paid assassins . . . is that all we want to be?" Joseph sighed. "Remember the night we arrived outside Marseilles? Where are our dreams now, Cesar?"

Cesar finally said, "A bank is what *you* want. It's your idea."

"Ours, Cesar, *ours!*"

"And some night I'll get shot in the back?"

"Not if you figure it out! You're good at such things, Cesar. It's your forte. Plan it carefully, exactly. I promise you . . . someday, with the bank, you'll be a *cavaliere!*"

"I'll think on it," Cesar said abruptly. He arose, almost in anger, and left the bar. At the door to the lobby, Galon gave him a half salute. Cesar walked on.

Heloise called from behind the desk. Her voice was light. "So early, *M'sieur?* Upstairs and to bed without company?"

Cesar returned a few steps to stand before her. Heloise dimpled. She lifted her hands to pat her hair, her large breasts jiggling beneath the demure black dress. "I don't like whores," Cesar said.

The smile faded from the girl's face. "Who *really* does?"

"Business," Cesar said. "It's simply business. From now on, if Gio and Anse—or the other *mecs*—want a woman . . . here! . . . they pay for it!"

Heloise's eyes dulled, her tone bitter but polite. "I understand. Would you prefer that I charge them higher prices?"

Cesar stared at her coldly. "That's up to you." He turned away from the desk and started up the stairs. Galon watched from the doorway of the bar, then strolled over to Heloise.

"What the hell's wrong with the boss tonight?" Galon asked.

"Son of a bitch! I don't think he's ever had a woman in his life!" Heloise said. "When he stares at me out of those goddamned eyes of his, he gives me the chills!"

Cesar entered his room on the top floor. It too had been painted, and a large rug almost completey covered the floor. The ancient shabby bed and table were replaced with newer, more ornate ones. Before the window stood a still beautiful rosewood desk. Cesar turned on the desk lamp and sat in a comfortable chair before it. His chin, sunk in thought, rested on his chest.

Joseph's words rang in his ears. "Whoremaster! Assassin! But a bank . . . a banker!" Yet somehow, in his mind, he was not convinced that the bank was the source of power for which he was searching. Le Marin was simply a step toward something, a goal not yet defined. The goodwill of Nastacio in Ajaccio and Gozy in Marseilles must be carefully hoarded. It would be a priceless asset repaid many ways, many times, in the years to come. Why risk squandering it now?

Yet it was Joseph's shrewdness that had first pointed the way in Ghisonacia. It was Joseph's skill that ran Hegan's money into a respectable fortune in Le Bélier. Joseph had purchased Le Marin at a price making it possible to turn the hotel into a highly profitable project. Dammit! Joseph was probably right again.

Slowly, Cesar pulled open the drawer of his desk and took out a pad of paper and a pencil. Placing them on the desk top, beneath the lamp, he stared at them for a while. Planning . . . like a campaign

. . . that was his business, his "forte," Joseph had said. When it came down to it, he—Cesar—could outwit and outmaneuver Nastacio or Gozy . . . or whoever else was necessary! Nothing was impossible, if a man sets his mind to it!

Cesar began to doodle on the paper with his pencil.

Chapter 17

The sign, partly rotted away by age and elements, read:
... ARD & FILS. It hung awry above the door in a stained
concrete-block building, the boards cracking open, the original red faded to a soft and dusty pink. The broken, gaping
windows were nailed over with planks, and brown clusters
of weeds grew up along the foundations. Once it had been
a factory, but even before the war it had long been closed.

Cesar sat in the black depths of the empty building, near
a rear entrance from which the rusty locks had been
knocked loose and the door pried open. He sat patiently,
without light, smoking. Eventually he heard a car pull up
and the sound of approaching footsteps. The door squealed
as it was pushed back, and momentarily three figures were
silhouetted against the night as they entered. When the
door closed, Cesar snapped on a flashlight, its rays spotting
the group.

Gio held a graying, dignified man firmly by an arm. He
shoved him forward toward Cesar. "Here he is," Gio said.
Behind him, Anse's face and figure blended into the darkness.

"M'sieur Durand," Cesar greeted the elderly man.

Jullien Durand disdained to peer into the light flashing
in his eyes. Turning his head, he said, "Yes." And waited.

"We need more light, now that you're here, *M'sieur*,"
Cesar said. "Let's have it," he ordered Gio. Gio lit a kero-

sene lantern, and in its yellow light a few objects took form in the darkness: a cot, several folding chairs, a tiny primus stove, half a case with bottles of wine, and a basket of tinned goods. "Sit down," Cesar said to Durand.

The banker sat down. "What're you waiting for?" he asked. "I know I've been proscribed. Known it for some time."

"Really?" Cesar was interested. "Why did you wait around so long?"

Durand took a deep breath. "At my age, it's not so easy to run. I'd have been stopped at my first move. Without plans. I've been waiting for . . . connections . . . to make arrangements. I need papers. It takes time." He added, "Obviously, it took too much."

Cesar made a pretense of looking at his wristwatch. "According to our plans, you should've been a dead man. An hour ago."

"Well, that's something that's never too late," Durand said with a humorless smile.

"M'sieur," Cesar said, "you're a brave man. That's to be admired. Possibly we can ease your fears a little. Let's talk some business."

"Business?" A flicker crossed Durand's face. "Any business at this time would seem trivial to *me*, wouldn't it?"

"If it saved your life? Make no mistake, M'sieur Durand, I'm willing to kill you now and have it over." Cesar gestured toward the two silent figures of Gio and Anse standing in the shadows. "On the other hand, I can save your life and arrange your escape to safety."

Durand's thin body stiffened. "In return for everything I have? Leave my family starving and helpless?"

Cesar shrugged. "I imagine they'll have sufficient—without your bank."

"Crédit de Berre?"

"Yes. It'll be quite useless to you if you're dead. And your family has hidden funds in other places." Joseph had dug deeply into Durand's past record. The banker had been instrumental in transferring large sums between the Nazis and their French political henchmen. Durand's memory and his bank records were a menace that could prove disastrous. "You see," Cesar told the banker with calm assurance, "you and I have friends. Powerful ones who can't afford to let you or your bank continue—most certainly, not remain in the hands of your family."

144

Durand's thin, narrow head slowly bent in agreement. "I see that . . ." He lifted his face and looked squarely at Cesar. "Nonetheless, why should I give the bank to you? What assurance do I have that you won't do me in . . . afterwards?"

"No assurance at all, *M'sieur*. But *if* you don't trust me, you have no hope, either. The choice is yours."

"I hoped Odessa might help me," Durand said, referring to the international underground operation which had successfully spirited many notorious Nazis to safety in the Argentine.

"Odessa's too busy concentrating on its own genuine Nazi bastards to bother with you. You've already found that out!"

Durand stared into the shadows at the menacing figures of Gio and Anse—waiting, motionless, inexorable. "What . . . how . . . would you get me to Argentina?" he asked. "Odessa has the organization," he added.

"I have ways, too." Cesar deliberately lit another cigarette. "I can arrange to smuggle you to Lisbon . . ." he waved aside Durand's attempted interruption, "in my own boat. From Portugal you book passage to South America on the first available ship. From anyplace in South America you make your way to Argentina . . . or wherever you want."

"That will take time . . . and money," Durand said.

Cesar's lazy hand indicated the dank shell of the room around them. "You hide here. No one'll find you. One of my men will stay with you," he said. "When we're ready to move, I'll furnish you all your papers and passport, deposit you safely in Lisbon—with a paid passage to South America. And I'll give you a thousand dollars cash in American money. In Argentina, your Nazi friends can look after your future comfort."

"In return for a bank worth several million?"

"Yes. You may not have many more years of life to look forward to, *M'sieur*, but certainly they can extend beyond tonight."

Durand said, "Let me think. May I have time to consider it?"

"If I were in your shoes, it wouldn't take me long to decide," Cesar replied. "But don't use up too much time. If I have to kill you, I prefer to do it before morning." He left the elderly banker alone on his chair and walked across to join Gio and Anse. The three lit cigarettes . . . and waited.

After some minutes, Durand lifted his head and called softly. "I have only your word? Nothing else?"

"That's all!" Cesar replied.

The banker fell once again into deep thought. After some minutes he shook his head as if attempting to clear it. "My family?" he asked. "Will you help them escape . . . follow me?"

"No," Cesar told him, "I won't help, but I won't try to stop them either. It seems to me that if you're in Argentina, your friends can help you make your plans for them from there."

"Yes," Durand agreed slowly, "I'll certainly be of more use alive than dead." Then slowly, reluctantly he shook his head. "It can't be done. Transferring my interest in the bank requires more than just my say-so. It's a complicated process, all the legal papers and things."

Cesar left his companions and crossed back to stand before the banker. "I thought of that." He raised his voice slightly and called to Joseph. "Bring the contracts." Joseph left the shadows and stepped into the circle of light.

"These were drawn up by an attorney," Joseph said, handing the papers to Durand. "You'll find all the legal technicalities covered."

Durand studied the papers carefully, reading each line of the carefully typed manuscript. "They seem to cover everything," he said finally ". . . even to the impressive witnesses already sworn to my forthcoming signature." He cast a cynical glance at Joseph, then back to the contracts. "Of course, this will have to be notarized, but I suppose you can arrange that too."

"Naturally, *M'sieur,*" Cesar said. But he did not explain that the nearest the papers would come to a notary would be Luigi Venito's expert hands.

The thin aristocratic face of the elderly man lifted to look into the eyes of Cesar. "If I keep my part of this agreement . . . sign these papers, you will keep your part . . . let me escape?" The banker waited for additional reassurance. "And do no harm to my family?"

"Yes," said Cesar. "I give you my word."

Reaching a decision, Durand stood up. "I accept your deal," he said. "But first . . . just an old man's curiosity . . . who is this new partner taking over my interests? This Joseph Tasera?"

Joseph bowed slightly. "I am Tasera, *M'sieur.*" He handed Durand a fountain pen. "Now if you'll please sign."

Durand crossed to the table. Leaning on it, as if to help support his slight weight, he scrawled a signature on the indicated lines. Dropping the pen beside the contracts, he straightened. Erect. "What next?" he asked.

"Your clothes, please. Take off your suit and vest," Cesar said.

A shadow of fear flitted quickly across the thin, aquiline face of the banker. But his voice was steady. "I should've known," he said. "Now that I've signed, you're going to murder me." He shook his head wearily. "Not that it makes much difference—you could've forged my signature anyway . . ."

"No, *M'sieur*," Cesar corrected Durand. "I keep my promises. I need your clothes for *my* protection!" He gestured to Joseph. "M'sieur Tasera has others for you."

"How long'll I remain here?"

"A few days, a week at most, while we wait for the boat to take you to Lisbon. You'll be in no danger, but don't show yourself. Don't go out. One of my men'll be here all the time to take care of trouble if it turns up."

"Meanwhile," said Joseph, "you'll spend some time with me. It's unfortunate we don't have the books for your bank. But you can brief me, give me information. Fill me in about your partners and employees."

"That would help, wouldn't it?" asked Durand with a slight smile.

"Very much," Joseph agreed.

The next afternoon, Passe, the brown shadow of a man, edged up to Cesar at the bar in Le Marin. "You wanted to see me?" Passe asked.

"Come with me," Cesar said. "I've something to show you." He walked from the bar and started for the stairs in the lobby. After a moment of hesitation, Passe followed him. In Cesar's room, on the top floor, Cesar closed the door behind them and crossed to the armoire. Taking out a bundle of clothes, he tossed it on the floor, retaining the vest. Holding it up, he said, "This belonged to a distinguished banker. He no longer needs it." He handed the vest to Passe.

Passe examined the knife slashes and caked blood on the garment. His expression questioned Cesar. Cesar leaned forward and picked up the suit coat, also stained, and turned it to display the lining. A label carried the monogrammed initials JVD. Passe nodded. "Why are you showing me?" he asked.

"Because no one'll probably ever see JVD again."

"No? Where is he?"

Cesar fixed his opaque glance on Passe. "Maybe the fish know."

"Oh?" Passe dropped the vest. "A bit unusual, isn't it? Some people might doubt he's really dead."

Cesar opened the drawer of his desk and took out an initialed leather wallet, a *carte nationale d'identité,* and a gold watch. Placing them on top of the desk, he said, "They'd recognize these. Take them along."

"It's not my job to prove things," Passe said. "I don't want evidence in my possession . . ." He indicated the clothes and personal items. "Get rid of them!"

"You'll remember what I've shown you."

"Yes."

"And if you're asked, you'll describe what you've seen."

"I'd do that," Passe said. "What I can't understand, why's this necessary? Other times the proof was *there!* In the street."

"Reasons, good ones—which I won't explain to you." Cesar paused, swept the items back into the desk, and closed the drawer. "I want to speak to your man. He may not want me at his office . . . or want to talk on the phone. But you'll arrange it."

"I'll let you know," Passe said.

Cesar stood beneath the columns of the curving sweep of promenade to the Palais Longchamp. Neptune leaned on his trident, flanked by two graceful water nymphs, but the fountain threw no water on their stone figures. The ascending flights of steps were empty except for a single figure making its way to the higher level of the walk between the columns. When he reached the promenade, he paused and looked around.

Cesar stepped from behind one of the pillars. The two men were alone in the monumental emptiness of the ornate walk.

Gozy's light gray eyes were cold, although his lips smiled. "There you are," he said. "A pleasure to see you again." His voice did not mean it.

Cesar ground out his cigarette beneath his shoe. "I thought, after the last report, you might have a few questions."

Gozy smiled smoothly. "Are any necessary?"

"Did Passe tell you the things I showed him?"

"Yes."

"There's something I didn't show him," Cesar said. "Here it is." Cesar handed Gozy a copy of the transfer of interests in Crédit de Berre. Puzzled, the politician began to read the contracts. He frowned. Cesar waited. Gozy glanced up to stare briefly at him, then returned to his reading. Abruptly, he crushed the papers together, clenching his hand.

"You assume a great deal, Satisanni," Gozy said. His voice was flat.

Cesar's tone matched the politician's when he replied. "Let's cut out the *merde*. I'm not in this thing for a few sous. Neither are you." He reached out and took the contract from Gozy's hand, carefully straightening out the papers before putting them back in his pocket. "You wanted Durand out of the way. He's *out!* If you're worried about the old records in the bank involving your people, stop worrying! I guarantee every damned sheet will be destroyed. That's your main concern, isn't it?"

"You had to make a deal with Durand. You had to give him his life to get him to sign that!"

"Certainly," agreed Cesar. "But afterwards . . ." His finger described the slice of a knife.

"Where's his body? You claim it's in the sea. Prove it!"

"You forget. I can't afford to have his body found," Cesar said. "His family, heirs, business associates—they'll contest the transfer if they can prove him dead. He simply disappears. What can they do? They can't be sure . . . it'll take them years."

"I don't like it." Gozy gestured impatiently. "It wasn't part of our agreement."

"There was no agreement against it," Cesar said. "So far I've filled the contracts. I'll continue to do so."

The wind lifted Gozy's hair, revealing his bald spot. He looked down at the palace grounds surrounding the fountains. "The bank," he said. "That's what worries my people."

"You can't knock off everyone working in it," Cesar said. "My

149

man'll handle them. If he can't, then I will!"

"There are other plans for the bank."

"It's mine now," Cesar said. He leaned against a column, folding his arms. "It'd be too much trouble to try to take it away again."

"Would it?" Gozy's face was turned to Cesar, but he did not see him.

"Yes," Cesar assured him, simply.

"Perhaps you're right." Gozy suddenly assumed his polished smile. "I won't underestimate you again. I'm sure there'll be more business in the future."

"We both understand business. Your people should be pleased that Crédit de Berre is in *friendly* hands. If I should make a little money from it, is that unreasonable?"

"Of course not." While Gozy shook a friendly hand with Cesar, his thoughts were less warm: "A tough bastard. We can afford to let him get away with this—for a while. We'll wait. He can't run a bank. When the time's right . . ." But none of his thoughts were reflected in Gozy's smiling face. A politician, he never burned bridges needlessly. Cesar was still useful as a tool. "I've heard about Le Marin," Gozy said. "Perhaps I should drop in some night . . ." The words were merely polite ritual.

"And bring your friends," Cesar replied with an equally empty welcome.

"I'll see you then." Gozy flashed his smile and walked down the columned way.

"*À bientôt,*" Cesar said. His stare followed Gozy as the politician descended the wide sweeping stairs. Gozy had accepted Durand's death. The shredded vest stained with chicken blood. Amusing! He had swallowed the bitter pill of losing the plunder—Crédit de Berre. Why? Cesar had anticipated the acceptance, which proved his theory: power! Already, Gozy was reluctant to cross Cesar—and his growing "family." Gozy would not turn the authorities loose against him, not unless he became desperate, or as a last resort against too great a provocation. Cesar realized that with the acquisition of the bank, he must now hire more men. His danger lay in the Rampini and Volanti families—who were also doing business with Gozy's people.

150

Chapter 18

Jullien Durand had long since arrived in Argentina and disappeared into anonymous safety among his friends. In the months following the transfer, Joseph took over complete management of Crédit de Berre. This privately owned bank controlled by a limited partnership of investors, of which Durand had been the senior and largest, had relatively modest assets—several million dollars. The bank was an old, established name, with a conservative reputation. Perhaps its semiobscurity in banking circles had appealed to the Germans, who had funneled funds through it in secret—deposits to numbered accounts of their own in Switzerland, as well as bribes and payoffs to French industry, military, and state officials.

The offices of Crédit de Berre were located on Cours St. Louis near La Canebiere. Like many French banks, the rooms were dark and unpretentious, filled with long, stained counters, small desks, and low glass partitions. A somber, sober air clothed the elderly employees, who spent their working days hunched over large ledgers, scribbling figures in fine archaic hands. Very little cash was kept on hand, but this did not prevent Cesar from hiring two tough guards—over Joseph's protests. "First, we'll never be held up," Joseph said. "And second, their salaries go against our overhead—and aren't worth it!"

Cesar was adamant. "Perhaps the bank doesn't need

them, but I do. They'll be there if I want them." Consequently, the guards were hired—Corsicans, tough *bandits* from the underworld of Marseilles. Each morning they reported to work when the bank opened, then sat through the day staring blankly at the dark green walls. Their presence intimidated the employees and officers of the bank, who gave prompt cooperation to Joseph when he took over the operation. Jobs were scarce in Marseilles and no one quit.

However, one of the junior partners, Monsieur Farinole, resisted Joseph's authority. Farinole questioned the legality of the entire transaction. With other business interests, Farinole was not dependent on Crédit de Berre. Shortly thereafter, the junior partner received a visit from a very large man with massive hands, and a silent black. Farinole did not recognize either of them when he came out of a restaurant, after a satisfactory lunch, to go to his car parked some distance down the street. As he opened the door to get in, a hand clamped across his mouth from behind, holding him helpless. A black hand grasped his wrist and placed Farinole's hand in the open door.

The door slammed shut across Farinole's fingers.

Soundlessly, Farinole screamed. And screamed again.

The door opened to release the red, pulpy mass of broken fingers. The big man holding Farinole said, "Next time it'll be your head." Farinole, doubled over in agony, held his mangled hand. Gasping with the excruciating pain, he did not see them leave.

The next day, Joseph made arrangements to buy out Farinole's partnership in the Crédit de Berre.

But the Farinole incident, in addition to the hiring of the two guards, brought a separation between Joseph and Cesar.

Joseph, wearing the suit of a conservative businessman, entered Cesar's room in Le Marin. Cesar, seated at his desk, looked up at his cousin. Joseph hesitated, then slowly sat down. Cesar swing his chair around to face him. "Cesar," Joseph began, not sure of his words, "it's about you . . . me . . . and the bank."

"Something wrong? Trouble with Farinole again?" The desk lamp etched Cesar's strong features in lines of black and white. "I'll take care of it."

Joseph studied his hands. "No, affairs are straightened out now." He lifted his head to meet Cesar's questioning look. "I'm moving away from Le Marin. It has to be that way."

"Why?"

"We can't afford for rumors to start. Gossip about Farinole . . . the *milieu* in the bank . . . the fact that we're *casseurs*. What happens when it becomes known I live in a waterfront whorehouse?" Joseph shook his head. "I, at least, have to appear respectable."

"I see . . ." Cesar was thoughtful.

"I'll find a decent address. During the day, during business hours, it'll be advisable we have no contact. Don't come to the bank . . . or send Gio or Anse," Joseph added, "or any of the others."

"I don't like it. We've been together from the beginning."

"It'll still be that way," Joseph assured him. "After all, it's your bank in reality. We'll meet whenever you say."

Cesar inclined his head. "When will you move?"

"Soon as possible. To a hotel, perhaps, on La Canebiere . . . at first. Close to the office."

"All right." Cesar's brusqueness hid his regret. Joseph was right, but he sensed that they would never be so close again.

Joseph stood beside Cesar's chair and placed a hand on his shoulder. He understood something of what Cesar was feeling. "Believe me," he said, "now that we have Crédit de Berre—it has to be protected. It's the base for everything you do in the future. Through it, someday, you'll get what you want."

"No," Cesar disagreed, "the bank's not the answer. You think figures and numbers in your books are too important. They're not. They don't have the final say!"

"What does?"

"I'll tell you when I find out." Cesar turned to his desk, his back to Joseph.

In the months that followed, Marseilles was a city of contradictions. Although it was in the throes of rebuilding, a city rife with activity, it still had high unemployment. Crédit de Berre invested in real estate, the building trades, wholesale fruit and vegetable markets. It bought an interest in a small meat packing company. All legitimate investments. Joseph's prophecy about the bank seemed to be coming true.

Cesar, too, became more active, but concerned himself with busi-

153

ness that he understood. His so-called distant uncle, Angelo Fenne-chi, resumed his smuggling runs to bring whiskey and tobacco from North Africa, plus an occasional load of German arms—rifles, revolvers, and submachine guns constantly turned up after the war. Cesar fenced Angelo's loads for resale into the black market. He also bought cattle from the rustlers operating throughout the Midi and sold them to the packing house controlled by Joseph.

His most lucrative business was loan-sharking. The port was filled with shipping, the docks and warehouses busy as never before. However, the longshoremen, stevedores, and warehousemen were constantly in need of money. Cesar made them small loans at an interest rate of twenty percent a week—"six on five" as the men called it. Gio and Anse were the collectors, and few customers turned into dead beats.

With the widening of his activities, Cesar continued to remain in the background, avoiding the limelight. He changed his name, shortening it to Sati. More men were hired to operate and protect his interests. Although most of the men he hired were Corsicans, some were French. At no time were the Corsican "families" so strictly bound, or limited in membership, as the Mafia in Sicily. While a hard core of blood or friendship remained in each Corsican family, outsiders on the underworld fringe came and went so long as they remained silent. The Corsican *patriarches* had a live-and-let-live attitude toward small-fry criminals. The Corsicans often did business with them without absorbing them into their private groups and circles.

When Cesar left Ajaccio, he brought with him the core of his future family—Joseph, Gio, and Anse. These three always remained his nucleus. As his interests and business increased, he added to the family: first, Luigi Venito; next, Galon, Franco, and Beni Turnella; then the two guards at Crédit de Berre. His group had increased to nine. After Cesar rented a small warehouse, he hired more men to protect and dispose of the smuggled goods from North Africa. Then he needed—and got—men to protect delivery of the stolen cattle. His soaring loans and shylocking eventually required more collectors also.

Cesar's *bandits* grew to fifteen.

Business at Le Marin prospered. Prostitutes and their stunts filled it almost round the clock. The police were paid off regularly and left the hotel's habitués and customers alone—especially since the hotel presented them with no problems. In the early days of its operation, Cesar encouraged calculated violence from the bouncers. Retribution for drunks and troublemakers was sudden and brutal. Galon, Franco, and Beni knew their bruising business well. Individually, each was a terror; collectively, when necessary, they were a tornado of disaster. The news quickly spread along the waterfront: "At Le Marin, *mec*, take it easy . . ." Within a short time, the transactions of sex and liquor were conducted quietly. Disturbances were infrequent. Under new instructions from Cesar, the three *videurs* remained vigilant, alert to suppress trouble before it exploded, but they were under orders to remain quiet and unobtrusive until going into action.

The entire fourth floor of Le Marin, occupied by Cesar and his original three companions, became more valuable with the passing weeks. Although Joseph moved out, his room remained empty. The four chambers represented one third of the potential space of the hotel and a proportionate amount of income if they were rented out. Too, Cesar found it increasingly inconvenient to live at Le Marin and conduct his other interests from the bar or his bedroom. He needed privacy to meet callers, free from the eyes of drinkers in the bar, arrivals in the lobby, and the inquisitive prostitutes in the halls.

Once a week, Cesar, accompanied by Anse or Gio, went to Crédit de Berre to deposit his cash receipts. Each Monday, Joseph waited in the empty offices of the bank, after closing hours, for Cesar's arrival. Following the transfer of funds to a special account held in the name of "Mar-Col," a dummy corporation set up by Joseph, the two cousins discussed current plans.

On one Monday, Cesar brought up the subject of finding a new headquarters for himself. Joseph agreed; the bank held a mortgage on a vacant two-storey building which, before the war, had been a small private boys' school. The school had not reopened and could be picked up for the balance of the overdue mortgage. Almost without grounds, except for a tiny playyard, the property was located in a commercial area not far from the old cathedral of St. Vincent de Paul—considerably distant from Le Marin and the waterfront. The building was not large, for it originally had been a day school, requiring only half a dozen classrooms. Joseph assured Cesar that it

155

could be remodeled to contain an outer office and meeting room, a private office, and a dormitory large enough to sleep four of the *casseurs*. The second storey would convert into a comfortable apartment and an additional private bedroom. Also, Joseph pointed out, the old school offered good security with thick walls, deep windows with heavy shutters, and only two entrances—front and back.

Cesar told Joseph to make the necessary arrangements. However, the move to new headquarters presented other problems. After further discussions with Joseph, Cesar decided to leave Anse at Le Marin to oversee its operations. Anse's cooler head was preferable to Gio's sullen moods and sudden bursts of anger. Gio would take over the loan-sharking end completely, but he would move with Cesar to the new quarters and be kept under supervision and control. The moving and shifting of responsibilities also required hiring more men. Joseph offered his usual resistance to additions on the payroll, but Cesar insisted. Money was still a nebulous commodity to Cesar, but men were tangible signs of authority.

Joseph offered a compromise. At this time he was considering the purchase of some available trucks to form a trucking company and transport fruit and vegetables to the markets and haul rustled cattle to their packing house. Sometimes Cesar was reluctant to invest present capital against future profits. Joseph pointed out that trucks required more men. Joseph got his trucks; Cesar got his men.

The last night before he moved, Heloise came to Cesar's room in Le Marin. It was the first time that she had been in it. After knocking, she entered with hesitation. Standing just inside the door, she grasped her arms, hugging them against her swelling bosom. "You're going tomorrow. Getting out . . ." she said.

"I'm moving, if that's what you mean," Cesar said.

"You're on your way. You won't came back here again."

"Why should I? Anse'll handle everything."

"Good for Anse!" she said bitterly.

"You don't like it?" Cesar regarded her. "You're making more money than you've ever made."

"It'll never be enough!" Heloise's voice was low. "You're a fool when it comes to women, Cesar!"

Cesar said quietly, sardonically, "Am I?"

"Why do you think I'm here? To save my money and retire? To

156

gather a *dot* so a respectable man will marry me? Do I want a nice little shop someplace . . . or a lousy farm with chickens and sell eggs?"

"That's up to you."

Heloise suddenly kicked the door. It slammed shut. Her voice rose. "I'll tell you why I'm here!" She laughed sharply. "For the same reason every whore comes here. H . . . big H! Keep the sheets hot to buy another fix!"

"No one's making you stay."

"Oh, I'll stay! And so will the rest of us. And more new ones every day. We'll hang on till we kill ourselves, or get so damned ugly we can't give it away free to the stunts." Heloise's voice cracked. "You talk about money! The more I make, the more H I can buy!" Tears gathered suddenly in her eyes. Her voice softened. "Cesar . . . Cesar . . . I just came to tell you goodbye . . ."

"Goodbye," Cesar said.

The girl's shoulders slumped. "Besides H, there was another reason. That first night . . . when I picked up Gio. You talked to me in the bar. I thought you had style! Class! I hoped maybe . . ." Her voice trailed away. Her head was lowered. "But you've never given me a glance." Her face flooded with embarrassment. "I don't have a disease . . ."

"I hadn't thought about whether you have or haven't. But I don't want a woman."

"What are you, a priest? A monk? A hermit?" Her voice rose again. "Or a goddamned fag without balls!"

Cesar's face was impassive. "Don't say that again," he said coldly. "There's a place in my life for a woman, but not now. When the time comes, I'll find her."

"Certainly! One who goes to Mass on Sunday. And raises brats. And hasn't a thought in her damned, stupid head!"

Cesar shoved back his chair. "She'll be what I want. And she won't be a whore!" he said, standing up, his face white with anger.

Heloise threw open the door. Without another glance, she stumbled from the room and ran to the lobby. Cesar turned on the light at his desk. Sitting down, he took out his pad of paper and began scrawling marks and doodles. Preoccupied, his face thoughtful, he weighed Heloise's angry words. That they were also pathetic did not touch him. Cesar felt no pity, but he did feel a sense of excitement building in him. The idea—what she had said—was there, everywhere around him. He had never seriously considered it, not because of moral or ethical reasons but because of the danger without a good organization and plenty of muscle behind him. The Rampini and Volanti, so far quiet, had permitted him to attend his own business without interference because he had not cut into theirs. But this new venture? He would step on a lot of toes!

Then there was Gozy. There were limits, too, to what Gozy would tolerate. Cesar knew the politician had not forgotten about Crédit de Berre. And Roncin . . . always in the background waiting.

But there it was, by God! The source, the root of real power! Slowly, slowly, Cesar cautioned himself. Think it out, plan it most carefully. Build for it before the first move. More men. Add more of the *milieu!* Of course, Joseph would object, but to hell with Joseph! He wouldn't tell Joseph what he had in mind until he was ready. When the money started rolling in, then Joseph would agree quickly enough.

Chapter 19

The new headquarters was called "La Tour," named in honor of the low, massive Genoese guard towers squatting on the coasts of Corsica, the old ruins that were a reminder of Italy's former power. For several weeks, shipping in the port of Marseilles had been tied up by a strike. Longshoremen and stevedores were hungry, desperate, and broke, but firmly resolved not to go back to work until an agreement had been reached. Consequently, loan-sharking had leaped to new heights. Gio and his squad of collectors were busy and harassed.

Passe, wearing his habitual brown suit, appeared one day at La Tour to see Cesar. The little contact man inched his way through the crowded outer room to Cesar's office. He was stopped by one of the *gorilles* at the door.

"I want to see Sati," Passe said.

The *casseur* looked Passe over with insolent eyes. "He expecting you?"

"No, but he'll see me. Tell him Passe's here."

The *casseur* disappeared behind the closed door, reappeared, and nodded. Passe entered Cesar's office. Across from the door, Cesar sat behind a large desk facing Passe. Cesar had not forgotten his first visit to Vito Nastacio's library in Ajaccio. It was reflected in this room—high cases lined with books, unread by Cesar; leather furniture; framed hunting prints on the walls; lamps with parchment shades; a thick, imitation Persian rug on the floor. Only the carved marble fireplace was missing—the room could not accommodate one. In place of the massive original, an electrical fireplace had been substituted, complete with a false mantle and glowing glass coals.

Passe slipped into a chair, giving no indication of Cesar's new surroundings. "There's going to be a meeting," Passe said as if picking up a recent conversation and avoiding names.

"Where? *His* office? The Palais?"

"*He* won't attend. But his people have arranged to hold it."

"Who'll be there?"

"The Rampini and the Volanti," Passe said, unblinking.

Cesar leaned back in his chair, his hands resting quietly on top of the desk. "Do you think I'm anxious to get hassled?"

"There'll be no trouble. Depend on it! Both families want you to come."

A blank mask hid Cesar's thoughts. He had always realized that eventually he must face the Families. Sooner or later, their paths would collide. It was inevitable. Both the Rampini and the Volanti had been busy rebuilding their forces and fortunes—were they out to get him now? "What do they want to see me about?" Cesar asked.

"You'll find out at the meeting," Passe said. "It's business."

"It's always business."

"This is important. Believe me, it'll pay you to attend."

Cesar was still suspicious. "Where will it be held?"

"In the country. Tomorrow. Fortuno Rampini has a villa at the beach."

"I won't be there," Cesar said.

"Bring as many of your *bande* as you want," Passe told him. "Will that assure you?"

"It would help," Cesar was sardonic.

"How many you bring . . . they'll only have the same number. No one wants a fight."

Cesar thought it over. "Has Volanti agreed to go to Rampini's?"

"Why not?" Passe appeared surprised at the question. "I told you this is business. Sometimes it's necessary for all parties to do business together."

"What other parties?"

160

"You'll meet him, but I assure you he is a real big-shot—high up!"

"All right," Cesar agreed slowly. "I'll be there. With two men. That means Rampini and Volanti will each have one. Correct?"

"Exactly," Passe said.

"When?" asked Cesar.

"In the morning. Eleven o'clock," Passe told him.

Fifty kilometers or so below Marseilles, the Villa Rampini squatted on a small finger of land near the conjunction of the Bay of Lions and the Mediterranean. Of elderly design, the building gleamed whitely, with a slate-blue tile roof and sea-blue shutters. A curved drive led to its low portico and a main door flanked by two sphinxes of poured concrete. The house sat alone above a rocky beach, its back to the waters.

Several cars were parked in the drive when Cesar arrived with Gio and Anse. The heavy door to the villa opened promptly at Cesar's knock. "*M'sieur...*" a *casseur* stood to one side while the three men entered. The floor of the reception hall was tiled with a reproduction of a Roman mosaic—an amphora, brick red, edged in black. To one side, an arched door led to a large drawing room in which another hard-faced thug was lounging. "You *mecs* will wait in there," the *casseur* said to Gio and Anse, indicating the drawing room. "This way," he said to Cesar, heading toward a set of closed doors on the opposite side of the hall.

Cesar stepped inside the doors, which were closed behind him. He stood inside a dining salon, furnished with heavy pieces of Victorian furniture, and faced three men seated at a long table. To one side a massive, carved buffet was loaded with platters and dishes of food —covered and, as yet, untouched. The seated men stood up at the table, a gesture of respect that did not pass unnoticed by Cesar. Cesar, suspicious and alert, slowly relaxed.

"Welcome, M'sieur Sati. I'm Fortuno Rampini." *Le Patriarche* of the Rampini family was well into middle age, with beefy shoulders, belly going to fat, and a slight silvering of gray at his temples. He wore an expensive gray flannel suit with chalk stripes. A heavy hand, its back tufted with hair, gestured slightly. "Do you know my other guests? M'sieur Volanti . . . and M'sieur Savon?"

161

"No," said Cesar politely. *"M'sieurs . . ."* They exchanged nods. As the men seated themselves again, Rampini asked, "Would you care for something to eat? Now? Later?"

"Later," replied Cesar. He took the few moments to size up his other companions. Ruggiero Volanti was only slightly older than himself. His father, Ignazio, had died in the war during the occupation, and young Ruggiero inherited the mantle and leadership of the Volanti. Quiet, with a thin face, a long lantern jaw, and wearing glasses with heavy, dark frames, Volanti appeared more a scholar than the patriarch of a powerful family. Unlike the business attire of Rampini, Volanti wore a pullover sweater, slacks, and sport shoes. Cesar's own expensive casual clothes fit comfortably with Volanti's, which satisfied his pride.

The third man, Savon, was difficult to place. He was about the same age as Rampini, but his round face was underslung with a double chin and his hair was well flecked with gray. Hazel eyes, round like two coins, stared from both sides of a thick nose. A thin, nearly invisible upper lip was supported by a surprising bright pink, moist lower lip. When he smiled he gave the impression of only half trying. Like Rampini, Savon wore a business suit—a herringbone of British cut. He also wore the authority of a big-shot—which Passe had assured Cesar the government man was.

"Now that we're all here," Rampini said, "M'sieur Savon will explain why we're getting together." Reaching to the center of the table, Rampini picked up a box of large Cuban cigars. He offered them silently to the others. They refused politely. While Rampini selected one, Cesar took out a heavy gold cigarette case and lit a long, dark brown, imported cigarette.

Savon cleared his throat. "As you gentlemen may know, I'm a . . . a labor consultant. Some of our friends are so kind as to call me an expert. I won't argue with them." Savon smiled, calm, assured. "For several weeks now, we've been in conferences or meetings. The government is vitally concerned. This strike in Marseilles is costing the country and the economy of France millions of pounds—dollars! —a day. The little people of our country can't afford this strike. The franc is continuing to drop. Soon the effects will reach into every home and every breadbasket."

Savon's three listeners sat silent, listening, their attention fixed on the government emissary.

"On the docks, the labor unions are all Communist controlled," Savon continued. "The strike is politically motivated. The Reds want to grab power here as they've already done so successfully in Italy. If this strike continues long enough, it can cause many problems among your friends in the government. Damned serious ones!"

Rampini nodded. "New elections, and out they go."

"Right, *M'sieur*. However, *our* friends are thinking not only of themselves but of the poor people of France," Savon said, his voice evangelical.

Volanti took off his glasses and wiped them. "Of course," he murmured. Cesar remained silent.

"My concern, the concern of *all* our friends, is to end this strike as quickly as possible. It can't be permitted to drag on for months —as the Communists wish. The longer the better, so far as the Reds are concerned. It's impossible to bargain with them, as they constantly increase, or shift, their demands. In time, our whole economy will be wrecked. That's what they want. Then they'll take over!"

Cesar drew on his dark cigarette, then exhaled slowly. "You're the labor expert, M'sieur Savon. You must've made recommendations . . . of some kind . . . to your people."

"Naturally, certainly, M'sieur Sati. I recommended that this strike be stopped! Somehow, someway! My friends most positively agreed. They're as one. Anything within reason, any means that offers the slightest hope of success to break it." Savon paused and looked at the three men around the table. "When I say within reason . . . you understand? The government can't afford to be embarrassed. Officially, it can extend no legal help."

"Unofficially?" Rampini asked.

"Unofficially, it won't raise any obstacles, either," said Savon.

"With millions at stake every day, I assume your friends will come up with financing to aid those who help them?" Volanti asked.

"All expense will be covered," Savon said. "Gentlemen, you've kindly listened to the problem. Is there a solution? Perhaps you will find an answer among yourselves. I hope so! Certainly, I would not presume to propose any special course of action."

"I suggest we have lunch," Rampini said. "We can think about it while we eat. I think better while my digestion's at work."

The men sat at the table before loaded plates. At the touch of a button beneath Rampini's shoe, a maid scurried into the dining room and deposited a number of glasses on the table with half a dozen bottles of wine. She hurried out again. The men ate in silence except for an occasional polite remark by Rampini concerning the weather, the salutary effects of salt air, and the benefits of a beach villa for occasional weekends. When they had finished eating, Savon arose, pleading the necessity of an immediate return to the city. He politely said goodbye to his host and the two guests and left.

Rampini, Volanti, and Cesar remained at the table. After it was cleared by the same hurrying maid, the men lit their smokes and sat with delicate snifters of brandy. "Savon discussed this with you before you called the meeting," Cesar said to Rampini.

"Yes," Rampini agreed.

"Was it your idea to ask me here? Or was it Savon's?"

Rampini paused for a moment. "Savon's," he said, glancing at Volanti.

"Savon was anxious that if the Rampini and my people get together on this, that you come in, too," Volanti said. "He didn't want the unions hiring *you* to fight *us.*"

Rampini said, "You have twenty *men* now. It's bad business for Corsican to fight Corsican."

"What'd you have in mind about the strike?" Cesar asked.

Rampini stood up heavily from the table. Opening the door to the entry hall, he gave a brisk order. Within moments, he returned to the table with a large map. Unfolding it, Rampini spread it out. The harbor and waterfront areas were marked with a heavy pencil, dividing them into two sections. Pointing with his finger, Rampini said, "I'll take this area . . . all alone here, up to this point. From there on the Volanti will be responsible."

Cesar studied the map. "That's half for you and half for Volanti. Where do I come in?"

"You and your *bande* will work for me, in my section," Rampini glanced at Volanti. "Or with him and the Volanti."

"I won't work in either," Cesar said.

The two *Patriarches* were silent. The silence stretched until Rampini finally said, "You'll fight against us?"

"If I have to," Cesar said. "But that shouldn't be necessary."

"What do you want?" Volanti asked.

"My own section. Divide that waterfront into thirds—a part for each of us. I won't work for you . . . or for Rampini. But I'll work for myself."

"Volanti and I, we each have twice as many men as you. Why should we be partners?" Rampini asked.

"Because I can hire as many more *mecs* as I need. Enough to match you and Volanti," Cesar said, his voice flat. "And besides, there's Savon. He wants this thing over as soon as possible. His people . . . Gozy's . . . aren't going to stand still for a fight with you and Volanti against me on one hand, and against the Reds on the other."

"We'd take care of you!" Rampini warned.

"It might take longer than you think," Cesar said. Suddenly he assumed a tone of reason. "Why fight? There's enough for us all." Taking a pen from his sports jacket, he divided the pencil line on the map into three parts. "Simple as that! A scratch of the pen and we're partners." He stared with a slight smile at Rampini.

"You're assuming a lot," Rampini said.

"I'm assuming that I get *respect*. I'm entitled to it. The Sati won't be pushed around . . . hired like peasants. You want my help, need it. I offer it to you. As an equal."

Volanti leaned forward, arms resting on the table. "You claim that you have a family now?"

"Yes." Cesar's eyes were opaque. "Prove me wrong?"

"Gangs, mobs . . . come and go." Volanti said. "*Relégués* with guns can be hired for a drink," he added with disdain.

"You started with Nastacio. You and your *milieu* can claim him for your *Patriarche*. We respect him. We'll do business with him," Rampini said.

"In Corsica you do business with Nastacio. In Marseilles you do business with me, Sati."

"Listen to me," Rampini said. "You have things against you. You don't talk our language, you're not part of us. You didn't come up the hard way. You're too young, too inexperienced!"

"I get older every day," Cesar said.

"These things I said. They'll destroy you."

"You know how I feel about it."

Rampini stared at the table. "If Vito Nastacio recommends it . . ."

Cesar interrupted, his voice flat. "I have respect for Nastacio. I kiss his hand. I kiss your hand. I kiss Volanti's hand. But I also respect myself. I expect you to do the same!"

Rampini lifted his eyes to look at Volanti. Volanti shrugged, then nodded. "All right," Rampini said to Cesar. "Each will respect the others."

"Agreed," said Volanti.

"Agreed," said Cesar.

"Now we get to work." Rampini pulled the map to the center of the table. Cesar and Volanti rose from their chairs to stand beside the older man. Staring at the map, Rampini poked a hairy finger at the waterfront, moving it slowly. "Each will have a section . . . here, here, and here."

Late in the afternoon the meeting broke up. Cesar was met in the entrance hall by Gio and Anse. Flanked by his two men, Cesar took polite leave of the others. Outside the villa, he paused briefly to look at the two sphinxes crouching beside the main door. Cesar's enigmatic stare matched that of the stone beasts. He continued on after a moment, passing Volanti's Mercedes parked in the drive, and climbed into his own black Citröen. Anse took his place behind the wheel, Gio beside him. Cesar shifted in his seat to stare at Volanti's big limousine. "We need a car like that," Cesar said.

Gio turned in the front seat to look back at Cesar. "A Mercedes?"

"Or a Bentley." A thin smile of satisfaction rested on Cesar's lips.

"Huh, Cesar?" Gio asked.

Cesar's laughter was hard and clear. "From now on, show me more respect. Address me as *Le Patriarche.*"

"Why, sure . . ." Gio said, confused.

Anse's white smile gleamed wickedly. He shoved a black hand against Gio's massive shoulder. "You . . . me . . . we're now members of the Sati *Family,* you dumb bastard!"

Chapter 20

The piers erupted in flames and violence. Angelo Fennechi's boat hauled recruits from Corsica to work as strikebreakers in the harbor of Marseilles. They were distant relatives, family friends, and sturdy peasants lured by the high pay offered by Cesar. With funds furnished secretly by the authorities, and funneled into Crédit de Berre, Cesar paid off the willing scabs after taking a ten percent employment fee from their wages.

The strikers and their union leaders did not stand by in impotent rage. The picket lines fought back with fury; first with fists, then with clubs, pipes, and cargo hooks. To protect his workers on the docks, Cesar hired more and more members of the *milieu* . . . strongarm men, mugs, thugs, and killers. His army doubled, tripled, then doubled again. At a meeting with Rampini and Volanti, the three families decided on a program of elimination, to gun down the defiant union leaders. Their assassins roamed the waterfront.

So long as the violence did not spill over into the streets and business areas of the city, the police did little to restore peace. Roncin, the detective inspector, stood by helpless, his scorn and hatred of Cesar unabated. In a report that Roncin filed, left unread by his superiors, he wrote:

167

Cesar Satisanni, now calling himself Sati, must be considered a threat to law, order, and justice . . . equal to that of the Rampini and Volanti. Originally, Sati was an outsider, a small-time criminal with no arrests or convictions. He is now firmly established as a third family of the Unione Corse in Marseilles.

In my opinion, from what I have seen and heard, as well as what other officers have told me, Sati lives in a world completely alien to other men or, for that matter, humanity. He has no close friends, no known women associates—other than the prostitutes frequenting his properties.

Sati is shrewd, intelligent, and completely amoral. He believes he is a gentleman, a cut above the criminals around him. He thinks he can do no wrong because he doesn't know what wrong is! He is not immoral as he has no conscience. He exists for today, and today only, because every day adds to his power and wealth. Sati lives in the best of all possible worlds simply because there is no other world he can imagine or live in.

At present, Sati has approximately 125 to 150 members of the *milieu* under his command. I urge that every effort be made to apprehend him.

Roncin's report disappeared in the bureaucratic wasteland without trace. He was not alone. Reports on Cesar, as well as the usual and continuing reports on Rampini and Volanti by other conscientious officers, rested briefly in police files, then vanished.

During the weeks that the strike raged, Joseph met with Cesar only once. On that occasion Joseph arrived at La Tour late at night, to see Cesar alone in his apartment. Below them, the building was dark, silent except for the *gorilles* on guard at the doors and their relief asleep in the dormitory. Cesar was wearing silk pajamas and a silk robe; his slippers were glove-leather soft. He greeted Joseph abruptly. "I know. There's sixty thousand dollars out in the streets we haven't collected!"

"How can you? The longshoremen aren't working. They have no money. How can they pay?" Joseph asked mildly.

"When the strike's over, they'll pay!" Cesar said grimly.

168

"Forget it for now. But remember, money has to work. Keep it working . . . circulating. Fortunately, the cuts from your scabs' salaries will offset your losses and show a substantial profit. But that isn't why I'm here."

Cesar sat down heavily on a rose-velvet sofa. "Then, why?"

"When this . . . thing . . . is over, what're your plans?"

"I don't want to talk about them now."

"I'm talking about the piers. Will you hand them back to the labor unions again?"

Cesar settled against the sofa, sprawling his legs. "There won't be much of the unions left."

"Exactly." Joseph sat quietly. "I have an opportunity to pick up control of an insurance company. Small. Very small, not much business."

"Why bother with it?" Cesar asked.

"Because, under the right circumstances, it could do a lot of business." Joseph paused, then added, "*If* you controlled part of the piers." He walked across the thick carpet and examined a large oil painting hanging on the wall. A bucolic landscape of Provence. Turning back again to Cesar, Joseph said, "And we already have the trucking company."

"Lay it out."

"Do I have to, Cesar?"

Cesar thought a moment. "The ships unload in our area. They carry our insurance—or they don't get unloaded. Cargoes stolen blind." He glanced at Joseph. "They use our trucks—or the loads don't arrive . . ." Cesar nodded slowly. "Not bad, Joseph. Not bad."

When the strike was over, the labor unions assumed control in name only. The waterfront was owned by the Sati, Volanti, and Rampini. But the strike's most important result was the attitude of both the national officials and the local Marseilles authorities: the political powers of France did not forget the favors extended them by the Corsicans.

Part
Three

Chapter 21

Peace returned to the piers and docks. Many strikebreakers, richer in purse, returned to Corsica. But the extra *bandits* added to Cesar's family during the strike were retained. The men were parceled out in jobs and permitted to participate in the family's growing rackets. Some were given positions of authority in the defeated labor unions; others went on the payrolls of the new insurance company and the hauling and trucking lines. Those with limited ability collected the old debts from the longshoremen; loan-sharking flourished as new loans were made to the men on the waterfront, desperate after the long strike. Two new brothels opened based on the success of Le Marin. Operating under the guise of small transient hotels, they absorbed others of the *milieu* as bouncers and enforcers.

Cesar's elevation to the patriarchy of a recognized Family forced him to assume new responsibilities, not the least of which was maintaining peace in the ranks of the *milieu*. Personal disputes constantly arose between the brutal, argumentative men. In all cases, Cesar's decision was final. Too, there was swift retribution meted out to *mouchards* who broke the law of silence.

The increased ranks of men under his command forced Cesar to restructure his organization. His original, loosely knit group was unable to function efficiently with the vastly enlarged Family interests. Organization became necessary.

The changes evolved slowly over the months. For two hundred years Corsican gangs had existed in the underworld. The gangs were small and usually transient; the members banded together through mutual interests and activities, coming and going as the individual members pleased. Even the older, powerful, established Families had little formal structure except for the *patriarche* and his assigned captains.

Cesar, however, recognized the need for an order of command. He was now at the head of an invisible army, and the difference between an army and rabble was discipline. Drawing his ranks together, Cesar finally put them in order. He, as *Le Patriarche,* was in supreme command. Directly beneath him was Joseph—his advisor, his one-man general staff. But Joseph remained out of sight, unknown to the rank-and-file *milieu* except for those who remembered him from the early days of Le Marin; these few had strict orders never to refer to Joseph by name.

As was to be expected, Cesar's general field officers were his two trusted companions from the early days, Gio and Anse. Acting as under-bosses, they were responsible for the men beneath them. Each had a company of approximately seventy men. The companies, in turn, were made up of squads of ten *casseurs.* Each squad had an acting leader, sometimes called a *picciotto,* (ruffian).

Luigi Venito, the forger, was elevated to the position of "fixer." He paid off police, bribed authorities, and compensated other interested parties, under the supervision of Cesar. Venito also performed another important function: with a lifetime career of crime, in and out of prisons, he possessed lines of intelligence deep into the underworld of *relégués,* criminals working alone, and the small shifting gangs. This information Venito passed on to Cesar.

The Sati Family was a formidable power. The strike had permitted Cesar to build his forces quickly and without opposition from the other Families or the government authorities. Consequently, he was able to put his new plans into action sooner than he expected after the strike. After careful preparation, he made his final move. Gio set it in operation.

Accompanied by a *picciotto* and two of his squad, Gio drove into the Arabian District. Even Gio did not care to venture alone into this squalid section, a narrow area below the Gare St. Charles. The filthy, dark streets are bounded between the Rue Bernard du Bois and the Rue des Dominicaines. The Renault drove carefully through the foul-smelling streets housing cheap and dirty whores, thugs, footpads, cutthroats, and perverts. The car stopped in front of a four-storey tenement that faced an open gutter with evil, stinking water and garbage. "You sure this is the place?" the *picciotto* asked.

"This is it," Gio said. Information gathered by Luigi Venito and passed on to Cesar was explicit.

Gio left the car carrying a large pillow. He was followed by Tonio, the *picciotto,* together with one of the *milieu.* The other remained in the car, the motor running. The three men entered the building, immediately stepping into a dark hallway reeking of decay and filth. Gio led the way down a steep stairway to the even darker basement. Tonio snapped on his flashlight. They walked slowly down a narrow concrete hall moldy with dampness. At the far end of the hall, near the back of the building, stood a heavy wooden door. Gio tried the door. It was solidly locked from within.

"Williot! Paul Williot!" Gio called. His massive fist thumped the wood. When he received no reply, Gio removed a .45 from his shoulder holster, wrapped it in the pillow, and expertly placed five shots into the locks of the door. The reports, muffled by the pillow, remained in the hallway. Gio's heavy shoe crashed into the panels and the door swung open.

Momentarily, the three men pressed against the walls of the hall, avoiding the open space of the doorway. The interior of the room was black. Gio's hand worked around the frame of the door and snapped on the switch.

The room sprang into light, revealing a low ceiling and peeling plaster walls. The cluttered room was filled with wooden tables, burners, bottles, tubes, and retorts—mostly makeshift—converted to the purpose of making heroin. The lab contained only one window, small and high up, in the wall at ground level. It was boarded over.

Directly beneath the window, Paul Williot cowered against the wall, red-rimmed eyes wide with fear. Stringy hair fell in his face. "All right," Gio said, "come with me."

"What do you want?" Williot's fingers, stained with chemicals, plucked nervously at his shirt.

175

"Somebody wants to see you," Gio said.

"I know you . . ." Williot's words held recognition. "You're from the Sati!"

"Get started." Gio nodded to Tonio and the *gorilles*. The two *casseurs* closed the door and began smashing the lab. The floor became a bog of broken glass, shattered tubing, twisted equipment, and spilled chemicals. They grunted with exertion. In the midst of the havoc, Williot made a sudden dash for the doorway. Gio's heavy blow crashed against the chemist's thin back, sending him sprawling. The big Corsican plucked up the helpless man and shoved him out into the hall. "We're going now," Gio said.

Holding Williot erect, the three Sati left the building and climbed into their waiting car. The miserable chemist sat in the back seat between Gio and Tonio. After Williot's hands were tied behind his back, and his eyes covered with tape, he was forced to lie on the floor of the car.

Leaving the Arabian District, the car stopped. Tonio and the two others of their *milieu* got out. Gio climbed behind the wheel and continued to drive.

Twenty kilometers beyond the outskirts of Marseilles, Gio turned from the main highway to follow a small country road. He approached a plain low farmhouse with decrepit outbuildings, some distance from the turnoff. The farm squatted on a few hectares of land, just large enough to support a cow, several sows, and a flock of chickens. Behind it was a scraggly garden and a small field of corn. In its mediocrity, the farm deserved no second glance. There was little to distinguish it from thousands of other farms scattered over the broad countryside of France. Gio stopped the car in the rear of the house beneath a single large apple tree. He dragged the bound Williot across the dirt farmyard and in the back door. Then he loosened the chemist's hands. "Here he is," Gio announced.

Williot peeled the tape from his eyes. Blinking, he looked around. He stood in a tiled, completely modern, fully equipped laboratory representing an investment of thousands. "Surprised?" Cesar asked, sardonically.

"Christ!"

"You begin now," Cesar said. "In a real lab."

Williot stared. "I can't, *M'sieur* . . ."

176

Cesar impaled the chemist with a cold stare. He knew little of Williot's background other than at one time the chemist owned a legitimate pharmacist's degree. Cesar had no idea what events had brought Williot to his present low status, and he was not interested in the chemist's misfortunes. The man standing before him was unprepossessing, wearing a filthy shirt and stained trousers, but he was a capable chemist. Cesar needed his services. "You'll be well paid," Cesar said.

Williot's sallow, dyspeptic face twitched. "I'm all tied up. Others depend on me. If I walk out . . . cut off their supply . . . they'll fix me . . . take care of me all right!"

"I'll take care of you if you don't," Cesar said.

The chemist ran his fingers through his lank hair. *"M'sieur,"* he pleaded, "you must understand!"

"Do you understand?" Cesar asked Gio.

"Sure," said Gio. He backhanded Williot across the mouth.

A trickle of blood ran down the side of Williot's chin. "All right." He cringed. "I'll go back, get ready to leave." Distraught, his eyes sought the door.

"You stay . . . don't go back. No one knows where this place is."

"Live here?"

"Yes." After the original owner had moved out, Cesar brought in a Corsican farmer and his wife, distant relatives of the Fennechi, to maintain the appearance of a working farm. "You'll have a room and enough to eat," Cesar said. "Also . . . company." An ironic smile touched Cesar's lips. "One or two of the *mecs* will be around in case you need help."

"So don't take a *cavale!*" Gio warned. "If I got to dig you up again, then I got to bury you."

Williot looked around the room. The new equipment glistened. His face slowly took on a look of interest, his thin shoulders squared. "I haven't seen a lab like this in years," he said.

"Use it right. I want nothing but the pure white. You'll get ten percent of each kilo wholesale price. You'll be a rich man," Cesar told him.

That night, on one of Joseph's weekly nighttime visits to La Tour, he reported to Cesar the acquisition of several cleaning and dyeing shops. "How're their supplies of acetic anhydride?" Cesar asked.

"They're ordering more," Joseph said.

"Plenty more! We'll need it. Acetic anhydride may be used to treat cloth fabrics, but it's also used to convert raw opium into morphine base, and from morphine into heroin." Because of his cleaning and dyeing shops, Cesar could now order sure supplies of the chemical through legitimate channels without questions or excuses.

Cesar walked to a cabinet bar and took out two glasses and a bottle. Pouring the wine, he handed a glass to Joseph. "Did you ever take a good look at this place?" Cesar asked.

The apartment in La Tour was too cramped for Cesar's taste. It had been filled with furniture most easily available at the time he moved from Le Marin. Although he had copied carefully Vito Nastacio's office, he had given no thought to his own living quarters. Cesar knew little about style and decoration, and considered them inconsequential. As a result, his apartment was jumbled with provincial, prewar modern, and late Victorian pieces without discrimination. Paintings hung on walls merely to cover empty spaces.

Cesar had remained satisfied, however, until his acceptance as an equal by Fortuno Rampini and Ruggiero Volanti. During the strike he had met on several occasions in the townhouses of the other two Families. He had been impressed by their opulence. Now he wanted the same.

"Look at it!" Cesar said.

"What do you want me to see?" Joseph asked mildly.

"*Cette merde!* I don't like it."

"What do you like?"

"I want a townhouse. A mansion."

"You can afford one," Joseph said.

"Certainly I can! No more dumps like this. I want it done right —by some *mec* who knows what he's doing!"

"There are plenty of professional decorators for hire."

"And in a good neighborhood," Cesar said. "A place with éclat. I want the best!" A heavy gold signet ring glittered on Cesar's finger. On it was the Moor's head crest of Corsica. It was also the insignia of the Unione Corse—worn only by the *patriarches*.

Joseph finished his glass of wine. Placing the glass on the table, he said, "I'll see what I can find."

Chapter 22

Cesar stared from the window of the plane on the flight from Athens. Beneath lay Turkey—the end of Europe and the beginning of Asia. The DC-3 prepared to land at Istanbul where the two worlds met. Despite his wealth and growing power, Cesar had never been out of France; never, for that matter, been farther than a hundred kilometers from Marseilles, with the exception of Corsica. From the viewpoint of an eagle, he watched the unfolding scene below. Istanbul stood on a great promontory jutting out into the Sea of Marmora—the Bosporus on the east, and the Golden Horn, an inlet, on the north. The city was surrounded by water on all sides except the west, where an ancient and lofty double wall, four miles in length, stretched across the promontory.

Minarets rose from hundreds of mosques, silhouetted against the sky in the heart of Stamboul, the old city. Wide boulevards slashed through ancient districts of narrow, dark, ill-paved, tortuous streets. Great modern buildings stood high in Beyoglu, the newer quarter, and in Taksim Square, its center. On the extreme point of the promontory glistened the elegant Seraglio, the former palace of sultans, with its lovely pavilions, gardens, and groves.

Cesar passed through customs without trouble. With him were Franco and Beni Turnella, two of the original *casseurs* at the Le Marin. Both were now *picciotti*. All three traveled

179

with false papers supplied by Luigi Venito. Cesar would have preferred to bring Gio and Anse, but the former's size and the later's color made them too easily identifiable. While the Turkish police were lax in multitudinous ways, they were strict in many others and were considered tough by the underworld. Cesar wanted his trip to Istanbul kept secret; he wished for no hangups at entry, or to be kept under surveillance while going about his business.

With his two bodyguards, Cesar checked into the Garden—an older Turkish hotel catering to a semi-European trade—and took a suite of rooms on the sixth floor. A balcony overlooked the Bosporus. Franco and Turnella, with the enthusiasm of tourists, ordered a supply of *lokum*, Turkish Delight, in all its fabled gooey glory, and a bottle of *arraik*. Cesar sprawled out in an overstuffed chair and watched the two men gorge themselves with sweets, washing down the *lokum* with the fiery liquor.

"Franco," Cesar said to the ex-paratrooper, "you speak some English, don't you?"

"Not much. A little. From the army."

"There's a bar called the Ekos. Find it. Contact an American who hangs out there. His name is Augie. I want to talk to him."

Franco nodded and stood up. "Good as done," he said. He strolled toward the door.

Cesar had not risked bringing weapons through customs. He told Turnella, "We might need *flingues*. See what you can find."

"Sure," said Beni.

"Don't raise suspicions. If they're too hard to come by, we'll settle for knives."

Alone in the small drawing room, Cesar strolled to the balcony. In the distance the river was filled with sleek white yachts from the oil-rich countries of the Near East. After a few moments, Cesar no longer saw them. He was deep in thought, again considering the reasons for this trip to Istanbul: the heroin lab at the farm, under Williot's skill, was operating successfully. But it took kilos of raw opium to produce a few grams of pure heroin. Securing delivery of sufficient amounts of the crude black opium, or partly refined crystalline morphine, was haphazard and uncertain. For maximum efficiency and highest profit, the lab must operate at capacity around the clock. Cesar was in Istanbul to establish an adequate and constant source of supply. For centuries, Turkish opium held the reputation for being the world's finest.

The underworld of Marseilles rumbled that a shadowy American living in Istanbul arranged shipments of opium around the world to gangs in Italy, France, and America. Luigi Venito attempted to get details about him, but details were few. He was known only as Augie, and he frequented the Ekos bar; no deal was too large for him to handle. Before traveling to Istanbul, Cesar attempted to contact Augie, but without success. Now Cesar waited for Franco to locate the American.

Franco was trying. He walked down steps to the Ekos, a cellar café in the Golden Horn—the port of the city with vessels from the Black Sea, Mediterranean, and oceans of the world crowding its wharves. Franco approached the bar. A dark-haired barmaid spoke broken English and took his order. Holding his drink, Franco looked around. The bar appeared to be empty except for two seamen sitting over beers in a corner. The barmaid appeared interested in Franco —if only to break the monotony. Franco smiled and asked her name. She told him; with her heavy accent, it sounded vaguely like "Sheri'a." He promptly called her Cheri. They talked for some time, slowly, hesitant, grappling with their strange English. Finally Franco said, "A man. Very much I want to see. Much business. Name is Augie. He is *Américain.*"

Cheri shrugged. "Perhap he come here. Perhap he no come."

"You know of him?"

"I know of many men," Cheri said.

"But no many of the *Americains.*"

Cheri carefully studied Franco's rugged face. She lifted his drink, wiping away the wetness on the bar. "Perhap I know man who know *l'Americain.*" She struggled with her vocabulary. "No promise he know *l'Americain.*"

Franco grinned. Cheri's broad face smiled back. "Where is this man?" he asked. "Much business. *Très formidable!* Important!"

Cheri called to the men at the table. She began speaking rapidly in utterly uncomprehensible Turkish. One of them left the table and went out the door. "Wait," Cheri told Franco. "We see."

In ten minutes the seaman returned with another man. Somewhat nervously, Cheri introduced him to Franco as Elias. The Greek spoke French, which eased the communication strain on Franco. "Why do you want to see the American?" Elias asked. A gold front tooth gleamed.

"Skag," Franco said bluntly. "A lot of it."

"For you?" Elias was skeptical. "You have the *blé?*"

"My boss. *Le Patriarche* of the Sati."

"Let's take a walk," Elias said.

They left the Ekos and walked to another café, a place called the Valjac. It was noisy, in a babble of a dozen tongues and a blasting jukebox, and jammed with seamen and waterfront characters; street-walkers hustled customers among the boisterous drinkers. A fight was in progress when Franco and Elias arrived. Two bloody combatants were tossed sprawling to the street while Franco and his companion found a table. Franco ordered *arraik.* Elias drank *ouzo.*

"How much does your boss want to buy?" Elias asked.

"Plenty. He'll tell Augie when they meet."

"Who sent you to the American?"

"I don't know. Have Augie ask *Le Patriarche,*" Franco said coldly.

Elias ate a tiny red tomato, took a bite from a sliver of goat cheese, and washed it down with *ouzo.* "Don't get pissed off, I got to pass this on . . ."

"Look, I got orders, too. I don't ask questions. All I know is I'm to set up a meet with Augie." Franco's voice was tight. "You can bet your sweet ass it'll be worth his time."

"Have to use a phone," Elias said, and left the café. He reappeared in a short time and sat down. The two men continued drinking. The stream of liquor warmed up their relationship; Elias became more cordial. At six o'clock he placed another telephone call and returned to the table, smiling. "Go on back to the hotel," the Greek said. "Tell your boss he's going to get a telephone call in about an hour."

Early darkness filled the hotel suite when the call came through. Cesar answered it. "You the boss?" It was Elias' voice.

"Yes," said Cesar.

"It's fixed at nine tonight. I'll pick you up . . . front of the hotel."

"All right," Cesar agreed.

"You come alone," Elias warned.

Cesar hesitated. "Why?"

"Either you do it, or you don't," Elias said.

"Alone. Nine o'clock." Cesar hung up the phone.

"You're not going to do it?" Franco asked, surprised.

"Set me up? What reason would he have?" Cesar shook his head.

"Maybe I can cop a car. We'll tail you," Beni said.

Cesar gave a short laugh. "In a strange town? He'd lose you whenever he wanted. He's probably expecting it, anyway. If he catches you tailing me, it'll mess up the meet."

"At least you'll take along a *flingue*." Beni had bought two guns and three knives during the afternoon.

"No. No knife, either. I'll be searched." Cesar left the two *picciotti* and went into his bedroom. He changed his clothes, donning a plain dark flannel suit, dark shoes, a white shirt, and a thin black tie. He selected solid gold cufflinks, collar pin, and tie clasp. Finally, he picked up a handmade black Borsalino hat. He put it on, snapping down the brim in front. He thought: "Christ, except for the collar, I look like a priest!"

Promptly at nine, a small Fiat pulled up in front of the Garden. Cesar was waiting. The Greek swung open the door and said, "I'm Elias."

Cesar, with only the briefest glance at the Greek, sat down beside him. Elias looked him over carefully. "Here. Put these on," Elias said, handing Cesar a pair of glasses with black smoked lenses.

Cesar adjusted the glasses to his face. The lenses were a blindfold, filtering out the street entirely except for tiny points of light. Elias pulled the car away from the curb and started down the street. From the sides of his eyes, behind the large frames, Cesar was able to see blurs of lighted signs passing swiftly in the night, but he could not identify them. Elias pursued a tortuous course, winding through streets, turning often, sometimes stopping to back and reverse his trail. Cesar eventually lost all sense of direction and was unable to distinguish the areas through which they drove. They continued in silence, the sounds of traffic thinning out, and Cesar guessed they were in a residential area when the car finally stopped.

"Don't take 'em off," Elias warned, helping Cesar out of the car. The Greek quickly brushed down Cesar's clothes for concealed weapons, then led him by the arm up a low flight of stone steps. Elias knocked. Cesar stood blindly until he heard a door open. Elias conducted him inside and the door closed behind them. "Okay," an American voice said.

Cesar took off the glasses. He stood in a hallway that ran the length of a long, narrow house. All the rooms on the main floor opened off it from the right. Old-fashioned, ornamented brass fixtures cast a glow of light. A high, intricately carved wooden screen, layed with gold leaf, partly blocked the view of the farthest end of the hall.

A short, swarthy American extended a hand. "Nice to meet you," he said.

"Pardon me. I speak no English," Cesar replied slowly.

"Dago, then?" Augie asked in Italian. "Hell, learned to speak it when I was a kid in Brooklyn. My old man and lady come from the old country." He paused, then started down the hall. "Come in . . ." he said over his shoulder.

Cesar followed, entering a room with a superb Turkish carpet. Although furnished with heavy American and European furniture, including a large radio and phonograph, it was filled with Near East bric-a-brac—a copper coffee server, Kutahya ceramics, a heavy brass brazier, a painted tin trunk, burnished ashtrays, small figures of silver camels, and tiny ornamental dolls. An icon and a number of old Turkish water colors hung on the walls. "Drink?" Augie asked. When Cesar declined, the American said, "How about some coffee? Learned to like the stuff." He turned to Elias. "Get some," he ordered.

Cesar sat down and lit a long black cigarette. "You've checked me out?"

"Sure." Augie grinned. "That's what's kept me so long. Gotta be careful. No law against growing the stuff, but the government buys the whole goddamn crop. Raises hell when the son-of-a-bitchin' peasants sell to outsiders. Lose their shitty taxes."

"I know," Cesar said.

"Crummy bastards shoot you for anything in this country. Tough."

Elias came in with two tiny cups of very sweet, very thick coffee and placed them on a table. He sat down in a chair slightly behind Cesar. Cesar politely took a sip. "I didn't make this trip to talk about politics," he said.

184

"Okay. Let's talk business."

"We'll start with a thousand kilos a month. Top grade, raw black."

"How long?"

"Year round. Later I'll want more."

Augie gazed thoughtfully into the thick black depths of his cup. "Paid where . . .?"

"Here. Istanbul on delivery."

"That's a lot of shit to haul away."

"I'll haul it," Cesar said quietly.

"What'll you pay in?"

"Any currency you want." Cesar flicked an ash into a tray. "But you guarantee delivery to us . . . and at a fixed price. Same every month."

"That's tough to do. Prices don't stay steady. You know—up and down. Cops . . . weather . . . how big a crop . . ."

"We'll agree on a price, a fair one—high enough you can stay inside it."

Augie shifted uneasily. "That'll depend on the price."

"We'll discuss it now."

"I got to think about it."

Cesar stared at Augie in the silence that followed. Then he said, "Too big a deal? I heard you can handle anything."

"Hell, yes! I can handle it," Augie said expansively. "But I got a lot of things I got to figure out first." His eyes flicked toward a desk, then away.

"Figure them," Cesar said.

"A day . . . or two. What's the difference?"

"None," Cesar said, rising from his chair, "so long as I get this settled." He nodded to Elias. "Take me back to the hotel."

"I'll call you," Augie said.

Cesar walked to the front of the hall. "Put on them glasses 'fore we go out," Elias spoke up.

Cesar shrugged. He took out the glasses, fumbling them. They fell to the floor beside a gas meter set beside the front door. Cesar leaned over to pick them up. Straightening, he put them on. Again, Elias grasped his arm, led him outside, and helped him into the car. They drove back to the Garden without speaking a word.

Inside his suite, Cesar ordered dinner sent up. He and the two *picciotti* ate kebab from copper skewers and rice wrapped in grape leaves. Cesar remained deep in thought through the meal. When it was over, he said, "Augie's a *filou*. I don't trust the bastard."

"Why not?" Franco asked.

"He's willing to hear about the deal, but he can't discuss the most important thing. Price! Why? Because he's got to go to somebody else first! I don't do business with people I don't know."

"How're you going to find out?"

"He has some kind of records in his desk. I'm going to see them."

Beni Turnella said, "I could lift 'em, maybe. But where's the goddamned desk? You don't even know where the bastard lives."

"We can find out," Cesar said calmly. His gaze rested lazily on his two bodyguards as if only partly seeing them. "I got the number on the gas meter in his house. Tomorrow you *mecs* are going to find out the address."

Chapter 23

Money found its way through the hands of the Garden Hotel's hall porter, a Turk named Emin, and passed through two intermediaries until some of it arrived at the desk of a minor official at the Istanbul gas company. The registration number of the meter in Augie's house, in the company's files, was checked and its location fixed.

That night Franco knocked on the door of the residence. Elias opened it. His mouth gaped with surprise. "How'd you . . .?" he started to ask.

Franco's gun nuzzled into the Greek's belly. "Shut up," he said. He peered past Elias; the hall was empty. Shoving the door open further, he nodded briskly. Cesar detached himself from the shadows of the street and climbed the low front steps. He was followed by Turnella. They entered the house, and the heavy front door closed behind them. "Keep him here," Cesar told Franco. "Look through the rest of the house," he ordered Turnella, and started toward the living room.

Augie, disturbed by the slight commotion in the hall, was rising from his desk when Cesar entered. When he saw Cesar, the American scrambled quickly to his feet. "What the hell!" he demanded angrily.

"Sit down," Cesar said. "You didn't call. Maybe you're not interested."

"I said I got to see about it. Take a little time." Augie seated himself behind his desk, eyes wary.

"You've had enough. What about it?" Cesar remained standing a short distance in front of the American.

"I still need more . . ."

"You don't have the skag," Cesar said. "It's too big a deal for you. But you're stalling, trying to cut yourself in, take a free ride."

"Look," Augie said, his anger again rising, "who the hell you think you're telling what to do!"

"Do you take me for a fool? Anyone can see you're laying the stuff off for somebody else. I want to know who!"

"Go shit in your hat!" Augie yanked open the drawer and his hand snatched at a .38 as Cesar coiled.

Cesar's arm flashed across the desk. His knife slashed deep into Augie's neck. Clutching at his throat, the American partly rose from his chair, then slumped forward on his desk. His face lay in a widening stain of blood. Then, very slowly, he rolled off his chair and thudded to the floor.

Cesar leaned over and wiped his blade on Augie's shirt. He returned it to a sheath strapped to his arm beneath his coat. Wrapping a handkerchief around his fingers to prevent prints, he reached into the drawer and took out a small, thick, leather-bound book. Cesar put the book in his pocket and picked up Augie's revolver, carrying it in his wrapped hand.

Returning to the hall, Cesar found Franco guarding Elias. Beni Turnella stood nearby. "Place is empty," Turnella said. Cesar nodded and handed Augie's revolver to Franco.

"Use this," Cesar said, his opaque stare fixed on Elias.

"Hey, wait!" Elias took a step forward. Turnella grabbed him by the arm and shoved him face to the wall. Franco quickly placed the .38 against the back of Elias' head and pulled the trigger. The slug traveled through the Greek's head, splattering membranes and blood against the plaster. While the fading reverberations of the shot lingered in the hall, Franco wiped the gun clean and dropped it beside the body of Elias. "Let's go," Cesar said. The three men left the house.

They made no effort to find a taxi, but walked through the dark streets of the city until, two hours later, they reached the Garden.

They avoided the lobby, slipping into the hotel by a side entrance and climbing the stairs back to their suite. They poured themselves a drink of brandy. "That girl . . ." Cesar said. "The one in the bar."

"Cheri." Franco nodded.

"She could make you," Cesar said. "Better take her."

A touch of regret flitted over Franco's face. He quickly erased it. "When it closes," he agreed.

"And the *mec* she sent to find Elias? How about him?"

"I don't know . . ." Franco said slowly.

"But you can make him?" Cesar asked.

"Yes."

"Then he can make you." Cesar turned to speak to Beni. "Go with Franco. That *mec's* probably there all the time. Part of the setup to make contacts. Take him out, too, along with the *nana.*"

The two *picciotti* left the suite. Cesar opened Augie's notebook and began to study it. It was filled with pages of numbers—numbers, nothing else:

47, 187, 22

53, 634, 133

74, 235, 274

65, 381, 45

19, 348, 186

The first two digits appeared many times, as well as many other two-number combinations. But the second three digits varied, as did the final figures, which ranged from two to four numerals. Cesar decided it was a code . . . simple, perhaps, but effective. The first two numbers designated a buyer or destination, the next series listed the amount sent, and the final numbers were the date. He figured that the entire series of 47, 187, 22 probably broke down to mean:

47 = Naples, Palermo, Marseilles, etc.

187 = 187 kilos of skag

22 = February 2nd

Toward the back of the book was a second section with a different code. The same identification numbers were used, but the second series differed. Cesar found 47,555, or 53,2011, and 74,725. These figures, Cesar thought, designated payment from the buyer: number 47 paid 555 . . . hundreds, thousands, of what? Dollars, pounds, Swiss francs, Turkish lira? Cesar did not know, and was not especially interested. The total amount of all sales ran to a staggering sum in any or all currencies.

Augie's book proved conclusively to Cesar that the American had been either a front or a figurehead. Someone else took the vast amounts of money involved, and Augie skimmed his commission.

Cesar frowned. The book contained no lead to Augie's higher-up, the tremendous supplier. The long lists of entries, covering the pages, were made in a scrawling hand—some in pencil, others with a ballpoint pen. Inside the cover, in the upper left-hand corner, an entry had been made in pencil, then heavily marked over in ink completely obliterating it. Cesar examined it closely, holding it at angles to the light, but his scrutiny solved nothing. He had a hunch, though, that it was important; otherwise it would not have been so carefully blotted out. Picking up the phone, he called the desk. "I want to send a cable," he said. "Seacoast Trucking Company, Marseilles, France. 'Need expert mechanic.' Signed, La Tour."

Late the following afternoon, Luigi Venito arrived in Istanbul and reported to Cesar at the Garden Hotel. Cesar gave him Augie's book and pointed to the inked-over entry. "Find out what's underneath that," he said.

"I can try," the forger said. "But I'll need some stuff to do it."

"Get it," Cesar told him.

The rest of the evening, Venito worked in the bathroom with solvents and a black light. Cesar and the two *picciotti* hired a taxi and drove past the corner of the Ekos bar. It was dark, unopened. "We took 'em out clean," Franco said.

"No trouble at all," Turnella added.

Cesar shook his head, indicating the driver, and set his lips in silence. They continued some blocks further, then got out of the cab. They entered a street café and ordered coffee. "Now we talk," Cesar said. "Sure there was no slipup?"

"There wasn't none," Franco assured him.

"How do you know?" Cesar snapped. "We can't understand the

radio. We can't read the papers. Give it to me again."

"The bistro was closed," Franco said. "Empty . . . except for the *mec,* the runner. And the girl back of the bar . . . she's counting the *blé* for the night. The *mec* comes out and I give him to Beni 'cause he never seen Turnella."

"That's right," Beni said. "I let him have the gun—side of his head. Out cold. Haul him down the street like a drunk. In an alley I give him this." The *picciotto* made a stabbing gesture. "No noise. Nothing. Never knew what hit him."

"Meantime, I tap on the door and the *nana* recognizes me," Franco continued. "She comes over and opens it—to tell me they're closed for the night. I push in and . . ." the former paratrooper chopped a commando blow, "that's that—'cept another *mec,* big bastard, comes out of a door someplace near the bar. He sees me same time I see him. He dives for the floor behind the bar and I know he's got to have a *flingue.* I'm laying low waiting for him to move. He's waiting for me. I ease open the door, then slam it—like I'm getting out. He pops up over the bar and I get him." Franco paused, then added. "Just one shot."

"You sure he was dead?" Cesar asked.

"With half his head all over the bar?"

"No one heard the shot?"

"I didn't wait to find out," Franco said. "Beni and me took off."

"I was only a couple doors down the street when Franco comes out," Turnella said. "And I just barely heard it. Nobody on the street at four in the morning."

"We're halfway back to the hotel before we find a taxi," Franco added.

Cesar appeared satisfied. "All right," he said. He placed some silver on the table. "Let's see what Luigi has found out."

At the hotel Venito was waiting with the book cover. "I think I made it," he told Cesar. "A telephone number, I'd guess. Hard to raise, but it looks like 47–27–86." Luigi paused and frowned. "One thing. If it was an important number, why didn't he memorize it?"

"Maybe a new number—changed from an old one," Cesar said. "Kept it till he was sure he wouldn't forget, then tried to get rid of it."

In the morning Cesar lazily eyed the hall porter, an alert, energetic, middle-aged Turk. Cesar, still in pajamas, wore a silk dressing gown while he enjoyed one of his dark cigarettes and sipped his morning coffee. He tried to make up his mind how far the porter, Emin, could be trusted. Emin had set in motion the procedure necessary to secure Augie's address from the numbered gas meter; whether the Turk knew about the two murders there, Cesar did not know. Or, if the fellow knew, did Emin connect them with the hotel guests? It was possible the police had not yet made the news public and the hall porter was still in the dark. Like most hall porters, Emin was shrewd and knowledgeable—qualities necessary to survive in his business. It was not improbable that Emin was on the payroll of the police; many were. Fortunately, informers could be bought both ways, with the party offering the most money being the more successful. Cesar needed a man who knew his way around Istanbul, one who could perform small but necessary services and keep his mouth shut. And speaking of mouths reminded Cesar that he also needed a translator. The utterly confounding sounds of the Turkish language fell strangely on his European ear. Emin was in command of half a dozen languages, possibly more, and fluent in them all.

Emin, summoned to Cesar's suite, smiled ingratiatingly in his dark blue jacket faced with red and laced with gold braid. With a slight bow, he said, *"M'sieur,* at your service."

Cesar applied both the carrot and the stick to the situation. With the gesture of a grand *cavaliere,* Cesar took a thick roll of bills from the pocket of his gown and casually handed several of large denominations to Emin. "I appreciate good service," he said.

Emin looked at the bills with pleased surprise. "Thank you, *M'sieur.* A thousand thanks."

"It's nothing." Cesar was indifferent. "I don't expect something for nothing." He handed his cup to Franco, who quickly filled it with steaming coffee. "We're French businessmen here on business," he went on, explaining to the hall porter. "We don't want our business known . . . to anyone . . . as there are competitors who would like to take our business away."

"I understand, *M'sieur.*" Emin put the bills in his pocket.

"We stand to make money—eventually—if we're successful. We're strangers in this city. A little help, now and then, will not be forgotten." Cesar smiled. "For instance, when we leave, you could arrange to drive us to the airport. See us safely on our plane. Such a service would be worth . . . say, five thousand lira."

Emin's eyes gleamed briefly at the idea of five hundred dollars. He smiled, teeth white in his dark, tanned face. "Any time, *M'sieur.*"

"That doesn't mean that between now and the time we conclude our business here, that there won't be other payments for services."

"Very good, *M'sieur.*"

"But you keep your mouth shut, your eyes closed, and hear nothing!" Cesar snapped unexpectedly, now applying the stick. Emin blinked. "We have a large company. A big one! Friends are remembered. People who aren't our friends sometimes regret it. Even here in Istanbul." The edge in Cesar's voice was unmistakable.

"Oh, you're doing *me* a big favor, *M'sieur!*" Emil protested. "I deeply value your friendship. I'll do my best to deserve it."

"Thank you, Emin." Cesar smiled easily. He peeled off more large bills and handed them to the porter. When Emin started a polite protest, Cesar gestured toward the telephone. "No, take the money. Something I want you to do." Cesar scribbled out the phone number raised from Augie's book. "Call this. I don't know who it's for . . . where it is. It might even be a wrong number," he added, covering his tracks. "Find out as much as you can. If it isn't the right number, don't make whoever it is suspicious."

"Certainly, *M'sieur,*" Emin agreed quickly. "Shall I say who's calling?"

Although Cesar was registered as Jean Hubert Vlaislour, he shook his head. "Act as if it's a local call. You're not sure of the number."

The hall porter got the desk clerk, then dialed. After a few rings, the call was answered. Emin began to speak rapidly in his own tongue. He paused for replies, then asked additional questions. Cesar calmly continued with his cigarette. Emin hung up the receiver and addressed Cesar. "It is an antique jewelry shop in the Istiklal Caddesi. Much gold jewelry. There are many like it in the city, *M'sieur.*"

"I don't care about the others. What about this one?"

"It has been there for five years. The telephone number was changed about three months ago."

"Who owns it?"

"That's not entirely clear. There's a man who runs it, but I think

193

the proprietor is . . . Hamid Osmar." Emin shook his head. "I said I had a friend who owned a *souk* . . . gold jewelry, too. Trying to locate him again. Was it the same? No, it wasn't! Then who did own it?" Emin shrugged. "The fellow didn't want to say, but I think he said, when I kept after him, it was Hamid Osmar."

"Have you ever heard of Hamid Osmar?"

"No, *M'sieur.*"

"Was he at the *souk* when you called?"

Emin shook his head. "He seldom comes in."

"All right," Cesar said. "Find out who Osmar is. And where he lives."

"Right away, *M'sieur!*" Emin said. He bowed politely and started for the door. Cesar watched him leave the suite.

"Is he wise?" Franco asked.

"If he is," Cesar said, "he'll keep it to himself. He can't collect more than a few sous from the *flics*—if he is a *mouchard*. Five thousand Turkish lira will keep him honest till we're back on the plane."

Chapter 24

In the city behind them, Cesar recognized the beautiful dome of Santa Sophia arching against white clouds as fleecy as the snowy wool of cropped Anatolian lambs. He had grown more familiar with Istanbul and could make out another landmark: the deep azure dome of the Blue Mosque, reflecting a more intense duplicate of the sky above. He relaxed in the back seat of a large Mercedes, rented by Emin for the occasion and driven by a French-speaking chauffeur. The limousine sped along the banks of the Bosporus heading for the hillsides overlooking the strait and the shores of Asia. Scattered along the seventeen-mile neck of water were lovely villas—the former homes of Turkish nobility, built before the time of Kemal Atatürk and the revolution a quarter of a century earlier.

It had not been easy to arrange a meeting with Hamid Osmar. Cesar was almost certain that Osmar was the power behind Augie. Emin had conducted his research well. Hamid Osmar, fifty-five, was an *aga*—a feudal landlord possessing thousands of hectares in an eastern province, together with four villages located on his land. In addition, he owned hotels, restaurants, stores, and other businesses. At one time Osmar was a member of the provincial assembly of his province, which meant that he had powerful political connections. For many years he had not set foot on his landed possessions, preferring to live in Istanbul. Not much was known about Osmar's personal life; he maintained a secluded privacy, living quietly and avoiding the public eye. Land to grow opium poppies, peasants to harvest them, and political contacts to cover illicit sales added up, at least in Cesar's mind, to the man behind Augie's huge operation—Hamid Osmar. But in setting up a meeting with the Turk, Cesar had not revealed his true reason—it would have blown the deal sky-high. Instead, through Emin and the manager of the shop, Cesar insisted that he wanted to buy gold: antique gold jewelry, dinner service, coins—anything of value in gold speculation. He had finally offered to buy the jewelry shop, at an outrageous price, and this led to Osmar's agreement for a personal discussion.

The Mercedes turned off the road. It drove through gardens to stop before an exquisite building of slender twisted columns and fretted marble. Gracefully curving arches and illuminated apertures ornamented the vaulted roof. A footman hurried from the villa to open the door of the car. "Wait here," Cesar told the chauffeur and the *picciotti* accompanying him in the limousine.

Inside the door the footman turned Cesar over to a majordomo who conducted him through a huge room with cushioned ottomans covered with Bursa silk. *Kilims* of beautifully woven and designed cotton covered the floor of exotic Kutahya tiles. Brass and copper gleamed in the cool darkness of the shuttered room.

Osmar greeted Cesar in a small court shaded with towering plants and clipped trees. Fragrant flowers grew in blue-glazed ceramic pots. A tiny fountain sprayed the air with scented water. Enclosed on four sides by the main structure of the house, the court was a place of privacy, of serenity. "Sit down, please," Osmar said, waving a soft hand at a low-slung metal chair heaped with cushions. He clapped his hands; a servant brought a glass of *ayran,* an ancient Turkish refreshment, and placed it on a round marble table by Cesar's arm. The Turk seated himself facing Cesar, heavy-lidded eyes mere slits in his pudgy face. A full black mustache drooped from his upper lip. Osmar's fingers fondled a string of amber "think" beads ... counting and sorting them in relaxation. "Perhaps ... it is not too polite ... if we speak quickly of business," Osmar said in French, very slowly, with an extremely heavy accent. "As I grow older ... I do not speak too well. I forget."

Cesar laughed. "Your French is better than my Turk."

Osmar smiled. "Very good! Now, you are here. I say to myself: He is businessman. Why does he offer me much more than my *souk* is worth? I am curious. You answer my question, please?"

"Certainly. Because I have no intention of buying it." Cesar stared idly at the spray of the fountain.

Osmar digested Cesar's reply in silence. Finally, he said, "Why so important . . . to see me?"

"Because we have a mutual friend. An American." Cesar shifted his glance to stare Osmar squarely in the face.

"An American?" Osmar was expressionless.

"You haven't heard from him recently," Cesar said. "You're wondering what happened to him. I've heard he's had a fatal accident."

The beads paused in Osmar's fingers, then began to run again. "His name? You know it?"

"Augie," Cesar said.

"Is it possible I recall the name?" Osmar shrugged. "You had business with him?"

"I offered him plenty. Maybe he had other ideas."

"Why do you say this to me?"

"I offer you the same business. A thousand kilos of black a month."

The mustache on the Turk's lip wiggled like a hairy caterpillar. "I am growing to be an old man." Osmar's tone belied his words. "Business does not interest me—especially small business."

"Two thousand kilos a month." Cesar watched the Turk. There was no reaction. "All right," Cesar continued, "how do you like this? I'll take every kilo you ship!"

"A year's supply? The entire crop?"

"All you can steal from your government." Cesar picked up the glass of *ayran* and moistened his lips. "This way there will be no details . . . no middleman . . . no wholesaler. Cash on each pickup in Istanbul."

Osmar opened his slits of eyes. He yawned, then politely covered his mouth with his hand. "Pardon . . ." he murmured,

"Are you interested?"

"Very," Osmar said. "It is time for my nap. We'll discuss details at dinner. If you please . . .?"

"I'm easy to please!" Cesar said.

Final agreement was reached that night. Cesar agreed to buy each crop at a price fixed in advance per thousand kilos—slightly more than a ton, but covering the annual crop in its entirety. Fixing of price from one year to another depended on the quality of the raw opium, as its potency varied from crop to crop. Secondly, the size of the crop determined the amount available for smuggling. As Augie had pointed out to Cesar, the government, in theory, bought the country's entire yield at a price set by the government—supposedly for international sale of medicinal morphine. However, the illegal demand for the drug exceeded the legitimate market twenty times over. Poppy fields were inspected by government buyers to estimate the yearly harvest. The big producers, such as Hamid Osmar, bribed the inspectors to sharply reduce their estimates of volume. The difference between what Osmar was forced to sell to the government and his actual crop was what he had left to sell to Cesar. But even this was cut into by his own peasants, who stole the raw gum opium for their own use or personal resale. This thieving had gone on for centuries and was impossible to stop. Consequently, exact tonnage was difficult to estimate in advance and would be sold to Cesar on a per-thousand-kilo basis.

Cesar, or the Sati men, would take possession of the crude opium, paying for it on delivery in Istanbul. The manager of the jewelry *souk* would continue as contact man, as he had done with Augie, between the Sati and Osmar. No future personal contacts between the two principals were to be made except in an emergency. Cesar was satisfied, although much was left to be done.

Owning raw opium in Istanbul was one thing; owning the same drug in Marseilles was something else. Cesar's problem was to get it to his lab. Furthermore, the huge amounts were too large for one lab to handle, and he realized he would have to build more. But the urgent question was how to ensure dependable transportation and safe delivery of the cargoes from Istanbul to Marseilles. This required another organization—small, perhaps, but trustworthy. Millions of dollars, eventually hundreds of millions, would be involved. First, he needed a front; time was pressing and his choice was limited to one man. He would have preferred a wider choice of candidates, but he took care to protect himself if he were wrong in his selection.

The *picciotti* sat silently against a wall of the living room in the hotel suite. The doors to the balcony were open and an early evening breeze tugged gently at the drapes, swinging them softly to the draft of the river. One of the intricate brass lamps, lined with silk, cast a soft glow on Cesar, who was seated behind a library table serving as a desk. Before him stood Emin, off duty, dressed now in a shabby European suit, waiting to go home, to disappear into the shabby maw of the city. Emin sensed a hidden tension and moved uneasily. He cleared his throat. "You are pleased with my services, *M'sieur?*" he asked nervously.

"No complaints, Emin," Cesar said. The silence strung out before he spoke again. "How much money do you make here at the hotel?"

"Not much. Only on occasion does a rich and generous gentleman like yourself arrive." Emin glanced at the *picciotti*, then back to Cesar.

"How would you like to make a lot of money? A regular salary?"

"And leave the hotel?"

"Yes."

"I have been here for nearly twenty years, *M'sieur.*"

"Do you plan to die here? To work out the rest of your life for a few lira?"

"I hope not, *M'sieur.*"

Cesar leaned forward, resting his arms on the table. His face was impassive in the rosy glow of the lamp. "My business has been successful," he told Emin. "All has gone well. I plan to open a small office here. Would you like to work in it? Be manager of it?"

"Why me, *M'sieur?*"

"Because I need someone who can speak the language, someone who knows his way around the city," Cesar said bluntly. "A man who'll do what he's told and keep his mouth shut."

"I know nothing about business," Emin said.

"You don't have to!" Cesar stared at the uncomfortable Turk. "I assure you that you'll be well paid. Ten times what you make here. Every month." Emin's involuntary start did not escape Cesar's notice. "Am I wasting my time? Or do you want to talk about it some more?"

"No, *M'sieur!* Please . . . I will most certainly listen," Emin protested.

"I plan to open a travel agency," Cesar said. "We'll have small yachts to charter for cruises, for rich men to haul their asses around —if they want. Is that too difficult for you to keep an eye on?"

"No," said Emin, "but I don't think you'll get much business either. Rich men can afford their own yachts."

Cesar stared thoughtfully at the Turk, then smiled slowly. "I like you better as I get to know you. You're not so stupid."

Emin shrugged. "If I change . . . I want a steady job."

"It'll be steady, even if you don't rent out one damned boat."

Emin straightened, his face assuming a new dignity. "Perhaps it is better that I don't ask questions. I'm a poor man, *M'sieur*. My family . . . we could use the money, so I want the job. There are things I've done to earn a few lira . . . things I won't talk about. So, why not again?"

"Good!" Cesar lit a dark cigarette. "Right now you go to work for me. Quit your job at the Garden." Cesar again peeled a number of bills from his roll and handed them to Emin. "Advance on your first month's salary. Tomorrow, find us an attorney to form a Turkish company. You'll be head of it—in your name."

Emin stared at the amount in his hands. "Yes, *M'sieur* . . ." he said in a low voice.

After the Turk left, Franco spoke for the first time. "Can you trust that bastard?" he asked Cesar.

"Yes," Cesar said. "He's been around long enough to figure most of the angles. He knows he's not hired to pass out business cards." Cesar rubbed his fingers together gently. "The *blé!* His first chance to make some—and he already likes the feel."

"Are you sure?" Franco was not convinced.

"He already knows too much—if he's put Augie, Cheri, the *souk*, and the rest all together. I have a choice: rub him out or use him. We'll use him and see what happens."

"Maybe it'll be too late," Franco said.

"Never too late." Cesar stared opaquely at Franco. "We need a Turkish front. Emin's it! But you're staying here to see that he doesn't forget that he's a front and nothing else."

"Alone?"

"For now. Till we get shipments underway. I'll send some *durs* back to help you. Lay low, the *mecs* too. Let Emin take the bows

—that's what he's paid for. But you're in charge. *You're* responsible!"

Franco frowned. "How long do I stay here?"

"Why so anxious to get back to Marseilles? I'll set up a bonus for you . . . each load that comes through."

"Christ!" said Turnella. "You'll be rich, Franco. If you don't want the job I'll take it."

Cesar shook his head. "Franco's the man for here. I have other plans for you."

"If I don't like it . . . change my mind?" Franco said, undecided.

"I'll send someone else to take over." Cesar's eyes were flat and hard. "But you'll like it, at least for a while." His voice was cold.

Franco sighed, shrugged in resignation. "Sure."

"Do you want to quit?" Cesar asked quietly.

"No!" Franco's protest hung in the room. Unlike the Sicilian Mafia, who sometimes made deals with their dissenters or occasionally lost interest in them if they were difficult to find, the Unione Corse never forgot. Retribution was inevitable.

"All right. So be it," Cesar said.

A week later Cesar and Beni Turnella stopped over briefly at the Rome airport, on their return flight to Marseilles. Old Angelo Fennechi met them. The Corsican smuggler's salt-tanned face, wrinkled as a winter apple, broke into a broad smile. He threw his arms around Cesar, kissing him on both sides of the face. *"Patriarche!"* Angelo exclaimed. They sat down on a hard wooden bench in the busy, noisy airport. "I received your message . . . and so I am here," Fennechi said.

"Zió Angelo," Cesar said, "we meet here because my *picciotto* will return with you on your boat to Ajaccio."

"Eh? He's welcome enough." The old man grinned at Turnella. "Long as you don't get sick, you don't puke on me!"

"From now on," Cesar told his distant uncle, "I'll hire your boat by the year. You'll work for no one but me. It'll be worth it."

"Well," replied Fennechi, scratching his gray thatch, "that's as it should be. I'm fed up with hustling my own deals, and I like money as well as the next man." He squinted at Cesar. "What do I haul?"

"Opium. Istanbul to Marseilles."

"I've done it often enough," the old man said.

"Also," Cesar continued, "I want you to recruit other crews and boats. Smuggling or fishing boats . . . I don't care which. Half a dozen of them, possibly more. Good ones . . . boats I can depend on. I'll lease the crafts and pay the men by the year. They'll keep busy making regular runs."

Angelo nodded. "How'll you bring the stuff in?"

"You're the old fox," Cesar said. "I'll leave that up to you . . ."

"Between partitions, under deck planking, engine room, shaft alleys, dunnage piles, bunkers, lifeboats, chain lockers, sail lockers . . ." Angelo began to enumerate.

"That's your job," Cesar said.

"Crates—olives, olive oil, salted nuts, fish, furniture, rugs . . ." the old man continued.

Cesar interrupted. "Fine! Fine, *Zió!* Also, I'll need some dependable skippers and crews for pleasure craft I'm buying in Istanbul. They'll make the run, too."

"No problem," Fennechi assured him. "Enough good men sitting on the beach at home to man the whole damned French navy."

"One thing more," Cesar said. "Turnella will stay in Ajaccio to keep things straight . . . fix any problems you might have."

Fennechi's face sobered. "How about *Le Patriarche* . . . Vito Nastacio? He may not like that."

"We're not stepping on his toes," Cesar said. "We're not interfering with his business. No cutting in on his rackets. All we do is base our boats on the island. The boats are there anyway—so are the men. If they weren't working for me, they'd be working for themselves."

"Maybe . . ." Fennechi was doubtful.

Cesar tapped the old man on the knee. "Besides, I'll talk to Nastacio. There're favors I can do him, too."

Angelo pulled his shapeless captain's cap to a jaunty angle and grinned. "When do I start?"

"You've started," Cesar said.

Chapter 25

Following the pattern set by his first lab, Cesar built two additional ones outside the city of Marseilles. Both were in isolated areas; one was hidden in a long-unused beach villa, the other in a small gristmill no longer in operation. The new conversion laboratories were inconspicuous, but accessible to cars making nighttime deliveries and pickups. Although all the labs were outfitted with the latest equipment, the conversion rate was high—a ratio of about eleven to one, requiring seven kilos of raw opium for reduction to morphine and—finally—to one kilo of heroin. The profit to Cesar, as manufacturer, was enormous. He sold the nearly pure heroin to wholesalers, who cut it to about eighteen percent potency before passing the H on to pushers. The pushers, in turn, debased the heroin to two percent in individual doses, the standard fix.

Fennechi's fleet of fishing boats and Franco's vacation yachts made regular scheduled runs to keep the labs supplied. With his controlled unions on the waterfront and friendly Corsicans in the Customs service, Cesar faced few problems getting the skag into Marseilles.

His problems came from elsewhere.

Marseilles' heroin began to flood Europe. A tidal wave of white crystalline powder engulfed the Mediterranean countries, then spread in widening circles to the United States and South America. But it was more than an addicting drug, it was powdered gold! More gold than was ever mined, or could be mined, from the greatest gold mine in the world. The easy availability of the drug found new users; the new users increased demand; the price of a fix continued to climb because it was priceless to the addict. The market was worth millions—tens, scores, hundreds of millions of dollars. Eventually it reached a billion.

This did not pass unnoticed in Italy.

For years the Sicilian Mafia had manufactured heroin. Its main seats of power were Rome, Naples, and Palermo. From these points the Mafia directed the traffic. The conversion plants, however, were in Milan. Milan heroin, although pure, was brownish in color, and to the smugglers who took it abroad, it was not so desirable as the white Marseilles. French competition was becoming too hot. Something had to be done about it.

A round mahogany table was set up in Cesar's office in La Tour, for the occasion. Cesar had not yet found the mansion he was seeking, and he was reluctant, embarrassed, to entertain his peers in the apartment on the second floor. The table was covered with a starched linen cloth and set with solid silver service. The three *patriarches*— Cesar, Fortuno Rampini, and Ruggiero Volanti—dined quietly on the heavy meal. A chef and waitress, hired for the event, kept busy: the chef cooked upstairs in Cesar's kitchen, the waitress ran the courses from the kitchen to the table. She brought a tray with six antipasti and a bottle of white Corsican wine. The antipasti was followed by scampi. After the shrimp came eggplant parmigiana with red chianti. Clearing the eggplant, she served chicken marsala and filled the glasses with white Asti Spumante. The men continued to eat. Following the chicken came *braciola,* a fragrant cartwheel of beef rolled around hard-boiled eggs, cheese, peppers, and mushrooms. She filled more glasses of red chianti, served a fresh basket of bread and creamy butter, and side plates of zucchini.

Finally the men leaned back in their chairs, completed. "Dessert?" asked Cesar.

Rampini patted his belly, gave a small belch, and shook his head. Volanti said, "No, I've had sufficient."

The waitress cleared the table and brought cups of espresso and snifters of brandy.

"Close the door," Cesar told her. "Don't come back again. You can clean up later." The waitress left the room, closing the door behind her.

"An excellent meal," Rampini said.

"Thank you," Cesar acknowledged the compliment.

"Most excellent," agreed Volanti. He cleaned his glasses on a napkin and tossed the cloth on the table.

Cesar took a sip of brandy. "I've got problems."

"Do they concern us?" Rampini asked.

"They could," Cesar said. "Might cost you millions." He took a sip of espresso. "We're all dealing in skag. You have your customers, I have mine. You go your way, I go mine. There's been no trouble."

"Our 'cousins,'" Volanti said to no one in particular.

Cesar nodded. "My wholesalers are being hustled. I've lost four *mecs* in the streets this last month. Two trucks of pure H hijacked. Three loads of black stuff . . . off the boats between Istanbul and here."

"I've had a few losses, too," Rampini admitted. Volanti nodded agreement. "Maybe not as much as yours," Rampini added.

"You will have," Cesar said. "Our cousins from Sicily are moving in."

"We've always gotten along together," Volanti said.

"That's because they've stayed out, left you alone." Cesar shoved aside his coffee and brandy in irritation. He leaned his arms on the table. "Our stuff is our stuff! If we let them take what they want now, they'll shove us out entirely. Do you want to kiss their asses?"

"You've got more going than we have," Rampini said.

"Sure, but that's your fault, not mine!" Cesar offered a box of cigars to the older man, then to Volanti. Cesar waited until Rampini had lighted up. "H is the biggest thing around. I'm going to build more cookers. Why don't you?" Cesar paused and looked around the table. "There's enough black stuff in Turkey . . . Iran, too . . . to keep us supplied even if we had seven labs apiece. Enough business for all of us. Hell! We can't begin to handle it even if we wanted to!"

"Then why start a war with our cousins?" Rampini's middle-aged face wore a mild expression.

"They take over our skag, they take over the rest of Marseilles.

Paris, too!" Cesar said. "They'll get all our other things. You name it—whatever you've got! When it's all over, our cousins will have it!" Cesar warned.

"I think he's right," Volanti said to Rampini. He adjusted the glasses on his nose. "I don't like trouble any better than you do," he continued. "But Sati's got a point. Our cousins, once they've moved in, won't move out."

"If it's got to be done, so be it," Rampini said heavily. "But it's going to take some killing. Maybe too much."

"The Sicilians can't match us," Cesar's voice was flat. "If we combine all our *milieu,* they can't possibly bring in enough *soldati* to outgun us."

"How many are here now?" Rampini asked.

"I don't know for sure," Cesar said. "Thirty . . . maybe forty. There's a rumble that Don Bello is the *capo* in charge. But they're all laying low, just leaning on us now and then till they build up to really lay on the arm!"

"We'll have to clear it with our friend . . ." Rampini said cautiously, not naming Gozy.

"If you like." Cesar was indifferent. "As long as we don't hit any *flics* or outsiders, he doesn't care *merde.*"

"How do you plan to do it?" Volanti peered through his glasses at Cesar.

"We need more information. Put out the word to your *milieu* to find where the bastards are staying. You find some. Rampini finds some. I find some. We put the names all together and go to work. When we're through, there won't be a Sicilian son of a bitch left in Marseilles." Cesar picked up one of the silver table knives and wiped it on the cloth, then threw it down.

Rampini sighed. "Yes," he agreed. He belched again. With a hairy hand on his belly, he stood up. "That was an excellent meal," he repeated.

"I thank you, too," Volanti said, also rising.

"My pleasure," Cesar politely replied to both.

The meeting was over.

Cesar's concern regarding the Mafia was substantiated again that night after his meeting with Rampini and Volanti.

A dark green, panel, pick-up truck rolled along a stretch of lonely road leading from the beach house-heroin lab to the city. The *Golfe du Lion* stretched to the right, beyond the coast, a flat sheet of dark slate in the night. The two *bandits* had made the drive numerous times along the dirt road to haul the loads of heroin into Marseilles for distribution. The operation had become a routine so far as they were concerned. The driver sat behind the wheel, a cigarette dangling loosely between his lips, his eyes watching without interest the path cut by his headlights. His companion lounged, bored, on the seat beside him.

Two explosions ripped the night as both front tires blew out. "Son of a bitch!" the driver shouted as he fought the wheel to prevent the truck hurtling from the road. He brought it to a stop and climbed out. His companion joined him and both stared at the ripped flattened tires. "Never heard of both going at the same time . . . before," the driver said.

"It sure as hell didn't just happen!" the other *dur* said.

They walked back down the road, behind the truck, examining the stretch as they went. In the darkness it was difficult to see the dirt at their feet, and both said little until the driver's foot stepped on a heavy wooden plank that stretched across the width of the road. With a muttered oath, the driver squatted and his fingers explored the board buried beneath a thin covering of earth. His fingers quickly identified heavy metal spikes driven through the wood so that their sharp ends projected upwards to rip tires of passing cars. "Hi-jack!" he exclaimed loudly, reaching for his gun and turning around.

Two powerful flood lights blazed suddenly on each side of the road blinding the *durs*. Two shotguns blasted the night. Two *durs* fell dead, their bellies strewn along the road.

Minutes later, the spiked board was put in the back of the truck. New tires were mounted. The bodies of the *bandits* were dragged some distance away from the road and the corpses covered with sand. The truck resumed its run to Marseilles with fifty kilos of pure heroin. But the load would never reach Cesar's distributors. It was now the property of Don Bello.

At approximately the time the truck was hit, Gervais Husereau named 'le canard,' the duck, by the underworld because of his straddling gait, patted his paunch after a good dinner, kissed his wife, and left his apartment. In the basement of the building, he climbed into a sleek Jaguar preparatory to making his nightly round of drops. The Duck was one of Cesar's largest local wholesalers and he did not deal on the street. His sales were limited strictly to distributors who, in turn, dealt off the stuff in small quantities to the pushers. Months of quiet business had dulled Husereau's natural wariness. Built into his new car, of which he was inordinately proud, were concealed compartments to carry large supplies of H. *Le Canard's* usual procedure was to drive cautiously through the streets, and park at predetermined spots where he would be met by his distributor . . . at an appointed time. The transfer of cash and dope took place within the dark security of Husereau's sedan. It was a simple, uncomplicated method of distribution that had always worked successfully in the past. The Duck had little fear of a heist. Despite his rotund build and comic appearance, Husereau was a hardened criminal and a dangerous man. In the security of his Jaguar, he conducted his business with a loaded revolver in his lap. His distributors knew that he would not hesitate to use it.

As Husereau started the motor of his car, a figure stepped from behind a cement pillar of the garage and held a .38 at his head through the window. The front door, on the passenger side opened, and Inspector Roncin slipped into the seat beside him. "Good evening, Duck," he said.

Husereau looked at the detective then at the cop standing outside the door with the revolver. "Get in," Roncin ordered, and his man got in the backseat still holding the gun.

"What the hell is this?" Husereau demanded.

No indecision registered in Roncin's expression. The inspector was not yet quite sure of his grounds for arrest. He had received a phone call, a 'tip' from an unidentified informer that Husereau would be making his run that night with a sizable amount of stuff. Roncin was aware of Husereau's record and he was convinced that for some time the Duck was part of the Sati organization. But a hunch was not enough for an arrest. He needed proof. The informer had spoken with a strong Sicilian accent which also disturbed Roncin. The detective had been around too long not to know that the underworld often hassled each other—just for the sake of harassment. He decided it was worth the risk to bluff the fat wholesaler. "Head for the police garage," he told Husereau. "Get going!"

"I'm clean!" the Duck protested.

"We'll find out." Roncin's heavy face settled into a grim mask. "We're going to take your godamned Jag apart—bolt by bolt. Screw by frigging screw! If I find one gram of shit in your heap . . . then, Duck, my fat friend, I'm going to bust your big ass in *le frigo* and keep it there!"

The police mechanics found nearly fifteen kilos cleverly concealed in Husereau's car. And Roncin kept his word: the Duck was out of action for a long time. All of Luigi Venito's efforts could not spring him, but . . . to Roncin's disappointment . . . Husereau did not squeal on Cesar and the organization. While Husereau served his term, he consoled himself with two facts; first, if he broke the code of silence, he was a dead man whether he was in prison or not—and he preferred to stay alive. Second, his wife and family received handsome monthly support money from the Family until he was a free man again.

The heist of the truck, and Husereau's arrest were only part of the activity that night. *Dauphin,* dolphin, a fishing boat owned by the Rampini, cut her motors and drifted up to a small yellow buoy bobbing in the bay. Attached to the buoy by a long line was a large package of crudely refined morphine sealed in waterproof wrappings. The shipment of morphine rested on the sea bottom and was raised to the *Dauphin* by hauling in the line on the marker. Earlier it had been cast overboard by a crewman on a freighter entering the port.

After retrieving the skag, the *Dauphin* headed for shore. She proceded only a short distance and was cut off by a fast launch which appeared from out of the night. Four men, carrying short burpguns, leaped aboard the old boat before the captain and his single crewman, the engineer, could evade them. The two Rampini men were cut in half, below decks, by the pirates' guns and the bodies dumped in the sea. The running lights on the *Dauphin* were doused, the load of morphine transfered to the launch, and the old boat was left wallowing in the bay while the launch sped toward the distant city.

Cesar waited impatiently for news of the Mafiosi to come in. Luigi Venito's lines of intelligence stretched deeper and deeper into the underworld—listening for a word here, a whisper there. Squads of the *milieu* on the streets kept their eyes and ears open and reported bits of news to their *picciotti*. The *picciotti* passed the information to the underbosses, Gio and Anse, who kept Cesar informed. This underworld intelligence came in bits and pieces from the twilight fringe of society surrounding the family—the dock workers, the truckers, the loan-shark debtors, the pushers, the collectors for gambling tickets, the whores, the clerks in the cleaning shops, the vegetable vendors, the seamen drinking in the bars, the scores—the hundreds—of featureless faces dependent on or doing business with the family's rackets. The machine was as efficient as a formal military apparatus gleaming intelligence by moving in the shadows. Dealing in whispers, the apparatus was invisible because it was there and was accepted, which also meant it was unseen.

And while the Sati used its resources to locate the infiltrating Mafiosi, the Rampini and Volanti were also busy using their manpower for the same purpose. Although many names were duplicated, new ones appeared exclusively on each family's lists.

A bloodbath was in the making, but it did not worry Cesar. He was not a cruel man; rather, he was unaware—or uncomprehending—of physical pain and human suffering. Violence and death existed in this world and always had—from the peasants' fields to the squalid streets of the cities into the palaces of presidents and kings. The fit survived, the others fell. What difference if they fell from a bullet, knife, sickness, or starvation?

Cesar had no intention of giving up the drug empire he was building. The traffic was not immoral so far as he was concerned; it was merely illegal. And laws were made to be broken if a man were clever enough, or strong enough, to break them. Cesar did not use drugs and regarded heads who did with contempt. A man or woman who gave up his freedom for a life of slavery to H was not only stupid, but weak. And Cesar disdained weakness, any weakness. But out there . . . in France, Europe, around the world . . . existed a large market for the deadly wares he sold. If Cesar did not sell his heroin to it, someone else would. Cesar's amorality was simple: He supplied an existing demand.

Let those who would try to stop him beware! From the earliest days when he set foot in Marseilles, his fortunes had risen. Slowly at first, then soaring until he commanded wealth and power comparable to few others. He sometimes amused himself with a parallel to the Bonapartes. When they left Corsica, the family first settled in Marseilles. For a long time they lived on the border of poverty. Madame Bonaparte, Napoleon's mother, had to do the menial housework herself. Napoleon's sisters, all future queens of Europe, were gamins in the streets. Years later, after the rise and fall of the Empire, one of the sisters defended her brother: "I'll never let anyone speak ill about a man without whom I should have been selling oranges on the quays of Ajaccio."

No one would force Cesar to peddle oranges . . . not so long as there was heroin to sell.

The lists of the proscribed Mafiosi grew. Cesar held strategy meetings with his two lieutenants, Gio and Anse, in the privacy of his apartment. La Tour's thick walls had been turned into an impregnable fortress. Four *mecs* slept in the downstairs dormitory; a fifth occupied the guest bedroom, behind the apartment on the second floor. Guards were posted around the clock at the front and rear entrances to the building.

Gio, angry and impatient, demanded, "How much longer you going to wait? They're hustling us hard! We're losing two or three *mecs* nearly every week."

"Yeah," Anse agreed. "They been hitting our trucks, muscling our dealers, cutting in everywhere. Our *mecs* don't like it."

"I don't either," Cesar told his underbosses.

"Then what're we waiting for?" Gio asked again.

Cesar pointed to the list. It was divided into two columns of names. He pointed to the first column. "You sure of these?" he asked.

Anse nodded. "All twenty-seven of 'em."

"These others?" Cesar indicated the second column, which listed an additional seventeen names.

"Sicilians . . . Neapolitans . . . and French," Anse said. "Not so certain. Maybe yes, maybe no. But they sure got contacts with the Dago bastards."

Cesar was thoughtful. Don Bello had brought many of his own *soldati* with him; he had recruited other *casseurs* among the French criminals in Marseilles. Cesar was not sure exactly who or how many were hired guns for the Mafia. Some might simply be opportunists lining up to do business with it. "If they're not with us, then they're against us," he said. "We'll take them out, too." He lit a brown cigarette. "You know where to finger them?"

"Most of 'em," Gio said. "They've got *gourbis* all over town. They come and go."

"How about Don Bello?" Cesar asked.

Anse shook his head. "He's down. Deep under. Haven't dug him up yet."

"Keep at it," Cesar said.

"What're the other families doing?" Gio grumbled. "We're doing all the work . . ."

"They've got their own lists," Cesar said. "When the time comes, they'll take out as many as we do."

Gio shifted his heavy weight. "And when's that?"

Cesar stared grimly at his huge companion. "When the lists are as complete as we can make them. Between us and the Volanti and Rampini, maybe a hundred names to hit. One by one . . . couple at a time . . . it'll take a hell of a long time. And we're going to lose a lot of *mecs* when the shooting starts in the streets." Cesar continued to fix Gio with his stare. "Maybe we have friends, but our protection doesn't cover a civil war this time around."

The two lieutenants sat in silence. "I'll get a drink," Anse said at a nod from Cesar. He walked to the bar, poured glasses of brandy, and passed them around. "How do you plan to do it . . ." his black face was impassive, "*Patriarche?*"

"Knock them out. One blow. One time," Cesar said calmly.

"All of 'em? Ain't possible!" Anse was surprised.

"Not all of them," Cesar agreed, "but enough to wipe out their guts. We'll mop up afterwards." He took a sip of his brandy. "Bello won't be expecting it. Not on that scale. When we move, we move fast. We cover as many names on that list as we can . . . in one night! Volanti and Rampini'll do the same." A tiny red spark seemed to flicker in Cesar's black eyes. "Next day, the bastards better be swimming back to Palermo!"

"Sweet Jesus!" Anse exhaled slowly. "That's a lot of killing. More'n I done all the time I was in the army."

Gio grinned. "I'll be getting the *sulfateuse* warmed up."

212

"No!" Cesar warned grimly. "No more shooting than's necessary. There are plenty of other ways."

"Shooting's quickest," Gio said.

"Quietly! Quietly!" Cesar warned. "So the *flics* will stay out of it." He looked impassively at his two underbosses. "If they don't hear anything, how'll they know to interfere?"

Chapter 26

The city lay in sleep. The last workers in the shops, offices, and businesses along the boulevards were long home, abed in the shabbily respectable residential districts and suburbs. The old mansions of the Prado and along the Corniche were darkened for the night. Waterfront bars and bistros, empty of customers, were finally closed.

But certain streets were not without clandestine activity.

Cars, lights dimmed, drove slowly and quietly into the Arabian quarter, into *Le Panier* behind the Quai du Port —an area of toughs and criminals—and around *L' Opéra*, a district of prostitutes and gangsters. Other cars probed further from the downtown sections in widening circles to include the industrial areas behind the vast expanse of commercial docks.

More than a score of cars nosed through the silent, deserted streets, their slits of light picking a cautious way, as if they were hounds hunting a trail on the cold, damp paving stones. Within each car was a *picciotto* and three selected men from his squad. The *picciotto* had a list of addresses; at each address was a name—or two or three. Streets were assigned to the individual *picciotto* according to his familiarity with them. In the winding morass of short streets and cul-de-sacs, especially in the dead of night without light, an address easily became a will-o'-the-wisp.

A car under the command of Galon, the *picciotto*, nosed

to a stop in front of an aged stone tenement. The street, barely wide enough for two small cars to pass, was a black chasm walled within cliffs of decaying buildings. Windows were shuttered against the night; the few that stared blindly into the street disclosed no light behind them. Nothing stirred; no one moved. Only the homeless or the foolhardy were abroad on the Rue de Peche at this time of night. Galon and two of his *bande* quietly left the car, silently easing closed the doors. The third *casseur* remained behind the wheel.

Galon and his men entered the building. They used a flashlight as they tread noiselessly up a cracked concrete stairway to the third floor. In the corridor Galon carefully examined the closed doors with his flash until he located one with an inconspicuous chalkmark checked very low on the door jamb. For days, similar marks had been surreptitiously chalked on other doors in tenements, lodgings, boarding houses, rooms, small apartments, and tiny hotels around the city. Urchins, streetwalkers, pushers, collectors, delivery boys, and countless others dependent on the goodwill and bounty of the Sati located and identified the *gourbis* of the Sicilians. To the *picciotti* and the *milieu* tracking down the Mafiosi, their prey was, in most instances, faceless. The men of the Unione Corse did not know the *soldati* by sight, and identification would be difficult. If too much time was lost finding the Mafiosi in the warrens of rooms and chambers of strange buildings, the Corsicans would lose their advantage of midnight surprise.

Thus, in a terrible way, the unobtrusive, unnoted chalkmarks became a black parody of a Passover. While the blood-red marks above the doors of the ancient Jews brought them life, the white marks on the doors of the Sicilians brought them death.

After checking the mark, Galon nodded. Planting himself solidly before the door, he slammed his foot against the aged lock. The flimsy door crashed open and the three Corsicans rushed into the tiny, dark apartment.

The *picciotto's* flash fixed a man sleeping, in drawers, on a sagging couch in the filthy boxlike room. A *gorille* with drawn gun, prodded him awake in the darkness, while Galon and his companion continued into an adjoining room. Two Sicilians sprawled on army cots were partly awakened by the sudden disturbance. They stared blindly into the stabbing beam of light held by Galon. One made a quick lunge for a gun beneath his pillow. The *dur* beside him whipped the barrel of his revolver across the *soldati's* face, knocking him aside on the cot.

"In the other room!" Galon said, keeping behind the beam of light. The Sicilians stood up and moved slowly toward the living room. "Hands against the wall. All of you!" the *picciotto* ordered.

"Christ, man," one of the Sicilians said, the long gash from the pistol dripping blood, "think we got a rod hidden up our ass?"

"Face the wall. Lean against your hands!" Galon ordered. "Which of you *mecs* is Erra and Massi?"

The Sicilians did not reply.

Galon held his list in the light of his flash, checking it again. "It says Erra and Massi. Where'd the other son of a bitch come from?"

The man awakened on the couch shivered. Turning his head, he spoke over his shoulder, his voice tight with fear. "Just met 'em tonight. In a bar . . . don't know 'em. Never seen 'em before . . ."

A *dur* snorted. "Yeah, sure!"

Galon said, "What's the difference? You're here, *mec.*"

The one who had been pistol whipped took a deep breath. It sounded loud in the dark room. He started to straighten up. "Hands on wall! Don't move!" Galon's voice rapped out. The Sicilian leaned forward again.

The third man, short, heavy-set, spoke for the first time. The light reflecting from the flash made his eyes gleam wildly. "Listen, this is a bum rap! What the shit is this all about?"

Galon did not reply. He raised his heavy revolver and brought it crashing down on the back of the man's head. His two *gorilles* instantly repeated the action on the other Sicilians. The faces of the three victims were smashed into the wall. Their bodies spun off and dropped to the floor. Galon played his flash over the upturned, unconscious faces. "Finish it," he said.

The Corsicans squatted, grasping the fallen men by their hair and lifting their heads. With swift strokes they slit the throats from ear to ear, severing the jugular veins.

The three Sati left the apartment, descended the stairs through the silent building, and went out in the street. They entered the waiting car. Galon checked his list for the next address. "Rue Chatal," he said.

Throughout the dark streets of the silent city, other cars with other squads—Sati, Volanti, and Rampini—were driving to other addresses. Not all the Mafiosi were at their designated locales; these more fortunate ones escaped, at least temporarily. Some of the hunted men were in bed with mistresses and prostitutes; the women suffered the same fate as the men, for the words from the *Patriarches* were "No witnesses." Sometimes the *soldati* were not caught unaware and put up a desperate fight for their lives, wounding—and in some instances killing—a number of the *milieu*. But gunplay during the night was rare, and the secret raids continued until dawn.

The first cold streaks of morning light found the might of the Mafia broken in Marseilles.

Cesar, however, was not completely satisfied. For once his iron control slipped. In his office at La Tour, he raged at Gio and Anse. The two underbosses were responsible for the Sati squads' activities of the night. "Goddamn it!" he swore. "I want Bello! I'll personally crucify the son of a bitch! Cut his balls off and shove them down his throat!"

"He wasn't there," Gio attempted to explain. "We got to this joint where he was supposed to be staying. He'd taken a *cavale* . . . maybe ten minutes 'fore we got there . . ."

"He was tipped," Anse said.

Cesar swung to face the black. "How the hell do you know if he was? He should've been staked out. When he left he should've been followed!"

"We looked for him all night," Gio said.

"Merde!"

"We'll find him," Anse said. "He can't get away . . . without we find him."

"Get the hell out of here and keep looking!" Cesar sat down, face pale with fury, as his two lieutenants hurriedly left. Luigi Venito slipped into the office, standing quietly just inside the door. Cesar looked up. "What do you want?" he snapped.

The little fixer flinched before the baleful stare. "There's going to be a lot of stiffs found around town this morning . . ."

"I know that!"

"Well, the fix is in."

"That's what you're paid for."

Venito shifted uneasily. "It cost a hell of a lot of *blé*," he said. Cesar continued to stare at him. "Here's the official line," Venito went on. "Authorities'll claim all the killings are sort of an inter-family thing. Strictly between the Mafia. Leave out our *mecs* entirely. That's the story from Hôtel de Ville [City Hall] straight on down. Newspapers'll go along with it . . . mostly, that is. Maybe some of the foreign correspondents, maybe some of the news services might ask some questions . . ." Venito shrugged. "What the hell if they do? Won't hurt *us* none, long as they don't have answers."

Cesar did not appear as if he had heard a word. Venito was impaled on his opaque stare. "Get your ass moving. Put out your lines for Bello. I want him—fast!"

Bobbing his head in agreement, Venito scurried from the room.

Late in the afternoon the *milieu* still ranged the streets, not in squads or cars but unobtrusively, singly and in pairs. They were sniffing out, tracking down the surviving *soldati*. In alleys, deserted hallways, dark basements a knife flashed briefly, or a short length of rope tightened in a garrote. Cesar paced impatiently in his apartment most of the day. Finally his private phone rang. He snatched it up. Gio's voice told him. "We got Bello."

"Alive?"

"Yeah. Shall we wipe him out?"

"Where'd you find him?"

"A *gourbi*—above a gambling joint."

"One of ours?" Cesar asked.

"Yeah. Le Chat."

Cesar thought for a moment. Le Chat, a bar, sold gambling tickets. Cesar did not want to lose the revenue from Le Chat, yet it was apparent that the bar owner had been bribed by the Mafia boss, Bello, to hide him. "Cordet owns the joint?" Cesar asked.

"Yeah. Take him out, too?"

"No . . ." Cesar said slowly. But Cordet's defection could not be ignored. "The swine! Work him over."

"Good," agreed Gio. "Real good."

"Don't lay him up," Cesar warned, "so he can't work. Keep the bar open."

"What about the Don?"

"Who knows you have him?"

"Nobody 'cept me and Anse. Cordet, of course."

"It's safe? You can hold him there for a while?"

"Yeah. Private room upstairs over Le Chat."

"Stay with him. Wait till you hear from me."

"We'll wait."

"And listen . . .!" Cesar's voice held the chill of steel. "You're not going to like what'll happen if he gets away, Gio!"

"He won't!" Gio said.

Cesar hung up. He had the instincts of Genghis Khan—never leave a powerful enemy alive, or a less powerful one at your back. A word to Gio, or the flick of his own knife, would remove the threat of Don Bello for good. Unfortunately, others might follow Bello's footsteps. A continuing war with the Mafia would not benefit the Corsicans. A feud lasting months or years would force the authorities to take action—eventually. For one of the few times in his life, Cesar was willing to kill through personal emotion: anger! His dignity had been hurt, his pride humbled, by the Sicilian's arrogant encroachment on family territory. Cesar enjoyed the thought of watching Bello die. Yet, as *Patriarche,* Cesar must concern himself with considerations other than his own pleasure. He must talk to Joseph.

Joseph came to La Tour. He knew of Cesar's plan, from its early conception, to oust the Mafia. Wishing to avoid violence and bloodshed, Joseph had nevertheless agreed that the Sicilian invasion of the Corsicans' interests must be stopped. Now that it had, what was the next step? Peace.

"Don't kill Don Bello," Joseph said, the figure of a prim banker in conservative clothes. "He's far more valuable to you alive."

"I can't trust him," Cesar replied.

"Use him to advantage." Joseph hunched his chair closer to Cesar, lowering his voice as if in deep confidence, although the two men were alone in the apartment. "Will you listen to me?"

"I'll listen."

"The Mafia has a far greater organization than the Unione. All through Europe, the United States, South America . . . the world." Joseph's hands rounded an invisible globe. "They have connections that we don't. They have their payrolls, make their payoffs. They

220

collect, they protect. That takes men and money. Are you following me?"

"You aren't telling me anything new."

"I know that, but keep it in mind!" Joseph paused. "Now, if you can escape those costs," he continued slowly, "you'll greatly increase your margin of profit. Agree to sell all your dope to them . . . all Bello and the other Sicilian dons will buy. Let them wholesale it around the world. Let them take the heat, the pressure . . . and the raps. You manufacture . . . they wholesale and distribute. You're safe here, Cesar. Out there . . ." Joseph lifted his chin indicating the boundaries of the world beyond, "let the Mafia take the risks. In the long run you'll make more money than they!"

"Give them a handshake and they'll take your fingers," Cesar said.

"Not now. Not for a long time," Joseph said. "They won't try to come back into Marseilles. It's cost them too much already. Make it plain that they stay out. Bello and the others'll listen—it'll pay them. After all, they're getting a good deal, too."

Cesar nodded. "I'd still like to wipe out the bastard." He relaxed and smiled coldly. "But business is business."

"And never forget it," Joseph said. "When it gets down to it, business comes first—regardless of your own feelings."

"Yes," Cesar agreed. "We'll do business with Bello."

"Two things," Joseph cautioned. "Don't forget that Bello is a don . . . he has his pride, too. Don't humiliate him. Treat him with respect so he'll carry no grudge back with him."

"The other?"

"Be sure that you discuss this first with Fortuno Rampini and Ruggiero Volanti. They helped you with this and they must be included in any deal you make with Don Bello."

"They will be," Cesar said.

The café Lis D'Or was a quiet, sedate restaurant owned by Rampini. Located not far from the Rond-Point du Prado, its customers came from the well-to-do districts below the Boulevard Michelet. They knew nothing of the owners. Rampini bought it not only as an investment but also as a place to dine for himself and a few intimate friends. The service and food were excellent. His own *bande* or other members of the *milieu* never frequented it.

The banquet in honor of Don Bello was held in a private dining room of the restaurant, behind doors, and the Lis D'Or was closed for the evening to other customers. The small, intimate room was decorated with red, white, and blue streamers in honor of France, and red, white, and green streamers for Italy. Large banks of red and white carnations and white carnations dyed blue and green ranged the walls and filled the corners of the room. Tables, arranged to form a *T*, occupied the center and were covered with white linen. Red, blue, and green napkins alternated at the place settings. The occasion might have been to honor patriotic veterans of foreign wars; in fact, it did—but the war had been a private one.

At the head of the *T* sat Rampini as the oldest *patriarche* of the Unione present. To his right, as guest of honor, was Bello Rosato, a middle-aged Sicilian, swarthy, with graying hair cut short and a neatly trimmed gray mustache. To Rosato's right was Ruggiero Volanti; to Rampini's left, as the youngest, was Cesar Sati. The trio of *patriarches* each wore a large fob of gold engraved with the black moor's head of Corsica—the symbol of their authority.

Down the length of the table sat the three families' lieutenants and underbosses, including Gio and Anse. Leaders, guest of honor, and all the followers wore tuxedos. Don Bello's own tux had been bought and furnished by Cesar while the Mafioso chieftain was held prisoner at Le Chat. Although the fit of the tuxedo left something to be desired, the gesture of respect was appreciated by Don Bello; he did not have to appear in street clothes. The Sicilian's own business suit, following his capture and two days of captivity, was badly soiled and rumpled. The Don would have lost face if he had been forced to wear it in public.

The elaborate series of courses were consumed in almost complete silence. Protocol required that no business be discussed during the meal. At the conclusion of each course, however, Don Bello politely remarked on its delicacy, flavor, and content. As politely, Rampini modestly acknowledged the compliment. Down the length of the table, the lieutenants and underbosses, as wary of their peers as strange pit-bulls, kept their attention fixed on their plates and ignored all conversation. A phonograph, in a corner, played stringed themes of Italian melodies. A waiter turned the records at the conclusion of each number, pointing up the few moments of silence in the room between selections, a silence broken only by the scraping of silver and the occasional clink of glasses.

When the meal was finished, the table cleared of dishes, the phonograph silenced, bottles of champagne appeared at the tables. Fresh glasses were poured. All eyes fixed on the *patriarche* Rampini as he stood up at the head of the table. "A toast," he said, "to the health of our cousin . . . and cousins . . . in Italy!" All at the table raised their glasses, "Health!" and drank. Glasses were refilled.

Don Bello rose to his feet. "To the health of our cousins in France!" The glasses rose. "Health!" and were drained and filled again.

Cesar rose, lifting his glass. "Health to the Rampini."

"Rampini!"

Rampini rose again. "Health to the Volanti."

"Volanti!"

Volanti rose. He held high his glass. "Health to the Sati."

"Sati!"

The circle of toasts was complete. Rampini again stood up. "Don Bello, our respected friend, returns to his home with our heartfelt wishes. May his journey be pleasant. His welcome as our guest is assured—anytime he cares to honor us with a visit." Rampini sat down.

The irony of Rampini's remark was not lost on Rosato. Bodies of his *soldati* continued to be discovered daily. His small army had dwindled to a handful; those few still in hiding were waiting for the opportunity to escape home alive. None of this showed on his dark face as he arose. He smiled, continuing the charade. "The advantage of travel is to make new friends. As I look around me, I am proud of the ones I have made. I will remember all of them warmly. The *Patriarches* and I . . . we've discussed new opportunities. We'll make the most of them. It is to our advantage to work together. Thank you." He sat down to scattered applause.

Ruggiero Volanti stood up. "I'm sure all of us have learned many things just knowing Don Bello. I can understand why he is held in such high regard. Our good fortune is his good fortune. His good fortune is ours. In the future, we look forward to doing much business together." Volanti resumed his seat while Cesar arose.

"We have given Don Bello our word. He has given us his. Let us remember that, and not forget," Cesar said. He sat down.

The bluntness of Cesar's words caught the listeners at the table by surprise. The room was silent for a moment, then Gio, followed immediately by Anse, started to applaud.

Don Bello, seated at the head of the table, nodded and smiled.

Chapter 27

The area of the city roughly bounded by the Avenue du Prado and part of the long boulevard which changes names from Corniche to Promenade, but bordering the beach of Plage du Prado, is an old aristocratic section. In it are many expensive and exclusive mansions. A townhouse owned by a wealthy, fifth-generation wine merchant was for sale. The land the house occupied was not extensive; it sat close to the street behind a line of neatly trimmed trees bordering the curbing. A portecochere projected over a driveway that ran along the side of the mansion and led to a large coach house and servants' quarters in the rear. Behind the mansion was a small enclosed garden beautifully tended and manicured, with a delightfully florid gazebo—the kind of background Seurat might have painted on a lazy afternoon in French summer.

Although the wine merchant was willing to sell the furnishings of the house—mostly of heavy nineteenth-century Victorian vintage—Cesar declined the opportunity. Perhaps his heritage of generations of landowners was again asserting itself; howsoever, he wanted a house strictly of his own. Cesar was not insensitive to his own shortcomings; he acknowledged his own lack of formal education and was aware of his cultural ignorance. In his early days it had not bothered him. But he had seen the use of money in Marseilles and he valued the esteem it established. The esteem brought a status which he wanted. That status, he realized, was based on pretentions he had not yet achieved. Joseph was content to live in a large, comfortable hotel suite, leasing a limousine with a chauffeur, secure in the knowledge that he controlled millions in his bank and accounts. Cesar, on the other hand, demanded the trappings of a satrap.

Cesar would have liked to have bought a large estate with wide grounds, curving drives, formal gardens, and a sprawling palace. But Joseph advised against it—firmly! A too gaudy display of pomp and wealth attracts attention. And uninvited attention and envy eventually brings ruin to anyone unable to withstand the prying of the public eye. The old mansion, anonymous among others, might pass unremarked for years. Cesar agreed reluctantly to Joseph's logic, but insisted that the interior be redesigned, refurbished, and refurnished regardless of expense.

A shy architectural designer, M. Alexandre Moutte, undertook the assignment. He was a diminutive man, not much larger than a storybook conception of an elf, with grandiose ideas and impeccable taste. Laboring under the impression that his employer was M. Joseph Tasera, the banker, Moutte asked Joseph about his preference of styles and periods. Joseph recalled Cesar's admiration for the Bonapartes and replied, "Napoleonic." Moutte was somewhat startled by the selection, but fell to his task with great enthusiasm.

The result of Moutte's labors was a magnificent period piece of Empire elegance. Stateliness and dignity were the main features of the furniture; the straight line was dominant, with a return to the classic lines of Greece, Rome, and Egypt. The pieces displayed large surfaces of highly polished mahogany with ornamentation either inlaid or appliquéd. Gilt and other metal detail animated the dark, rich color schemes. Round marble tables mounted on a pedestal or tripod base, consoles topped with porphyry and supported by obelisks, bronze caryatids, and Egyptian motifs were carefully selected. Beds were classic ceremonial couches with scrolled ends. Chaise lounges and love seats appeared as furnishings. And everywhere, Moutte followed classic motifs and decorations—acanthus leaves, laurel wreathes, winged victories, torches, cornucopias, and imperial eagles. Small bronze busts and heads, marble obelisks, and sphinxes stood on consoles and tables.

226

The splash of royal purple in velvets, stripes of gold satin, and the mellow luster of fine worked leather all impressed the eye. The little decorator searched the country for pieces to fit exactly into the columned rooms and circular areas of the newly remodeled interior. What he could not find, he ordered made in the fine cabinetworking shops of Paris.

To Cesar, a pragmatist, living in a museum did not bother him. The impersonal rooms failed to touch him because he, too, was impersonal. His only reaction was one of satisfaction: Bonaparte himself could not have had better quarters—larger perhaps, but certainly no better! Cesar was not discontent.

A staff was required to maintain the new establishment. Again Cesar's nature asserted itself. Secretive and reticent, yet paternal, he surrounded himself with servitors he could trust—those as instinctively secretive as himself: Corsicans. Business demanded that he have bodyguards. Gio and Anse no longer lived with him; they had apartments of their own. In the converted coach house, long a garage before Cesar acquired it, stood four autos. Three of them were for Cesar's use—a Bentley, a Mercedes, and an inconspicuous Citröen. The fourth, a Renault, was for the use of the staff. Two chauffeurs maintained the cars. Both were drawn from the ranks of the *milieu* and had formerly had jobs in the Family's truck lines. Good mechanics, excellent drivers, and tough *mecs,* they doubled as chauffeur-bodyguards.

The combination gardener-handyman was a former farmer from near Calvi, on the island, and a very distant relative of Gio's; the gardener's wife did the heavy cleaning in the house. Two sturdy girls, recommended by the widow Proto in Ajaccio, served as upstairs and downstairs maids. A burly bartender, once an assistant to Jean in Le Marin, was butler and majordomo; he also added muscle, if necessary, to the chauffeurs.

The only exception to the group of Corsicans was the cook—a thin, almost anemic Frenchwoman who, uncomplaining, spent her life before a stove. Perhaps the continual preparation of food soured her, for she ate little of the French and Italian dishes she prepared. Évangeline appeared to suffer from malnutrition, but her thin arms and pipe-stem legs moved her pots and pans with the grace of an artist.

Cesar continued to maintain his office in La Tour, but he seldom remained in his old apartment overnight. With the completion of his townhouse, he found time on his hands. A dummy corporation, simply called Marseilles et Cie, operated behind the scenes by Joseph, handled nearly all of the family's far-flung interests—real estate, hotels, bars, nightclubs, cleaning establishments, trucking, insurance, labor, food processing, and other investments. Only *tierce*, loan sharking, and drugs required Cesar's personal attention, and these rackets were again running smoothly.

Tourism was recovering faster each year, and the Riviera again bloomed. Joseph anticipated a building boom along the Côte d'Azur. Always interested in sound investments, and especially real estate, Joseph worked out a way to take advantage of a quirk in the law by which cooperative apartment houses were tax free for twenty years. Buyers were French colonials who already were beginning to return to France and were willing to pay high prices. Cesar, as usual, expressed little interest in Joseph's proposal to buy or build cooperatives in the sun-bathed strip of Cannes, Antibes, Juan-les-Pins, and Nice.

Cesar, however, was interested in gambling. Although some casinos operated in France, they were tightly controlled by the government. The Sati, as well as others in the Unione Corse, were heavy contributors to political campaigns—from the local level extending up to the National Assembly. These large sums, which often directly determined the outcome of elections, were carefully concealed in mazes of names, companies, and accounting practices. But, as yet, Cesar was unable to get into French casino operations. He had invested as a limited partner in casinos operating in England and Lebanon, but the income from these operations merely whetted his appetite for more. In Cannes were two casinos—one "winter" and one "summer"—but both operated most of the year. In Nice was another. Cesar thought it might be possible to open a second in Nice, although he admitted it was a distant possibility. If not possible, there was Cap d'Antibes . . . or any one of half a dozen other resort towns along the coast. Impossible? Cesar was convinced that enough money, the right connections, and sufficient pressure backed by naked power accomplished the impossible.

Cesar, with time and opportunity, decided to go to cote d'Azur to look over both possibilities—Joseph's cooperatives and his own casinos.

By car, Nice is approximately two hundred kilometers from Marseilles, and is the closest port to Corsica. It lies bathed in color—brilliant whites, greens, reds, yellows, and the blues of sky and sea. Nice is a lady of taste concerned less with her commerce than with entertaining her wealthy guests. To them she offers a racetrack, opera house, casino, golf, tennis, boating, nightclubs, and fine hotels. Her Promenade des Anglais extends for kilometers along the sparkling waterfront.

Cesar felt a sense of ease upon arriving in Nice. Its people spoke with a Niçoís accent, a certain Italianate quality, for the city belonged to Italy until the last half of the nineteenth century. He also recalled that Napoleon had once lived in Nice at the Rue. St. Francois de Paule, and he made a note to look it up. Cesar, with his chauffeur-bodyguard Roux, took a two-room suite in the Savoie. Their rooms, in the luxurious old hotel on the Promenade, overlooked the water. The rocky beach did not concern Cesar; he had never learned to swim in the mountains of Corsica.

In the old-fashioned bar of the Savoie, a group of foreigners waited impatiently. Drinking, laughing, chatting, they occasionally glanced restlessly at their watches. Two young couples were seated in a line at the bar. Cesar entered wearing slacks and a sports jacket, and took a stool at the far end, ordering a brandy. He paid little attention to the others until one of the girls leaned forward and called down the length of the bar . . . a question . . . in English. Cesar shook his head.

"Very sorry," the girl said in fluent French, "thought you were American."

"I'm not," Cesar said.

"Are you familiar with the countryside around here?"

"No." Cesar wanted to stare at the girl. Instead, he smiled and lit a cigarette. He had never seen a girl quite like her before. She was not beautiful in a classic sense, but she was lovely nevertheless, with light brown hair glistening to her shoulders, an extremely fair complexion, and inexpressibly delightful blue eyes.

"What a dreadful shame!" She smiled. "We wanted you to settle an argument. How far is Gourdon from here?"

"I don't know. It's in the hills behind Cannes," Cesar replied.

229

"Of course," the girl said, "but can we get there and back today? Everything's gone quite wrong. We hired a car—and it's over two hours late. No one seems to know what happened to the blinking driver."

"Probably drunker than a lord by now," one of the Britishers said.

The girl laughed. "I've heard the road zigs and zags all the way to the peak. If he were drunk enough, he should make it quite easily."

"Come off it, Vivian," the second girl said. "Who wants to see another old castle? I'd rather have another drink."

"It's not a castle," Vivian said. "It's supposed to be a fourteenth-century fortress . . . or something. The Seigneurial." Her eyes crinkled. "Do you suppose that's where the Seigneurs demanded their rights?"

"If they did, there must've been a bit of deflowering going on," the second girl said. All the Britishers laughed. The joke merely puzzled Cesar.

To his surprise, Cesar heard himself saying, somewhat stiffly, "I have a car. You're welcome to use it."

Vivian said, "Oh, we couldn't do that."

"Why not? I don't need it today."

"Awfully decent, old chap," the man beside Vivian said. "But too generous."

Vivian swung around on her stool and stood up. Carrying her drink, she walked gracefully to Cesar. For an instant her eyes held his. "If you really mean that, I'll accept . . . on one condition. You must join us."

Cesar felt a warm glow of pleasure flooding him. He wanted his words to be gracious, to match hers. Instead they sounded short. "All right." He picked up his glass and drank the brandy. "I'll go."

"I'm Vivian Burke," she said, extending her hand. Cesar, embarrassed, touched it briefly. "And over there is Sally Lang," she continued, "and Ted Crawford and Bob Miles." The three acknowledged the introduction with nods and somewhat restrained "hellos."

"I'm . . . Vlaislour," Cesar said, using his old pseudonym from Istanbul.

"Well, what're we waiting for?" Sally asked in a bright voice. "We need one for the road, wouldn't you say?"

"I'll drink to that," Miles said. He straightened his lanky frame and motioned to the bartender. "Another round."

Cesar picked up the phone, by the end of the bar, and called his room. "Bring the car around," he told Roux.

Fifteen minutes later when the party came out of the Savoie, the Bentley was waiting in the drive. "I'll take it," Cesar said, sliding behind the wheel. The red-haired bodyguard stood back, his hard face without expression. Vivian sat in the front seat beside Cesar and the others climbed into the back. Vivian glanced at Roux. "Why's he so grumpy?" she asked.

Cesar smiled. "He'd like to come along. Wouldn't you, Roux?"

"That's up to you," Roux said.

"I won't need you."

Roux shrugged and walked back into the hotel.

"Odd chap," Crawford observed from the back seat. "Afraid for his job, what?"

"No," said Cesar. "He takes his job too seriously." He headed the car down the curving drive.

"I remember, before the war," Vivian chatted easily, "my father had a driver. Old duffer named Harley. Dear old man . . . been driving Daddy simply for years and years. Finally, whenever it rained, Harley didn't want to take out the car. Raindrops and all that splattering it and making such a mess. He'd make up the most marvelous excuses . . ."

"What'd your father do?" Cesar asked.

Vivian laughed. "What could he do? He daren't hurt Harley's feeling, you know. He'd grumble—then put on a waterproof, grasp his umbrella . . . and call a cab."

"I'll tell you, though," said Crawford. "I wouldn't much care to argue with that bloody chauffeur of yours, Vlaislour."

"He's a hard 'um," Sally piped in.

On the drive from Nice to Cannes, the bouquets of mimosa, jasmine, carnations, roses, and violets filled the air as the car passed collections of villas unequaled in France. Cesar slouched behind the wheel, listening with wonder to the casual conversation of his companions. All spoke French, although the men were not so fluent as the women. Occasionally they lapsed into English, and then Cesar felt both deaf and dumb. Vivian, realizing his plight at such times, politely switched the conversation back to French.

The party never reached Gourdon. No one minded. They stopped to eat *pissaladière*, onions tarts, and drank Bellet—the pleasant rosé wine of the region. In Cannes the girls insisted that they visit the shops on La Croisette, the avenue that runs along the shore. However, they did little shopping. England permitted them to take out only £50 of currency each, and this they needed for their hotel and meals.

A new . . . and unknown . . . euphoria took possession of Cesar. His eyes and ears were for Vivian Burke alone. Her companions were merely faces and voices to which names were attached. For her sake, he offered to loan all the party unlimited amounts of francs or dollars. His offer was politely declined.

In one of the fine shops on La Croisette, Vivian was entranced by a magnificent bracelet of gold and amber. She tried it on, eyes sparkling with desire, then reluctantly returned it to the saleswoman. The price was more than the combined allotments of the four British. Leaving the shop, they walked to the beach. The sand was covered by tanned bodies, concealed only by brief strips of cloth, exposed in grotesque positions to the sun. The girls had not brought along their swimsuits and were reluctant to buy new ones. After a brief debate, they settled on a drink at the Carlton.

Cesar made an excuse to meet them later at the bar. When Vivian and her friends left the beach, he returned to the shop on La Croisette and bought the bracelet.

Late that night, when they returned to the Savoie, Cesar left the piece of jewelry at the desk to be placed in the mailbox of Vivian's room.

Chapter 28

Cesar looked up from his lunch in the dining room of the Savoie. Vivian approached him, smiling, and sat down. She held out her wrist, the bracelet encircling it in a golden pool of light. "Lovely, isn't it?"

"I'm pleased you liked it."

"Quite one of the nicest things I've ever received," Vivian said. She unclasped the bracelet and placed it on the table. "Unfortunately, I can't accept it . . ."

"Why not?" Cesar was puzzled.

"It cost too much . . . and I don't know you that well." Her blue eyes were level across the table.

"To hell with the *blé*." Cesar waved a disdainful hand at the bracelet. "I know you're not just another . . . *nana.*"

"I'm glad of that." She did not smile. "I don't think you did. But I simply won't take it."

"I can't wear it," Cesar said, attempting lightness. "I don't know anyone else to give it to . . ,"

"What a pity!"

"You won't take it? You think I'm trying to buy you? Or . . . something?"

"Aren't you . . . really? I suggest you return it to the shop and get your money back."

Cesar picked up the bracelet and rose from the table. "Come on," he said.

Vivian stared at him for a moment, surprised. "Why?"

"We'll go to the beach!" Cesar's voice was suddenly hard.

After a slight pause, Vivian stood up. Cesar walked through the dining room and the girl followed him. They remained silent as they left the great double doors of the hotel facing the sea and walked to the stony beach. Cesar stared out at the water, gently tossing the bracelet in his hand. He turned his attention to the girl. "You won't take it?"

"No. It was generous. A gesture," she said. "I suppose . . . you wanted to be kind."

Cesar turned and hurled the bracelet far out into the sea. It sailed as far as his strength could carry it. With a slight splash, it disappeared beneath the blue water.

Vivian was very quiet. Finally she said, "That was unnecessary. A . . . cruel thing to do. Why? To give me my comeuppance?"

"I bought it for you," Cesar said. "If you won't wear it, nobody will!"

"I don't understand you . . ."

"You think I'm con . . . nuts? Maybe I am. Maybe I belong locked in the *taule!*"

Vivian laughed, breaking the tension. "My French isn't up to your argot, Cesar. But why should we be angry? Tomorrow I'm returning to London."

Cesar stood motionless. Despair gripped him. "Tomorrow? Stay awhile. You . . . we . . . just got here."

"I've been here five days," Vivian said. "I've just enough to get home."

"How about the others?"

"Sally'll go back with me. Ted and Bob . . . I think they have friends in Paris."

"Listen," said Cesar, reaching for her hands and holding them. His voice was earnest, pleading. "I know a *mec* . . . a chap . . . who has a boat. Nice one . . . near here. I'll borrow it. Few days . . . a week! It won't cost anything. All of us can sail . . . live on it."

Vivian disengaged her hands. "That would be jolly fun," she admitted slowly. "Are you sure your friend won't mind?"

"I'm sure!" Cesar was positive.

"Well, if Sally and the fellows . . ." Vivian gave in slowly. Then she smiled, eyes crinkling. "I'd love it!"

They hurried back to the hotel. Cesar, in the privacy of his suite, placed a call to Beni Turnella in Ajaccio. "What's in?" he asked the *picciotto* abruptly.

"Huh?" Turnella replied, confused.

"What boats . . . yachts are there?"

"The *Seramis*. Just in."

Cesar thought rapidly. The *Seramis* was one of the yachts operated by the Turkish travel agency under Emin and Franco. It had undoubtedly arrived in Corsica loaded to the gunwales with raw opium. At the right time, it would complete its run to Marseilles. "Strip her," Cesar said. "Clean!"

"But . . ." protested Beni, "she ain't through . . ."

"You heard!" Cesar interrupted. "Is Angelo Fennechi around?"

"Yeah."

"I want him to captain her. Have her in Nice tomorrow!"

"Sure . . ." agreed Turnella, wondering how to salvage the treasure of cargo on short notice and keep clear of the authorities. "Maybe if we . . ."

"I don't care *merde* . . . how! Do it! Another thing: Tell Angelo my name's Vlaislour. And he better be here!" Cesar hung up on the unhappy Beni Turnella.

Late the following afternoon the *Seramis* arrived in Nice. She was somewhat travel-stained from her recent trips between Istanbul, Ajaccio, and Marseilles. Her metalwork was dull, her white paint tinged with gray. The main salon and two guest cabins were the worse for wear, but clean and in order. When Cesar and his party arrived on board, Angelo gave Cesar a half salute. "M'sieur Vlaislour," he said, emphasizing the name and grinning. "At your service."

Cesar turned toward Vivian. "You and Sally take what cabin you like," he told her. "Crawford and Miles can have the other."

"What about you?" Vivian asked.

"There's more room forward," Cesar assured her. In the bow was the crew's forecastle with extra bunks. "While you settle in, I'll stow my things." He gave a discreet nod to Fennechi to follow him.

Alone with Angelo, Cesar asked, "Who'd you bring with you?"

"Three from my own crew. And a cook."

Cesar grimaced. "I hope he doesn't poison us."

Angelo shrugged. "Limeys don't know good cooking anyway."

"None of that!" Cesar warned, his voice cold. "Keep your mouth shut. No remarks. That goes for the men, too. You understand?"

"Yes . . . sir." Fennechi was no longer smiling.

"They're my guests!"

"Yes, sir."

"Anything they want, anything they ask for—you get for them!" Fennechi nodded. Cesar continued. "And if Miss Burke asks questions about me, play dumb."

"That won't be hard," said Fennechi. "When do we sail?"

"Send the cook and one of the men ashore for provisions. Wine. And scotch—my guests like it. When they get back, I'll decide." Cesar returned to the salon looking for Vivian.

It was apparent to everyone except Cesar that he was in love. Now past thirty, he was moved by a new and novel excitement whenever he saw her, when he heard the sound of her voice. She was one of the generation of English women coming to maturity in the first decade following the great war. She maintained a free and easy relationship with Cesar and with the other men in her party, a relationship of equality. That she had a mind of her own and maintained an independence of thought was quite evident. Yet, oddly enough, she still held to some degree a link with the traditions of her class, although those traditions had been bent badly, and sometimes broken, by the war. She was sophisticated and at the same time a bit naïve. Like centuries of British women before her, she had a will of iron beneath a fragile, quite deceptive beauty.

Cesar put together bits and pieces of her past through the casual, often witty, conversations between Vivian and the two British men. Direct questions, Cesar discovered, were often met with polite reticence, so he listened and hoarded his small personal discoveries—more precious than all his numbered bank accounts in Switzerland.

Vivian Burke, Cesar guessed her to be in her early twenties, belonged to a Norman English family, upper class; the cadet branch and not a member of nobility. Her father, Marion, a barrister, twice had been elected to Parliament from Shrewsbury—in the county of Shropshire where the family owned land. She had two brothers, both older. One of them had been killed in the war; the second had gone to school at Cambridge, where he was friends with Crawford and Miles. At present, the surviving brother was practicing law with his father.

Ted Crawford worked for the government in the Forestry Department—his exact position was not clear. Bob Miles was interested in journalism, although he was not currently employed. Sally Lang, a displaced Scot in London to study music, was a close friend of Vivian.

Cesar thought there might be a romantic involvement between Sally and Miles, although there was no outward display of affection. Between Vivian and Crawford, Cesar could detect nothing except a long-time friendship. However, the random, almost aimless interrelationships among the group were confusing. And Cesar could not, in the slightest, understand Vivian.

It was apparent that Vivian was used to money, yet she seemed to have very little. The lack of it did not especially disturb her. The same attitude was true of the others. They had friends—many of them celebrities or near famous—on the stage, in the cinema, in sports, in Academe, in publishing, and in politics. Also scions and playboys. Some few of the names Cesar recognized—those in the theater, movies, and sports.

One of the mysteries that baffled Cesar was the party's complete acceptance of the *Seramis*. For a yacht to suddenly appear over the horizon and be placed at their convenience might seem a daily occurrence. It was accepted, apparently, by Divine Right—received with indifference, without question, and enjoyed through the Grace of God. Yet there were no pretensions, only a calm unruffled acknowledgment of a means to prolong their vacation. All of them, Cesar knew, had scraped and saved the money to make the trip to the Riviera. Heretofore, their excursions had not extended beyond Paris or, in the case of the men, to Spain, where prices were still low and the pound sterling went a long way. The four travelers meeting on the Continent was accidental. Vivian and Sally made the trip together from London. It was a coincidence that Miles and Crawford were already in Nice.

Cesar had never met a girl like Vivian. She was an unknown quality who attracted and intrigued him. Until meeting her, Cesar's conception of women was black and white. There were good women;

girls who were virgins until marriage, then they became mothers. Their property and rights vanished beneath the law of their husbands and sons. But they were *good* . . . dearly loved . . . and respected. They lived with frugality that their families might have more; they went to Mass regularly; they asked for very little—and gave much.

Then there were bad woman. It made little difference how they first lost their virginity—either through love or necessity. Once they had fallen, there was no redemption. As a matter of fact, the more depraved were considered hardly human. Heloise, for example! Cesar never considered the possibility that she possessed emotions or held the capability to love. She failed to exist as a woman. And Heloise's slightly less tarred sisters—the girls working as waitresses, in laundries, or doing menial tasks of scrubbing and cleaning, who eked out their humble wages with an occasional pickup off the streets —were only slightly less inhuman than the whores bringing business to his hotels.

And there were women of the demimonde—the divorcées, the paramours, and the mistresses. The kept women! They were permitted on the outer edges of society but never taken into the intimacy of a man's family. The women could be used, might even be cherished, but were never to be regarded seriously. They were not entirely bad, and so long as they remained faithful, they served a purpose. But under no circumstance did they approach the category of a *good* woman. No man in his right mind married one.

Vivian seemed to fall into none of these categories. Cesar's Latin instincts told him that beneath the flowerlike skin, behind the pansy blue eyes, buried under the calm breeding and cool manners, fires smoldered. Passion? Love? He sensed that if the desire moved her, she would take a man for the same purpose that a man might take her—pleasure. She would discard him as quickly and without remorse or lowering her self-esteem. However, he did not believe her promiscuous. She refused to let him buy her with the bracelet— something she coveted; the jewelry was a price of which no woman need be ashamed. Yet she accepted the hospitality of the yacht without question—from a mythical "friend" of Cesar. She could not be unaware that the cost of maintaining the *Seramis,* the entertaining, and all the ensuing expenses ran many times the cost of the bracelet. In her code of ethics, this seemed to be satisfactory. However, at the casinos she refused to permit him to stake her at play on the tables.

Cesar was confused. If he were blindly infatuated, he was also blindly in love. Love was a completely new experience to him. Cesar, with his contempt for the women available to him in Marseilles, led an almost monastic sex life. He had little knowledge of women; his contacts with them were brusque and coldly condescending. But now it was different! Vivian's smile brought new brightness to the day. The brush of her shoulder, the passing touch of her fingers, the flashing glimpse of a long, slender body enflamed him. He was filled with desire, a desire that engulfed him when he was with her; a desire that smoldered . . . lusted . . . gnawed at his emotions when they were apart.

He maintained enough sanity, however, to realize that he must keep himself under control. He could not afford the luxury of a demonstration. He aped the cool, casual demeanor of the Britishers and made no overt gestures toward Vivian. His usual impassive features, he hoped, concealed the afflictions raging within him.

There were times when Cesar was convinced that he was not entirely successful. Sometimes Vivian and her friends chatted in English and occasionally burst into peals of laughter. It was natural, he supposed, that they grew tired of speaking French on his account. But what was so amusing? Did they consider him a tongue-tied, clowning oaf . . . a love-struck peasant? If they *were* laughing at him . . . ! Cesar choked back the frustration and fury that gathered in his throat.

The *Seramis* cruised for a bittersweet week toward the Italian border . . . past the fishermen's salty little town of Villefranche, around the lovely peninsula of Saint-Jean-Cap-Ferrat, then on to Ese-sur-Mer and beyond to Cap d'Ail.

And finally, Monte Carlo.

Chapter 29

The *Seramis* returned to Nice and dropped off the party at the Savoie before continuing on to Ajaccio. Angelo Fennechi blasted a breath of relief through his nose as the fast yacht cleaved through the waters to resume her career of smuggling and prowling. He tugged at his shapeless, weathered captain's cap—which he refused to discard for a new one—and glanced with disgust at his recently purchased blue shirt and trousers. Cesar had insisted that the captain and crew spruce up and assume a semblance of respectability. Unshaven and in worn, battered deck clothes, they looked more like pirates than the crew of a private yacht. Cesar outfitted them with blue and white striped shirts and white pants, and navy blues for the captain—standard uniforms worn by other crews on yachts anchored in the basin. Although the men grumbled among themselves, contemptuously calling the uniforms "monkey suits," they wore them. Except for Angelo's cap. He would not have exchanged it under direct orders from the Admiral of France.

Bobo, a crewman named because of a large permanent lump over his right eye, entered the enclosed flying bridge to relieve Fennechi at the wheel. "Christ!" Bobo said. "I'm glad that's over."

The captain spit on the deck. "Yes, *M'sieur*. No, *Madame!*" he mimicked. "A bunch of goddamned tourists! I'd rather haul a load of stinking fish any day."

A camaraderie existed between Fennechi and his crew based on years of sailing together and participation in numerous evil adventures. When Angelo received orders to take over the captaincy of the *Seramis* and sail her to meet Cesar in Nice, he had temporarily beached the *Seramis*'s original crew and brought his own men. It was more comfortable that way. Bobo spoke familiarly in the Corsican dialect. "Dead fish or not, I liked that one with the nice tits and blue eyes. Wouldn't mind having some of that myself." Bobo grinned and shook his head.

"Keep it to yourself," Fennechi grunted, "or some morning you'll wake up with your balls stuffed down your throat."

"Cesar's *con* about her," the seaman agreed.

Fennechi lit a large, cheap cigar. He took his time. "I take it you know *Le Patriarche* pretty well," he said slowly.

Bobo glanced at Fennechi. "Never met him before . . ."

"The next time you meet him, call him Cesar to his face."

"What're you getting up the wind about? You call him Cesar."

"I'm family," Fennechi said, his voice stiff. "You're not." He left the bridge.

Cesar and Vivian sat in a padded leather booth in the Savoie bar. Crawford and Miles had left for Paris. Sally Lang was upstairs in the room she shared with Vivian, packing for the girls' morning flight to London. It was early evening, not yet the dinner hour, the sad part of the dying day before its death into night. The sadness gripped Cesar; there were many things he wanted to say. Somehow, he could not find the words to say them. Vivian toyed with her French 75, a combination of champagne and brandy. She felt ill at ease, reacting to Cesar's bleak moodiness. Her graceful hand brushed back the hair from her face, and she shook her head as if to throw off the depression surrounding her thoughts. She forced a smile, assuming a brief gaiety. "Cheers! To you! For a lovely vacation!" She lifted the long-stemmed glass to her lips.

Cesar's spirits did not rise to her words. His eyes remained fixed on his glass of brandy. "Tomorrow," he said, "I can drive you to Paris . . . on to Calais. You can catch a channel steamer from there." In his mind he thought: two days . . . three days more.

"Oh, no!" Vivian's smile faded. "I must be getting back."

"Why?" Cesar asked bluntly.

"Well, I just must . . ." The girl's tone was evasive. "I simply must, and all that . . ."

"All right," Cesar said bluntly, "I'll fly back with you."

Vivian was silent. She took a careful sip of the 75 and cast a wary glance at Cesar. She said firmly, "That wouldn't do at all."

"I want to see you again. I don't want to say goodbye."

"We'll run into each other again. Sometime," Vivian replied, vaguely. "Things—money, that sort of thing—it's getting better. I'll be traveling more . . . loads more."

"I can travel now," Cesar said. He stared at the girl. Abruptly, he asked, "You don't want me to go back with you? Is that it?"

Vivian was embarrassed, squirming inwardly at the pressure of Cesar's insistence. "You wouldn't like London. It's not like here. You don't speak any English—you'd have a dreadful time."

"I don't care what the others speak, so long as I can talk to you." Cesar angrily gulped down his brandy. "I want to marry you!"

"How nice!" Vivian said. She realized she was being rude but she could think of nothing to say. She stumbled on, "I mean, it's a compliment . . . and what not . . . and . . ." Her voice trailed away.

"I'm rich!" Cesar said, his voice too loud. He forced himself to lower it. "I'll give you anything you want. The best. No *camelote!* What do you think I am? A *filou?* All the *fric* in the world— whenever you want it!" Cesar, in his excitement, had dropped into the argot of the underworld. "Think about it! You can live here . . . in London . . . or Paris . . . or Marseilles. Any damned place you want!" He reached for her hands, grasping them as if to press home his points.

Vivian stared at Cesar, her eyes wide with surprise. Then she pulled away her hands. Her embarrassment slowly turned to anger. "People don't get married—just like *that! I* know nothing about you!"

"What do you want to know?" Cesar's anger rose to meet hers.

"I can't place you as a person," Vivian replied, defensive under the necessity to explain, as she tried to put her thoughts into words. "You don't seem to be a man of any *place* or any *time.* You don't identify with *anything.*" She forced a mirthless smile. "You can't escape yourself. What controls you I don't know . . . only my guess

. . . is your past. You should know what I mean . . ." Vivian sighed and leaned back against the booth.

"I don't," Cesar said, his voice grim although his face was blank and expressionless.

"It's his lack of emotion," Vivian thought. "He's frozen into a caricature of himself, into two dimensions. It's all surface. Yet, blast it, in loads of ways he's larger than life and I simply can't identify his emotions even when he's acting out whatever it is that he feels. He makes me *uncomfortable.*" She sipped her 75, her resentment building. "Oh, what's the bloody use of trying to explain!" she said aloud. "You wouldn't understand!"

"What're you talking about? I don't know!" Cesar replied, reacting to Vivian's frown. "Do *you* know?"

"I know this . . . there's something awfully odd about you! You speak French with an accent thick enough to slice like bacon. And sometimes you talk like . . . a gutter rat. You haven't the slightest idea of what's going on in the world! Frankly, you're a bore!"

"But you liked the Bentley . . . you liked the *Seramis!*"

"With a chauffeur who looks like a thug . . . and a crew of pirates!" Vivian laughed scornfully. "There's *one* more thing: I don't love you!" She slipped quickly from behind the table, out of the booth. "A vacation's just a vacation. We thought you amusing. Understand that! Go impress one of your . . ." she paused, then added, *"nanas!"* Turning on her heel, she swung gracefully on lovely legs from the bar.

Cesar remained frozen at the table. His face was drawn taut, and he was pale with fury. After some minutes he arose and walked to the lobby, placing his feet carefully as if crossing ice. He saw nothing, neither the stares of the bellman nor of the elevator man observing the terrible expression on his face.

Alone in his suite, he exploded.

A lamp crashed against a wall. His foot overturned a writing desk, splintering it. "Bitch!" he shouted. "Dirty, filthy bitch! *Grisette!* Tart! Whore!" He yanked the coverings from the bed, strewing the spread and sheets along the floor. His inflamed imagination visualized a naked Vivian lying on the carpet, breasts inviting, hips rounded and parted—awaiting him like the stag movies, and the live sex-circuses staged in Marseilles. Her lips were moist, panting, eager for his kiss. He covered her, raping her brutally until she cried in despair. And he continued—stabbing her again and again with both his penis and his knife, until the carpet was blood red.

Panting, eyes glazed, Cesar looked around the room. It lay in complete ruin. The fantasy gone, Cesar sank to the bed. His head fell to his chest and he gulped in deep breaths of air. His shoulders slumped. He closed his eyes. "No," he said aloud, "I love her. And not even a kiss . . ."

He stood up and went into the bathroom. Standing in front of the medicine cabinet, he stared in the mirror. A haggard, hawklike face stared back. "Fool! Sucker! Why should she love you? Pimp! Shit peddler!" Turning on the taps, he bathed his face with cold water. After combing his hair, he again looked in the mirror. "There are others. Others just like her. Even better. I won't forget it!"

Cesar returned to the bedroom as Roux entered. The red-haired chauffeur stared at the shattered room. "What happened?"

"Shut up!" said Cesar. "Get the car. We're starting back."

"Tonight?"

"Tonight!"

Cesar rode in misery, suffering all the pangs of a rejected lover. His spirit ached; a great weight pressed against his lungs until the act of breathing seemed a chore. Within was a void of loneliness and despair. The time with Vivian had been one of enchanted days; even now, with the magic gone, he wished for their return. For a while he had lived in a world he had never known. He did not yet realize that his enchantment had been based on love; what he remembered was only the glitter of the strange circles in which he had moved for a short time. In addition to the wounds of rejection, Cesar was suffering from humiliation. He had nothing.

Cesar was more crusty than a Mandarin about losing face. His pride, his dignity, his manhood were humbled. He felt he had been ridiculed; his speech, education, money, and background held in contempt. Vivian had called him a bore. She considered him a peasant! Yet the name of the Satisanni extended back through the centuries—back to the great days of Genoa, and even before. Certainly it was as good as that of some unlettered Norman with a sword, a descendant of the detested Norse, invading the shores of England!

Cesar's native tongue was not illiterate, neither was it ungrammatical. It was plain, precise, and simple—the speech of a hardy people left with little time for the niceties and adornments of social graces. The structure of his Corsican carried over into his French. It, too, was starkly plain as he spoke it, without the subtleties and inflections so greatly admired by the educated French. Unfortunately, he carried with his speech not only the heritage of the Italian inflection of his native Corsica, but also the slow, thick accent of the Midi—the type of French heard most often on the island and on the Mediterranean coast of France. More unfortunately, he had picked up the street jargon, the criminal argot, of Marseilles and unconsciously dropped the idioms into his speech. Unless he were careful when he spoke in polite society, he was a marked man. He must watch it!

And he squirmed at the other thought that crowded his mind: what a lout he must have appeared to Vivian and the British. A lout . . . even greater than he considered Gio! Cesar seldom read newspapers, unless the story somehow touched his own activities. He had not read a dozen magazines in his life. And books! He could not name six great writers among the classics of France and Italy combined. He had listened to the rapid exchanges of conversation, the easy give and take of repartee aboard the *Semaris*, shut out of the group's communications. Cesar had few points of reference to what they were saying—names were mostly unrecognized; jokes passed over his head.

But, by God, he still had his money! And money could change anything. In the light of his recent experience, Cesar modified that belief: Money could change *almost* everything!

Upon his return to Marseilles, Cesar immediately took up the subject with Joseph. Joseph listened patiently while Cesar paced the tiled floor of the mansion's reception salon. Cesar spoke with an intensity Joseph had seldom heard in his cousin. "You're right," Cesar said. "You learned English a long time ago. Back in Ghisonacia!"

"Good business," Joseph admitted quietly.

"I'll speak it, too!"

Joseph eyed his cousin thoughtfully. "It may not be so easy. I learned from the Americans at the airfield—they were all around. Then they and the British were in Ajaccio, and I could practice. In

246

business, at the bank, and in other affairs I use it every day. Just studying it a few hours a week won't help much. You'll find that out."

"Dammit, stop objecting! I've made up my mind."

"If you have . . . good."

Cesar sat down on a brass and velvet chair. "I'm not a student like you, Joseph," he said slowly, almost in apology. "Me . . . with a tutor?" His voice tinged with anger. *"Merde!* I'm not a schoolboy learning my lessons and reciting to please my teacher!" His hand included the luxurious room. "Imagine some supercilious schoolmaster standing over me!" He shook his head.

"What do you want to do?"

"You have any . . . suggestions?"

"Possibly," said Joseph. "You may not like them. And, as a matter of fact, they might not be practical."

"Go ahead!" Cesar said.

"Get rid of your staff here. All of them. Replace them with persons who speak English. Insist that nothing be spoken here, at any time, except English. And when you and I meet, we'll do the same."

Cesar shook his head. "Roux . . . and the others. Someone might try to make a hit here sometime. I need them."

"I said my suggestions might not be practical. On the other hand, among the *milieu,* how many speak English? A few, perhaps. Find the ones who do. Or simply have those here remain as *casseurs* and nothing else. But your chauffeur, housekeeper, maids, cook, and all the rest—they must speak English to you all the time!"

Cesar considered Joseph's words. Finally he agreed. "Yes. Pay them off. Pay them well—and find other jobs for them if you can." Unconsciously, Cesar's paternalism rose to the situation.

"I'll take care of it," Joseph said. He started to rise.

"Wait. There's something else . . ." Cesar glanced around the room—the objets d'art, the magnificent paintings, the fine busts and sculpture. "I don't know much about these things." Beside him on a marble table lay three books bound in Moroccan leather, with titles tooled in gilt. He picked one up. "Voltaire," he read the name aloud, then looked at the others. "Balzac, Rabelais . . . you ever hear of these *mecs?"*

"Yes," said Joseph.

Cesar tossed the book back on the table. "I want to learn about them," he said. "There are a lot of things I want to find out. But, as I said, I'm not going back to school to do it." He paused, continuing slowly, sorting out his ideas. "Somewhere there's a *mec* who knows all about such things. And he speaks French like they do in Paris—or wherever the hell it's supposed to be so damned smart. Not like we do, Joseph!" Cesar's voice was harsh.

"There are probably many like that," Joseph agreed.

"I've got to have something he wants, so he's not doing me a favor! You understand?" Cesar stared at his cousin intently. Joseph nodded. "And he can't know who I am, so he won't laugh and talk behind my back." Cesar's voice was tense. "Maybe I'm ignorant, Joseph, but I'm not stupid. Find just the right man!"

"I'll find him," Joseph assured him. He waited, then asked, "Anything else?"

"Yes . . ." Cesar started to speak. He paused, shook his head. "I'll take care of it myself."

The last floor show of the night was over at the Lapin Pourpre, an undistinguished nightclub near the Quai des Belges. The club was not a criminal hangout, and it catered—in a fairly successful way—to the flow of businessmen visiting the city. The drinks were too high, the music mediocre, the performing talent uninspired, and the decor second-rate, but the service was excellent—provided by eager waiters anticipating large tips. Cesar did not own an interest in the club, but one of the companies operated by Joseph covered its insurance—or, quite simply, its protection. The Lapin Pourpre continued to do business, not very securely, from one year to another, with an established credit rating of "slow payment."

The captain of waiters, having pocketed a large tip, brought Juliette to the table where Cesar was seated alone. That the captain was aware of his guest's identity was apparent in the obsequious manner in which he performed the introductions. And the singer was equally impressed as she sat down. The star of the show, Juliette wore heavy makeup and had not had time to remove it before the summons came. A young Lebanese woman, with a French mother, she was small, softly rounded, with large, dark eyes enlarged with mascara.

Her hair was dyed to a glinting silver and did nothing to soften her thirty some years.

A large bottle of champagne was nestled in an ice bucket beside the table. The captain quickly poured a glass for the woman and, still bowing, backed away.

"You sing very well," Cesar said stiffly.

Juliette accepted the compliment, knowing quite well that she possessed only a slightly better than ordinary voice. "Thank you," she said, exposing a row of very regular, very white teeth.

"I don't come here often." Cesar had never been in the club before.

"I've been here three weeks," she replied. "Next week is my last."

"Then where do you go?"

Juliette shrugged. She had played in most of the cheap clubs around the Mediterranean. Some were better than others, but most were the same. Usually she had lengthy layoffs between jobs. "Paris," she said, "at least I think so." She lied. At first there had been the hope that someday she might play in Paris. As the years slipped by, the hope dimmed, then faded. But she could still pretend.

Cesar ignored the lie, sensing its falseness but leaving the girl her dignity. "You sang some songs in American tonight?"

"Yes. *Le jazz!* You like it?"

"Did you just memorize them, or do you speak English?" Cesar asked.

"Oh, I speak it. And very well. I learned it in school." Juliette had learned it, through necessity, as a small girl helping tend her father's shop in Beirut.

Cesar looked around the club. It was thinning out, and he felt uncomfortable. The waiters, hearing of his presence, cast fleeting glances at his table with ill-concealed curiosity. "My car's outside," Cesar said abruptly. "I'll drive you home."

"Not like this!" Juliette protested. She was wearing the low-cut evening gown of her last set of numbers.

"Change it," Cesar said.

"Yes. Yes, of course!" Juliette rose quickly to her feet, tossed a mechanical smile, and disappeared into a door behind the small stage.

Cesar stood up and dropped a number of bills on the table, not

249

waiting for the check. He nodded to Roux standing at the back of the room. Roux went to bring the Mercedes to the club entrance. Cesar strolled to the lobby and stopped to examine an enlarged, highly retouched photo displaying the charms of Juliette. He lit a dark cigarette and was smoking it when the girl touched his shoulder. "I'm here," she said brightly.

Cesar helped her into the front seat of the large limousine. He walked around to the driver's side. "I'll take it," he told Roux. "Go home."

Roux slipped from behind the wheel and started walking toward a stand of taxis some distance down the street.

"Where do you live?" Cesar asked the girl. She named a small commercial hotel on the Boulevard d'Athénes, not far from the Gare St. Charles. The big car purred softly as they drove; its two occupants were silent. Cesar stopped in front of the hotel—an old, very narrow building with a bleak lobby. Juliette looked at Cesar, then started to open the door. He stopped her. "I have something to say," he told her.

"Yes?" She leaned back against the soft leather seat. Her eyes were fixed straight ahead, watching the night-deserted street.

Cesar's hands clenched the steering wheel. "You don't need to live in a dump like this!" His words seemed to explode in the car.

"Just another week," Juliette said, pretending not to understand.

"You can work at the Lapin Pourpre . . . long as you like. Twice your salary." He looked at the girl. She still avoided his eyes. His words tumbled out. "Get new clothes. Have a car to drive. Find a nice apartment. Whatever you want!"

Juliette finally turned to look at him. In the dim light of the street lamps his face was softer and nearly handsome. The fear she had felt upon first meeting him began to fade away. A surprising thought flashed to her mind: "He's embarrassed! He doesn't even know how to go about propositioning a woman." Juliette's charms were not regularly on sale to any bidder. In her drab corner of the world of cabarets, she had enjoyed a number of both lovers and protectors. But they had always been men she *liked!* In a way, they had looked up to her, impressed by the supposed tinsel and glamor of her career. But this one, this racketeer, this boss who everyone feared, would never look up to her. Never really enjoy her as a woman. He would merely use her—for whatever purposes of his own. Unexpectedly, however, she felt a surge of pity for him. He was lonely—even more than she. While she thought she knew plenty about men, she realized he knew nothing about women. Unknowingly, Cesar presented the greatest, the most irresistible attraction possible to present to a woman. *He needed her!*

"That would be nice. What you said . . ." Juliette still watched the impassive features of the man. "What would you want from me . . . besides the usual thing?"

"Plenty." Suddenly Cesar smiled as he turned toward her. She thought he looked almost boyish . . . uncertain and awkward. "This won't be all one way, you know . . ."

"I'm glad of that," she said. She leaned over to kiss him.

Cesar kissed his new mistress back.

But in his mind he was kissing Vivian.

Chapter 30

Almost due west from Marseilles, across the Gulf of Lions, lies the city of Carcassonne in the province of Languedoc. As a plane flies it is about two hundred and fifty kilometers —hardly more than the flip of ailerons and rudder—yet Carcassone is centuries distant from Marseilles. The ancient walled city's battlements, towers, and spires thrust against the translucent sapphire dusk like hand-illuminated pages from the manuscripts of history. The setting sun washes traverses and watchtowers with unbelievable reds, while the facades of the castle and the Visigoth tower present their barbicans to be gilded with molten gold. And above them towers the Cathedral of Saint-Nazaire, stately and the color of mellow ivory, gathering her buttresses around her in a mantle.

The lower town contains the living and business sections, with trading and wine markets spread out across the plain. The high town is the old walled city, the city of history; it has heard the echo of Rome's marching legions and the triumphant, barbaric shouts of King Euric's Visigoths. It has not yet forgotten the jangling silver armor of Charlemagne, the fanfare of trumpets announcing the pomp of Simon de Montfort.

The old city is located on a steep hill rising next to the bank of the River Aude and is completely encircled by a series of two great walls; from the top of these walls, on a clear day, it is possible to see the Pyrenees on the border of Spain. Within the inner wall are the castle, cathedral, wells, great living halls and guards towers, courtyards, and a honeycomb of small, twisting, cobblestone streets lined with tiny stone and stucco houses. Scores of persons live within the walls of the old city—just as people have always lived within them down through history. At night the ancient city is a cavern of darkness, the streets unlighted, the shadows of the buildings piling blackness on blackness. It is as quiet as if it were buried in the tomb of its own past.

Approximately twenty kilometers outside Carcasonne was another tomb—a living one, inhabited by Edmond Hubert St. Xavier Villecrosse, Comte de Tassigny. He lived in the Château Barthélémy.

A cursory glance disappointed anyone expecting to see one of the famed and graceful châteaux of the Loire. Barthélémy was an extra large, sprawling farmhouse, embellished with a low semitower pierced with a large wooden door. The roof was missing numerous tiles, and the thick walls of the house were falling apart stone by stone. Behind it stood a vast barn beyond mending, with a scattering of partly ruined outbuildings no longer in use, their original purpose long forgotten. It was apparent that Barthélémy was once a working farm that had assumed a short pretense of importance before being caught up by fortune and giving up in despair. The buildings now occupied less than a hectare of land. Gardens and lawn were long overrun, the surviving trees half dead through lack of pruning.

Edmond Villecrosse was forty-two, nine years Cesar's senior. The same basic Latin-Mediterranean strains gave both men a similarity of build and complexion. They were the same height, weight, and coloring. But there all resemblance ended. Villecrosse's brown eyes were slightly slanted, almost Oriental; his nose thinner and longer, the nostrils slightly flared; his chin heavier and a little protruding, as opposed to Cesar's equally firm but more rounded Roman type. Possibly, in the comte's background, were Basque characteristics inherited from those mysterious people of the Pyrenees.

Edmond, Comte de Tassigny, was a man of such contrasting traits that he had lost his own identity—a scholar, a dreamer, a wastrel, completely devoid of any ambition (a disease he considered on a level with Saint Vitus's dance and tarantella), lazy, embittered, cynical, and a recluse. But with the slightest effort he could be amusing, witty, and entertaining.

He was also a completely dedicated alcoholic.

A graduate of the Sorbonne, before the war, Edmond had attended a postgraduate year at Oxford. He still subscribed to the *London Times* as well as an assortment of Paris newspapers and weeklies. His days were spent in the soporific shadow of the vine, reading everything he could lay his eyes on in four languages—including Italian and Spanish; listening to the news and music on a battered radio, sleeping when exhausted, and sobering up on the rare occasions when no liquor was left in the cellar.

He lived on a pittance derived from a few municipal bonds. The once broad hectares of land belonging to Barthélémy had been sold off piece by piece over the decades by the preceding comtes. All that remained was the "château" and the attendant buildings on the small piece of ground. Edmond could afford no servants; in fact, he wanted none. Occasionally an aged farmer from a neighboring farm came in to haul off the accumulation of trash, and for a few extra francs cleaned out the kitchen. The old man's name was Boilly, and he also delivered cheese and eggs. Once every two weeks, on Monday, a grocer's truck deposited a carton of supplies from the city—mostly bottles of cheap brandy and a few cans of food. In a financial crisis forcing a choice between liquor and food, the liquor won.

The comte, one of a number of unsuspecting candidates for the job of coaching Cesar, had been located by Joseph after a long thorough search. The list was narrowed until only three remained. Their backgrounds carefully checked, Joseph told Cesar, "I think this Villecrosse is the man you want. He's well educated and informed."

"All right, but what's wrong with him?" Cesar asked.

"First, he's hard up. Practically broke. His title carries no money or weight. It's a nouveau patent—only about a hundred and fifty years old."

"From the Napoleonic Empire?"

Joseph nodded. "The original Villecrosse was a general."

Cesar thought complacently: Our paths cross again. Bonaparte's and mine! He said, "How do you know he'll go for it?"

"Haven't talked to him yet, but he needs your money. Villecrosse is also a lonely man. He sees no one, goes nowhere. He'll be glad to have someone to talk to."

"That's good. He can't gossip," Cesar said.

"There's a seldom-used dirt road by the château. If you want to fly your own plane, you can land on it—less than a two-hour flight from Marseilles."

Cesar shrugged. "Make the arrangements. I'll see him and approve them."

On their first meeting the comte was unimpressed with Cesar. Villecrosse sprawled in a huge old wooden chair filled with cushions. The square, low-beamed drawing room was filled with a clutter of dusty provincial furniture, both French and Spanish; several faded tapestries hung unevenly on the walls, together with oil portraits of former comtes de Tassigny and their ladies, the paintings obviously idealized by amateurish hands. The crest of the family coat of arms was incised in the mantle of the fireplace. The room was cheerless, threadbare, and filled with a musty, moldering odor that brought back to Cesar the memory of Col Pietro and the old house in the Valle. But where the manor of the Satisanni was a collection of the life and growth of generations, the château of the de Tassignys was the memory of the death of a family.

"M'sieur Landeau," Villecrosse said lazily, "we need stand on no formality here. Your business . . . uh, what . . .?"

"Manager," Cesar said.

"Your business manager said you need a place to vacation . . . relax. You'll find it here—and not much else." Joseph, in arranging the meeting, had concealed Cesar's identity, using the name of Auguste Landeau, a businessman of Marseilles. "Your comfort will depend on your ability to help yourself," Villecrosse continued. "I have no servants and I certainly have no intention of waiting on you myself."

Cesar shrugged. "It's not important."

The comte lifted a cynical brow. "Don't be impressed by me . . ."

"I'm not," said Cesar.

Villecrosse laughed. "That's good! I inherited this Godforsaken place from a distant relative. Frankly, I wish I hadn't, but it was going begging and I'm the last of the line." Villecrosse lifted a large snifter of brandy; its cheap, raw fumes reached to Cesar. "And good riddance! Fortunately, I have no intentions of perpetuating the fraud."

"You're not married?" Cesar asked. He already knew that Villecrosse was single and, probably, as many chronic alcoholics, impotent.

"No wife," said Villecrosse. "I have enough problems supporting myself. Which brings up the arrangements. They're agreeable enough, I suppose. It's understood, though, that you furnish your own food and drink."

"Sixty thousand francs a month," Cesar said. The sum was equivalent to one hundred dollars. "I'll come up as often or as seldom as I please." Cesar added, "There are several cases of brandy in my plane and sufficient food to last awhile."

"Ah! Business must be good!"

"Not bad," agreed Cesar, referring to his supposed business of importing olive oil and pasta.

Villecrosse rose quickly from his chair, standing a bit unsteadily. "I'll help bring them in . . . Auguste."

"Is there any hurry, Edmond?"

Villecrosse looked at his empty glass still reeking of cheap brandy. He shuddered. "Ever love fans it/Ever life feeds it/Time cannot age it/Death cannot slay," he said, quoting Sir William Watson. Cesar did not recognize the lines but they sounded appropriate—and impressive. He made a note to remember them. "I hope your brandy is worth my effort to carry it," Edmond continued.

"Carry it as it pleases you," Cesar said, "inside or out."

"Hah!" Villecrosse laughed. "I'll tuck some of it away immediately!" His long nose twitched as if in anticipation of the brandy's fine bouquet.

On that initial visit to Barthélémy, Cesar stayed for three days. Villecrosse remained pleasantly and glibly drunk. Most of the time was spent within the house; there was nothing of interest outside, and there were no visitors. The days set a pattern for following visits to be made by Cesar over the months and years—sometimes for only a day, occasionally for a week. No one, with the exception of Joseph, knew of Cesar's destination or purpose when he left Marseilles for Barthélémy. He always arrived with a welcome supply of brandy and food. Cesar listened quietly to his loquacious host. Gradually he began to assimilate Villecrosse's sophisticated views and wry values; he absorbed Edmond's reminiscences and family history; he began to read the newspapers and listen to the radio when he returned to Marseilles; he accepted the comte's evaluations of art, literature, and music. Alone, and in private, Cesar copied and practiced Villecrosse's cultivated Parisian accent. When his own efforts to learn English, in Marseilles, reached a level of semifluency, Cesar also began to speak in that tongue with the comte.

Cesar possessed a quick and retentive memory. Villecrosse was delighted to have an appreciative audience. Still motivated by memories of Vivian and his past humiliation, Cesar clung tenaciously to his course. He began to take pleasure in his enlarging education. And Edmond Villecrosse took pleasure in his brandy and his expositions.

Cesar received a course in the humanities, without benefit of a collegiate degree. He was surprised by the range of topics upon which Villecrosse rambled, and by the oddments the comte offered. Cesar, cooking over the huge old wood and coal range in the dreary kitchen at Barthélémy, expressed admiration for the brilliance of Curie, who Villecrosse was discussing. The comte straddled a wooden chair pulled near to the stove, holding his inevitable glass of brandy. He was not at all interested in the meal Cesar was preparing. Edmond paused and studied an evening shaft of light slicing into the darkening room. "Curie . . .?" he said and laughed. "How about Giordano Bruno?"

The name of the sixteenth-century Italian philosopher meant nothing to Cesar. Cesar shrugged. "What about him?"

"Bruno was neither an astronomer nor a mathematician," Edmond said. "He was a philosopher . . . only! But he went beyond Copernicus. Do you have any idea what that means?"

"No."

"Intellect! Pure, brilliant thought!" Villecrosse stood up from his chair, carried away by wonder. "Bruno was the first man to conceive 'space' as a boundless universe. That's the underlying idea of infinity!" He staggered, spilling drops of his brandy. "Infinity . . . the most majestic concept of our culture and civilization." Villecrosse took a drink. "There has never been a more inspired inspiration of man," he added quietly.

"What happened to Giordano Bruno?" Cesar asked.

Villecrosse laughed, drained his glass, and again straddled the chair. "As a heretic, he was burned at the stake."

In the evenings the two men sprawled in the living room, its confines filled with dunes of shadows piled high against the walls and ceiling. A single weak glow of a lamp, the proud triumph of rural electrification, broke the darkness beneath a salmon-colored shade. Sometimes they sat drinking and talking through the night, for Villecrosse was an insomniac. They listened to music on the radio. When the comte found no programs to his liking, he played classical records on an old, hand-wound Victrola, his Oriental eyes squinting in concentration. His tastes were catholic, and once while expounding on the eccentricities of Beethoven, he paused to stare at Cesar. "Beethoven, Brahms, Bach, Mozart . . . where would they have been without Pythagoras?"

Cesar smoked his dark cigarette. Pythagoras? The fellow was undoubtedly a Greek . . . tell that by his name. Cesar waited, knowing that Villecrosse would continue. The comte did not disappoint him.

"Back in 500 B.C. or so, here's this Pythagoras. Another philosopher. He had a lyre . . . you know, 'plunk, plunk'!" Edmond held up the brandy glass against the glow of light, admiring the firey depths. "So what did he do? He discovered the harmony of musical tones. He could produce the octave, fifth, fourth, and third. By mathematics. By subdivision, no less." The comte leaned forward, thrusting out his prominent jaw. "I'll tell you what Pythagoras did, my friend. He discovered the invisible fluid of sound!"

"I must remember that," Cesar thought.

The "rent," paid regularly from Marseilles through one of Joseph's accounts, took the blunt edge of stark need from Villecrosse, but it left the comte still dependent on Cesar's goodwill. Villecrosse had no margin to travel or entertain others. He remained sealed in Barthélémy. Oddly enough, he had little interest in Cesar—his past or his present. Edmond asked few questions, although on occasion he was slightly puzzled why a man of Cesar's apparent wealth wanted to visit Barthélémy's less than pastoral acres. In passing, he sometimes wondered at Cesar's solitary arrival, piloting his own small plane, unaccompanied by friends, or his lack of references to activities in Marseilles. On the whole, Villecrosse permitted these questions to pass unanswered, and remained in his haven of brandy bottles. But Villecrosse's alcoholic haze never interfered with his constant reading, or his charm as a conversationalist and raconteur.

Cesar inched into a life that consisted of two separate parts. He was, first, the *patriarche* of the Sati—the blunt, simple, argot-speaking crime lord; his relations with his underbosses and *bande* remained unchanged. On the other hand, in his empire mansion he practiced his English; if it were necessary to speak French, he copied the style of Villecrosse. And following the lead of the comte, Cesar's extensive library no longer remained unread.

Juliette, the first of his mistresses, was supplanted by another, then another, and finally a string of willing and often interesting women. While Cesar learned much from Villecrosse, he learned more from his paramours. To his surprise, he discovered that women had much to teach him. Often their genuine tenderness and sympathy touched him. Their circumlocutions of reasoning intrigued him. Their instincts and intuition amazed him. He discovered the feminine world, heretofore unexplored, where gentleness was more powerful than brute force, generosity of spirit was more important than generosity of purse. In that world, laughter, gaiety, the tender demonstration of emotion were not signs of unmanly weakness.

Cesar learned much, but much of what he learned he did not spend. He saved it, tucking it away in his mind; the human insights discovered in his bedroom did not spill over into the jungle world of his business. It was as if his soul were calloused by the attrition of his family, yet he knew the alchemic salve by which to remove the callous. He never displayed this knowledge, or attempted to use it. He kept it secretly buried in his own character. The old Cesar, the campaigner, the *patriarche*, remained the same to his peers and *milieu*.

Chapter 31

In the late 1940's and early 1950's, the United States government deported a number of criminal aliens to Italy. Many of these were rich, powerful overlords of the American Cosa Nostra. They brought back to the old country American know-how and efficiency in criminal operations. Their connections with their American families remained intact, although the newly dispossessed mobsters cast their lot with the Sicilian Mafia.

The Mafia did not forget the terrible beating it had taken in Marseilles. But the Americans dangled an irresistible bait before their eyes: the billion-dollar drug market in the United States. Once again the Sicilians, now combined with the American-Italians, began buying huge supplies of opium from Turkey and the Middle East—Iran, Iraq, and Afghanistan. Wholesale prices of the black stuff rose. The Unione Corse's sources were threatened. Osmar's contract with Cesar was not always filled; the Turk often sold to independent buyers of the Mafia for higher prices. Deliveries to the Marseilles heroin labs were uncertain. The crisis grew, threatening not only Cesar but the other patriarchs as well.

The Marseilles Families met to discuss the situation. They sat behind the locked doors of a study in Cesar's mansion. The house staff had been given the evening off. Cesar's hands toyed with the gold medallion of the black

Moor's head. "Mafia!" he said, his voice sneering. "It's a word supposed to mean 'men of honor'! What about their promises? They're not worth *merde!*"

Rampini sighed. His voice was heavy. "What do you propose to do? Fight them on the sea? Start wars in Italy? Our cousins have all their own protection there."

"Maybe we were wrong," Volanti said, adjusting his glasses. "We can still distribute the skag ourselves."

"We can . . . *if* we have it!" Cesar said thoughtfully. "But first we've got to have something to sell. We're filling in on C." His labs were now manufacturing cocaine. "Luckily there are plenty of coca leaves in Peru and Bolivia." His fist closed in anger. "But H is better. Easier. More profit!"

"Agreed, agreed," said Rampini. He added slowly, "I don't suppose we should call in a *giùdice?*"

"What's the use?" asked Cesar in return. One of the differences in organization between the Mafia and Unione Corse was the method of settling internal disputes. The Mafia usually submitted their quarrels to other Mafiosi; the Corsicans called in expert outsiders— *giùdice*, "judges"—to arbitrate their arguments. "We meet with Don Bello and his *mecs*. The *giùdice* says 'this . . . and so-and-so.' And our cousins agree . . . all fine. All great. What happens next? They break their word whenever it pleases them!"

"Then we must wait," Rampini said heavily.

"We'll wait, but not forever!" Cesar's face was grim. "The time'll come—and we'll be waiting!"

That time arrived sooner than Cesar expected.

In 1954 the French withdrew from Indo-China, leaving a vacuum in southeast Asia. The retreat of the French forces was compounded with administrative confusion. "We have men over there—high-ranking army officers we're paying off. S.D.E.C.E., too!" Cesar told Joseph. The *Service de Documentation Exterieure et du Contre-Espionage* is the French equivalent of the CIA. "Laos will supply us with opium—as much as Turkey! Now's the time to grab it."

"How'll you get it out? There's no transportation," Joseph asked.

"I'll arrange it," Cesar said with assurance. "There's Vietnam— take it out through there. I'll need letters of credit. Unlimited funds.

You take care of that. And when I'm through, we'll have so god-damned much black stuff we'll pump it like oil!"

Cesar, accompanied by Gio, checked into a European hotel, topped by a roof garden, on Lam-Son Square near the center of Saigon. Luigi's forged passport identified Cesar as Jean Mouren of Lyons, France; another set of counterfeit papers held Gio to be Émile Duplan, also from Lyons. From the bar on the roof garden, Cesar saw Saigon stretched out below—wide Parisian boulevards and mean, twisting Oriental streets. A freighter nosed slowly up the Saigon River, from the sea some kilometers distant, to drop a rusty anchor in the muddy waters. Swarms of rickety sampans, sculled by weather-beaten boatmen, hovered close to the river's shores. Flat, high-sterned, evil-smelling junks carrying kapok, maize, and pepper bobbled like flocks of ancient ducks on the wide expanse of water.

In his mind's eye, however, Cesar was trying to visualize Laos. It was the least developed country in Southeast Asia as well as the most sparsely populated. For over sixteen hundred kilometers it bordered the north of newly divided Vietnam. The entire border area consisted of an impenetrable jungle covering flatlands, hills, and mountains. Landlocked Laos had no railways and practically no motor roads. Its nearest shipping point was Hanoi, now the capital of the Communist Viet Minh. Cesar doubted that he could do business with the north. He decided that he would not even make the attempt.

The one important fact, in Cesar's still forming plans, was that Laos grew opium poppies. Millions of them . . . millions and millions!

In the days that followed, Cesar became familiar with the city. Vendors carts filled the side streets, displaying steaming rice, dried meat, and sugarcane juice. In the Cholon district, a wedge-shaped Chinese section some distance from downtown Saigon, existed a tight, rapacious world. Bicycles, rickshaws, bicycle-propelled tri-shaws, motor scooters, blue and cream-colored taxis, small cars with high whining motors, and a mass of pedestrians flowed through the streets. The slap-slap-slap of bare feet and the clacking wooden clogs of farmers underscored the din of voices and machines.

On the streets everything was for sale: black-market material from • the withdrawing French army—food, medicine, clothes, arms; drugs

263

such as opium; roots and herbs; charcoal, cheap candles, and kerosene. Baking odors floated from various ovens; tailors stitched endlessly in tiny holes in the wall. In the doors of massage parlors, masseurs shouted out their skills; peddlers of porcelain spoons and bowls clattered their wares. In the alleys and twisting streets, Eurasian, Vietnamese, and Chinese whores solicited openly.

In the southern capital, confusion existed, political as well as social. Bao Dai, chief of state with France's support, was soon to be ousted by Ngo Dinh Diem. Through the chaos, Cesar picked his way —making contacts, buying favors, bribing officials, acting with impunity. Where Archimedes had asked for a place to stand to move the world, Cesar merely asked for enough money to accomplish the same. He had enough, at least, to accomplish his task of moving tons of drugs halfway across the world to the heroin labs of Marseilles.

Soldiers, civilians, administrators, and officials of French colonialism still remained throughout the south of Vietnam, mixed in the turmoil of the corrupt government. A key man in Cesar's plans was Captain Charles Nembriny, a pilot in the French Air Corps. Wounded and discharged, Nembriny remained in Saigon after recovering, hoping to better his fortune. The fortunes of war had brought him little. However, Nembriny had maintained his contacts in the army—some of them reaching to staff level. A hard, tough, shrewd Norman, he knew his Calvados from soft cider.

From the roof garden, the screaming, naked children playing and urinating in the streets could not be heard; the snaking, narrow passages lined with coffinmakers' shops, brass and copper bazaars, and food hawkers could not be seen. The bar was well filled with officers in uniform, both Vietnamese and French. A few Vietnamese women were sprinkled among the tables wearing neck-to-ankle gowns split up to the waist, with silken pantaloons beneath. Rich, wispy-bearded taipans in stiffly brocaded robes, from the Cholon Chinese district, entertained customers. Cesar and Gio sat at a table with Captain Nembriny. It was not the first discussion with the ex-army pilot, nor would it be the last.

"You can land and take off with a small loaded plane in Laos?" Cesar asked.

Nembriny nodded. Short, stocky, well muscled, he spoke with

assurance. "Chop out . . . smooth over . . . make our own runways. No problem."

"With how much weight?" Cesar asked.

Nembriny considered the question. Four-passenger, single engine?" Cesar nodded. Nembriny said, "Two hundred and fifty kilos . . . not including pilot and essence."

Cesar calculated. Slightly more than five hundred pounds of opium, in addition to the weight of the pilot and gasoline. Perhaps Nembriny was being conservative, but planes are expensive to replace. "How about more cargo and less essence?" Cesar asked the pilot.

"That'd mean refueling."

"Is that impossible?"

"No," Nembriny said. French planters still operated plantations —coffee, tea, and rubber—where gasoline could be stockpiled and planes serviced.

Cesar signaled to the waiter for another round of cognac. "Planes we need are available. Can you help me get them?" Light observation, reconnaissance, and private transport planes for ranking officers stood deteriorating on the airfields. They were still the property of the French army, but with the right connections could be bought as surplus.

"It'll cost money," Nembriny said. He wiped the cognac from his stiff military mustache. "But not so much as new planes. Besides, they're already here."

"You'll buy them at the price I want," Cesar said. He already had arranged for their purchase through a high-placed civilian administrator connected with the army. The administrator, indebted to the Unione, was closely related to a general. Cesar did not want to buy the planes in his own name; as usual, he preferred a front.

The dream of a sizable profit on the transaction faded from Nembriny's mind. Concealing his disappointment, he said, "Then why do you need me?"

"To form an airline," Cesar said. "You'll head it. I don't know what we'll call it yet."

"Air Opium," Gio said unexpectedly.

Surprised, Cesar stared at the big man, then smiled. "Good idea,

Gio, but a bit gaudy. We'll think of something else." He turned his attention to Nembriny again. "We'll start with five planes, get more when we need them. How about men to fly them?"

"I know plenty," Nembriny said.

"The pay is one thousand dollars a month. You'll draw two," Cesar said casually.

Nembriny jumped at the excellent pay. "I'll keep them flying," he said.

"You know this place, I don't," Cesar continued. "You go on the payroll right now. Make arrangements to buy the planes and recruit your men. Figure out your logistics—clear what runways you need in Laos. Give me the approximate points you want to refuel." His eyes fixed Nembriny with a stare. "I'll take no *merde* on this. If you take my money, you're in for good."

"Agreed," Nembriny said.

"When we're ready to operate, I'll send my men over to handle the skag . . . keep it moving from here to Marseilles. You concern yourself only with heading the airline company. Keep up appearances! Make it as respectable as possible. You don't have to worry about the government or the damned authorities. They're paid off and will stay that way." Cesar paused, then added, "They'll leave you alone so long as *I* don't worry about you."

The lightly veiled threat did not escape Nembriny. Although the captain did not yet know Cesar's true identity, he knew Cesar was not a man to cross. Obviously Nembriny realized he was getting into the drug business, but he did not care. The pecuniary sparseness of his military days was too recent to be forgotten. The smell of money —*real* money—was great, especially when there was no money in his pocket! The captain gave a hard, tight-lipped grin. "Worry? Worry about what?" he asked.

Cesar and Gio walked toward the single-engine plane squatting on the hard-packed dirt road. Behind them lay the wooden house, its paint peeling, enclosed on three sides by a low veranda. The plantation belonged to a destitute planter, one Alard, brought to the point of ruin by the recent war. Beyond the main house stood clusters of small, one-storey cottages with wattled walls and thatched roofs— for the long-vanished workers of the deserted coffee field. The land gave way to thin stands of trees, then gradually thickened with timber and underbrush as it neared the foothills. The plantation required years of rebuilding and money—much money—to be profitable again.

Alard had been most receptive to Cesar's proposition. Planes could land on the road. Supplies of essence might easily be stored in the outbuildings on the farm. But a morphine refinery? He, Alard, was an honest businessman!

But how long would he be able to remain in business?

That was a question, of course. A small laboratory might be built —far distant from the road or main house, where no one would see it. Who would know? Or, for that matter, who would care?

Alard, fair-skinned and badly burned by the hot Asian sun, scratched his head. "Perhaps no one."

"And a lot of *blé*," Gio said. "Build this dump from the ground up."

Cesar said, "Look at it this way, M'sieur Alard. You sell coffee, I sell opium. Your coffee is ground, my opium is refined. Raw opium's heavy and bulky to ship. By refining it, even crudely, I make it into morphine—which is much easier to handle. None of it'll be sold on your land. For that matter, you need never see it. You don't even have to know it's around. And every month, year after year, you'll receive a steady income—as much as you ever made the best year on your coffee!"

Alard accepted. Cesar returned to the plane he had flown himself from Saigon to the plantation, while Nembriny was busy buying additional aircraft. Affairs were progressing well. Alard's was the third plantation on which he planned to establish a crude refining lab. With easy-to-handle crystalline morphine, he would next arrange to smuggle it back to Marseilles aboard tramp steamers and freighters and perhaps passenger ships—the right ones! Eventually, crews of international airlines would be bribed to fly it in long transoceanic hops.

Cesar settled himself behind the controls. He nodded to Gio, who swung the propeller. The motor coughed, caught. Cesar warmed it, revving it, while Gio climbed into the small cabin and settled his big bulk in the copilot seat beside Cesar. The small plane moved down the dirt road gaining speed. Cesar pulled it into the air, nose up, gaining altitude. At ten meters the motor suddenly sputtered. The plane hung for an instant in the air, clawing to maintain itself.

Then the B-60 Mercury crashed into the hard, sun-dried Viet earth.

Chapter 32

Gio died in the crash.

Cesar was more fortunate: He escaped without serious injury. In a land where sudden death was a way of life, the accident passed almost unnoticed. Except for Cesar. He saw the results of the accident each time he faced the mirror to shave. His razor had hard going over the terrible scars that laced his face. His high, arched nose was replaced with a smashed and broken one that lay pushed toward his cheek. The full lower Roman lip was split at the corner, drawn down in an expression of perpetual disapproval.

Sometimes he spit at the grotesque image in the glass.

Cesar arranged for Gio's ashes to be shipped back to Col Pieto. He would be buried with his family in Valle Satisanni. Gio's death did not especially disturb Cesar, did not really sadden him. He missed the big, lumbering companion he had known as a boy, but felt no actual grief. What Cesar missed was a familiar prop—Gio was one of the few persons Cesar trusted. Now there were fewer: Joseph, of course, and Anse. They were all.

As soon as he was able to get about, Cesar resumed the business that had brought him to Saigon. Nembriny hired pilots; purchase of planes was completed, including a replacement for the one Cesar crashed. Supply dumps were set up and small garages were built to service the ships, and rudely equipped labs were erected. Personnel to operate the laboratories were already on their way.

When Cesar finally returned to France, a new, unlimited source of opium and morphine base soon followed him into the ever-operating labs of Marseilles.

Part
Four

Chapter 33

Victore Satisanni died in 1964. Cesar returned to the Valle, near Col Pieto, for the funeral. He had not been back to his birthplace since the death of his mother four years earlier. The death of his father was different; it presented problems that had to be answered.

Among the older generations of the island, life after death was more important than life itself. They were deeply religious, and many were as deeply superstitious. Once it had not been unusual for a family to abandon its home if too many deaths had occurred in it during a short period of time, for fear of spirits. That house was never lived in again. In the younger people, however, the deep religiosity and superstition were dying out. But the dead of the past were always present in the motley arrays of tombs—large and small, carefully crafted or crudely made, pretentious or humble—that dotted the roads, squatted on sheltered properties, or appeared unexpectedly at the curve of a path. All had the appearance of being extravagantly tended.

The Valle Satisanni had its tomb, too: a square, squat, windowless building of pink stone. Two plaster pillars, chipped and weathered, but painted pink, flanked a thick wooden door reinforced with strips of heavy metal. The door was barred with a great, hand-forged padlock. A low rock wall enclosed approximately half a hectare of land surrounding the tomb. In the land were buried generations of Satisanni—bloodlines close or distant. Many of the old graves had sunk to the level of the land that held them, and they had disappeared without trace except for small markers or crosses. Some were chiseled with names and dates; some revealed paint faded on eroded wood.

The pink stone tomb was reserved for the bodies of the *signori* of the Satisanni and their wives.

A heavy coffin containing the remains of Victore was carried into the tomb and deposited on the stone floor beside the one of Angela Andrea Fennechi Satisanni.

Cesar stood outside the tomb in the late afternoon sun. Around him were gathered a hundred or more relatives and friends. Some of the very old men wore their coarse woven suits of black with hued cummerbunds for the occasion; others wore their brown or black corduroy coats and dark scarves. The ancient women still clung to their ill-fitting skirts and blouses of black, with shawls and headcloths. The clothes of the younger generations differed little from those worn in Marseilles.

Father Massafra had long since joined the Diety he had served faithfully for nearly seventy years; he was replaced in Col Pieto by a younger, more intense priest. Like his predecessor, Father Polein served both the church and the tiny school. Many older members of the parish grumbled that he was too young, too inexperienced for the responsibility. He had conducted the final services and Mass for Victore Santisanni with dignity, and he stood now in a privileged position beside Cesar and Joseph at the front of the tomb, listening to the histrionic recital of Cesar's distant cousin, Paolo.

Corsica, over the centuries, never developed an art of its own. It borrowed what it needed from the countries of the Mediterranean. What it kept of art, literature, and architecture, the Corsicans stripped to lean simplicity. With one exception, which, oddly enough, was a form of poetry strictly its own. The poetry was written expressly for funerals and—for revenge.

With the days of the terrible vendettas over, only the panegyrics of burial remained.

Now as the long blue shadows lengthened in the Valle, painting the pink tomb a delicate lavender, young Paolo Satisanni delivered the final tribute to Victore. In strangely beautiful formal speech, with measured cadence and beat, he recited his carefully written eulogy. The superlative praise and laudation of the poem were no more out of place than the great piles of mountains surrounding the bowed heads of the silent listeners. Both, for a few last moments, seemed to touch the veil of infinity.

Paolo Santisanni finally stood silent. It was very still. Cesar stepped forward and closed the great padlock on the tomb. "May you rest with God," Cesar said, and turned away.

Cesar, with Joseph and the priest, walked slowly across the fields toward the old house. Behind him, with their husbands and children, were his sisters dressed in mourning. The crowd followed, speaking in low voices among themselves, and keeping a respectful distance. During the days of funeral activities, few had addressed him personally. He had assumed the proportions of a legend. Cesar was more than a *signore* or a *cavaliere*. He was *Le Patriarche* of a great and powerful family—a man richer than a king, a man who dealt in life and death. Peasants who had worked the docks during the strike told stories of his wealth and power. Were not his boats, uncounted, plying the seas? Did he not command an army to do his bidding? Did his property not include more buildings, more hectares, than the very city of Ajaccio?

And the ring on his finger, the Moor's head medallion for all to see—only the most powerful and feared of men wore the crest of the Unione . . . less than half a dozen anywhere in the world. Cesar, it appeared, had accomplished the impossible. The fierce, independent islanders extended him more than respect; they regarded him with awe.

Behind the mask of his fearfully scarred and disfigured face, Cesar was aware of the reactions he aroused in others. He wore his authority with indifference; the heady taste of privilege no longer thrilled him. He had lived long enough with power that it was a familiar companion. Money was no longer counted in francs, dollars, or pounds. His seven heroin labs manufactured the drug night and day. The output of one lab alone over a relatively short period of time was nine hundred kilograms of the pure drug—roughly a ton. After dilution for sale on the streets of New York, it was worth nearly four hundred million dollars. The unbelievable sums were beyond imagination. All the four hundred million was not Cesar's, but ten million of it was. After his costs of transportation, manufacturing, the protection of his *milieu*, the graft and payoffs, possibly four million tax-free dollars remained. During the course of a year, he imported over four hundred and fifty tons of opium—more than four times the legitimate need of the entire world! Cesar had no idea, no accurate estimate of his own wealth. But Joseph did.

Through accredited financial channels, Joseph continued to make legitimate investments in greatly diversified fields. However, there were huge sums of cash that could not be concealed easily, and these were deposited in blind and coded accounts around the world— Hong Kong, Beirut, Tehran, Berne, Buenos Aires, and even West Berlin. But not in the United States, not in New York, for there the banking laws did not permit easy concealment. Joseph submitted to Cesar a list of the account numbers and their coded names. Cesar memorized them carefully, then destroyed the list. The only record was in the memories of the two men.

So Cesar no longer thought of money as *money*. It had assumed the unreality of Joseph's own figures. However, he was not content. It was not that he wanted more power or more money. But he wanted —something! His long years of contact with Villecrosse enabled him to imagine that he, perhaps like Alexander, needed new worlds to conquer. But Cesar was realistic enough to recognize that while he might be a lion, he was also a lion in a cage—of his own making. Outside the cage of the criminal world was a society of hunters, backed by law and resources greater than his own, which would show him no mercy. He was safer inside his cage than out. Once, while reading, he had stumbled on the name of "Sati." Cesar had assumed the name by merely shortening his own—Satisanni. Now he discovered that in Hindu mythology Sati had voluntarily invited death by entering fire. That the name existed at all surprised Cesar. It pleased him that it had belonged to a supernatural being. But Sati's mythical end had left Cesar with a small superstitious doubt. Or perhaps it was a warning . . . before his life, too, went up in flames.

Walking toward the huge old stone house, Cesar recalled the incident of the name. He paused and turned to look back at a stone urn that stood a short distance to one side, and slightly behind, the tomb. The urn contained the token ashes of Gio, which Cesar had shipped back from faraway Saigon. Nearly ten years ago! In the

276

burning plane it had been Gio who was consumed, not Cesar. Cesar's scarred, slashed lip twitched in a cynical smile. "What's in a name?" he thought, and resumed his way.

Joseph and Father Polein paced silently beside him. Cesar fell once again into his thoughts: Tomorrow or the next day, he would return to Marseilles . . . and what? There was Theda, of course—the last in a long line of nearly forgotten mistresses. Some he could hardly recall, their faces and bodies dimmed by a decade, their names nearly forgotten. He remembered Juliette, the first woman who had taken him into her heart. She had been amusing. Their nights, at the beginning of the affair, had been delightful. The game and language of love were new to Cesar. And Juliette had been an instructoress of finesse. He had worked hard to follow and practice the rules. Yes, for a while the game had been great sport, but then . . . most unfortunately . . . Juliette had forgotten it was a game. She became serious, too serious. She claimed that she loved him. Cesar remembered he had at least been generous . . . most generous . . . when he told her to leave. She left for Paris with a purse heavily loaded with francs, and the promise of a job in a small bistro on the Left Bank. The café-bar was owned by the family of the Parisian branch of the Unione.

Perhaps Juliette had loved him, and some of the others who claimed they did. But that was before the accident. Since his return from setting up Air Opium in Vietnam, Cesar was convinced that no woman could love him—not with his face which might double as a gargoyle on Notre Dame. Once he had not been bad looking . . . even if he admitted it himself. Girls had always liked him back in those days, although, frankly, he had not paid too much attention. But now he bought his women, bought them as he might buy cars, or planes, or furniture. He asked for little; they asked only for money. So it was fair enough. When they were new, it was a pleasure to have them around. When the newness wore off, he got another.

But recalling Juliette revived the memories of Vivian Burke. Because of Vivian, he had taken Juliette in the first place. He had associated with Villecrosse, spending hours in flight, and days which totaled to months, in seclusion at the château, learning to be a gentleman. Hell! He now spoke fluent English—all on account of the British girl. Sometimes he wondered what had happened to her. Was she married? Did she have children? Would he even recognize her if they should meet again? Cesar was quite sure he would know her face anywhere. It had lived just around the corner of his memory for too long, and often the sound of her voice intruded on the lips of other women. No, he would never forget. After he learned enough English, he had read the London papers hoping to see her name. He never had, but once he saw an announcement that Sally Lang was giving a concert recital. It was enough to bring back the hurt of an old love lost. Occasionally, he had thought . . . back when the wound of losing Vivian was still open . . . that he might take a trip to London. Arrange . . most accidentally, of course . . . to see her. But he realized that would have been ridiculous.

So the years simply went by. Time did heal most wounds, hurts, disappointments, and reverses. And in their place, what did it leave? Just an easing. Not contentment even, but perhaps a lack of discontent. Was that enough to satisfy a man? Cesar was not sure.

The generations of inbred dogs rushed from around the old house, as always, to greet the approaching crowd. They were growling, showing their teeth, although wagging their tails. Ignoring the animals, Cesar climbed the three heavy wooden steps and entered the great main room of the house. He sat down, surrounded by his sisters and their families, and with Joseph and the priest. They sat in silence, waiting patiently for the supper to be served. A huge meal had been prepared to feed the assembled relatives and guests. Most would eat, then return up the mountain to Col Pieto, and beyond, to their homes. Others would stay the night.

Outside, swarms of children played in the farmyard—shouting, running, quarreling, darting in and out like dusk swallows, among the groups of men clustered in small talk. The women were in the kitchen helping dish-up and serve the food.

"I wish to speak to Paolo," Cesar said.

"I'll get him," one of the brothers-in-law said quickly. He stood up and went outside. In a few minutes he returned with the reluctant eulogist.

Cesar stared at the young man standing uneasily before him. In his early twenties, slender, with regular, sensitive features, he reminded Cesar of his own youth. But Paolo, Cesar thought, had a warmth which he had never possessed. He observed the friendly smiles that greeted the young man from the others in the room. The hidden strain of steel bred into so many of the Satisanni had been softened in Paolo. "The poem to my father was excellent," Cesar said.

"Thank you, *Signor,*" Paolo replied shyly.

"You wrote it?" When Paolo nodded, Cesar continued, "Where did you go to school?"

"At Col Pieto." Paolo became silent again.

"Speak up," Cesar said. "I'm interested. Don't make me question you." He realized his face disturbed the young man. If it did not frighten Paolo, at least it made him uneasy. Cesar felt the sympathy of his sisters for the awkward youth, and it brought an edge of irritation into his voice. "How long have you lived here in the Valle?"

"Three years, *Signor* . . ."

Agatha, Cesar's favorite sister, slipped into a hurried explanation. Paolo was the son of second cousin Piero, who had lived on the Golfe de Pere near Cargese. Unfortunately, Piero was aboard the ship of Uncle Angelo Fennechi when it went down in the Sea of Crete on a run from Istanbul. As Cesar knew, everyone was lost. Paolo's mother, an Archino also distantly related to the Fennechi, had died when he was still a boy. After his father's death, Paolo had visited the Valle—and remained.

Cesar nodded. "Would you like to study at Ajaccio?"

"Very much, Signor," Paolo said.

"What do you want to be? A doctor . . . judge . . . engineer, or what?"

"I would like to come back here," Paolo said.

Cesar was silent. The others watched him. Finally, he asked, "Why?"

"Because I like it," Paolo replied.

Cesar considered the simple, direct reply. He could not understand it. A farmer on hectares of tired land? A young man—with the choice of paths in a world before him—to return to Valle Satisanni? Cesar remembered the land too well. The mountains, of course, and the forests—they were different. The hidden falling streams, the sheer cathedral sides of the calanches; the remembered smell of smoke ascending over charcoal-makers in the green stands; the fragrance of arbutus and myrtle and rosemary. The great upswelling lift of spirit, the sweeping, swooping, mystic soaring of youthful soul to meet the dawning sun of a crystal day. Yes, Cesar remembered that —and then it was gone. With regret, he thought, "But no man can live forever in the mountains . . ."

Chapter 34

A log burned slowly in the great fireplace. The flicker of its flames was the only light in the wide expanse of the old room. The French chairs, Spanish tables, Italian chests, and English sofas were the same from Cesar's memories of childhood. The aquatints on the walls were perhaps a little more faded, the old photographs a bit more yellowed. The narrow shutters were closed in the thick walls. The rafters of the low ceiling occasionally groaned in the coolness of the night. Cesar sprawled in Victore's favorite chair with high carved wooden back and slung leather seat. Near him, Joseph sat with a glass of red Corsican wine. It was after midnight and the house had settled into sleep. The two men sat alone before the fire—a fire laid in honor of Cesar.

Joseph broke the silence that had held the two men for some time. "What do you do now, Cesar?" he asked.

Cesar shifted in his chair and lit a dark cigarette before replying. "Why do you ask?"

"There's no longer a *Signore* in Valle Satisanni, although there's a *Patriarche* in Marseilles." Joseph leaned back on the sofa. "I'll tell you what your family's asking. When will Cesar get married? When'll he return and have a son so the family and Valle can go on?"

"Tell them I'll marry when I damn please!" Cesar stared at Joseph. "When I find a woman . . . who pleases me." Cesar spoke around the brown cigarette held between his

lips. "I won't marry just to have a women whelp a litter of brats."
Cesar leaned forward. "You saw the women today . . . dumb, stupid
peasants! Who'd want to marry one like them?"

"I don't know . . ." Joseph said.

"You don't?" Cesar was scornful. "Then marry one. Why don't
you? Go ahead and have some brats of your own!"

"I wish I could," Joseph said. "We've come a long way together,
Cesar. And every step of it has been lonely."

Cesar relaxed slowly against the back of the chair. "Look, Joseph,
I mean this seriously. I'll never return to this Valle, but it deserves
better than to be forgotten. If you want to retire, get married, and
come back here, I'll give you the valley. Every centimeter!"

Joseph shook his head. "I can't retire. You should know that."

"Why not?"

"Because of you. You can never get out . . . which means I can't,
either. Once we split up, Cesar, neither of us will last for long." Cesar
frowned. Joseph continued, "If you step down as *Patriarche* of the
Sati, others will move in to take over. Either from within your own
organization . . . or the Volanti or the Rampini. They'd do it to
prevent Affinito in Paris from moving in. Even Nastacio, old as he
is, might have his own ideas. But once whoever is in, he'll have to
get *you* . . . put you out of the way for good. Otherwise he can never
be sure—you might change your mind and try to come back again."

"That still doesn't prevent you from getting out."

"Yes, it does! Like Jullien Durand, I know where too many bodies
are buried. I'd be racked up until I told everything I know . . .
revealed every last asset, every franc that's invested or hidden. And
afterwards, I'd get my throat cut anyway." Joseph gestured to the
signet ring on Cesar's finger. "That's *my* only protection, too."

"So long as I have it, you have nothing to worry about. You can
still retire and move to the Valle."

"For a while, perhaps," Joseph admitted. "But if I got out, that
would be the first breach in the dam. The breach would grow until,
finally, you couldn't stop it. Others would try to get out, too." He
stared thoughtfully at the fire. "Remember this, Cesar: Business is
business. It comes first. And first of all, without each other, we'll
both be dead men."

Cesar mashed out his cigarette on the top of a Spanish marble table. "About the Valle," he said. "I like that young Paolo."

"So do I," Joseph agreed.

"If he wants . . . arrange that he go on to school. When he likes, he can return to take over the Valle."

"As heir?" Joseph asked.

"Why not? He bears the name."

"And your sisters?"

Cesar shrugged. "Set up an estate for each of them. Enough that they can live well, and without worry, the rest of their lives." Joseph nodded, and the two sat in silence for a few minutes. Cesar aroused himself from thought. "And at the bank, in Ajaccio, guarantee a line of credit, establish a trust fund—or whatever . . . you know how to do it. Just be sure there'll always be sufficient money for Paolo to run the farm, pay taxes, and keep the Valle open for the families who wish to live here."

"I'll take care of it," Joseph said.

Perhaps Victore, in the pink tomb, would be placated if he knew. Not pleased, because Cesar was not carrying on—but at rest. The Valle Satisanni would continue with a Satisanni at its head, which was the way it should be. And the family—large and small, young and old—would be protected. Cesar had performed his duty as *Signore*, although his tenure had been brief. *Noblesse oblige.* Cesar was surprised that he still cared.

Cesar and Joseph returned to Ajaccio the following day. Cesar drove the car, rented in Ajaccio, down the narrow, winding coast road. The small capital had changed greatly, nearly doubling in population since the days of the war. Across the bay, an airport scheduled daily flights to Nice and Marseilles. Letting off Joseph at the bank to make the arrangements they had discussed for the Valle, Cesar drove on to the mansion of Vito Nastacio.

The old townhouse was not so impressive as Cesar remembered it, although it had not changed. The doors, shutters, and mansard roof still were neatly painted in black. Cesar pulled the bellcord and the door was opened by a burly, heavy-faced servant, elderly, but who might have been the same who had let him in twenty years before.

"Is *Le Patriarche* in?" Cesar inquired.

The man's eyes rested on the signet ring Cesar was wearing. "I will see," he said politely. He stepped aside and Cesar entered the entry hall. Closing the door, the servant hurried down the hall and returned with Cuomo . . . a Cuomo grayed by two decades and wearing fifty additional pounds of fat. His eyes had the old wariness as he tried to identify Cesar beneath the disfigured face. The Cesar that Cuomo remembered was of a different time. His eyes, like the servants, fixed on Cesar's ring finger. *"M'sieur . . . ?"* Cuomo asked, his voice without expression.

"Cesar Sati. I wish to speak to *Le Patriarche.*"

"Sati?" Cuomo's eyes flicked in recognition. "I apologize. I did not recognize you . . ." But his voice held no apology.

"It's hard for me to recognize you, Cuomo," Cesar said. "You've put on fat since I last saw you." Cuomo accepted the slight and nodded. "Now tell *Le Patriarche* I'm here . . . and wish to pay my respects to him."

"Yes. He's here. He'll see you," Cuomo said.

It was as if the years had slipped past without touching the room. The library with its shelves of books, the leather furniture, the glow of paneling, the marble fireplace were the same. Even the figure seated in a chair by the window overlooking the well-kept garden was in the same position that Cesar remembered. And Cuomo took up his old familiar position by the door.

But time had not really stood still. The room that had so greatly impressed the provincial Cesar was merely another comfortable study. The once strange, unknown books on the shelves Cesar had read by now. The gray-haired, middle-aged man, with a sallow face over a voice of steel, was a frail old man with white hair light as silk. The sallow skin stretched tightly across the bones of his face, turning almost to a nut brown. Only his eyes, alert behind heavy, wrinkled lids, remained young.

"*Patriarche* Vito," Cesar said, crossing the room.

"*Patriarche* Cesar," Nastacio replied politely. "You will excuse an old man if he does not rise to greet his guest."

"It is honor enough that you see me," Cesar said.

The old man smiled, his face suddenly etched with wrinkles. "Sit down, sit down, Cesar. The formalities are over. Will you have one of my Havanas?" The thin, almost transparent hand waved to Cuomo.

284

"The first Havana I ever saw smoked was in this room." Cesar's lips twisted into a smile. "And you didn't offer me one."

Nastacio laughed—surprisingly clear and ringing. "Ah! But I offered you something better—your life." Cuomo opened the box of cigars and presented it to the old man, waiting patiently until it was ready to be lit, then lighting it. "Cuomo, here, wanted to hit you, you know . . ." Nastacio continued behind a first cloud of smoke.

Cuomo offered the cigars to Cesar, who took one, bit off the end, and lighted it. He glanced up at Cuomo. "If he had tried, I'd have killed him," he said indifferently.

"Yes, you probably would," the old man agreed. "And then we would all have lost. Cuomo's my under-boss now. He wouldn't have been here to help me." He paused. "And, of course, you would never have reached Marseilles." Nastacio carefully nursed the ash on his cigar. "I'm only permitted two of these a day . . ." he said. Then, "You returned for your father's funeral?"

Cesar nodded. "I'm flying back to Marseilles. So long as I was in Ajaccio, I wanted to see you."

"If you wait again for twenty years, it'll be too late," the old man said. "About your father, the Signore Victore . . . I offer you my sympathy."

"Thank you," Cesar replied.

"I lunch early. Will you join me?"

"An honor. Nothing I'd like better, but I can't." Cesar's voice held true regret. He stood up. "I didn't forget. You helped me . . . back when I needed it . . . with Gozy. That was the start. If I . . . my people . . . can ever repay you—it is yours!"

The old man's eyebrows raised slowly. "What is there to ask, Cesar? I am alone . . . see no one except Cuomo. All that I can wish is enough time, each day, to enjoy . . ." his eyes wandered out the window to the garden, then back to his cigar, ". . . this."

The mausoleum mansion in Marseilles, upon Cesar's return, seemed more empty than usual. Theda's studied coquetries aroused no desire, no lust, and little response in Cesar. Restless, he decided to fly to Barthélémy to see Villecrosse again. He had not visited the comte for some time. Over the last few years his trips to the château were fewer and spaced at longer intervals. He had, however, continued to send the monthly remittance to the man so like him physically, but so different in all other ways.

When Cesar's plane, loaded with liquor and supplies, touched down on the road beside the château, Villecrosse stumbled across the unkept gardens to meet him. Usually Cesar's arrival was a moment of excitement in the comte's life; a splash of color in the dull, monotonous days eroding Villecrosse. Greeting Cesar, the comte's sardonic expression softened as he looked greedily at the cases of brandy in the cabin of the plane. "I had given you up," he said, "but I see you have arrived well supplied with the waters of Lethe, so . . . welcome!" Villecrosse picked up a heavy case, nearly tripped and fell, then staggered toward the house with the liquor.

Cesar followed him with cans of food. Inside the old house, the large drawing room reminded him of his own in Valle Satisanni— permeated by the smell of the past. For a fleeting moment Cesar wondered if ghosts smelled dusty. Stretching out on a large horsehair settee, Cesar lit a dark cigarette. "It's good to see you again, Edmond," he said.

Villecrosse, knocking off the top of a bottle, hoisted it in a casual salute and drank deeply. "Nepenthe!" He wiped his lips and stared at the brandy. "It doesn't do so good a job as it used to, Auguste. Still, it's better than nothing . . ." He drank again. The comte sat down abruptly on a chair and stared at Cesar. "This very well may be your last trip to Barthélémy—under the present management," he told Cesar.

"How's that?" Cesar asked.

"I've been thinking about selling this old barn," Villecrosse waved vaguely, "and moving to Paris. Why stay here . . . ?"

Cesar felt an unexplainable pang of regret. First the Valle, and now the château was going! The past is always a part of the present, and the present is the first step of the future! Change is unavoidable, but continuance is an intrinsic part of a man's soul. Like spider webs applied to a wound, memories of the past stop the bleeding of today —and tomorrow. Cesar was reluctant to see Barthélémy go. "You've decided? You won't change your mind?" he asked Villecrosse.

"I'm tired," the comte said. "It's not self-pity, but boredom. Life no longer amuses me. It is worse than death. I'm not afraid to die —actually, it would be quite a relief."

"It'll be no different in Paris," Cesar said. "And probably a lot worse. Your last francs will go quickly. You'll be broke." He watched Villecrosse's face. "Nothing left! No place to live . . . no friends. And no brandy!" he warned.

"For a little while, at least, I'll open a window and look outside. See something—even if it's nothing more than a scabby dog scratching himself." The comte lifted the bottle again.

Cesar remained silent. Finally, he said, slowly, "Remember when I crashed?"

Villecrosse stared at Cesar's face, and smiled—a look of complete indifference. "I haven't been able to forget it."

"During that time, when my face was chewed up and burned, the doctors gave me morphine. For the pain," Cesar said. "I still get prescriptions when I need them. You can have them."

"There's nothing wrong with my face, only my head," Villecrosse said, and took another drink.

Cesar shrugged. "Have it your way. You might try it, though. You'll feel different . . . about things."

Villecrosse grinned, his long, almost Oriental eyes slitting. "Perhaps I was cut out to be an opium eater—like De Quincey. Coleridge tried it, too! Hell, alcohol will kill me anyway," he said. "So if drugs do it first, why should I complain?" He glanced at Cesar, then away. "At least it'll be something new . . . a new experience. What bothers me, Auguste, is . . . how can I afford it?"

"Long as you live here at Barthélémy, I'll keep you supplied. Get the prescriptions filled in Marseilles and bring the stuff up with me. We'll make it a bonus . . . in addition to the rent," Cesar said.

"Shoot away!" Villecrosse rolled up his sleeve and extended his arm.

Cesar realized he was putting a monkey on Villecrosse's back that the comte was unable to carry. But Château Barthélémy was safe. Villecrosse was tied to it forever.

Chapter 35

Joseph said, "They're a different breed of cat. Dangerous. So far we've done business on our own ground, followed rules that we laid out. And, of course, we have our own political protection. Over there they'll call the shots. They'll have it their way . . . whether you like it or not."

Cesar nodded. When he replied, his voice was cold. "The bastards are cutting off our market. I won't stand by and see fifty-five million dollars of H shot to the devil. I'll shoot it up his fat ass first!" Cesar was referring to the dope situation existing in the United States, and especially New York City, in the first half of the 1960's. He was well aware of the history of the Cosa Nostra, although he had little direct experience with the organization. As a member of the far older Unione Corse, he regarded the American mobsters with some disdain . . . somewhat in the light of Johnnies-come-lately. Contrary to public belief, the American mobs were not simply outgrowths or transplants of the old Mafia. In 1919 the Sicilians controlled the rackets in East Harlem and Greenwich Village sections of Manhattan, while across the East River, in Brooklyn, Neapolitan gangsters staked out their territory.

The Sicilians held ties to the *Mafie;* the Neapolitans were *Camorrista* in background—a secret criminal society in Naples. The two gangs met in a blood war, and when it was over, the Mafia and Camorra merged into one family. This was the original, which was to divide, like an amoeba, into the five Cosa Nostra Families of New York City, as well as nineteen others in Boston, Buffalo, Newark, Chicago, St. Louis, Denver, Miami, New Orleans, San Francisco, and Los Angeles . . . to mention some of the strongholds.

The American mobsters were flexible. They were governed by a *commissionne* made up of nine to twelve members, who were also heads of their individual Families. The mobs were quite willing to do business with other ethnic gangs—Jews, Irish, Germans—although they insisted on Sicilian ancestry for membership in their own Families. This distant relationship had made it possible for the deported American-Italian ganglords to take up ties with the Mafia in Palermo.

U.S. authorities at both the federal and state levels were aghast at the tremendous rise of narcotics sales resulting from the new cooperation between the Mafia and the Cosa Nostra. New pressure . . . constant and heavy . . . was applied to the big men, the head of the Families and their under-bosses, which resulted in many going to prison—some for long terms. With the top chiefs away serving years, reorganization took place in the Families. Some of the dethroned crime lords tried to rule from prison; others had their power taken over by their subordinates—with the approval of the *commissionne.*

All the New York families trafficked in dope; it was a huge source of income, but many of the top men, especially among the older generation, wanted to discontinue the sale and get out of the market. At least for a while. Opposition to this plan came from the younger gang members, although they were too discreet to object openly. They merely agreed—and continued to import the H and sell it on the sly! The established dons, however, tried to shut down the import of wholesale quantities by agreement with the Sicilian Mafia.

After Cesar had opened up new alternate supply routes from Indo-China, the Marseilles Families of the Unione continued to smuggle drugs to independent New York gangs and distributors through South American and Mexico, bypassing the Mafia. Cesar's business did not suffer, although he was still angry with Don Bello for the Sicilian's supposed doublecross of the peace agreement. Consequently, when Cesar learned of the break between the New

York Families, he was eager to take over Bello's markets with the dissenting factions of the Cosa Nostra.

Cesar arrived in New York via Canada, traveling as a French-Canadian businessman from Quebec. Sewn in the bottom and lining of a cheap airline boarding bag were two alternate passports, expertly forged by Luigi Venito, who had not lost his old skill, as well as thousands of dollars, and genuine traveler's checks supplied by Joseph. Anse, and a *picciotto* called Cuir because of his thick hide, landed in Manhattan aboard the Greek liner *Olympia,* out of Piraeus. Both were traveling on tourist visas. All three men checked into the St. George Hotel in Brooklyn Heights, an old, quiet hotel, once fashionable but now lapsed into semiobscurity. It still attracted conventioneers, and Cesar hoped that he and his *casseurs* might escape publicity in the crowded, out-of-the-way hostelry.

Cesar had selected his companions with care. After Gio's death, years before in Indo-China, Galon was elevated to replace him. Anse and Galon were the two under-bosses. Cesar had been faced with the choice of bringing either Anse or Galon; he would have preferred to have brought both, but one had to remain in Marseilles to run the family during Cesar's absence. He chose Anse, his old friend and companion. Cuir was a brutal, unimaginative killer who followed orders quickly, efficiently, and without questions.

Unfortunately, neither Anse nor Cuir would pass unnoticed in a crowd—the Moroccon with his gleaming black face and porcelain smile; Cuir, Italian-Portuguese, with the leatherlike skin that gave him his nickname. But more important, Cesar felt, they were both dependable and he could count on their loyalty.

Cesar was ill-at-ease in New York. Smoke mixed with the damp ocean air to lay soggy, gray felt blankets over the city and cut off the tops of the huge, tall buildings. The sheer canyon walls of Manhattan reminded Cesar of the Calanches—rising straight up in precipices of colored stone. But the skyscrapers were not the city. The city was made up of innumerable streets lined with small, dirty, two and three-storey buildings straggling along as far as he could see. The buildings were crowded with little shops displaying hand-lettered cardboard signs through grime-streaked windows: men's clothing slightly used, shoes repaired, gent's suits cleaned while-U-wait, quick lunches, orange drinks, beer on tap, swap stamps and coins, and ten thousand other offerings by which men struggled to earn a living.

Lines of autos, honking taxis, and lumbering trucks moved with the inevitable purpose of endless columns of army ants marching through a jungle. Rusty iron fire escapes projected from the second storeys over the streets, their end steps balancing like aerialists above the crowds on the sidewalks below. Late sunlight drew patterns of black and white designs through the webs of rusty metal, and cast them on the faces of the small buildings. But no one saw them. No one looked up and smiled at the creations of the mad etcher.

The harbor, the busy port of New York, was a more familiar world. The miles of piers and docks, the majestic liners, the tiny, bustling, nudging tugs with the power of behemoths and the deep-laden freighters—this was not unlike Marseilles. In the St. George, Cesar heard the deep-throated horns of the ships and buoys calling in the night. In France, he had heard them many times.

Cesar, however, remembered an axiom from his youth. Who was it that told him, "You'll live longer if you know two ways out!" Raphael? Of course! That old bar fighter deluxe, his mentor . . . *Zió* Raphael, the wizard of the blade. Cesar patted his own knife, sheathed to the belt at his back, as he recalled Raphael's advice. The old man sat on a crumbling rock, high on a mountain slope above Valle Satisanni. His weathered face was alive with memories. "So there you are, my boy. Back against the bar. And you want out. So what do you do? You look for the door, that's what! Right?" Cesar had nodded and murmured agreement. "But this guy you've just put away—he has half a dozen pals already between you and that door. And you're not going to get there! So then what do you do?" Raphael paused dramatically. "Now, there's either another door . . . *some-place* . . . you know about, or you damned better start making your own door!"

That afternoon Cesar rented a room located off Washington Square, near New York University. He paid three months' rent in advance for the small room in a remodeled brownstone turned into a students' quarters. He did not arouse the landlady's suspicions. Speaking fluent English with a French accent, Cesar explained that he was a graduate student from the University of Orléans, with the intent of studying at New York University. Furthermore, he had relatives living in Bridgeport, Connecticut, and would probably spend most of his time with them until the new semester began. So, if Mrs. Curry, the landlady, did not see him too often, she was not to be concerned. Mrs. Curry assured him that she would not be concerned; in fact, she had little interest in the activities of the students living in her house so long as they were quiet, and paid their rent. And, yes, she would keep an eye on his room while he was away.

Before Cesar returned to the St. George, he securely locked a suitcase of clothes and the airline bag in the closet, then bolted the hall door to his room in the rooming house.

Dominick's Steak House, near the end of Elizabeth Street beneath the Brooklyn Bridge, remained hidden and unsung by the passing world. Within the confines of its soot-plastered, red-brick walls, Tony Deboli and Rocco Sapulla occupied a corner booth far in the back—a position from which they could watch all entrances to the restaurant. Both men were *caporegimes*, captains, in the six-hundred-man army of Don Leo Consonno. With Frank Liardi (one thousand members) and James Mangello (three hundred members), Consonno divided the rich, natural, criminal resources of the Borough of Brooklyn between their families. The nineteen hundred buttons the dons commanded between them participated in the profits of smuggling, loan-sharking, extortion, union racketeering, pilferage, contraband cigarettes, heroin, bars, nightclubs, policy, untaxed alcohol, bolita, car thefts to order, and bookmaking. When the Brooklyn action in the bookie bank reached seventy-five million dollars a year, and Bedford-Stuyvesant received an eighty-eight-million-dollar-a-year play, the profits were not inconsiderable. But among any well-run organization, dissenters will be found. Tony Deboli and Rocco Sapulla were included in this group. Hard-pressed for money to raise bail, retain lawyers, keep mistresses, support their families, and maintain their own florid standards of living, the two captains often speculated in ventures of their own. The code demanded that they share their profits with Don Leo Consonno—which they seldom, if ever, did. Luckily for them, this oversight had not yet been noted by their active boss.

However, the edict from the *commissionne* against further pushing of heroin, an order supported by the Consonno family, caught the two captains sorely hurting for money.

"Where the hair's short," Tony said, glancing past the bar to the front door of the steak house.

"Yeah," agreed Rocco, "the fat bastards! Where're they when you need the dough? You ask 'em for a loan and what do you get? I tell you—they say 'kiss my ass! Know what I feel like tellin' 'em? I feel like saying you want me to suck hind-tit all my life. To hell with you. I'll make my own!"

"You don't tell 'em nothing," Tony grunted. "You kiss their ass same as anybody else. That's what you do. Me too. But now, maybe we don't need Leo Consonno no more. Maybe we fix up our own connection. Huh?" He stared at the front door, then quickly around the room of tables. No one paid any attention to the three men who had entered and were making their way toward Tony's table.

"That the frog?" asked Rocco.

"Yeah. Think so. He's spotted the newspaper on the table."

"Ugly bastard," Rocco said, then fell silent. Cesar picked up the newspaper lying on the table beside Deboli. Unfolding it, he gave it a glance, then folded it again and replaced it. "No front page," Cesar said, according to the prearranged recognition signal.

"No news is good news," Tony gave the required reply. "Sit down."

Cesar, Anse, and Cuir crowded into the booth with the two men. The Consonno buttons and the Sati *milieu* regarded each other warily. A waiter hurried up to the table, took orders for five steak sandwiches with French fries, and hurried away. Cesar leveled an opaque stare at Tony Deboli and waited. Deboli shifted, picked up his silverware, wiped it on his sleeve and carefully lined up the silver in place before him, then said, "I understand you got some stuff."

"All you want," Cesar told him.

"I can use maybe eighteen . . . twenty kilos. Pure. Cash onna line."

"It's hardly worth my time," Cesar said.

Rocco started angrily. "Hey, waita minute! Big-shottin' don't go down 'round here!" he interrupted.

Cesar switched his attention to Sapulla. "I mean it," he said, his voice cold. "A hundred kilos. Minimum."

Tony nodded to Rocco. The two rose from the table and walked to the washroom. They turned on the water taps and conversed in low voices. "That guy's pushin' us! Who he thinks he is? Not gonna get away with it," Rocco muttered.

"You gotta better idea?" Tony asked.

"Where we raisin' the scratch for a hunnerd kilos?" Rocco demanded.

"Maybe we lay it off with Elmo," Tony replied. Elmo Lyttel was the most important black heroin dealer in Brooklyn . . . in the United States, for that matter.

"What if Big Mo don't want none of the action?" Rocco persisted.

"He'll take it. If he don't, we go to Harlem. The spades and the spics'll always come in," Tony said with assurance.

Rocco was not so sure. He shook his head and dried his hands on a damp roll towel. "Too much talk, Tony, and you know what happens—the ole crap hits the street and somebody's ears get filled, and then we get trouble. You know that, you know . . . the word gets out."

"Nobody believes the Puerto Ricans anyway," Tony said. "This guy, Sati, ain't no new boy. I got it—he's one of the biggest dons in Europe. Maybe we level with him . . . and we do business?"

They returned to the table. Cesar was calmly eating the steak and continued without glancing up. Slipping into the seat, Tony said, "We're gonna give it to you straight. A hunnerd kilos we can't handle, not by ourselves. Maybe we gotta bring in somebody else."

Cesar nodded. "Like Mo Lyttel . . . and Ramon Arriquez?" Ray Arriquez was a power in the Puerto Rican and Cuban rackets, holding the Broadway district between 131st and 181st Streets in Manhattan. Tony glanced at Rocco and shrugged. Cesar wiped his lips and took a sip of wine. "Not a bad idea," he told Deboli. "Set up your own system. What've you been paying?" When Deboli told him, Cesar continued, "I'll go along with you, help you get started. Supply you with all the H you can get rid of. With only half the cash on the line. Is that fair?"

"Sure! Fairer'n hell!" Tony agreed.

"You need an organization. Get with it," Cesar said. He looked thoughtfully at Deboli. "In case of trouble, how many men can you put on the street?"

Tony switched a glance at Rocco before replying. "Between him and me," Deboli told Cesar, "we got friends. Good ones. That right, Rocco?"

"Yeah, good ones," Rocco said.

"How many?" Cesar asked again.

"Maybe twenty . . ."

"Every family—five thousand goddamned members—will be out for you," Cesar cautioned. "And you think you can fight back with twenty buttons?"

"Well," said Tony, his voice defensive. "Big Mo's got a lotta spades he can put out, and if Ray Arriquez . . ."

Cesar's impatient words cut into Deboli's reply. "*If!* If . . . if . . . if!" He lowered his voice and continued, his tone again conversational. "I'll back you—you won't have to worry about money. But don't *depend* on Lyttel and Arriquez to do your work for you. You need them, they don't need you. You and Sapulla," Cesar jerked his head toward Rocco, "line up your own muscle. Put them on a payroll to start. That'll hold them with you. Get the blacks and the Spanish to commit themselves. Get them so damned involved *they can't get out!* Then you have a chance."

"Sure, sure!" Deboli agreed. He looked at the three impassive faces watching him—Cesar's scarred features, Anse's black countenance, Cuir's leatherlike skin. Tony felt a tingle of fear. "You ain't no Santa Claus," he told Cesar. "How come you're getting your neck stretched out . . . to here?" Deboli's hands spread.

"Because you and Rocco are going to be worth half a billion dollars a year to me." Cesar spoke coldly, pronouncing each word clearly and distinctly. He paused, then added, "Sometime."

At the bar, a nondescript man finished his boilermaker and set the beer glass down on the bar. Known simply as Skinny Mike, he was a numbers runner. Mike slipped off the barstool and edged into a phone booth. He sorted through a handful of quarters to find a dime. Depositing a coin, he dialed a number.

Chapter 36

The Acme Air-conditioning Company's offices are located on Knickerbocker Avenue near Myrtle. Myrtle Avenue is a strip of real estate so depraved that even its mice hire large rats for bodyguards. The president of Acme is Leo Consonno, a citizen well known to the authorities-at-large. He is equally well known to his associates, a somewhat more tightly knit group than the police, among whom his word is regarded as good as his bond—although, to be frank, most of them preferred his bond. At fifty-eight, Leo Consonno had not served time in forty-six years. His first run-in with the law occurred when he was twelve—for busting and grabbing. Leo had hefted a brick through a pawn shop window, at an age most boys are trooping to Boy Scout colors, grabbed every item his short arms could reach, and flamed down the street in a burst of speed which dazzled, but did not deter, the pursuing cop who had heard the sound of breaking glass in the shade of the three gold balls.

Since the unforgotten days of reform school, Leo Consonno had continued active in devious and illegal ways by operating on a solid legal premise: stay the hell away from where the action is! Or, as he succinctly phrased it to the board of directors of Acme, "If you ain't around, the cops ain't gonna slam your ass in the can for what maybe . . . you don't know . . . happened. Get me?" The board, under the chairmanship of Carmine Zappinzano, voted approval.

Zappinzano was also, incidentally, under-boss of the Consonno family. He, together with Mrs. Leo (Natalie) Consonno, the two sons Consonno—Ernesto and Georgie—and the highly regarded *Consigliere,* Michael Mancuso, comprised the board of the family-owned corporation.

Acme operated under a charter of the sterling state of Delaware, and had a certificate and stamp to prove it. The company afforded Leo a legitimate front from behind which he participated in his more nefarious endeavors. It must be understood and appreciated, however, that Acme stood on its own feet as a business enterprise—and did very well for itself. There was always plenty of business for the Brooklyn-based company, even when older, larger, and well-established air-conditioning outfits were sometimes crying so loud that their tears watered down their own dividends. Although Leo Consonno had never taken a course in executive management, he devised a method—sure-fire! no misses!—that might have impressed a graduate of the Harvard School of Business, even if it might not have received his unqualified approval.

The method was simplicity itself and required no sales force and no advertising agency. It did require, however, a few contacts in City Hall. When construction licenses were applied for—hotels, office buildings, hospitals, apartments, motel units, and public-financed construction of any kind—a retainer in the Department of Building and Safety, on the Consonno payroll, quickly notified the president and sales manager of Acme. Leo immediately called the contractor, requesting an opportunity to bid on installing the air-conditioning system in the new project.

The contractor, or developer, usually had his head screwed on tightly enough not to reject Leo's polite request. In a series of following meetings, Leo convinced him that Acme would underbid any other competitor. All the contractor would have to do was to slip Acme the lowest bid received—so Leo could undercut it. By this time the contractor was well aware of Leo's close contacts in the building trades unions. If he wanted no labor trouble on his job, then the contractor wanted Leo . . . needed him! . . . as a friend. Consequently, Leo always got the bid.

On completion of the job, the contractor viewed with despair and dismay the final air-conditioning costs—which far exceeded the original bid. Leo would gently explain that a building inspector had insisted on unforeseen alterations due to shoddy building methods. He also added that only through his, Leo's, own personal interest in the project, did the department grant final approval—or the contractor would have been in *real* trouble, the whole building condemned before completion. Leo did not explain, naturally, that the inspector was also on his payroll.

So Acme Air-conditioning prospered. Leo lounged behind a Danish modern desk in an office that displayed a wide expanse of expensive carpet with extremely thick nap. Carmine Zappinzano sat in a contour chair that enclosed his bulky body firmly in its fine natural-grained wood. Leo toyed with an onyx desk set and occasionally scratched his head with its monogrammed pencil. His upper lip supported a thin, hairline mustache. After speaking, he brushed the individual hairs back in place as if proffering an example of order to the chaos of bushy eyebrows growing wildly across his nose. "You sure?" he asked Carmine.

The under-boss said, "Sure, I'm sure." Zappinzano looked around for an ashtray, then tipped his ash into the cuff of his trousers. "I ain't trusted this son of a bitch Deboli. He's a hustler and he's always bitchin' he don't take home enough. You know what I mean, Leo . . . not right out, but always sumthing a little extra. Like maybe a couple more jukes which we already got promised away. So I'm figuring, if he's got sumthing goin', he ain't coming across with us neither. You get it?"

Leo nodded. "I don't like stingy bastards," he agreed. He scratched his head with the pencil before jamming it back into the holder beside the pen. "You think Mike is giving it to you straight? He ain't just tryin' to pull the rug out from under Tony? He ain't got no score to settle . . . through you, maybe?"

Carmine shook his head. "No. I onny passed out the word to some of the boys. I don't say nothing . . . just 'What's that guy doin' in alla his spare time when he ain't bitchin?' Maybe he's got more important friends than his own family which treats him so bad, huh?"

"So? When Mike called, what'd he say?"

Zappinzano leaned forward, his heavy face screwed into a scowl. "He says that Deboli and Rocco Sapulla are meetin' these creeps in

Dominick's. Mike ain't never seen 'em before. Three ugly bastards —one's a spade. After Tony and Rocco leave, they sit around jabbering in some kinda lingo like foreigners, you know, Leo." Carmine set back in his chair, satisfied with his explanation.

"Hell," Leo said. "That dumb Skinny Mike, he wouldn't recognize Dago if he heard it."

"No, he would all right," Zappinzano disagreed. "He's been 'round long enough he ain't no stranger. I kept askin' him 'bout that. Mike was real positive he said there was a lot of 'wee-wee's' . . . French like. 'Course that was all he could unnerstand anyway." Zappinzano shrugged, no mean feat within the tight confines of the chair.

"French? Frogs . . .?" Leo sat very still. "I heard something. Maybe the Unione ain't so happy. Some of our guys ain't so happy, either." Consonno's voice trailed away as he stared, deep in thought, at his onyx pen and pencil. "So maybe they come over to do some business?" He lifted his eyes. "One was a spade, you said. What'd the others look like?"

"There was this mug . . . hot-shot! Alla boys listened when he opened his mouth. Ugly bastard . . . face all chopped up. You know, scars and all that crap. Him and the spade with halfa ear missin' . . . I tole you that." Carmine thought a moment. "An' another . . . maybe a spic Mike thinks, real soft voice like them guys have, you know, Leo . . ."

"The guy with the funny face . . .?" Leo closed his eyes.

"All dressed up like you. You know, plentya class. Acted like he owned the joint."

"I . . . think . . ." Leo said, his voice low and slow, "I think I make him." He opened his eyes and reached for the phone. "Now maybe I make a mistake, Carmine. Sometimes I do . . . everybody's human, right, Carmine?" Leo silenced Carmine's polite protest and continued, "But then maybe I ain't. And if I ain't, I call the *commissionne* right now!"

Anse said, "I don't like it. What I saw gave me the creeps. Never seen so many black men in my life. More'n I ever saw in Afrique! I tell you right out, they *scared* me!" He shook his head, remembering the grim, rotting streets of Harlem, the hopeless faces staring from windows, the fleeting, furtive shadows in doorways, the lowered, secretive voices—planning, waiting. For what?

Cesar stretched out his legs. His hand held a snifter of brandy. From outside came the muted roar of traffic. He listened to it as if it were speaking, the voice of a strange and terrible city, but he could not understand the words. Anse had heard part of it . . . understood what it was saying . . . up in Harlem. And what he had heard, he had not liked. Cesar shook off the idea—in the comfort of his hotel room at the St. George. "Did you talk to Mo Lyttel?" he asked.

"Not for long," Anse said. "He took me up there. Introduced me to another *mec*, but he didn't hang around." Anse grinned evilly and scratched his mutilated ear. "Fancy pants . . . all duded up. Suede shoes. Name of Zod." Anse grunted. "And full of *merde!*"

"Why'd Mo leave?"

"Don't know. Told me that Zod was one of the biggest dealers in the business . . . next to himself, that is. Sometimes they split up a load together, but usually they work alone. This *mec* in Harlem has his own organization, got all his own pushers. Makes his own deals. So Mo left it up to him and me."

"How'd you get along with Zod?"

"We couldn't talk much." Anse spoke no English. Mo Lyttel spoke some Italian, but after Mo left Anse alone with Zod, communications broke down completely.

"What'd you do?" Cesar asked.

"Zod sent out for a *nana.* Some gal from Haiti who spoke a little French."

Cesar shook his head. "I don't like that. She heard everything you said?"

"How could I help it? Otherwise we'd both still be up there eyeballing each other."

"Where was Deboli all this time?"

"He went on after he drove me to meet Mo."

Cesar swore softly. "This thing's coming apart," he said. "Deboli knows Mo. I figured you'd get along better with Mo and his people than I would. You'd all work together. What happens? Deboli takes off; Mo takes off; and Zod brings in some whore off the street! No one knows what the hell the others are planning." Cesar paused, then added, "Or maybe everyone knows *too* much about what's going on."

"This Zod," Anse said. "He's anxious to do business. He don't like the Di Carlo mob. They . . . supposed to claim Harlem. Dudes stuck him a couple of times."

"How anxious?"

"He'll take all or any part of the hundred kilos."

Cesar nodded. At street value an uncut kilo was worth nearly half a million dollars. "When?"

"Sooner the better. Wants a test on delivery." Anse shrugged. "Told him sure . . . our stuff was pure. Test all he wanted." He glanced at Cesar. "How'd Cuir make out?"

"Don't know. He's not back yet," Cesar said. The *picciotto* had attended a meeting with Ray Arriquez that afternoon in the Puerto Rican and Cuban territory above 131st Street. Part Portuguese, Cuir had some understanding of Spanish.

Shortly afterwards, Cuir knocked on the door and entered. He poured himself a drink and sat down. "Tough *mecs!*" he said, shaking his head. "I got a real pushing around." He took a drink of the liquor. "Suspicious as hell!"

"Of what?" Cesar asked.

"How good's the stuff? Where's the muscle coming from?"

"You tell them that's their goddamned problem?" Cesar said.

"Di Carlo's people haven't cut 'em off entirely. Not yet. But Arriquez says that if they start buying from outside, there's going to be trouble. He don't want to put his *mecs* out on the streets."

"Big Mo . . . Zod. Deboli and Sapulla! Their *mecs* will be out there," Cesar said.

"Yeah, but Arriquez—he wasn't too impressed. Says they're not enough guns. They'll get burned up!"

Cesar thought to himself that Arriquez was probably right. On the other hand, the *commissionne* preferred to stay away from open warfare in the streets. Not only was fighting costly, it besmirched the clean name of business. The word for his operation, he decided, was "pressure." He would apply pressure . . . a little here in Brooklyn, some in Harlem and upper Manhattan. Then wait and see what happened. How would the Cosa Nostra react? Quite possibly it would make a deal. Peace. Business for all. Meanwhile, he would do nothing to openly challenge or anger the organization. Perhaps it had a weak spot of which he was not yet aware. With enough time, he would find it. However, he missed Luigi Venito; he wished he knew what everybody was thinking out there!

Nine men, grave as Justices of the Supreme Court, sat at a long, highly polished, mahogany table. Before each was a yellow pad of legal-size paper and a matching yellow pencil. Twelve floors below, traffic flowed along Fifth Avenue, starting and stopping at the lights as if controlled in huge spurts by a gigantic hose. Most of the men listened intently to the speakers, although a few doodled on the yellow paper, building elaborate designs but taking no notes. The *commissionne* was in session.

Leo Consonno spoke earnestly. "I know what I'm talking about. He's from Marseilles . . . patriarch of the Sati Family there. He's got a couple of his buttons with him. I got reports he's already trying to put together a deal with a couple of my boys. The stinkin' bastards got him together with Big Mo Lyttel. You know what that means?" He looked around the table at the serious, heavy faces. No one spoke. "*I* know what it means," Leo went on. "It means there'll be enough H in Brooklyn—up to our balls! The Feds are giving me 'nuff trouble already . . . so I should go out askin' for more?" He shook his head in disbelief.

Don Albert leaned forward, resting his arms on the table. As head of the Di Carlo Family, he spoke with assurance. "With all my respects to Don Leo, he ain't hardly put it strong enough. Now I been sitting on a situation . . . jess waitin' to explode . . . for a long time. You gentlemen know, of course, I'm referring to niggertown and Little Cuba. When this *commissionne* decided to put the clamps on H, them meatheads didn't like it. But what could they do?" Albert spread his hands expansively and shrugged. "Nothing. They had to get the stuff from me, or they didn't get it. Right?"

Eight heads nodded agreement around the table.

"Okay," Di Carlo continued. "So now Zod Henry and Ray Arriquez can tell me to go piss in my hat. They can buy . . ." Albert paused and spaced out his words with deliberation, "direct . . . from . . . Sati. Enough goddamn, pure, one hundred percent, white H to plaster the frigging walls of *The New York Times!*" His eyes flared with anger as he looked at his peers. "You get it? If not, I'll tell you. It means once them bastards get out from under, I ain't never going to get 'em back under control again! And . . . you gentlemen won't neither!" Breathless from his oratory, Albert leaned back in his chair.

Don Carlo Mascotti, from Buffalo and acting chairman of the meeting, glanced down the table. "Anybody else got something to say. How about you, Frank?"

Don Frank Liardi was seated next to James Mangello, who was drawing an intricate series of *X*'s on his pad. Liardi turned his thin, dark face toward the chairman. "I think Leo Consonno said alla it. I agree . . . except maybe I got one thing to add. So, okay, everybody says 'Forget the shit. Too hot to handle. To hell with the dough coming in—it ain't worth the heat from the Narcs.' But that don't mean some goddamned *foreigner* walks in and cops the business, does it? We built it up. It's ours!" He looked at Mangello. "Right, Jimmy?"

Mangello stopped doodling long enough to nod and say, "Yeah, that's right . . ."

Mascotti made a steeple of his fingers and regarded them in silence. Finally, he said to Consonno, "I guess maybe you plan to take care of Deboli and Sapulla yourself?"

"Yeah," agreed Leo. "I got plans—if the *commissionne* approves."

"It's entirely a matter inside your own Family," Mascotti told him. "Them are your boys—don't concern us."

"How about Sati?" Di Carlo asked.

"Well," said the chairman, "we better talk about him."

Chapter 37

The subway in the St. George disgorged a crowd of com-
muters into the bowels of the hotel. They climbed the stairs
and swarmed into the street, continuing homeward on foot
in the dusk of the Brooklyn night. The old brownstone
houses of the Heights, lining the narrow, quiet streets,
seemed part of another era—as indeed they were when once
they housed merchants and importers whose clippers
ranged the seas. From the captains-walks on the Heights,
the first sight of their sails could be glimpsed on their return
voyage home.

Cesar emerged from the lobby of the hotel accompanied
by Anse and Cuir. They were quickly absorbed by the
crowd hurrying along the sidewalk. Cesar lit a dark cigarette as he strolled, glancing occasionally into the shop
windows as he passed. He paused to cross at an intersection,
and stepped back quickly into the crowd on the curb as a
cream-colored truck with a sign 'HOME BAKERY' reck-
lessly ran a light.

Further down the block, Cesar and his companions entered the Amsterdam Grill. The restaurant was still nearly
deserted at the early dinner hour, and they were quickly
seated in a booth along one wall. An aquarium, lighted and
filled with large lobsters, stood to one side and partly
blocked the view of the front entrance. "We've two more

to join us," Cesar told the waiter. "Meantime, we'll have three cognacs."

Well into their second drink, Cesar glanced at his wristwatch. "Deboli and Sapulla are late." The swinging doors of the kitchen opened and two men, dressed in white uniforms, entered carrying large canvas breadbaskets stenciled "Amalfie—Home Bakery." They set the baskets on the floor and looked around, then began to unpack long loaves and stack them on a rack by a waiter's station.

A latent instinct suddenly warned Cesar. He upended the heavy table and threw himself on the floor as a burp gun began to cough and spit lead. Almost immediately it was joined by a second.

The table splintered, and tufts of leather from the booth floated like black leaves around the men. Anse, gun in hand, shouted, "Son of a bitch!" and got off a shot before he fell, half cut in two by a riveting line of bullets. One of the killers in white dropped his weapon and grabbed his belly, where a stain blossomed into a red camellia. His companion poured another round into the booth, grasped the wounded man, and fled back into the kitchen. The last hurried shots smashed the aquarium, and a flood of water poured into the room, carrying seaweed, oyster shells, and lobsters along the floor.

Cesar lay very still. Finally he moved, drawing himself to his knees behind the wreckage of the table. "Anse . . .?" Anse, beside him, lay on his back, his lips drawn in a grin of death; the porcelain white eyes stared, unseeing, at the ceiling. His belly, gaping with rough edges, looked as if a great tree-saw had been drawn through it. The thick red pools of blood, thinning out with seawater, were assuming the delicate pastel color of a pink birthday cake. Cesar lifted the black head. "Anse?" He could think of nothing to say. He loosened the black hand still gripping the revolver.

Cuir lay a step or two further away from the shambles. He had been shot in the back, part of his head missing, as he stood up from the table when Cesar upset it. The *picciotto* had caught the first blast of the guns, temporarily saving the other two in the booth. Cesar was unable to distinguish Cuir's features beneath the blood and brains besplattering them.

It seemed to Cesar that time had stopped. After the blasting rattle and spit of the machine guns, all was silence. Action was suspended in the room. Abruptly it came to life again. Waiters, busboys, and cooks ran shouting to the street.

Cesar looked at Anse's gun in his hand. He tried to remember something. Important! He forced himself to think . . . recall. Just before the shooting, he had looked at his watch. What time was it now? He looked at his watch again. Seven twenty!

His assassins did not yet know that he had not been killed. How much time did that give him before they found out? Half an hour, forty-five minutes? Be safe . . . say, thirty minutes. The two gunmen had already fled, but there would be plants around to listen . . . and report back. When the Dons heard he was still alive, they would try again—quickly as possible! Next time, he might not be so lucky.

Cesar had thirty minutes of grace, half an hour's jump on them, to save his life.

In the distance, he heard the sound of police sirens.

Get moving, man! Get moving!

Grasping the revolver, Cesar ran toward the kitchen. He burst through the doors, a terrible and horrendous sight caked in blood. A chef and pot boy backed away from him as he grasped a towel and dipped it in hot water to wipe off his face. A topcoat hung from a hook behind a door and he tore it down, changing it for the blood-stained jacket he was wearing. Nothing was said. Nothing needed to be said. Cesar waved his gun and disappeared through the back door into the alley behind the restaurant.

His feet pounded the pavement as he circled back toward the St. George. He forced himself to resume walking and made his way to the subway. He rode it beneath the river and got off at the Wall Street stop. From there, he took a taxi to Washington Square.

In the rooming house he showered, freeing himself of the last bloodstains, and completely changed his clothes. His face, dammit! The police and the mob would recognize his description anywhere. They would be waiting . . . expecting him . . . at the airports, train stations, and bus depots. How much time did he have left? No time!

It was already eight o'clock. The news was out.

He forced himself to sit down on the bed and think—quietly, calmly. He could not remain there, hiding; it was only a matter of time until he was traced. And if he did leave, where would he go?

Canada? Mexico? Too obvious. That would be anticipated, too. Besides, the mob connections were good in both countries. They would get him in either place.

But he was certain of one thing: He had to get out of New York. Rising, he picked up his airline bag, put the gun in his pocket, and left the rooming house. He walked down University Place until he passed a small grocery. It was closed, but a young man, wearing overalls, was unloading crates of vegetables from a rusty red pickup truck. Cesar paused and watched him for a few moments. "Is that your truck?" he asked.

The youth shook his head. "Belongs to my old man."

"Want to make some money with it?"

"Doing what?" The youth stopped and regarded Cesar with a quizzical look.

"Giving me a ride," Cesar said.

"Where?" The youth lifted another crate from the open deck of the truck and placed it on the pavement.

Cesar thought a moment, trying to recall the maps he had memorized of the area. New Jersey was strong Cosa Nostra territory. Connecticut wasn't much better. He wanted to jump out of New York in one leap. "Pennsylvania," he said.

"Where in Pennsy?"

Cesar pulled a name off the map. "Easton," he said.

"That's maybe . . . like . . . a hundred miles."

"I'll pay you a dollar per mile."

"A hundred bucks?"

Cesar nodded. "And the same for your trip back."

The youth whistled softly. "You must be real anxious to get there."

"I am," Cesar agreed.

"Look," the boy said, "you really mean that? You're not kidding? You'll give me two hundred bucks to drive you to Easton? 'Course, I'll drive you, but I gotta get back by noon 'cause my old man needs the truck, and I gotta call him and tell him why I'm not coming back tonight. We gotta truck farm . . ."

Cesar handed him two fifty-dollar bills. "That's for the trip over," he said. "You get two more . . . just like them . . . when you start back."

The boy stuffed the bills in his overalls. "I'll call my dad from inside there . . ." he motioned toward the grocery. "When I come back, we'll get rolling."

Cesar nodded, tossed his airline bag into the cab of the truck, and climbed in. "Hey, what's your name, mister?" the boy called from the door of the grocery.

"Baker," Cesar replied laconically. "Holmes Baker."

After leaving Newark, the black line of the highway pointed west, leading forever to nowhere and everywhere, across the state of New Jersey. Signs pointed to towns: South Bound Brook, Mountainside, Millstone; earthy American names of Bernardsville, Pottersville, Stewardsville; Long Valley, Middle Valley, Far Hills; and the "burgs"—Stephensburg, Pattenburg, and Phillipsburg. The red Ford pickup raced behind the path of its lamps through the night.

The boy's name, Cesar discovered, was Clinton Pollock. Young Pollock drove with the practiced ease of a boy raised behind the wheel of a car. In the cab of the truck was a radio, assembled and installed by the youth, and it was tuned to a station that played records through the hours of the drive. At eleven o'clock the schedule was interrupted for a news and weather forecast. "Tonight," the newscaster read, "violence and sudden death erupted in a quiet Brooklyn eatery. Two men were left dead. How many were wounded is not known. Police are looking for a third man—one of the intended victims, who apparently escaped. The dead have not been identified, but they are believed to have been involved in a Mafia feud. Meanwhile, two other well-known gangsters have been found dead in a parking lot in the Williamsburg district. Authorities say they are Anthony (Tony) Deboli and Rocco (Rocky) Sapulla, both members of the Consonno Family. The two men were killed by shotgun blasts as they walked to Deboli's car parked in the lot. Police do not know if the killings in the restaurant and parking lot are related. And now for the weather. Tonight will be clear and slightly cooler for New York and vicinity . . ." The newsman's voice droned on.

Cesar thought: "The *flics!* They'll find our passports in the St. George." He tried to remember the names Anse and Cuir had used, but they had traveled under so many, during the long years, that it was difficult to recall. Not that it really made that much difference anyway. There were more passports and more names in the airline bag beneath his feet on the floor of the cab.

"Those guys sure are pros," young Pollock said suddenly.

The music, again blasting in the truck, returned Cesar to the present. He looked at the young face, staring straight ahead through the path of light, down the highway. "What?"

"Those gangsters. Killers. They know what they're doing," the boy said. "Real professionals . . . like doctors or lawyers, or anybody else earning a living. They know their business." He patted the wheel of the truck. "Take me for instance. Like, my dad says there's good money to be made in truck farmin'. But you gotta know what you're doing. Make every inch of ground count. Be scientific!" He glanced rather shyly at Cesar. "He wants me to go to agricultural college . . ."

"Are you going?"

Clinton Pollock smiled. "I guess so. It's not such a bad life. I . . . sorta like the farm. Nobody around to boss you." He laughed. "And no time clocks to punch."

Cesar suddenly remembered another young face, Paolo, who also loved the land. The lucky ones in life, he decided, were those who had something to love. What had he, Cesar, ever loved? Certainly not Valle Satisanni, or he would not have given it away. Not his father who he had buried without a tear. Not lumbering Gio or black Anse. All of them had died and he had felt no grief, because he had never felt love. But that was not entirely true! Once . . . he had loved Vivian. Had he really? Or had her rebuff so injured his pride that he had cloaked the incident in colors of romance? Yet, even now, fleeing for his life in a rattling, rusty truck through the New Jersey countryside, he would have returned to New York to spend the night with her. "Ridiculous!" he said aloud. "This is sheer bathos," he added to himself. "Right now, your one problem is to stay alive long enough to get back home."

Cesar's exclamation caused Clinton to look at him. "Ridiculous?" the boy asked.

"Yes. I meant . . . it's ridiculous to be tied down to a job . . . like you said," Cesar explained.

The boy appeared satisfied with the answer. "Yeah, that's not for me. What do you do?"

"I don't have a regular job either. I'm an . . . importer."

"Of what?"

They were talking about olives, and olive oil, tomatoes and artichokes, when the truck reached Easton, Pennsylvania, in the early hours of the morning. "Where do you want off?" Clinton asked as they drove through the darkened, empty streets.

"The hotel," Cesar said.

The truck pulled up in front of a rambling, low, wooden building with a wide porch. Cesar looked at it, picked up his airline bag and opened the door. He paused, then stopped. Reaching into his pocket, he took out another hundred dollars and handed them to the waiting youth. "Nearly forgot . . ." Cesar said.

"Thanks, Mr. Baker," Clinton said. "Hope you have a good trip west."

"So do I," said Cesar. On a sudden impulse, he gave the boy another fifty dollars.

Young Pollock was surprised. "You don't need . . ." he started to protest.

Cesar interrupted him. "That's in case you get back late. Perhaps your father won't be so angry."

Clinton grinned. "My old man's a pretty good guy," he said. "But we can sure use the dough all right."

Cesar watched the red eye of the taillight diminish down the street. When it was gone, he felt a sense of regret, as though its disappearance had severed his final tie with the past—with Anse and Cuir and New York and the great expanse of ocean that separated him from France. Here he was alone; finally, completely, utterly. Oddly enough, he felt no particular fear; it was as if he were a young man again alone in the mountains of Corsica . . . the days when he followed the hidden trails from Ghisonacia to Col Pieto by instinct alone. Now he would follow an unfamiliar trail again—to California.

Picking up his airline case, he entered the hotel. A sleeping clerk aroused to register him and assign him a room. "Kinda late," the desk clerk said.

"Car broke down," Cesar replied.

His room was old but comfortable. He undressed, placed Anse's gun beneath the pillow, and climbed into the large bed. Stretching out, he tried to blank out the last twelve hours, but he could not forget the sound of the guns and the sight of his men lying in their blood on the floor. Who would claim the chewed-up bodies of Anse and Cuir? Who would bury them? Or would they be buried among the other nameless of potter's field? Not that it made much difference, anymore, to Anse and Cuir. Where the hell would Anse have been buried anyway? Morocco . . . Algeria? Anse had spent all of his life running—from nowhere to final obscurity.

Perhaps . . . just possibly . . . Joseph might read about Anse's death and make arrangements. Safe, from the distance of Marseilles, Joseph could handle it. With that comforting thought, Cesar fell asleep.

In the morning Cesar got up, showered, and dressed. He bought shaving supplies at a drugstore and a pair of dark sunglasses. The glasses were not much of a disguise, he realized, but he also knew that descriptions of him, sent out by the police or the mobs, were verbal. No pictures of him existed in the United States, and it would take several days, a week perhaps, to get a photo from Europe. He must make use of that time lag. There was nothing he could do about his broken nose or the scars on his face—at least not for the present. But an idea was developing in Cesar's mind. A plan . . . now vague . . . that could be elaborated by which he would evade arrest by the police, or death by the Cosa Nostra. He was good at planning; very good! The more he thought about it, the more he saw its possibilities. Once started, it led to many things. The plan would take some doing, but Cesar assured himself it could be done. . . .

He bought a bus ticket to Ohio.

Chapter 38

A week later Cesar arrived in Los Angeles. The bus was caught up in a heavy stream of traffic far outside the limits of the city. Cesar dozed in his seat beside the tinted window through which a gray expanse of desert steamed beneath a near tropical sun. When he started his cross-country trip, he had no idea of the enormity of distance he would travel. Since then he had traveled nearly three thousand miles across endless acres of rolling farmlands; ridden past awe-inspiring mountains that made the high passes of Col Pieto seem little more than the work of ambitious moles; traversed deserts with wild, twisted cactuses, joshua trees, yucca, and sagebrush. He had crossed the gray, rolling flood of the Mississippi, seen the multicolored buttes rising like monolithic sculpture from the hands of a stone god.

The buses had all been alike; he had changed so often that he could no longer remember or differentiate between them. The passengers, even the drivers in their gray uniforms, seemed to be the same. Cesar had been careful in selecting his route, avoiding the large cities where he might possibly be identified by an alert policeman at the bus station. Consequently, his journey had taken longer and been more circuitous than if he had taken a transcontinental bus directly across the country.

But the long hours, riding alone in his seat, had given him time to formulate his new plan. To work it out in detail.

He was convinced that his trail had been lost, although the story was still carried in the newspapers. He bought papers when the bus stopped and read them carefully. Anse and Cuir were identified and their connection with the Sati Family established. He, Cesar, was also tentatively identified, but was thought either to be hiding out in New York or had made his escape to Mexico or Canada. Well enough for the authorities, but it was the Cosa Nostra that Cesar still feared. The organization would know better than the police that he was not laying low in New York, and had, most probably, not yet left the country. The *commissionne* was still waiting for him to make a move by plane or ship—there was simply no other way he could get back to Europe.

Los Angeles and San Francisco also had West Coast Cosa Nostra Families. These would cooperate with the east. The western buttons would still be watching the airports from which flights to Europe originated. But Los Angeles was also a city of tourists, people with eccentricities, a metropolis flung up and down the coast with little central cohesion. Beneath its veneer of flamboyance, a man—with money—would find anything for which he looked and could pay for. In Los Angeles, Cesar did not believe that he would be conspicuous.

The bus pulled into the downtown Los Angeles bus station—noisy, crowded, and littered with the debris of weary travelers. Cesar alighted, carrying his airline bag, and walked out into the street. He took a taxi to Hollywood.

His first sight of the famous movie capital disappointed him. Quiet, nondescript, unglamorous, the miscellany of buildings, traffic and crowds were unlike what he had expected. The taxi pulled up and stopped before the doors of a large hotel and Cesar got out. He was registered at a busy desk without a glance and assigned a room. It was furnished with modern furniture, boasted piped-in stereo music and color TV, and overlooked a swimming pool at which guests were trying for instant sunburn.

After the bellman had departed with his tip, Cesar ripped open the airline bag to count the money and traveler's checks in it. He had nearly twenty thousand dollars left, as well as two unused passports. Again selecting a Canadian forgery—carrying the name of Romain Dubois, occupation engineer, age forty-two, unmarried, home Quebec—he destroyed the second passport and burned it in an ashtray.

For some minutes Cesar stood before a mirror studying himself. He shook his head in disapproval at the dusty, wrinkled dark suit, white shirt, and conservative tie. Stuffing the traveler's checks into his pocket, he turned on his heel and left the room.

Off the lobby of the hotel, an expensive men's clothing store took care of Cesar's immediate shopping needs. He ordered a number of sport shirts, jackets, slacks, and several pairs of casual shoes, with instructions that the purchases be delivered to his room. Leaving the shop, he stopped at a desk in the lobby to arrange to lease a car. An attractive girl, wearing a chic baby-blue uniform, efficiently made out the necessary papers. "May I see your driver's license?" she asked.

Cesar hesitated, only momentarily, as he realized his driver's license was not Canadian to match his passport. He patted his pocket as if trying to locate it. "International . . ." he said apologetically. "Must've left it in my room. I'll get it—and be back."

"I'll keep your papers ready," the girl smiled.

Cesar returned to his room. Christ, he thought, I've got to be careful. Nearly slipped—next time I might be in trouble. He took out the small, brown, bookletlike international license issued to him in Marseilles. He studied it carefully, then shrugged. He would have to forge another name—even if he ruined the license. It was useless as it was now made out. A simple job for Luigi Venito; Cesar wished for him now. He had watched the little forger work many times, and he tried to remember, in detail, the materials Venito had used. A fine-line lettering brush, pen, solvents, bleach, ink . . . and what else?

He left the hotel and walked down Sunset Boulevard to buy the materials, stopping in a drugstore and an art supply shop. Passing a large department store, he remembered the other items he needed. In it he bought a small clothes steamer about the size of a coffee cup, and a tiny electric pressing iron.

Returning to his room, Cesar set to work—carefully and cautiously. He steamed the page with the name and address, loosening the ink, then carefully traced the lettering with solvent, repeating the process until the original markings disappeared. The solvents and bleach had whitened the background enough to be noticeable, so a dilution of brown ink and water brushed over the lines returned the paper very close to its original color.

A knock at the door interrupted him. His new clothes were delivered. He returned immediately to his task, printing in the name of Romain Dubois and the Quebec address and permitted the page to dry before pressing it flat with the iron. *Voilà!* Cesar inspected it closely—not perfect by any means, but fair enough to take a chance. He needed a car. Taxis keep records.

Cesar dressed himself in his new clothes and returned to the rent-a-car desk. The girl accepted the license and as she started to look at it, Cesar distracted her. Reaching into his pocket, he took out a thick roll of dollars. "I may want the car for some time," he said, "so I'll pay a deposit on it. How much?"

The girl looked up, surprised. "You don't want to charge it to a credit card?"

"No, I'd rather pay for it," Cesar said. "This is my first trip to Los Angeles and I'll do a lot of driving. When I go home, where can I leave it?"

"Oh," the girl replied, indifferently. "Are you flying?"

"Probably," Cesar said.

"At the airport," the girl said. "We have an office out at LAX. Just turn the keys in there."

Cesar paid her three hundred dollars, took the keys to a Ford, and went to the bar to have a drink before making a phone call—to put into effect the primary step of his plan.

The County Medical Association office gave him the names of three doctors. The first one was Dr. Simon Sherman of Beverly Hills.

Dr. Sherman was a small, slender man with a deep suntan, sandy, sun-bleached hair, and mobile, delicate hands. His office, in an air-conditioned building behind towering palm trees, was soundproofed and filled with fine paintings—reflected into infinity by antique, gold-veined, mirrored walls. Elegant, carefully-selected furniture graced a waiting room filled with muted strains of joyous music. The usual antiseptic smell of disinfectant was missing; it was replaced by the intoxicating aroma of expensive perfume arising from the breast of a bosomy, long-legged nurse in a tight-fitting, form-tailored, white silk uniform.

Dr. Sherman motioned Cesar to stand by a window while he examined the scars on his face beneath direct sunlight. "Bad!" he told Cesar. "You've had them for some time."

"Yes," Cesar said. "Can you do anything about them?"

"Why'd you wait so long?" the doctor asked.

"Never had the time . . . or money . . . before," Cesar said, evasively. "Besides, I've always heard the best plastic surgeons are in New York and Hollywood."

"Some of the *best* are," Sherman agreed, his voice including himself in the select circle. "So this is your first trip out here?"

"Yes."

Sherman returned to his desk and waved Cesar to a chair facing him. "You're not on probation . . . don't have a police record?"

"No," Cesar said. "Why?"

"If you were, I can't legally perform an operation."

Cesar took out his passport and placed it on the desk. "That's who I am," he said. "If I were a criminal, I wouldn't be permitted to travel. You see what my face looks like. Who wouldn't want to get it changed? I've had to wear it for ten years. It's interfered with my business. And my social life.

Sherman nodded. "Reason enough."

Cesar sat back in his chair. "Can you . . . will you do it?"

"No problem with your nose," the doctor said thoughtfully. "Now we use hard plastics to replace bone for people with smashed-up noses . . . they're better than bone or cartilage. The scars are more of a problem. The deep scars have to be elevated. Planing will remove the raised ones with scar tissue." He nodded as if to himself. "It can be done."

"A new face?" Cesar asked.

Simon Sherman waved a hand. "Now you are talking about plastic surgery. I'm a cosmetic plastic surgeon. I don't do heavy reconstructive work."

"What's the difference?" Cesar asked.

"The difference between an architect and an artist. You're an engineer, you should recognize the difference. I don't rebuild faces . . . molding them from nothing with noses, chins, and ears. I simply take what you have and make it look better. A lot better!" He continued to stare at Cesar. "Matter of fact, I've never known a completely *ugly* person. Most of the so-called ones simply have one bad feature. Usually it's the nose—the nose is the key structure of the face. Fix it, and the man or woman is good-looking. Which reminds me . . . do you have an old photograph of yourself? One taken before the accident."

"No," Cesar said. The doctor looked disappointed. "I can tell you, though," Cesar continued quickly, "that my whole face looked entirely different."

Sherman was puzzled. "Leaving the nose and scars aside, how's that? Your face structure wasn't destroyed."

"For one thing," Cesar replied, "my eyes were more like this . . ." Cesar pressed his fingers at the corners of his eyes, slanting them slightly. "My nose was longer . . . and thinner. My chin was straighter, more square," Cesar explained, describing facial characteristics that were never his.

The doctor fixed his eyes on Cesar's face as if examining it under a microscope. "I can understand about your nose," he said. "But I don't get the rest of it. Your eyes . . . oriental?" He paused, then shrugged. "Possibly the scarring pulled the skin enough to change the shape. But I've never heard of it before. Interesting . . ."

"And the same on the chin." Cesar pointed to the deep scar at the corner of his lip. "Here! Where this pulls down."

"Was a muscle cut?"

"I don't know."

"If it's a muscle, it can be rejoined," Sherman said. "If it's a main nerve, you're in for trouble." He pushed a button on his desk. The nurse in the silk uniform strolled into the office. "Miss Cannon," the doctor said, "I think we would like some coffee. Coffee, Mr. Dubois?"

"Yes, thanks," Cesar said.

"Black?" asked Miss Cannon.

"Yes." Cesar watched the roll of her hips as she sauntered from the office.

"Incidentally," the doctor said. "Such an operation as you're anticipating will cost a little . . ."

"How much?"

"Five thousand dollars," Sherman said cheerfully. "Plus hospital expenses. I have my own hospital where you'll be quite comfortable."

Miss Cannon returned with the coffee in two bone-china cups with sterling silver spoons. She gave Cesar a soothing smile as she handed him his cup. Once more she made an exit, her hips rolling to the beat of silent drums.

The idea of a private hospital pleased Cesar. He would be safe in it—a welcome *planque*. "The price is all right," he told Sherman. "Only thing is—I want to know what I'm going to look like. If it isn't right, I can't very well exchange it for a new one."

Sherman smiled thinly. "I don't guarantee *anything*," he said. "However, before we start surgery, I'll make a sketch, according to your description. You'll approve it, and I'll follow it as best I can."

The following morning, Cesar checked out of the hotel and drove to the hospital. On a secluded side street, it was a low, two-storey building, a cheerful pastel pink, set in a green lawn with shrubs and flowering bushes. Behind it was a parking lot for staff and patients where he left his Ford, a stranger among Cadillacs and Continentals.

His hospital room was bright with wallpaper, a thick rug, and expensive bedroom furniture including a chaise lounge. A table held a number of new magazines and recent novels, as well as a vase of freshly cut flowers. All the boudoir lacked, Cesar thought, was a woman. She soon appeared, an attractive blonde in heavy eye shadow, silk uniform, and well-rounded figure. Breezily, she told him to shave, shower, and change to his pajamas. "Doctor will see you soon," she said.

"This doesn't look much like a hospital," Cesar said.

"Do you like it? Doctor tries to make this a *happy* experience. When a patient comes here, why be depressed? He's going to leave here—with a new life ahead of him."

"You don't know how right you are!" Cesar told her.

Dr. Sherman appeared shortly, dressed in immaculate white from jacket to shoes. He carried with him the sketch he had prepared under Cesar's supervision the day before. "You're sure this is right?" Sherman was still skeptical.

"Absolutely," Cesar assured him after examining the portrait of a Mediterranean male with long nose, jutting chin, and narrow slanting eyes. "But there's one thing more. Long as I'm having the operation, do I have to come out still looking like forty-two?"

Sherman laughed. "You want a face-lift, too?"

"Why not? I'll pay for it."

319

The doctor shrugged. "I can give you a breast transplant while I'm at it. A couple of big boobs that stick straight out."

Cesar smiled. "No. I'll find my own." He walked to the dresser and took five packets of one thousand dollars then handed them to Sherman. "How much extra for the face-lift?"

Sherman shook his head and pocketed the money. "Be my guest," he said.

Cesar, under a local anesthetic, lay on a slightly inclined operating table staring into a bank of overhead lights. His head was strapped, immovable. Dr. Sherman, aided by two nurses, peered into his face. Then the surgeon started to work.

In the next hour, an incision was made under Cesar's chin and a small molded sponge implanted beneath it; indented scars were also filled out with the plastic sponge; his skin was planed. Tiny incisions beneath the lower eyelashes loosened the skin, the baggy tissue tailored to fit the tightening slit of the tilting eyes, the excess skin snipped off, and the incisions resewn with very tiny nylon thread; much the same was done to the upper lids. Then the nose was rebuilt, while the doctor occasionally referred to his sketch. The nose was narrowed and lengthened, the nostrils carefully curved. Finally Sherman started the face-lift, with incisions around the ears and in the hairline at the back of the neck. The skin was pulled up, the excess clipped away, and the incision sewn up.

Collodion, a transparent dressing, was swabbed on the surgery of the eyes, and pressure bandages were applied to prevent swelling of the face.

"There you are!" Sherman exclaimed.

"Animal, vegetable, or mineral?" asked Cesar.

"You'll find out," the doctor said.

320

Chapter 39

Cesar remained in the hospital longer than required. While he might have left after two days, he preferred to stay until all swelling and discoloration disappeared and the stitches were removed. His room was comfortable, more so than his hotel, and the privacy of patients was strictly maintained. Many of the patients, Cesar discovered, were show business stars or aging, wealthy dowagers who dipped into Simon Sherman's pool of eternal youth and were not anxious for publicity. This suited Cesar perfectly, for his anonymity was not a matter of ego but of life and death.

He was satisfied with the operation. It was so successful that it presented a new problem. His new face did not resemble, in any way, the old photo in the passport of Romain Dubois. Cesar had a new passport picture taken and mounted one in the document after stamping it with an embossed seal—from a Canadian silver dollar.

On the day Cesar packed to leave the hospital, Dr. Sherman dropped into his room to say goodbye. He eyed his handiwork and said, with satisfaction, "Your own mother wouldn't recognize you."

"That's good," Cesar said. "I wouldn't want her to."

"You look ten . . . possibly fifteen . . . years younger."

Cesar nodded. "Any younger and I'd have to go into a foster home. For kids!" He locked his suitcase. "You did a good job, Doc. No complaints."

Sherman was slightly puzzled at Cesar's cool acceptance of his new image. "I'd better warn you," he said to Cesar, "your family, friends, girl friend are going to have to get used to you all over again."

Cesar looked at Sherman, but said nothing.

Cesar drove the Ford to Los Angeles International Airport and turned in the keys to the rent-a-car desk. He picked up his ticket and went to the staging area, where his passport was stamped after a punctilious glance. With his new face and American clothes, he was quickly absorbed into the crowd of waiting passengers.

Until his flight was announced, however, Cesar covertly searched the heavily trafficked premises for possible pursuers. His new face was being put to its first test and he wondered if it would pass inspection by the police and the Mafiosi who were, he knew, still watching the ports of exit from the United States. He sat quietly, although alertly, behind an open newspaper, watching the crowds around him. One traveler, he thought, might be a mobster. The man's appearance differed little from the other passengers, but he also seemed to be watching the crowd, examining each new arrival with hard, suspicious eyes.

With a feeling of relief, Cesar heard the metallic voice of the public address system announce, "TWA Flight Seven-O-Five to London, now ready for boarding. Gate Three . . ." Rising from the seat, he casually folded his paper and walked, without a backward glance, toward the gate.

He arrived in Orly Airfield in Paris, via London, and passed through customs without delay. It was the first time his feet had touched French soil in nearly two months—long ago, it seemed, when he and Anse and Cuir had left for New York. But that was past, and best forgotten. Other more important matters had to be taken care of, now: the second stage of his plan.

Cesar arranged, quickly, for another rent-a-car using his Romain Dubois passport and driver's license, and drove into the city. He checked into a hotel on the Left Bank, near the Quai des Grand Augustins. Across the Seine stood the lovely towers of Notre Dame in the dusk dissolving into night. After enjoying a leisurely dinner, he then drove to Montmartre and parked the car. Tourists thronged the streets, which were lined with cheap bistros, cafés, pornographic bookstalls, and striptease shows. Cesar was looking for one Jean le-Sport. He debated the risk of approaching the pimp and pusher once he found him, but decided he had no choice.

It was after midnight when Cesar finally located le-Sport in a poorly lit bar. The pusher, half-drunk, was wary. But Cesar, with knowledgeable talk and impressive display of cash, persisted. They had never met, so Cesar was not afraid that le-Sport would discover his true identity. The shifty street-dealer was so low in the hierarchy of the underworld that it was with great difficulty that Cesar had recalled his name. Jean le-Sport was the only small-time operator that Cesar could remember in Paris, for he wished to avoid the Unione chieftains of the Affinito Family in the city. Cesar feared that the pusher might later recall a mysterious sale to an unidentified stranger during this particular week. Rumors have an unpleasant habit of turning up to haunt the underworld—and to be remembered years later. His trip to Paris and his purchase of heroin must remain a secret.

Cesar paid the waiter for the third round of drinks and shoved the roll of francs back in his pocket. Across the table, le-Sport sat with a fixed, glazed expression on his face, staring through the cloud of smoke wreathing his head. "I'm not going through *cette merde* again," Cesar said. "I don't want one of your filthy whores. I'm here to have a good time—and I intend to have it! Now, do I get it or don't I?"

The pusher shook his head woozily as if to clear it. "How come you know I got the stuff?" he asked thickly. "Maybe you're a *flic.*" He shrugged. "I don't know you . . ."

Cesar displayed his passport. "Read! For yourself! That's who I am! I'm from Quebec. Arrived today. The concierge at Le Normandie, where I'm staying, said you sent a *nana* to the hotel one night. She told him you could always hustle up a deck or two. That's why I'm here!" Cesar returned the passport to his pocket and again took out his roll so the pusher could see it. "How about it?" His thumb riffled the bills.

The pusher appeared convinced. "How many . . .?" le-Sport asked, draining his glass.

At street level the white stuff was cut as much as ninety-eight percent—even more. Cesar calculated quickly. "Half a dozen."

The pusher turned his head and spoke over his shoulder. "'Nette!" A bargirl, horsey-faced, grotesque, with heavy makeup, slouched from the bar and came up to stand behind le-Sport. "Six decks," he told her. She reached inside the neck of her sweat-stained dress and took out six small cellophane packets from her brassiere. Each contained an ounce of heroin. She handed the envelopes to le-Sport, who palmed them from sight, and sauntered back to her stool at the bar.

Le-Sport motioned to Cesar with a jerk of his head and got up from the table. Cesar followed him into a filthy, reeking toilet. It was empty except for pools of urine on the floor and graffiti scrawled on the walls. The decks and money exchanged hands. Suddenly, le-Sport pushed Cesar's shoulders against a stall. "Gimme the rest of your *blé!*" the pusher snarled. His hand dropped menacingly toward his pocket.

Cesar's hand, in turn, shot out and his fingers clamped over le-Sport's lips, pinching them outward in the caricature of a kiss, while his knife stabbed into the pusher's belly, slicing upwards, to be stopped only by the bones of his chest.

He held his hand clamped over le-Sport's mouth to shut off his cries. The tableau of death held for a long moment; the pusher's eyes widened, strained, staring in wonderment and disbelief above the whitening fingers of Cesar's steel grip.

Cesar caught le-Sport as the pusher's knees buckled and he started sinking to the floor. Dragging the body into a stall, Cesar balanced it, seated, on a stool. Stepping back, Cesar regarded the corpse: "You won't remember anything, now," he thought, and closed the door to the partition.

He walked from the toilet into the bar. In the dim, smoke-filled room, he looked for the bargirl. She had disappeared. He continued toward the entrance, edging his way, without hurry, along a wall and between the tables. On the street, he blew through his nose to rid it of the stench of urine from the toilet. It was soon gone in the cool night air. Making his way casually through the still busy street, he reached his car and headed back to the hotel. While he drove, he suddenly laughed aloud. "Christ!" he exclaimed. "All this trouble just to get some H!? He shook his head, and patted the deadly decks in his pocket.

Château Barthélémy was a block of dark blue shadow in the lowering, translucent, blue dusk of the plains of Carcassonne. Cesar had driven from Paris without stopping, as if goaded by the realization that all was so near now. So far, his plans had gone without a hitch—except for killing le-Sport which really didn't matter. The third part was coming up and its success depended on Villecrosse being freaked out. He had passed Nevers, the "pointed city," without a glance at its many spires, steeples, and sharply angled roofs, until he reached Vichy with its parks and gardens. After a stop for gasoline, he pushed on to Le Puy, ignoring the centuries-old Cathedral of Notre Dame du Puy, built by superhuman effort high on a steep cliff. Then on to Nîmes, the beginning of the South. Here it almost seemed he was returning home. At Nîmes he turned east, angling toward Carcassonne.

Cesar stopped the car behind the old stone building and turned off the motor. For a moment he relaxed in the seat, weary from the drive . . . and somewhat disappointed. The château was dark—not even a faint glimmer of light from the dreary cavern of its drawing room. Getting out of the car, he walked slowly to the back entrance. He pushed open the door to the kitchen and listened for the sound of music. Usually, at this time of day, Edmond was playing either the radio or the old phonograph. But now all was quiet.

Cesar started when a cat jumped down from a counter by the zinc-covered sink, where she had been eating scraps. She landed, lightly as a fluff of dust, on padded paws and stalked past Cesar into the evening. "How long was she locked in the house?" Cesar wondered. The kitchen was a mess of dirty dishes, empty bottles, and dried food. And where was Villecrosse?

Cesar walked down the long back service corridor to the front of the house. He made his way through the litter of the drawing room and turned on the single droplight from the ceiling. Under its faint glow he looked around the room. It appeared to be empty. Then he heard a faint groan coming from an old settee with a high back. Cesar had to walk around it to see more.

Edmond Villecrosse was stretched out on the settee. The comte's face bristled with a week's growth of beard; his face was beaded with sweat. Tears trickled from the corners of his eyes. The front of his shirt was covered with dried vomit.

As Cesar watched, Villecrosse's muscles began to twitch uncontrollably. In pain, he drew up his legs to his belly, and grasped them with another groan.

Cesar reached down and shook Villecrosse's shoulder. "Edmond!"

"Cold!" Villecrosse muttered.

"Edmond! Sit up!" Cesar shook him harder, then pulled him upright.

Edmond opened his eyes and stared blankly at Cesar. "Who're you?" he gasped. Then he added, "You look . . . familiar . . ." He tried to focus his attention on Cesar's changed and altered features.

Villecrosse did not realize that he was looking at himself through a foreshortened mirror of his own years. He saw a remarkable duplicate of himself, a younger Edmond, half his lifetime before created by the knife and skill of a surgeon, Dr. Sherman, of whom he had never heard. The resemblance was striking, although not identical. The face of now is eroded by the years of ago, so that no man remembers exactly the twin of his former self.

"I'm Auguste," Cesar said. "Come on! Snap out of it!

Villecrosse was too sick, too tired, to wonder further. Wracked with withdrawal, physically wrung out, and tortured, he was left with but one desire: to escape the pain. "You son of a bitch!" he said, accusingly. "Get me hooked . . . then leave me. Dry!" He pulled his cracked lips back in a whine. "Where the hell have you been . . ."

"Busy," Cesar said. "But I didn't forget. I brought you some stuff . . . you'll be all right."

"If you hadn't . . . I would have died." Villecrosse wiped a finger beneath his dripping nose. "I'd have killed myself . . ." His hand shook so badly that he grasped it, holding it still in his lap.

"That won't be necessary," Cesar said. "Where's your artillery?"

"I'll get it." Villecrosse attempted to stand, then fell back against the settee.

"You've got the shakes. Take it easy! Tell me where."

"In the drawer. Chest near the fireplace." Villecrosse's eyes followed Cesar. "You're not kidding me, Auguste? You really brought it?"

Cesar returned with a hypodermic needle and a syringe. "Why should I joke with you, Edmond?" He looked around and found a small silver ashtray. "I'll mix the fix myself," he said, emptying the decks of heroin into the ashtray, adding water from a carafe, and mixing them. Cesar held his lighter beneath the metal tray until it was too hot to hold any longer. He tested the fix with his finger—it was lukewarm, about body temperature—then filled the large syringe. Villecrosse watched with avidity.

"Hurry!" Villecrosse urged.

"It won't be long now," Cesar said, seating himself on the settee beside the comte. He picked up one of Villecrosse's emaciated arms; it was covered with punctures and scabs from wrist to elbow. Cesar looked for a place to insert the needle.

"Go on!" Villecrosse cried.

Cesar quickly jabbed in the needle and pressed the plunger.

A euphoric smile crossed the comte's face. "Ahh . . ." he sighed, his tone a benediction.

Suddenly Villecrosse stiffened, then writhed on the settee. His eyes rolled up until only the whites remained. Cesar leaped to his feet, waiting.

In a coma, Edmond rolled off the settee and began a dry retching on the floor. The great snorts of his breathing blasted the silence.

A foul odor of defecation filled the room.

Cesar turned away, abruptly, to find a blanket.

When he returned, Edmond Villecrosse, Comte de Tassigny, was dead.

At least, Cesar thought, he died happy; he had owed Villecrosse that. Under the first euphoric glow of the drug, the comte had dropped down the dark tunnel of unconsciousness never realizing he was dying from a massive overdose.

Cesar knew the layout of the old château as well as he knew his own mansion in Marseilles. Wrapping the comte's body in a blanket, he carried it to the basement and deposited it on the flagstone floor of the wine cellar. He returned to the kitchen, lit a lantern, then went out to the barn. After a brief search he found a pick and shovel. With the implements he made his way back to the cellar. In the light of the lantern, the wine racks—long empty of bottles—stood like ghostly skeletons draped in dust and cobwebs. No one would spend much time in the cellar looking for a bottle of wine.

Cesar pried up several of the large, flat stones and began to dig. He dug deep. After depositing the body in the grave, Cesar refilled the hole and carefully reset the stones over it. The excess dirt he carried outdoors and scattered. Cleaning the pick and shovel, he returned them to their original positions in the clutter of the barn, then made a final visit to the wine cellar with a broom. He swept away the last vestiges of fresh dirt, blending it thoroughly with the thick layer of dust that already covered the floor.

He inspected the cellar carefully. No telltale trace of his activity was evident. Picking up the broom and lantern, he went upstairs.

Cesar hurried now. In the comte's bedroom on the second floor of the building, he packed Villecrosse's clothes in two old monogrammed suitcases. Extra clothing, which could not be fitted into the luggage, he wadded up in bundles. He sat down at a small desk and went through the drawers, putting aside an expired passport, a birth certificate, a few family papers and yellowed photographs, Villecrosse's ID card, and carefully hoarded items of jewelry—a heavy pocket watch engraved with the de Tassigny crest, gold cuff links initialed E.H.V., and a massive signet ring with the family coat of arms. These items he stuffed in his pockets.

Outdoors, he packed the bundles of clothing and suitcases in the trunk of the car. Cesar tried to remember: Oh yes! Don't forget the shaving kit, toothbrush—and set of silver hairbrushes! He returned upstairs and got them.

In the library off the drawing room he located a battered portable typewriter. Cesar sat on the arm of a chair to peck out a final message:

> As you know, I've planned to take a vacation for some time. I've decided that now is the time. I don't know when I'll be back. If I'm lucky, never!
>
> Lock up the place. Keep the keys—I'll get them when I want them. Meanwhile, I'm leaving you sufficient money for your services, and to pay the bills in the city.
>
> E.H.V.

Cesar signed the note with Villecrosse's initials in an imitation of his scrawl. Folding the note, he placed it in an envelope, together with a thick wad of bills, addressed to Boilly, the neighboring farmer who delivered supplies to the château and acted, on occasion, as part-time caretaker.

He nailed the envelope to the kitchen door where Boilly would be sure to find it on his next visit.

Cesar climbed into his car and drove away.

Chapter 40

The phone rang. It continued to ring for a long time—
sufficient time to be answered from anywhere in the mansion. Satisfied that his home was empty, Cesar hung up the
phone and left the public telephone booth. He drove to the
old townhouse and parked across from it on the quiet,
tree-lined street. He sat in the car for a while, watching the
house for any sign of life within. Then he got out and
walked toward it, climbing the slight elevation of the porte
cochere. Ringing the bell, he waited patiently before ringing
it a second time. When the door remained closed, he took
out his keys and let himself in.

He stood inside the entry hall, head slightly tipped—
listening. He heard nothing, no movement, no stirring of
life. The house held the slightly stale air of emptiness, of
being closed for some time. The staff had been sent on
vacation by Joseph, Cesar guessed, during his long absence
from Marseilles. However, he was still anxious that no one
know of his return to the city with his new face. Crossing
the hall, he walked through the formal, ornate dining room
to a small, informal breakfast room overlooking the back
garden and adjoining garage with servants' quarters. Standing behind a closed venetian blind, he peered between the
narrowed slits, observing the area closely. The garage was
closed. The windows in the quarters above it were shuttered. If there were a night watchman, he would be sleeping

there. Convinced, finally, that the grounds were unoccupied, he left the room and walked quickly to his study. Seating himself in a great leather and bronze campaign chair, he dialed a number. When the phone answered, he asked, "Joseph . . . ?"

"Cesar!" Joseph's voice held both warmth and surprise. "It's really you? Where are you?"

"I'm back," Cesar said.

"You made it!" Joseph exclaimed. "Aren't the American *flics* still looking?"

"Let'em look." Cesar laughed.

"We thought perhaps you were dead. Killed! Along with Anse and Cuir."

"Not yet," Cesar said easily. Then his voice assumed a more serious tone. "Can you talk freely? Is anyone around to overhear?"

"No," Joseph assured him, "go ahead."

"This is important. I want to see you, but I don't want anyone to see me yet. I'll explain later." Cesar did not intend to mention step four of his plan, although he was now putting it into effect.

"All right," Joseph agreed. "We'll meet. Where?"

"I'll get to that. Meantime, pass the word that I'm back. Spread it around. Make sure that Galon knows . . . and Volanti. Rampini, too. Tell them that after New York, I'm swearing vengeance on those Cosa Nostra bastards! See that the news gets out, Joseph!"

"I will," Joseph said.

"We'll wait until after dark," Cesar continued. "You know that launch we have? Number Three? Where do we keep it?" Cesar referred to a harbor launch owned by the waterfront union.

"Pier Forty-two," Joseph told him.

"Is it in running order?"

"I haven't heard to the contrary."

"I can't take a chance it's out of order. It's too damned important!" Cesar said. "Here's what you do. Find a marine mechanic and bring him along. I'll meet both of you aboard the launch . . ." he paused to look at his watch, ". . . at eleven tonight."

"All right . . ." Joseph's voice sounded slightly puzzled.

"Incidentally," Cesar added, "I don't want a mechanic who's married or has a family. And, preferably, some *mec* who isn't with us."

332

The line hummed emptily for a moment. Finally Joseph said, "I don't understand. What's up?"

"Look, Joseph!" Cesar snapped. "I'm going to take a trip. An important one. In that launch! Where I'm going—when, why—that's top secret. I don't want some *mec* who'll talk about it later. I'll fill you in on the details when I see you. Can you wait?" his voice held a bite of impatience.

"Yes," Joseph replied, ignoring Cesar's sarcasm. "We'll see you at eleven."

"If I'm not on the pier, go aboard the launch and wait for me," Cesar said, and hung up. He stared at the phone in its cradle, then got up and crossed to a stand of bookcases. A section of shelves swung out and he reached behind it where he kept a cache of weapons.

A night mist hung heavily over the harbor, muffling the sounds of small pleasure craft hurrying back to the sheltered security of Le Vieux Port. High above on its hill, floodlights illuminated the great golden statue atop the towering basilica of Notre Dame de la Garde. The huge stone mass of the church rested as a climax to a long sweep of ascending stairs, and pointed like a lighted finger to the heavens above. Somewhere in the distance across the harbor was a tiny pinpoint of land, the island with the ruins of the Château D'If, from which the Count of Monte Cristo escaped.

Pier Forty-two lay in shadows, wrapped in darkness, the waters of the harbor lapping gently against its creosote pilings. At the foot of a wooden ladder, a long gray launch was warped to the pier that loomed above it. Forward, toward the bow, a low, small cabin enclosed the instruments and controls of the craft and served as a wheelhouse; aft, the stern of the boat was open. Number Three was a sturdy, although quite unlovely, working launch.

Footsteps sounded hollowly on the pier. They followed the resounding boards to approach the ladder, which was located about half the distance between the land and the end of the pier. At the ladder, two figures stopped. In the darkness it was difficult to be sure of footing, and the shadowy forms hesitated before one carefully descended the ladder. The second followed and joined his companion on the gently rolling, open deck of the launch. Nearer the water, the

333

lights of the harbor were picked up and reflected to slightly dissolve the darkness.

Joseph looked around. "Are you here?" He did not speak loudly, but his voice carried. His companion, dressed in faded denim trousers, jersey, and dark pea jacket, put down a heavy metal box of tools on the deck. His name was Macky, and he was third engineer of the tramp freighter S.S. *Portius,* under Panamanian registry, then in port to pick up cargo. A fat bribe had persuaded Macky to leave his drinking, pick up his tools, and accompany Joseph to inspect the engine of launch Number Three.

Macky opened his toolbox and rummaged inside for a flashlight. "It's darker than the inside of a bat's ass," he told Joseph.

"Don't use that light!" Joseph warned.

"Huh?" Macky paused. "Got to have light to see what I'm doing."

"Not now," Joseph said. "Later . . . if you need it." He walked along the open deck of the launch toward the cabin, pulling together the lapels of his jacket against the coolness of the night. At the closed cabin door he stopped and held his wrist before his eyes, trying to make out the time. He slanted the face of the watch back and forth until he caught a reflection of light and could see the dial. "Late," he said to himself. A flurry of wind gusted across the water and he shivered. Opening the door, he stepped inside . . .

To eternity.

Cesar's silenced gun spat against Joseph's head. Joseph died instantly—without knowing it. Catching his cousin's body, Cesar lowered it quietly to the deck inside the cabin. Then, in a muffled voice, he called to Macky. "Hey! Come here!"

Unsuspecting, the engineer walked to the cabin. He was met at the door with a second bullet. Cesar made no effort to catch his falling body.

The interior of the cabin was not only dark, it was also cramped. Although he hurried, it took time for Cesar to strip Macky to the skin and dress him in Cesar's own clothes. He donned the engineer's garb, and . . . finally . . . transferred his own personal papers, ID card, and wallet to the dead man, and strapped his wristwatch to the cooling wrist. Last, he slipped his ring, the Moor's head medallion of authority, on Macky's stiffening finger.

334

When he had completed these tasks, he poured a large can of gasoline over the dead bodies, soaking them well and saturating the interior of the cabin. Cesar started the motor of the launch, but left it idling. Leaving the cabin, he hurried to the bow to cast off the line holding the launch. Still carrying the end of the fore line, he returned to the stern and released the aft line, too. He threw Macky's box of tools overboard.

Cesar looped the bowline around his wrist and climbed the ladder to the top of the pier. With the line, he towed the launch to the end of the dock. Looking down at the gently rolling boat, he waited until the angle of its bow swung slightly inward to expose the expanse of glass in front of the wheel.

With one deft toss, he lobbed a grenade through the glass into the cabin.

Turning, he raced down the pier.

Behind him a muffled explosion.

In a few seconds a great pillar of flame exploded into the sky, but Cesar was already safely protected in the street shadows of shore. Breathing heavily, he settled behind the wheel of the rented car and watched the rosy glow lifting from the fiercely burning launch. Joseph's voice seemed to speak to him again—the words he had told Cesar in the Valle that night after Victore's funeral.

Joseph's voice held no rancor as he repeated in Cesar's memory: "Remember this, Cesar. Business is business. It comes first."

Cesar nodded his head. "You understand, Joseph!" he spoke aloud. "You're a businessman. It was strictly business—that's all."

He started the car. Behind him, the flames of the launch were dying down.

The morning newspapers carried headlines and stories of the murders. The *Marseille Héraut* explained:

Last night the bodies of two crime lords were found in the burning wreckage of a launch foundering in the harbor near Le Vieux Port. The dead men are tentatively identified as Cesar Sati, or Satisanni, chief of the notorious Unione Corse family, and Joseph Tasera, well-known businessman, banker and industrialist.

Inspector Jacques Roncin, in charge of investigation, is quoted as saying, "We have known for some time that Tasera was the financial front-man for the organization."

At present the police have no leads to the killers. The motive is believed to be connected with recent gang wars over narcotics in the United States. According to M. Roncin, "Several months ago, two of Sati's men were shot down in New York. At that time, it was believed that Sati, who was with them, might also have been murdered, although his body was not found. It is evident that he escaped and returned to Marseilles.

"We are working on the theory that the New York mob followed him back here, and finally caught up with him. Identification of Satisanni and Tasera is difficult because the two bodies are so badly burned. Both men were shot. The launch was bombed in an attempt to prevent identification, but there is enough evidence to strongly indicate who they were."

Galon, surviving under-boss of the Sati, made arrangements for the bodies to be shipped back to Col Pieto.

Young Paolo Satisanni delivered another eulogy at the pink tomb . in Valle Satisanni.

Chapter 41

In the spring of 1973, the sleek yacht *Gloriosa* lay at anchor in the bay of Ajaccio. Her paint gleamed whitely, her brasswork sparkled. Gaily striped red and white awnings protected her spacious decks from the blazing sun. On a cruise to the Aegean, she had put in for additional supplies and fuel. Her one hundred and ten feet used a lot of diesel oil. Her twenty-some guests also used up a lot of food and liquor.

The owner of the *Gloriosa*, Edmond Villecrosse, Comte de Tassigny, took his ease in a deck chair beneath the awning on the afterdeck. He was a handsome, youthful-appearing man, with a muscular body. A steward, in natty nautical blues, served him a well-chilled drink. Near the comte's chair, his wife—the Comtesse Gloria, for whom the yacht was named—tanned herself in an open patch of sunlight. The Comtesse Gloria, née Gloria Langer, was heiress to the Langer Dime-a-Dozen Variety Stores' millions of Boston, Massachusetts.

Lolling around the deck in the heat of the day were three guests—one young woman and two men. From the hatchway of the main salon came the strains of music from a stereo, where the other guests were killing time with dice, backgammon, and sundry games mixed with liberal portions of highballs.

Arching a softly rounded hip, the comtesse rubbed it

with suntan oil—where it was not protected by her scrap of bikini —peered over the sunglasses on her nose to look at her husband, and said, "Darling . . . how much longer are we going to be here?"

The comte looked fondly at his wife. After eight years of marriage, he was familiar with her moods. Now she was restless. But she was nearly always restless, insatiable for color and adventure, alone unless encircled by a crowd of chattering friends. She adored the sun, although she did more than travel its path. Gloria created a splendid planet of her own around which she orbited, accompanied by her satellites to warm the little spheres of tradesmen, maître d's, and social columnists. Like all celestial bodies, she possessed her own field of gravitation and attracted the famous, notorious, talented, gifted, near-famous, poseurs, phonies, social bums, and hangers-on wherever she went. She preened, glowed, and thrived on their adulation—real and simulated.

Long ago, the comte had decided that she was worth it. What was the money? He did not have to worry about that, not with his secret numbered accounts scattered around the world—of which not even Gloria was aware. No, the comte was merely convinced that he could never find . . . or buy . . . another like her. Gloria was unique. She was a piece of living art. Only once, in how many thousands of human couplings, was such a masterpiece produced? Silver-gilt hair; a flawless, tanned skin; great, dazzling, near-purple eyes; and perfect delicate features. She was more than beautiful, she was Aphrodite beside whom all other woman paled into memory—or so, at least, the comte saw her. However, he was also realistic enough to recognize that in her vanity, Gloria prized her title most highly of all her possessions. After all, a title could not be purchased at Tiffany's.

"Dammit, Eddie," the comtesse swore prettily, "did you hear me? How much longer are we going to be stuck here?"

"Probably most of the day," the comte said.

"How boring!" Gloria glanced at the second girl sprawled comfortably in a deck chair reading a magazine. "I'd like a little action. Wouldn't you, Francie?"

Francie, a stunning brunette with an innocent face who had climbed to fame singing double-entendre ballads in exclusive nightclubs, yawned and put aside her magazine. "I've just been reading this article by a psychiatrist on sex," she said. "A very interesting case."

The two men playing gin at a table looked up. One of them, a seeded Wimbledon player named Rick, said, "What was so interesting?"

"Well," said Francie, "this girl . . . patient . . . told the doctor that every time she saw a handsome, well-built man on the beach, she got this funny feeling between her toes."

"Which toes?" asked the tennis player.

"The big ones," Francie said. Her voice held artless innuendo. She turned toward Gloria. "I can't see the beach from here. Can you?"

"No," Gloria laughed. "Perhaps Edmond can."

The comte finished his drink and placed the highball glass on the deck beside his chair. Looking toward the shoreline of the small port, he said, "I don't imagine there's much to do in Ajaccio . . ." The steward brought the comte a fresh drink. "Anyone else?" Edmond asked, looking at his companions. At their nods, he ordered another round, then said slowly, "I think—or I've been told, at least—there's a casino in Ajaccio . . ."

"All ashore who's going ashore!" Gloria scrambled quickly to her feet.

"Wait," the comte cautioned her. "I don't know if it's open this time of day."

"Find out. Please, darling?" Gloria turned to the others. "Wouldn't everyone like to go?"

"Ripping!" said Rick throwing down his cards.

His companion in gin gathered up the cards and said, "A break for you. You owe me thirty-two dollars, Rick."

Gloria shook the back of Francie's chair. "C'mon," she urged. "Let's put on some fresh faces."

"Why?" asked Francie. "For the fierce wild natives? I've heard that they're all a bunch of pirates . . . *corsaires.*" Francie clasped her hands as if in supplication. "No virgin is safe!"

"You haven't had to worry about that in years!" the comte told her sharply. Gloria thought her husband's voice sounded offended. He had been uncharacteristically abrupt. However, she pushed aside the thought and hurried into the main salon to alert the other guests to the trip ashore.

The comte concluded the arrangements with the steward.

Several hours later, three large, leased limousines pulled up and stopped by the casino. The large gambling building stood on one corner of the plaza with the great cast-bronze equestrian statue of the emperor surrounded by the gardens of Casone. The comte, comtesse, and guests climbed out and looked around, orienting themselves.

Gloria saw the statue and asked, "Who are those four men? Their statues . . . one on each corner around Napoleon?"

"His brothers," the comte explained. "He made three of them kings. The fourth didn't quite make it. He was an ambassador."

An attractive, slightly graying woman, in her mid-forties, descended the steps of the casino on the arm of her husband, Sir William Wakely Powers. The Lady Vivian Burke Powers wore a sleek, chic pants suit that helped to cleverly conceal the slightly blossoming lines of her rounding figure. Lady Vivian saw through the pink tinted lenses of her sun glasses the three large limousines that had just disgorged their lively party of twenty guests and were preparing to park in the shade of over-hanging trees down the street from the gambling establishment. "Look, William!" Vivian exclaimed. "I should imagine that's the Villecrosse entourage. I heard at the hotel that the *Gloriosa* pulled in this morning."

Sir William barely glanced in the direction of the square where the group was staring at the Napoleonic monuments. "A bit gaudy, don't you think, m'dear?" The famed British barrister was always tweaked by Vivian's continuing interest in what he disdainfully called the 'wet set.'

"Oh, but darling! I understand the comtesse gives such *lovely* parties!" Vivian said with reluctant envy.

"If her husband is bloody fool enough to squander his money, that's his business," William harumped. "We've better things to do with ours."

Vivian's eyes picked out the figure of the comte, at a distance, as he walked surrounded by a cluster of elegant sensuous women. His oddly different features she found attractive, even more than in his photographs which she had seen in the papers, but she did not recognize him. For merely a passing instant, his youthful athletic walk, the balanced forward swing of his carriage as if moving on steel springs reminded her of someone. A Swiss mountaineer? she wondered. And then the flash was gone—the memory too distant, too buried to be recalled distinctly. She shrugged. "I might inveigle an invitation to the yacht, if they stay over night," she said tentatively, hopefully.

"Who do you know aboard?" William demanded. "Certainly none of *our* friends."

"I think . . . I heard . . . that Rick's taking a cruise with them."

"Rick who?" asked William.

"Oh, you know . . . Ricky Marston. Plays tennis . . . that sort of thing. Billy knows him." Billy was their son, William Wakely Powers III, attending Cambridge.

Sir William snorted. "Wouldn't think of it!" He patted her hand. "C'mon, old dear. We'll stroll back to the hotel. Stop on the way. Have a drink. Perk us up."

With a sigh of regret, Vivian agreed. She cast one last look at the laughing, chattering group by the great bronze figure. She would have enjoyed visiting the yacht. She remembered once . . . over twenty years before . . . when she had sailed on the . . . what was its name? She searched her memory: the *Seramis!* That was it! And the impossible little oaf who had invited her. But try as she did, the Lady Vivian could not dredge up his name in memory. Nice to Monte Carlo . . . she had *loved* the trip. Actually, it was her first visit on a yacht. She recalled more distinctly now, back when money was really short. A real treat. A luxury! And she had been bananas about boats ever since. She wished that William could afford to buy one. But the way taxes were now, of course, he never would . . . or could.

The Comte de Tassigny turned away from the statue. For a moment he saw a rather distinguished, middle-aged, couple strolling on the sidewalk past the square. "British," he thought absently, "stuffy codger. The woman doesn't look too bad, but her face is getting plump and someone ought to tell her those big, round glasses don't help any." Then he forgot about them.

Francie started for the casino, paused, then turned around. With rounded eyes she stared at the figure of the emperor in the center of the high, raised, concrete pedestal. "To think . . ." she said in a small girl's voice, ". . . that such a teensy-weensy little man caused so much trouble. I mean, what would've happened if he weighed three hundred pounds?"

"Oh, Nappy got what was coming to him," the comtesse assured her.

"Don't speak ill of the emperor," the comte cautioned his wife calmly. "If it hadn't been for him, where would *we* be today?"

"Of course, you're right, darling!" Gloria pressed her palms together and bowed humbly. "I apologize." She bobbed up and down, alternately facing her husband and the statue.

The comte raised his voice for the benefit of his assembled guests. "I think as you enter the casino, you can all take a lesson from the emperor's mistakes," he announced. "Stop while you're ahead . . . !"

Laughing, the crowd moved toward the casino.

That Edmond . . . how droll!